Highway Don't Care

Freebirds II

Lani Lynn Vale

Dedication

To all of my family who supported me. My mom who encouraged me to write my book. My husband for watching the kids while I sat in the corner and typed away. To my beautiful babies, I love you like crazy! Finally, to the readers who bought my books and gave me a chance.

Table of Contents

Chapter 1

Sometimes you will never know the value of a moment until it becomes a memory.
-Dr. Seuss

Ember

Today had been a long day. It was the first day of two-a-day practices for the football team. I treated over fifteen kids for minor injuries that they'd sustained during practice, and one major who suffered a concussion. The player had been suffering from confusion and after a few tests on my part to confirm, he was transported to the local ER. My ass was officially dragging.

I loved being an athletic trainer. Since tearing three ligaments in my knee and being unable to go on my full ride volleyball scholarship to Texas A&M University, I've put every waking hour into keeping athletes healthy, or getting back in fighting form.

My phone buzzed in my pocket and my heart soared, but then quickly deflated after I glanced at the screen. Damn. It was Maximillian. My brother. Not that I didn't love and cherish him, but he just wasn't the one I wanted to hear from right now.

I wanted to hear from Gabriel. My heart longed to hear his voice, his husky laugh, the annoying tapping that he did incessantly, and, hell, even the sound of his breathing.

Me being me, I'd thrown the bitch fit of all bitch fits and we haven't spoken to each other in nearly a week. Every time the phone rang, I got my hopes up, only to have them come crashing down again when he wasn't the one on the phone.

I hit ignore on the screen and shoved the phone back into the front of my shirt. My usual spot for my phone is in between the strap of my sports bra and my chest; I find that it holds in place great, even when I'm running. Since I'm in some sort of athletic type apparel, nearly ninety percent of the time, I had to improvise on where to put things.

Cheyenne thought this was hilarious. She said I looked stupid because the phone was bigger than my boobs, but I took it in stride. I knew I had no boobs to speak of, but my ass more than made up for the lack of boobs. If I could transplant some ass fat into my boobs, I'd be batting a thousand.

Cheyenne was my best friend in the whole world. She was my lesbian lover when ugly guys hit on me during our nights out. She was the cheese to my macaroni. The ketchup to my scrambled eggs. She's the best friend that picked me up at the airport after a weeklong trip to England with a sign that said, 'Welcome home, loser'." She was the perfect best friend; I wouldn't trade her for the world. Except, maybe, for a night in Thor's bed. Who wouldn't?

After rounding the corner, I noticed the flood light, which normally blinded me when turning the corner, was out. A wave of fear ran through me, but I pushed it back. Grow a pair Tremaine, I thought to myself. However, I pulled my phone out, clicked the green phone app on the screen, and went to the keypad just in case.

I continued to walk until I could see my car, when it happened. A scuff of rocks on the sole of a shoe was the only warning I had before someone tackled me to the ground. Hard. My face slammed into the gravel, and I tasted dirt on my tongue.

My whole body smashed into the ground so hard that I was temporarily stunned. The breath left my body in a whoosh. Everything refused to work; I sat there stupidly blinking and trying to catch my breath. My head smacked against the pavement with a sickening thud, and gravel bit into my arms and hands. Feeling seemed to come back all at once and pain exploded everywhere. Everything hurt; my head, neck, arms, hands, pelvis, and knees.

The body that tackled me straddled my back, pushing my face further into the gravel as he leaned down and put his mouth near my ear. His breath smelled like garlic and made me want to throw up. Bile came up my throat, and I clenched my eyes tightly shut.

"You shouldn't walk alone at night. Someone could really hurt you." The man said.

The breath stalled in my lungs and all I could get out was a small whimper. The man's legs and one arm held me tight as he snuck his hand down between us.

"Nothing to say bitch? No matter. I don't want you to talk anyway."

I heard his belt buckle clink as he released it, then the rasp of a zipper as it he pulled it down.

Fear exploded in me and I clenched my hands. As I tightened my hand, it reminded me that I still had my phone. A shot of adrenaline coursed through my veins; I was amazed I was able to hang on to it through the struggle.

Doing some quick thinking, I held the button on the side of the phone, and screamed "Gabriel" loudly, and prayed that my auto dial worked. Then I shoved it underneath my thigh, hoping against hope that he didn't see it.

Fetid breath invaded my nostrils, and my stomach revolted once again. "Isn't that an angel? I'm no angel bitch."

"P-please don't h-hurt me. P-please." I said to him. "I can go back into the gym and get you some money. Or we can get in my car and I can take you to the ATM and get cash out for you. That's my car right there, in the corner where it says '*AT parking only*.'" I tried to give Gabriel as much information as I could about my whereabouts without being too obvious about it.
I hoped that he was on the line and was able to hear me, even though the phone was under my legs.

"Shut up, bitch. Or this will be worse in the long run." My attacker said.

With that statement, my bravado fled and I started sobbing. My attacker must not have liked criers, because he hit me in the temple with his meaty fist and everything went black.

Ω
Gabe

I had the impact wrench in my hand, unfastening some bolts on the exhaust manifold of a '78 Roadster, when my phone rang. I grabbed the red rag out of my back pocket and wiped my hands before I rescued it from my pocket.

A smile broke out over my face when I saw who was calling.

I hit speaker on my phone and said, "Decided not to be stubborn anymore and talk to me?"

Harsh breathing, the occasional scuffle of rocks, and grunting broke the silence of the line, and my demeanor instantly changed. I dropped my rag, the wrench, and shot up from my crouched position. My heart was pounding so hard I could almost hear it. Jack stood from his stool with a questioning look, but I didn't stop to explain.

At a jog, I turned and headed into the office from the main garage. Sam and Max were sharing a beer, laughing when I barreled inside. Suddenly, they were alert and ready, knowing something was wrong just by the look on my face.

Holding my finger up to my lips, I held out my hand so everyone could hear what was going on at the other end of the line.

"P-please don't h-hurt me. P-please." She said to him. "I can go back in to the gym and get you some money. Or we can get in my car and I can take you to the ATM and get cash out for you. That's my car right there, in the corner where it says 'AT parking only.' "

When Max heard Ember's voice, he bolted from his chair, hit the keyboard with a thump, and started typing away. He pulled up her cell phone position, as Sam was busy on the phone with Kilgore PD giving them the details that Ember had just relayed.

"Shut up, bitch. Or this will be worse in the long run." A low male voice said.

Ember must have lost the battle with her emotions because gut-wrenching sobs came through the speaker and a sick knot of fear lodged in the pit of my belly. Ember's attacker started hitting her then, and we could hear each sickening thud.

"Oh yeah, you like that baby?" The attacker asked.

Bile rose in my throat, and I could no longer stay put. I ran out to the truck I'd just purchased, hopped inside, and slammed the door. The sound of tires spinning on the pavement, and the smell of burnt rubber did nothing to my senses. Everything in my being was focused on the phone, and what I was hearing. The phone hooked up through my Bluetooth, and I could hear the sound of grunting, and the sounds of flesh meeting flesh. I prayed that nothing was as bad as I was imagining it, and that she was going to be all right.

I arrived at the college within five minutes, but was still beat there by dozens of police cars. Police cruisers were parked haphazardly in all directions. Getting as close as I could, before parking and getting out, I sprinted towards the group of people outside of the gym.

An officer did his best to stop me, but I was a force of nature. Plowing right through him, I ran up to the figure I saw huddled on the ground in a fetal position.

Ember's shock of blonde hair was the first thing I saw. The second was the fact that she had no shirt on. A police officer was just taking off his jacket and draping it over her when I dove in on my knees, skidding to a halt next to her head.

There was a commotion further away, but I paid it no mind as I concentrated on Ember. My heart was in my throat, and tears started pricking my eyes. I stifled a moan of despair, and took in the sight before me.

I started to place my hands on her head when she flinched away from me. Her eyes were squeezed shut and she was making heart wrenching whimpering noises.

"Emmie. It's okay. I'm here now. Can you look at me, baby?" I said quietly to her.

The whimpering stopped and those big hazel eyes snapped open. She looked at me with fear-clouded eyes. One second she was lying in a ball on the pavement, and the next she was throwing herself into my arms. Instinctively, I wrapped my arms around her and pulled her to me. She buried her face in my neck and started sobbing. Each and every sob broke my heart. Ember was a spitfire; I've never seen her look so defeated. Her tears were flowing hotly down my neck and sliding into the gap of my t-shirt.

Something slick trickled over my hands, and it registered in my mind that ember's entire back was bare and slick all over. I tried to place her down on the ground but she clung to me tightly.
The paramedics rolled up with their gurney and stopped beside the both of us.

"Please let her go, sir, so we can take a look at her." The young medic said.

Once again, I tried to put her down but she refused and clung even more tightly, wrapping her legs around my waist.

"Ember, honey, these guys would like to take a look at you to make sure you aren't hurt anywhere. Can you let them check you over?" I whispered to her.

"No." She moaned. "I'm not too bad. It's just my back. I think he scratched my back when he ripped my shirt off." She said into my neck

The paramedics must have been able to make out what she said; they nodded and bent down to take a closer look at her back. One of the officers turned on a large spotlight that lit the area up; now I could make out that the shirt she had been wearing was laying in tatters around her waist.

My blood was on a slow boil; I just prayed that I would find the strength to not go off and find the fucker that dared to hurt her.

The second medic let out a low whistle with his tongue and teeth while examining the wound. The first medic pulled out a bottle and some gauze. They went to work on her back; I tried not to think about the amount of blood I was seeing.

I knew it was bad without even looking at it. With the amount of years I served in the military, I knew that that much blood was only produced by something that was more significant than just a scratch. What I think happened was the POS cut the shirt off her with a knife and didn't care if he was slicing her skin along with the shirt in the process.

A short time later, the medics got her patched up and took her to the hospital. Again, I tried to let her go, but she was having none of it. Instead, I walked over to the bus, and took a seat on the bench, all the while holding onto her tightly.

Max and Sam were at the police barrier being held back by a rookie cop who refused to let them come to us. I nodded to them, letting them know, without words, that Ember was okay, and that I was going with her; they both nodded back to me. Max wore an expression that could only be described as devastation, as if his heart was being ripped slowly from his chest. He said he loved Ember, but she was beyond knowing it was her brother; they left shortly after to speak more in depth with the police.

We arrived at Free two hours later.

Ember had received a thorough examination, but never once let go of me. She had fifty-seven stitches put into her back. The cut started at the base of her neck, and flowed all the way down, until it met her jeans. It was around a quarter inch deep the whole way down. A scar was inevitable, and would forever be a reminder of what happened.

From what the officer in charge told us, once they received the call, cruisers were dispatched. The first officer that arrived reported seeing a man, but didn't give chase since he had a victim that needed medical attention. Although the officer arrived in time to prevent rape, she still had bruises from head to toe, as well as contusions and scrapes on her knees, elbows, hands, chest, and face.

I pulled up in front of my room and shut the truck off. Max was standing in front of his place with a blank face, and a beer bottle dangling from his thumb and pointer finger. I nodded at him as I rounded the truck and opened Em's door. She was knocked out on painkillers, thankfully; otherwise, she would have never let me go to drive us home.

Max stopped in to check on her when he dropped my truck off, and she told him to go home because she was a big girl. No one commented that she had yet to let me go. Max had given her a soft kiss on the forehead and then took off shortly after. He wasn't doing good, even though he was hiding it well. It was only obvious to us since we'd been in life or death situations more times than we could count, and knew each other very well. He was tied in knots, and if he didn't get himself straightened out, he would blow. Neither one of us was happy that Ember was beaten and almost raped; that put both of us so close to the edge I wasn't sure I could keep myself from falling over it.

Ember woke when we made it to the bedroom, and gave me a small smile.

"Can I borrow some clothes?" Ember whispered.

I turned and grabbed some basketball shorts from the top of

my dresser, as well as a t-shirt that I'd worn earlier that day. I handed them to her and she laughed.

"I told you I'd get this shirt from you!" She exclaimed jovially.

I smiled at her, kissed her nose, and left the room, giving her some space to get changed. I knew she needed to do this on her own and I left her to it
.

I couldn't help but smile when I remembered about the t-shirt.

I was working on my bike in the garage when she came up behind me and ran her hand over my back. She had never willingly touched me before and I was surprised that she had. According to Cheyenne, I made her nervous, and she didn't like being out of her comfort zone.

"I love this shirt. Can I have it?" Ember asked me.

"Over my dead body." I replied.
"It looks old anyhow, why does it matter. Please?" She whined, and then rolled her lower lip over and gave me a pleading look.

I rolled my eyes and ignored her. I was serious. This was my favorite shirt, and I'd have to have a really good reason to give it up, and she hasn't given me a good enough one yet.

"Why do you like it? You can go get one from a mall in Dallas easily." I explained.

"Because it looks so soft. I love the saying, too, though." She said.

The navy blue shirt had a star on the left breast and on the back, in white writing, it said, 'You all can go to hell. I'm going to Texas,' on it. My mother purchased it, and sent it to me in Afghanistan. I received the shirt, and three days later, I received the news that she'd died. It was as if she'd known she wasn't going to make it, and sent me some things that would make me think of her.

The shirt was more sentimental than anything else I owned, and I wore it sparingly now that it was looking so used and abused. During my army days, I would wear it under my BDUs, while on missions. It seemed to be my lucky shirt, on top of my favorite. It's a miracle that it's lasted so long. Pure luck. I'd been shot twice while wearing it, and neither time was it life threatening.

Ember came out a few minutes later, drowning in my clothes. She was gorgeous though. Her thick blonde hair hung to just above her pert ass, slightly curling at the bottom. Her face was void of makeup, and the scrapes and bruising stood out starkly against her white complexion. The shirt made her look like her chest was non-existent, but I knew there were two perky, beautiful breasts rubbing against the softness of my shirt. The green shorts fell below her knees, enabling me to see the bandages covering her scraped knees. When her eyes met mine, my knees shook. The color of her eyes looked dull, almost like there was little life left in them.

She came to a halt about three feet from me, looking so lost that I opened my arms for her; she didn't hesitate. She walked right into them, and wrapped her arms around my back, making fists while clenching the back of my shirt.

"Are you ready to talk about it?" I asked her.

"No. But I will anyway." She said.

17

I walked her to the kitchen chair and sat her down very carefully, avoiding the wound on her back.

"Are you hungry? Thirsty?" I asked.

"Have any coke?" She asked.
Walking to the fridge, I rolled my eyes. I wasn't even going to touch the 'coke' comment. Picking up a Mountain Dew from the top shelf, I handed it over.

Eyes wide at the realization that I had her favorite drink; she held out her hand and muttered, "Thanks."

I kept the drinks just in case she happened to show up. I wasn't going to go into why I did this, since it wasn't something I was ready to acknowledge quite yet.

Ω
Ember

"I was walking out to my car from the side entrance to the gym." I said.

I fiddled with the tab on the coke can and flicked it back and forth until it broke off at the letter '*g*.'

I've done this game since I was a little girl, normally breaking the tab off at the desired letter of the alphabet that was the first letter of my crush's name. This time I didn't have to, it came off on its own. Hell yes. I started to do a little shimmy until the stabbing pains from the knife slice on my back brought me back to the moment.

I looked up and saw that Gabe was patiently waiting for me to continue. Apparently, I've done this before. Often, at times, I find myself thinking about random stuff in the middle of conversations. It always starts little, before my mind wanders; and, before I know it, I'm thinking about what pair of panties would feel the most uncomfortable to wear.

A throat clearing brought me back the second time.

"Anyway, I saw two kids get in the car and drive off when I turned to lock the gym up. I walked around the corner of the gym, heading towards my car, when a large body slammed into me."

I took slow calming breaths, trying to slow my heart rate. My heartbeat didn't speed because of the attempted rape. No, it was speeding because Gabe was looking at me with death in his eyes. Don't get me wrong, I was scared that I was beaten and almost raped. I'm more upset because I wasn't able to defend myself. I never want to be that vulnerable again. I also never want to see Gabe look like this again. If I didn't know him as well as I did, I'd be freaking out. As it was, my heart and breathing sped up. It turned me on.

The fierce protective look in his eyes did something weird inside me. It was almost as if my heart knew that he was pissed off enough to kill someone, all because I was hurt. His fists clenched at his sides, veins popped out, skating like ropes all the way up his arm. His eyes sparked. His muscles bulged, then relaxed, as if he was physically keeping himself in the chair. All of this because of little old me.

Chapter 2

Four wheels move the body, two wheels move the soul.
-Biker truth

Gabe

"What next?" I asked her.

The question came out sounding calm and remote, which couldn't have been further from the truth. My mind was fighting my body; my body wanted to kill the "almost" rapist. To pull him apart with a pair of pliers, one chunk of flesh at a time. Starting with his dick.

My mind, however, knew that I needed to calm myself and focus on Ember.

I forced myself to sit on the kitchen chair, looking calm cool and collected. The can of Coors in my hand didn't receive the same fate. It had long since bit the dust. It was completely crushed; now that I thought about it, my hand ached from the grip I had around the crushed aluminum. Not like it mattered. There was a sharp pain somewhere in the vicinity of my heart that overshadowed any other pain I had.

I had a fucked up childhood. On top of my shit upbringing, my three tours in Iraq and Afghanistan only compounded my problems.

"He tackled me from behind. I was stunned at that point and didn't react much until he grabbed my hair and ground my face into the gravel. I was on my stomach when I felt the burn run down my back. I was screaming and trying to fight back, but he was a lot stronger than me. Luckily, I had my phone in my hand and was able to speed dial you. I got knocked out at some point; when I woke up, the guy was gone and there were a few police officers walking up to me. You know what happened from that point." She said in a flat voice with no emotion at all.

I studied her face, and sure, she looked frightened, but there was also fierce anger. The type of anger that makes you sloppy, and can get you into hot water if you're not careful. During a fight, anger can be used against you. I needed Em to get past the anger, because it was going to wear her down if she didn't get it under control.

"What's wrong? I mean other than the obvious. What else is going through that head of yours?" I asked her.

"I'm so fucking pissed at myself. I never should have left so late; since I did, I really should have had someone with me. I was useless. I couldn't fight back." She whispered.

I got up, and dropped to my knees in front of her. I traced the bruises on her jaw lightly with the knuckle of my pointer finger.

"I'll teach you how to defend yourself, honey. You'll never feel like this again. Do you know how to shoot a pistol?" I asked her, while staring into her eyes.

Ember's eyes were hazel. Sometimes they were blue, sometimes green, and even brown in the right light. Now they were a deep, vivid green. They looked like they were shooting emerald sparks with how intent she looked at me.

Ember leaned forward and ran her nose along the bridge of

mine.

"Thank you for coming, Gabe." She said and lightly kissed me on the cheek.

My hands itched to grab hold of her hair, to bury them within her luscious mane, just to see if her hair was as soft as it looked. Giving in to the urge, I let my fingers run thorough her hair that hung in waves down her back. It was so silky smooth. Most women's hair that I've touched had a stiff feeling to it, but Ember's was light, cool, and smooth. Her hair was an odd shade of blonde. It was a white blonde color with reddish hues to it when she moved, especially in the sunlight.

It wasn't usual for her to have her hair down either, so I continued to play with it. I never get to see it like this.

I've also never taken these types of privileges before. I knew that the likes of her was too good for the likes of me. However, after the scare tonight, I decided that she was going to be mine, whether I deserved her or not. I would give her everything and do anything she asked. Except let her go.

"And, yes, I can shoot a pistol. I can also shoot a rifle, a shot gun, and a submachine gun." She said with a smile.

"How do you know you can shoot a submachine gun?" I asked curiously.

She gave me a wide smile that showed off her beautiful straight teeth.

"James and Max took Cheyenne and I once. They got us guest passes and we drove up to their base over a long weekend. It was a blast." She said.

I let out a deep laugh when I saw the satisfaction on her face. She would enjoy something like that.

"Alright, in that case, I have a .38 you can have. I want you to carry it on you from now on; but not in your purse, on your person. We can get you a pancake holster for your back, or an ankle holster. Whatever you want, but I want you to carry it on you at all times from now on. We will go to the range as soon as you feel up to it and test your reaction time. Got it?" I asked.

She gave a nod, and I noticed she was fading fast. The pain meds were creeping in and she would be out like a light shortly.

"Time for bed, honey." I said as I helped her stand.

She stood slowly, and picked her can up to toss into the trash. She kept the tab though. She pulled the chain that was around her neck and unhooked it, then threaded the tab onto her necklace and re-latched it around her neck.

I gave her a quizzical look, but she waved me off.

I made my way to the hallway and turned towards the guest room, but Ember didn't follow me. She turned to the right instead and headed into my room. I waited a few minutes for her to come back, but she didn't reappear.

I broke down and strode to my room, only to freeze in the doorway at the sight that was before me. Ember was on her knees on my bed. My black shirt didn't leave much to the imagination, since it had ridden up over her bottom and exposed her plain white cotton bikini underwear; the shorts she wore on the floor next to the bed in a heap.

The position she was in was an odd one. Her ass was in the air, with her knees tucked under her. Her arms curled up tightly to her chest, and her hair was a mess all around her.

The position she was in reminded me of when Sam's girls fell asleep. They sleep in the exact same position that Ember was in right now. It didn't look the least bit comfortable, but it obviously had to be since she was dead to the world.

My cock hardened, painfully, behind the fly of my jeans. I pressed the heel of my palm down hard against it, looking for a little relief. Didn't help though, only made me that much more aware of it. It didn't matter anyway. Ember could be in a rag, throwing up with chicken pox and I would still want her.

Heaving a sigh, I walked to the bathroom, took a piss, brushed my teeth and changed into my pajama bottoms. I had to rip the tag off first since I never slept in anything but my underwear. Anyone who ever had to be up in a hurry knew better than to go naked to bed. *'Always be prepared,'* was my motto. Sure would look funny to be running out of the barracks and looking over to see a friend's dick swinging. The pants were entirely for Ember's benefit. I didn't want her getting upset with being in bed with me practically naked.

Grabbing my boots, I shoved my .45 into the left boot before opening the door. I turned off the light, and walked quietly to bed. There she was again. In the exact same position. Placing my boots and gun next to the bed, for easy access, I stared down at her sleeping form. I couldn't make much out other than her silhouette, but what I could see took my breath away.

I contemplated how to sleep around her since she was in the

middle of the bed, but decided to get in and shove her over some. Well, maybe not shove.

I eased down beside her and moved her carefully over to the other side of the bed. I laid there, stiffly, for five or so minutes before finally relaxing enough to reach for the covers. I pulled them over both of us and placed my arms behind my head.

I was nearly asleep when I felt her creeping towards me. I didn't think she was awake because she was making the funniest noises. They were somewhere in between whimpers and moans. It didn't take her long before she was straddling me with her head tucked underneath my chin. I left my arms right where they were. This was going to be a long night. At least the noises stopped when she finally settled.

Ω
Ember

If I didn't have to piss like a racehorse, I would never move. I was so very comfortable. I knew exactly where I was, too. Cracking an eye open, I searched the area for a clock. Finally spying it projecting onto the wall across the room, I focused on it until my eyes cleared of some of the bleariness. Ten till four.

Good. I had a reason to come back to bed.

I gently eased off my Gabe bed, and shuffled stiffly to the bathroom. I didn't bother closing the door, because I honestly didn't have the gumption to do anything more than walk straight to the bathroom.

Since I was already up, I popped a pain pill and drank it down with water from the sink. I hope that it kicked in soon because my back was throbbing. With each step I took, tiny sparks of pain shot down the length of the cut, and I had to grind my teeth to keep from whimpering.

It took me a few pain-filled minutes, but I was shuffling back to the bed in no time. I contemplated walking around the bed but decided I just might die if I had to walk any further, so I went to the same side where Gabe was.

I crawled back onto the bed and went back to the same exact position I'd just left. Straddling Gabe with my head tucked under his chin. I wasn't sure if he was awake or not, but I didn't want to take anything for granted. I was going to lay on Gabe, because this was the one time I could do it and actually have an excuse.

All the tension left my body, and I fell into a deep sleep once again.

Ω
Gabe

She was seriously trying to kill me.

I honestly thought it couldn't get any worse; however, I was mistaken. I've spent the last five hours in a light sleep, waking every time she moved slightly. At least, earlier, her crotch rested over my belly. This time, her crotch was nestled snugly against mine. It took absolutely everything I had to keep my cock from going rock hard.

I thought about the smell of rotting flesh, the sight of a gunshot wound, gray matter leaking out of a blown apart head, and everything else truly disgusting to keep my mind from the party that wanted to happen below my belt.

Fuck me.

I've thought about this for nearly a year. Every time I saw

her. If she was in the room, I could pound nails with my dick.

Not that I was good enough for her. I knew that and she knew that.

My step-father made sure to tell me every day that I wasn't good enough. Or smart enough. Or even halfway decent looking. I constantly heard from him that I was a mutt and would never amount to anything.

Apparently, half-Brazilian and half white were considered a mutt to him. My Brazilian father died when I was twelve, of cancer. My mother couldn't afford to work and support us, while paying his medical bills, and she married to make our life better. Little did she know that she was going to turn my life into a living hell, all the while thinking she was making everything better. She married for all the wrong reasons. She never loved Patrick. I never once heard her tell him she loved him. He used to say it all the time, but my mom would smile and go about what she was doing. This was what made it so bad for me.

I look a lot like my father. Tall, at two and a half inches over six feet, with a dark tan. Jet-black hair and a muscular build. Not too bulky, but nothing to sneeze at either. I was literally the carbon copy of my dad. I didn't have one ounce of my mom's features, except for her cerulean blue eyes; which looks totally fucked up with my dark features. Nevertheless, what do I know? He saw in me the reason my mom would never love him like he loved her. Therefore, he took it out on me.

He never hit me, but his words could be as cruel as a whip. I spent seven years living in an emotional hell, and my mom never even knew. I wouldn't have told her, though, and he knew that.

27

I set out in life to prove that bastard wrong. I kept to myself and tried to make myself invisible. I never spoke unless spoken to; I kept my head on straight, worked thirty hours a week at a local construction company after school and on weekends. I studied my ass off to graduate with honors, at sixteen, then joined the military. My mom wasn't too happy about that, but she knew that I was unhappy, and she'd do anything for me.

I left my stepfather's home and never looked back. My mom came to me every time I had leave. She would spend the two weeks with me, or, sometimes, the rare month at the location where I was stationed.

Her last visit I knew something was wrong as soon as I saw her. She waited to tell me until I was home that she had cancer. The same type of cancer that took my dad. Lung cancer.

What was ironic was that neither one of them smoked a day in their lives. They both were extremely healthy. We ate right, and we were very active outdoors. My dad worked as the supervisor for a local construction business, he was in peak shape at forty-two. My mom was also active, at forty-eight. She was a server at the local diner, and on her feet for hours a day. It was just a cosmic joke that they both died of the same thing. Just another fucked up thing that happened to the people I loved most in this world.

Ember shifted on top of me and brought me back from my wanderings. A quick glance at the clock showed that it was now five in the morning. Good, early enough that I could workout.

I slowly eased out from under Ember and stood. Adjusting myself in my god-awful pajama pants, I pulled the covers just to the top of her hips so I didn't agitate the wound on her back.

Spinning on my heels, I went to the closet and located my tennis shoes on the floor, grabbed a pair of running shorts from the shelf, along with a pair of socks and exited the bedroom. Something needed to be worked out, and it was obvious to me that I wasn't going to be getting what I really wanted. Treadmill, here I come.

Ω

An hour and seven miles later, I was dripping sweat. I had just climbed off the treadmill when Ember came into the room. She was adorable. Long hair tumbling down her shoulders, nearly to her hips. It looked like she just rolled out of bed, and didn't bother combing it in any fashion. The t-shirt was hanging off one shoulder. Still no pants, but the shirt came just to the top of her knees; nothing good was showing. She was rubbing her face with her hands and yawning.

"You can go back to bed, there was no reason you needed to get up so early." I said to her.

She continued to yawn, but spoke anyway, "I have to be at work in thirty minutes."

"I already called the director for you. They know what happened last night, and want you to take a week or two off work; pending until you're more comfortable and your stitches are out." I said.

"Dammit, Gabe." She said exasperated. "You had no right, I would've been okay!"

"I know you would have been good, but I also wanted them to address the security issue they have there. They won't have the cameras set up for another week. Therefore, it gives you a little time to heal. I also want to teach you some basic self-defense, just in case you run into this problem again."

"I don't think I'm up for anything to physical right now. My back is throbbing like a bitch, and the pain medication doesn't seem to be helping at all." She revealed.

"That's understandable. They only gave you what amounts to extra strength Motrin. It probably won't do much but take the edge off." I said.

"Well doesn't that just blow? I was nearly raped, my back is sliced from my shoulders to my ass, and all they can give me is a fucking Motrin? What the fuck. I think I deserve the good shit." She complained.

Rage started burning in my belly again at the flippant way she'd just said she was almost raped. Surely, she was taking this too easily.

"Don't make light of this, Ember. You could've been seriously injured, or even killed. You were a very lucky person last night. I got a message from Luke, not even ten minutes ago, saying that they think this is gang related, and they need your statement as soon as you're ready to give it." I ground out.

"I'm not making light of this, Gabriel. I'm just trying to blow some steam. I know what could've happened; I know I was lucky. I just want everything to go back to normal and to not think about it anymore. It didn't happen, so let's not dwell on this anymore. I'll go give a statement as soon as you can get me down there. But we better hurry because Cheyenne won't wait much longer before she's all up my ass."

"Alright, let's get going then. You aren't allowed to take a

30

shower as per doctor's orders. I have some of your clothes still here from when you changed here a while back. I'll set them out on the bed, and you get changed while I'm in the shower." I ordered.

With that, I left the room and headed for my bedroom closet. I pulled her clothes off the shelf at the top of the closet and tossed them onto the bed before heading into the bathroom. Once in the shower I soaped and rinsed. Palming my erection, I ran the soap over it, then stopped. What if she heard me? That only made me hotter. It wouldn't bother me a bit to have Ember join me in here. I would totally welcome it. Only wanting one woman put a damper on my sex life. I tried being with someone around six months ago, but I wasn't able to get it up; she just wasn't Ember. It was incredibly embarrassing, and the look on the other woman's face made me never try again.

Having only a door in between Ember and me was torture. Seeing her wearing my shirt set off something primal inside of me, and made me wish for things I've never had before. Deciding that a door and the shower were loud enough to balance out the sounds, I took my erection in hand again and gave it a rough tug. Reaching down with the other hand, I ran it over my balls, tugging on the sac lightly. Shutting my eyes firmly, and working up a good rhythm, I didn't notice the door crack open. Nor did I notice Ember peak her head in, and her eyes widen. Squeezing my balls a little tighter, I started crudely yanking on my dick. Lightening shot up my spine, and I groaned Ember's name quietly, shooting my semen all over the glass enclosure of the shower.

Fuck. I've never come that hard, and all I was doing was thinking about her in my clothes.

Grabbing the showerhead, I washed the mess I made off the

glass, then quickly shut off the shower. I toweled dry, and wrapped the towel around my waist before heading back into the bedroom.

Ember was on the bed, the jeans I'd dug out from the closet covering her nicely shaped ass. She didn't have a shirt on, only a sports bra. The bandage was starkly white against her tanned back. I walked over to her, and ran my finger lightly down her side. She shifted slightly away from my touch and giggled. Goosebumps broke out all down her side; I longed to run my tongue over them.

"That tickles." She giggled.

"We'll have to change this later when we get home." I noted, tapping the side of her bandage.

"Okay." She mumbled into the mattress.

"Why aren't you dressed yet?" I asked her.

"I can't get my pants buttoned. You must've dried these when you washed them, and now they're too tight." She announced miserably. "I don't dry any of my jeans because they'll shrink up in the dryer; then I have to lay down to snap them, which I can't do today because then I'd have to lay on my back."

"Well, stand up, and we will see what we can do." I instructed.

She stood up and turned around. Her first two buttons were undone, so I pulled her to me by the waist of her jeans. When I curled my fingers around the waistband, I quickly realized that she wasn't wearing anything underneath. My fingers encountered hair, and nothing else.

I inhaled sharply, and my eyes shot from the buttons on her jeans, to her eyes.

Ember was biting her lip while her eyes focused on my hand. I abruptly made the decision to go for it. I've been so strung out this last year that I knew something had to give. We've been skirting around the elephant in the room for too long. No more.

"I think we've denied this for too long, Ember. It's gonna happen. I don't think I can keep myself away from you for much longer. I'm running out of excuses to stay away from you." I said to her, while moving my fingers back and forth over her springy curls.

I found myself wanting to undo the last two buttons on her jeans, so I did. The fly of the jeans read *'Lucky you,'* and damned if I didn't feel like a lucky fuck.

Her voice quivered as she said, "Umm, you're supposed to be helping me button those, not unbuttoning them."

Of course, she didn't respond to my earlier statement, but that also wasn't a "no" coming out of her mouth.

My dick was making a tent out of the towel that was wrapped at my hips. Ember's eyes kept wandering down to it, before they shot back to mine.

"I only wanted to see if the upstairs and the downstairs matched." I hedged.

With that statement, I let my eyes wander down until they sought what they were looking for. Yes, the top matched the bottom. I let my hand drift off her waistband, and buried my fingers into her curls, tugging gently.

"Soon, maybe not tonight, or tomorrow, but soon." I declared, before reaching down and buttoning her jeans, all the way to the top.

When I straightened, the fold in the towel fell just right; my dick escaped the restricting confines of the towel. Ember's eyes widened when she saw it, but quickly averted her head. I laughed as she looked at the ceiling, then the curtains, while covertly looking down at my dick.

Yes, it would be soon. I wasn't holding back anymore. She was screwed. Literally.

Ω
Ember

Oh my god. Oh my god. OH MY GOD!

This was more than I ever could've hoped for; I'd fantasized about this very moment in time at least a hundred times. Gabe's been Mr. Stoic ever since I met him. He never spoke much. He's just the dark, formidable presence at your back. He's spoken to me more in the last twenty-four hours than he has in the last year. I never would've thought my feelings were returned by him. I thought I was the only one with the overactive imagination. Every time he walked into the room, my heart would start beating double time; the butterflies in my stomach felt more like hummingbirds zipping around, and sweat would start to form in the most awkward places. He always seemed so calm and cool. If today was anything to go by, he's been feeling it almost as bad as I have.

In an attempt to get my mind out of the gutter, I started giving orders. "Okay, I'm going to send Cheyenne a text message from the truck. You need to haul-" I informed me before pounding interrupted my request.

Fuck. Too late.

I let out a long-suffering sigh before walking to the door and swinging it wide. There she stood. My best friend in the whole entire world, and her two boob ornaments that were stuck to her tit ninety percent of the time. Don't get me wrong, I love those two girls from the bottom of my heart, but they seem to be attached to her boob the majority of the time. I mean, shouldn't they be done at a little over a year old? Not that I have a problem with others doing it, it just kinda creeps me out. Not to mention she tried to shoot me with her milk missiles once. I ran away from her just as I do when I see those nasty huge cockroaches scuttling across the floor.

The two boob ornaments wore matching outfits today. How surprising. They were cute though; sporting two Spiderman onesies with ruffles on the butt. They were supposed to be gag gifts, but Cheyenne loved them. Their hair was rather crazy today. It looked like mommy forgot how to use a comb.

Steeling my spine, I finally scrounged up the courage to look at Cheyenne. I flinched at the fury I saw there. I knew she was pissed, but she looked like I ran over her cat, and then backed up and did it again to make sure I really got it.

"I'm assuming you're pissy because I wouldn't let Sam bring you to the hospital last night?" I asked with feigned innocence.

"Pissy. Yea, bitch face, you could say that. How could you do this to me? I've been worried sick, and just look at you! You were going to try to sneak out weren't you?" Cheyenne seethed.

Motioning to Gabe with my thumb I said, "I have to go give a statement at the popo station. Gabriel here said I could hitch a ride with him. I'll explain everything when I get back, pinky promise."

Glaring at me, she turned and marched off without another word.

"That went well."

Gabe shook his head slowly and headed to the passenger door. He helped me inside carefully, and then walked to his own door, jumping in a lot more gracefully than I had. The truck started with a dull roar, vibrations started and gave me a little feeling of euphoria. There was something about a good sounding truck that did it for me.

"This sounds great! When did you get this?"

"Yesterday, actually. I needed to be able to do stuff that my bike couldn't do." He explained simply.

"Well that's cool. Can I drive it?" I asked sweetly.

"Absolutely not. I've known you for a year now, and you've gotten into two fender benders and sideswiped a car. No way will I let you touch my brand new truck." He told me firmly.

"Oh that's bullshit! None of those were my fault!"

"Whose fault was it?"

"Well the time I sideswiped a car, it was because there was this massive grasshopper in the car with me. He flew in my window and landed on my leg. I tried to flick it off, but he started going crazy and attacked me. I don't do bugs, and I swear to God this one was a mutant."

"Whatever. You're still not getting my truck in your crazy hands."

Sulking, now, because he could possibly be right, I watched as we passed all the sights and sounds of downtown Kilgore. The police station was located in the historical district. Flowers were dying in the potted plants that lined the middle of the road. Texas heat, in the summer, was a bitch, and when it didn't rain, it got worse. Everything was brown by the time summer ended.

Each bump Gabe hit jolted my back; tears threaten to spill out of my eyes, now that my painkillers were wearing off, not that I said anything. Gabe didn't mean to hit every fucking pothole on this side of the Texas line; he was just doing that naturally. I wasn't going to say anything because I knew he'd feel bad if I made him aware of it. I just wanted to get this shit over with as fast as possible and go back to Gabe's nice warm bed. Preferably with him in it. Underneath me, with that lovely cock I saw a quick preview of, inside of me.

Gabe found a parking space close to the front doors. I was a tad nervous. I'd never been to the police station before, and I didn't know what to expect. Gabe's presence at my side calmed me down some, as we walked through the double glass doors. It wasn't anything special. A lobby to the left, where there was a door with metal detectors on it. To the right there was another door with a locked keypad entry. Towards the front was a glass wall with women sitting behind the glass, waiting on the citizens.

I opened my mouth to ask Gabe where to go, when a man I've only met a handful of times walked out of the room to my right. Luke Roberts. He sure was a cutie. Tall, with a nice build. He had a shock of bleach blonde hair that was clipped in a no nonsense cut close to his scalp. He was wearing jeans and a KPD shirt, which stood for Kilgore Police

Department. He strode right on up to us and did the man hug-shake with Gabe.

They were nearly the same height; Gabe just a tad shorter than Luke. Where Luke was blonde, Gabe was dark. Where Luke had a light tan, Gabe was a nice golden brown. Luke looked like a golden warrior, where Gabe reminded me of a death angel. His looks were dark and menacing. Gabe was wearing a Black t-shirt with dark washed jeans and motorcycle boots.

Luke turned to me after his man hug and made eye contact.

"How ya' doin', Ember?" Luke asked me.

Glancing around, I scratched my arms with my nails. "I guess as good as I can be. Can we get this shit over with, please? This place is giving me hives."

Luke looked a tad startled by my blunt reply; Gabe wasn't. He was wearing a shit-eating grin.

Luke spun on his heel and headed back to the locked door; Gabe and I followed behind. He led us through a maze of hallways, passing through what looked like a huge room with desks everywhere, and finally coming to a stop at a small office. He held the door open for us, and closed it behind us. He made a gesture to a seat that was in front of a rickety old desk. We all took our spots.

"Alright, let's get this show on the road." I informed him, and then went into my tale without preamble.

As I spoke, Gabe stood behind me and gave me moral support. I didn't think I really needed it, though. Yes, it was a horrible thing that happened to me. Yes, it could've been a hundred times worse, but it wasn't. I was hurt, but I wasn't raped. I was roughed up, but I wasn't so bad that I needed a hospital stay. I think my mind was trying to protect me on the could-have-beens. Everyone was expecting me to fall apart, but I wasn't going to give the fucker the pleasure. I was royally pissed.

Luke spoke in gentle tones when asking me questions, and when we were through, he gave a long drawn out sigh and ran his hands over his face roughly.

"Alright, this is what's going on." He started. "Apparently, there is a new process the Blue Skulls are using when they initiate their newest members. Senior members follow the initiates around for a few days, and see the people that they hang with, or that they look up to the most. If they see that there is a certain someone that the initiates are close to, then the seniors think up acts that they know the initiates won't want to do; they're forced to do it so they can prove that they're loyal to the Blue Skulls. The victim has to be someone they know, or have helped. The reason we know all this is because we caught a perp, about a week and a half ago, beating the shit out of an older woman who gave him side work when she knew the boy could use the money. The neighbors heard the commotion and the cops got there in time to catch the little fucker. He was only thirteen, and was easy to crack. The old woman is dead, by the way. We aren't sure if another member did it, but she was released from the hospital on a Monday. Later that week, we got a well check on her when the granddaughter couldn't reach her while out of town; found her dead in the kitchen. Gunshot wound to the head. We can only assume that it was related. And that's how we end up with all of this." He explained as he waved his hands over the notes he took.

Gabe paced like a caged panther. His movements were graceful, yet calculated. I watched, mesmerized, as veins pulsed up and down his arms. His hands fisted at his side.

"Gabe." I whispered.

Gabe took a deep breath, then turned to me with his Terminator face. He looked like he was ready to kill someone, and I'm pretty sure he would've if the option had been available to him right now. The guy who'd done this to me wouldn't stand a chance.

"Okay, we're going to put round the clock surveillance on her. Do we need to worry about her friends?" he asked.

"Not that I'm aware of. The granddaughter lived with her and wasn't harmed." Luke told us.

"Okay. We're gonna get out of here. Here's my number, in case you need any more information, or you have anything more for us. Thanks for your time." Gabe stated as he handed Luke a card with his cell phone number on it.

A uniformed officer escorted us out to the lobby, and we left the building shortly after that. Gabe's eyes never stopped scanning. He looked like a man possessed. Gone was the Gabe that was a silent mountain at your shoulder. In his place was a man that terrified me. I've never seen anyone with such intense concentration. He was ready to kill if needed, and it was all for me.

Gabe came to a sudden halt about four car lengths from his truck. I was walking behind him, checking out his ass, when I smacked into his back. His arm hooked around my waist and he shoved me behind him tight, his body strung tight. My arms went around his waist reflexively and I stood waiting for what was about to happen. I chanced a peek over his shoulder and blanched at what I saw.

There was an older blue Buick, with those big wheels; you

know the kind, the ones where they look like monster truck rims with about an inch of tire. That's not what made my stomach feel like it dropped to my feet though. No, it was the two young kids, maybe sixteen, leaning against the trunk with a blue bandana wrapped around their heads. Their eyes were trained in a different direction, but it was obvious they were there to intimidate me. Show me that they hadn't forgotten about me. A quick glance around the parking lot showed that they were drawing the attention of the cops that came and went hourly for shift change. Two were leaned up against their own squad cars, just waiting to see if anything happened. They hadn't done anything wrong, so there was no reason to confront them. Apparently, it didn't mean they couldn't be watched like hawks.

Suddenly, they got up from their perches and rounded the car, got in, started it up, and roared away, bass thumping like all those cars do now these days. Gabe visibly relaxed, his arm disengaging from around my waist. He started walking again, making sure to have my hand in a firm grip.

Adrenaline pumping, I asked, "That was because of me wasn't it."

Thank you Captain Obvious!

"Yes, but now they know you have the support of me, and also of the KPD. They looked like scouters, sent to take in a situation before any decisions are made. We're gonna go by your house, get your shit, and then you *will* be moving in with me. This is too dangerous for you, and I don't want to lose you before I've even had you." He retorted angrily.

"Okay." I said back to him calmly.

I wasn't going to be arguing with him, I was creeped the fuck out. No arguments what so ever. No sir-ree-Bob. Plus, maybe it would get us where I really wanted, and that was in his bed. I've wanted him forever. I've been in love with the broody silent man for nearly a year now. I've also not had sex in twice that long, so I wasn't wasting any more time on the inevitable.

Chapter 3

Say hello to my little friend.
-Scarface

Ember

"Okay, when you go in, don't freak out. Hoochie is all meow, and no bite." I explained to Gabe.

Gabe gave me a funny look, but nodded in agreement, as he turned the key in the lock of my apartment door. I laughed inwardly. He was going to be in for a surprise when he walked in the door. Gabe insisted on being the first inside so he could check to make sure there weren't any gangs hiding out under my bed, or in my panty drawer. I told him I needed to come get my cat and some clothes if I was going to stay with him. He agreed, on one condition; that was that he went in first to check things out, and that Jack came for backup.

Hoochie let out a menacing growl, and started attacking Gabe's feet as soon as he stepped over the threshold. Gabe came to a halt. He just looked down at his feet, while Hoochie latched onto Gabe's boots, clawing and scratching like his life depended on it. It only lasted about thirty seconds or so before Hoochie got tired, and fell to his side panting.

Hoochie was my thirty-five pound monster of a house cat. I loved every delectable roll on his cute little chubby body.

Jack was chuckling behind me, as we both watched Hoochie lay on his side. He decided that this was as good as place as any and closed his eyes for some much-needed rest.

"This is not a house cat, this is an obese bobcat." Gabe stated.

"Don't call my baby fat, he's a very sensitive boy." I complained to Gabe as I scooped Hoochie up in my arms.

My back decided to make itself known and I bit back a moan. I wasn't going to let them see me cry. Crying was for babies and wieners. However, Gabe saw everything; he took the cat out of my arms, and continued inside in search of my underwear drawer.

"So, how are you doing these days Jacky boy?" I asked.

"I'm doing better. One day at a time I guess." He answered.

Jack's father passed away a little over a year ago, and he was still taking it hard. They were as close as a father and son could be. They acted more like best friends rather than father and son, from what I'd heard. Jack seemed to go into a depression, and only existed. Nevertheless, slowly, with the help of friends, he was returning to some semblance of his old self. I didn't know his old self, but I could definitely see him getting better as each day passed. I knew how it felt to lose a parent, and I even listened a time or two as he spoke so highly of his father. I gave him some Ember wisdom as well. I told him that the pain never fades; it just becomes more bearable over time.

"How is the new bike coming?" I asked him.

"It's coming along really well. I just installed the gas tank; it's almost ready for the paint to be applied." He expounded.

Jack was working on a custom bike, honoring Dougie. All of

the members of Free have put a little something into this bike. Sam designed it, James installed the mechanical and electrical components, Jack the body, Max the chrome and wheels, and, finally, Gabe will finish with the paint job. It was a wonderful team project for them to work on, trying to capture Dougie's essence in bike form. The proceeds would be donated to Dougie's daughter, for her college fund. The rally's in Tulsa in a few months, and the boys are scrambling to get everything finished in time.

This was a community effort as well. Local businesses donated parts, and money, to fund the project. The community outreach was simply amazing. When the locals realized they had a Soldier's daughter in need, they threw themselves lock, stock, and barrel into the project, helping any way they could. The auto-parts store Cheyenne and I used to work at donated all the parts. A lawyer set up all the legal work; the community bank set up a trust for the money to be donated into once the auction happened. It was an amazing thing to see so many helping a fallen soldier's family.

"Clear." Gabe barked gruffly.

Gabe still had Hoochie asleep in his arms, and I smiled inwardly. No one could resist my kitty. Max, the king of cat haters, even liked him. That was saying something since he used to go out of his way to torture the cats we had growing up.

I walked to my bedroom and grabbed the duffel bag that was in the back of my closet. I started stuffing it with underwear, bras, shirts, shorts, and flip-flops. I wasn't a big fan of dressing up.

I made sure to grab my old rabbit that I slept with every night. It definitely had seen better days, but it didn't stop me from cuddling him every night as I fell asleep. Poodle, my rabbit, was the very reason that Cheyenne and I had become best friends. We were young when we discovered that we slept with our stuffed animals every night, and we have been best friends ever since.

I left the bag on the bed and walked back out to the living room. Gabe and Jack were busy studying my picture collection. I was a picture hoarder. Photos covered three quarters of my living room wall. I had pictures of absolutely everything: birthdays, Christmases, weddings, and even one at a funeral. Gabe was stuck in front of one, in particular, and I blushed scarlet red.

The picture was of Gabe on his death machine. He looked badass with his black leather vest, black helmet, black jeans, black Oakley sunglasses, and the big black Harley Davidson. The motorcycle is a "*Fat Bob*;" I giggled to myself every time I thought about its name. I'd snapped the photo when he was riding out of Free, and immediately took it to Walgreen's and had it blown up. Then I bought a beautiful black frame, and plonked it down right in the middle of my mantel so I could see it every time I walked in the door. I did too. I admired it, drooled over it, and even kissed it once. Okay, maybe it was twice, but who's counting?

Gabe turned to me with a grin, when he noticed I was in the room. He took in my blush with a quick look; his smile got wider. Damn. There were those dimples.

"When did you take this?" he asked me.

"About eight or nine months ago, why?" I asked.

"I like it, that's all. I also like that you have it in such a prime location." He answered quietly.

I rolled my eyes, and made my way into the kitchen. Grabbing the binder that was on the table, as well as the lap top that was sitting beside it, I turned on my heels to go back into the living room, but was stopped by a brick wall named Gabe.

I sent him a glare, but that didn't deter him. He lifted his hands up to frame my face gently, then leaned forward slowly and placed a soft kiss on my lips. He backed away then, taking the things that I had in my hands with him. I stood frozen there for a good two minutes before my feet came unglued from the tile beneath my feet.

I walked back into the living room; Gabe had all my shit in his hands, while Jack had Hoochie and his litter box. I flipped all of the lights off, and we headed back down to the vehicles. I tried my hardest not to stare at the prime grade A ass that was walking down the stairs in front of me, but no matter what I did, my eyes wouldn't look away.

Soon Ember dear, soon.

Ω

After arriving at Gabe's home and getting Hoochie settled, I went to see Cheyenne while Gabe went to the main office to speak with the guys. I walked two doors down, and entered without knocking. Screams and shrill whines assaulted my eardrums upon opening the door. I took quick inventory on what was going on, then burst out laughing. Poor Chey looked miserable. She was face down on the couch, head buried into the couch cushions. Pru was sitting on her back, naked, pulling on her hair, bouncing up and down riding her like a pony. Piper, I couldn't see, but definitely could hear.

I walked to the couch and snagged Pru around the middle, tossing her up into the air and then catching her. Her shiny white blonde ringlet hair tickled my face as I gave her a smacking kiss on her cheek. She squealed and giggled wildly.

"What are you doing to your poor mama? And why are you naked?" I asked her, not that she answered me.

She was only a year and probably didn't understand half of what I said. Cheyenne moaned from the couch and I laughed. Slinging Pru onto my hip, I went in search of Piper, and found her in the kitchen. It wasn't a pretty sight.

"Oh. My. God." I exclaimed aloud.

I left the room and got Pru into a diaper. Their room was a mess, just like Cheyenne's normally was. Shoving the shit on the changing table to the floor, I quickly changed her and stuffed her into the first onesie I found. Grabbing one for Piper as well, I headed out of the room. Walking slowly, placing each foot onto a tile with the upmost precision, I bent and scooped up Piper, then made my way back out to the living room, and exited out the front door. I walked quickly, ignoring the pain in my back.

Walking into the side door of the garage, I heard voices coming from the office. I made my way towards them, ignoring the fact that Gabe was giving them a rundown of what happened at the police station.

Entering the office, all eyes swung to me, and then widened.

Yes, it was that bad. Piper was covered head to toe in oil, flour, and blue food coloring. She looked like a fucking Smurf. I marched directly to Sam, and deposited each kid onto his lap. His hands were held out at his sides at shoulder level, unsure what to do with what I placed in his arms. Turning, I tossed the clothes onto the desktop, and exited the office without a word.

Once back at Cheyenne's, I started tackling the mess that was the kitchen. It only took two towels, an industrial sized trash bag, and a bottle of Pine Sol. The kitchen smelled rolls of paper refreshing when I was finished with it, but my back was screaming like a bitch. I took a hit of Ibuprofen and made my way back to the couch where Cheyenne still had her head buried.

"What the fuck?" I asked her.

A garbled mess of words followed my question.

"Turn over and face me like a real man." I snipped to her, snickering silently.

She turned over in a flourish of arms and legs, tears covered her cheeks; they were still leaking out of her eyes.

"This is about me, isn't it?" I asked. "I didn't mean to not call you, but I was high on the good stuff last night, and I didn't even think about it. Apparently, I shunned Max too, but that's not really my fault. You know I would never leave you out intentionally. The good thing that's come out of this is that Gabe touched my girly parts, and told me he wanted me. I also got a kiss. I think I had an orgasm. I'm not sure, because I haven't felt anything like that before. Benny never gave me one, so I'm not real sure what it feels like to have one from someone besides myself."

My ramblings slowly faded as I watched Cheyenne start to cry harder on the couch.

"Get on with it already." I demanded.

"I'm pregnant!" she wailed.

49

Oh, lord Jesus. No wonder she was so upset. She was meticulous about birth control ever since she had the twins. Apparently, they were a lot of work. Who knew?

"Oh honey, this is a good thing. Babies are miracles. If you're pregnant, then it was meant to be." I whispered to her quietly.

Her tears dried, and she took a deep calming breath.

"I know, but I was so close to having a real job. So close. Now I'll have to wait another year to start working. If I'll be able to at all. Do you know how much childcare is?" she asked.

Well, no, I didn't. I didn't have any kids, so why would I need to know that juicy bit of information?

We gabbed for another hour. However, after the third time she said something bitchy to me, I told her to take her cranky ass to bed. She agreed with one condition.

"Tell Sam for me."

Once I agreed, I left her to sleep and made my way back to the office. Everything was quiet except the low hum of deep male voices.

Max had Pru in his arms, fast asleep on his shoulder. Gabe had Piper, who was asleep and drooling as well. The Smurf still had a blue tint to her, but she was otherwise clean.

"Awww, aren't y'all just too cute!" I announced to the group at large.

Pulling out my cell phone, I snapped a few pictures. A few protests went up when my phone appeared, but they stayed where they were and let me get a shot.

Smiling down at the photos, Sam interrupted me to ask, "So what happened?"

"Well….Cheyenne was having a breakdown on the couch while Piper played in the kitchen with the ingredients Cheyenne was using to make a cake. Apparently, she couldn't handle making it anymore when she found out you knocked her up again." I said nonchalantly.

Sam's boots hit the floor with a thud. You could hear a pin drop in that office. Sam actually looked scared, and I burst out laughing.

"She's going to kill me." He muttered, putting his head into his hands.

"Oh, yes; most certainly, my Dear Watson." I snickered, smiling wide. "You can go; I'll watch the girls for an hour until you can come get them."

Sam got up, walked over to me and kissed me on the forehead before going to Cheyenne. The silence remained for a few seconds, until chuckles filled the air from each of the men in the room. Jack, James, Max, Elliott, and Gabe all had wide smiles on their faces. This was a blessing, and everyone was happy, even if Cheyenne wasn't.

Ω
Gabe

The tiny duplex was filled to the brim with people. Everyone that meant something to me was in the room. Although I loved them, I hoped they would leave soon. I wanted to spend some time with Ember, and I couldn't do that with kids and people capturing her attention. We'd had an impromptu barbeque celebrating Sam and Cheyenne's exciting news.

Everyone was over the moon, and Cheyenne had come around once she spoke with Sam. I envied them at times. I'd always wanted kids, just hadn't met the right woman to have them with; that is, until I met Ember.

Cheyenne and Sam were the firsts to leave, followed shortly by James and Janie, Blaine and Elliott, Jack, and, finally, Max.

Max wrapped Ember in a tender hug, and spoke quietly into her ear. He rubbed his bearded face on her hair, gave her a kiss and walked out. Ember stood there for a few seconds before raising her eyes to mine and smiling slightly.

"I worried him last night, and he told me to stay close to you." She explained to me.

"You worried all of us last night. Max and me more than the rest. We'll figure this out though. Don't worry too much about it." I explained comfortingly.

I wasn't so sure this would all be figured out and wrapped up into a nice bow. I was being positive for Ember's sake, but I honestly didn't feel too good about this. I had a feeling this was going to get nasty and a whole lot more dangerous before it started to get better. From what I'd learned of the Blue Skulls over the past year, this was about to turn ugly, and I'd have to be constantly on guard.

They were a nasty gang, and had little regard for people outside of their gang. They went into a fight and didn't really care if they won or lost; they took out whoever was a danger to their gang. Just from local chatter, as well as findings from Luke, I knew that this wasn't just a minor gang. This was a small branch of a much larger gang, which spread across Texas, and flooded into Louisiana, Arkansas, Arizona, and Nevada. I just hoped to God that I could figure out how to fix this before anything bad happened.

I had faith that I could take care of Ember, but I knew they weren't going to give up without a fight. They would go after her family, kids she saw at work, even casual acquaintances if that's what it took. All I knew was that I'd die before anything happened to her; without her in my life, I'd be incomplete.

We headed to bed shortly after. Ember had a full day, and the pain and lack of sleep were catching up with her. I practically had to undress her and put her to bed, by the time it was all said and done.

She was sound asleep by the time I got out of the bathroom. I went to the drawers and looked for a pair of clean sleep pants, but didn't see any. I glanced at the bed, saw how dead to the world she was, and decided that I could get by with just the briefs.

Crawling in next to her, I covered us both with the blanket and fell into a deep sleep with the woman I may possibly love, by my side. Oh, who was I kidding? I was already gone.

Ω

This was a great dream.

Ember was grinding her pubic bone against my full length. I had a hold of her hips in a tight grip, helping her with her movements. She was moaning loudly in my ear, and then she suddenly grinded down and froze. Moaning even more loudly, she came in a rush.

I could feel her slick heat through my briefs, and decided that grinding wasn't good enough. Moving my hand down to my underwear, I shoved them down so my cock was now up tight against her cotton panties. It felt divine, but I wanted that juicy slickness as if I was dying of starvation.

Shoving her panties to the side, for convenience, I probed her entrance with my finger and found her wet and very ready for me. Lifting her up slightly, I positioned my cock at her entrance with one hand, and took her hip in the other. Simultaneously, I thrust up and pushed down, burying myself to the balls in one swift movement.

It was at that moment that I realized I wasn't dreaming. Nothing could feel this good in a dream. This was heaven. Nothing had ever felt better than this. I opened my eyes; Ember's dark eyes were staring back at me. She was so goddamn beautiful. Her hair fell over her shoulders and came to a rest on my bare chest. My shirt was riding up high on her waist.

It was still dark out; I glanced at the clock to see that it was a little after three in the morning. Turning back to her, I framed her face with my big hands.

"I've wanted to be inside of you for forever. Nothing compares to the feeling of being inside you." I exclaimed desperately, flexing my hips up into her once more.

When she let out a small whimper, I took that as my cue to start moving harder. When I couldn't reach the desired depth, I pulled her off my cock and set her gently beside me on her knees. She looked beautiful like this too. Underwear askew, only giving me a tiny peak at what I wanted. Pulling her underwear down to her knees, I left them there so she would have to keep her legs tight together.

Taking my cock in my hand, I slapped it against her pussy once, and then did it again when she moaned and pushed back against me, looking to bring me inside of her.

"You want my dick back, baby?" I asked, smacking her clit with the head of my cock.

When she didn't answer, and moaned in reply, I rubbed her clit with the head, back and forth, until finally she called out to me.

"Please, Gabe." She pleaded.

"Please what, amorzinho?"

"Please, Gabe. Please, fuck me."

"Such a dirty mouth on you. But it will be my pleasure." I said, before slamming back inside of her.

I fucked her long and hard. I gave each pump everything I had to give. Over and over again, I went balls deep, hitting her cervix with each thrust.

"I'm close. Oh, God." She exclaimed.

"Not God baby, just Gabe." I hissed, pumping my dick in and out.

Then a thought occurred to me, and I froze.

"Are you on birth control?" I rasped.

"Yes!" She keened.

Worries alleviated, I started to pound into her again. In and out. In and out. Suddenly, she peaked. The walls of her vagina clamped down on my dick with a force I've never experienced before. It was as if she wanted to hold me inside of her and never let go.

I wanted that too, but my climax didn't care. A zing shot down my spine and seemed to settle deep in my balls before I exploded. My come shot into Ember so hard that it literally took my breath away. I squeezed my eyes shut and pumped through it until it finally ended. I gave her hip a firm squeeze before pulling out of her and flopping down onto my back, panting.

"My god. That was a-fucking-mazing. Can we do it again?" Ember said from beside me.

She was flopped down onto her stomach, her panties still down around her knees, and her shirt rucked up to just under her breasts. Her hair was flying all around her, and she was smiling from ear to ear.

"I knew it would be like that with us. I knew it. Why the hell I waited so long to go after you, I don't know." I said to her, kissing my way down her spine. My lips brushed lightly over the gauze so I wouldn't hurt her.

"Oh, I think that the buildup was what made that so explosive. Just give me a few minutes to get my bearings, and I'll be ready for round two." She said, then her eyes closed, and she was back in la la land.

Figures. At least I knew that I could have her again anytime I wanted her. Yes, I would just rest my eyes here for a few minutes and catch my breath. Then I would wake her up and start that whole beautiful process over again.

Chapter 4

*Love is the feeling you get when you like something as much
as your motorcycle.
-Biker Truth*

Ember

One week later

I awoke to lips and a prickly beard running up the inside of my thigh. I was on my stomach on the bed. Somehow, I was naked, even though I specifically remembered putting underwear and one of Gabe's t-shirts on. I didn't sleep naked. I felt like if there was an emergency, in the middle of the night, I damn sure would have a clean pair of underwear and something covering my boobies.

Speaking of covering my boobies, hands slid in between the bed and my breasts. Massaging and kneading them, plucking at my nipples. He ground his erection into my ass, mimicking thrusting. I buried my head into the pillow and groaned. My god, we'd been going at it like bunnies for a freakin' week, and I still want him just as much, if not more, than I did the first time.

"Wake up, meu anjinho. You have to be at work in an hour, and I have plans for you before you go." He said gruffly.

I pushed my butt up against him, and he groaned in pleasure. Taking my hips in his rough grip, he pulled me until I was on my knees, face still in the mattress. We always seemed to end up in this position for some reason, I liked it deep and rough, and this way made it to where Gabe could take me roughly. It was also the way I slept. Therefore, when Gabe woke me in the morning, it was how I was situated when he started. We did this two to three times a day, and we both knew what positions worked the best for us.

Gabe was everything I could ever want and more. He knew how to work his rock hard body. He also knew how to work mine. I've had two other sexual partners, and neither one could hold a candle to how hot he made me.

His cock abruptly slammed into me from behind. A squeak emerged from my throat at the suddenness, but that didn't deter him. He pounded his cock into me, but pulled out a minute or so later, flipping me over to my back. Lifting my right leg over his shoulder, he positioned himself at my entrance again, sliding home with one smooth slick thrust. My leg was plastered against his rock hard abs and chest. His dog tags swung with each thrust of his body, making clinking sounds that sounded like music setting the tempo for our lovemaking.

He leaned down, took one of my nipples between his lips and sucked hard. My body arched off the bed, trying to get closer to his mouth. My leg was wedged between both of our bodies, and Gabe's cock was bottoming out inside of me. He released my nipple from the suction of his lips with an audible pop, and leaned back so he could watch his cock enter my wet heat. He reached his hand down and rubbed my entrance, while his cock was sliding in and out. He let the tip of his finger slip into me, and the added fullness set me off like a rocket.

He gave a few more hammering thrusts and then came himself, shooting into me in hot thick pulses. He stayed inside me while we caught our breath. He slowly shrunk inside me, pulling out, reluctantly, a few minutes later; his come slid out of me and onto the sheets. He watched as it trailed down my lips, past my anus, and pooled underneath my butt on the sheets. Reaching down, he used the side of his index finger, gathered some of our combined wetness, and rubbed it back up until he reached my clit. I jumped from the sensitivity and moaned because, surprisingly, it still felt unbelievable. Normally, I was too sensitive but he knew just how to work me.

He continued to rub and flick until I had a second orgasm, arching my spine and throwing my head back. Dropping my leg to his side, he leaned in and gave me a chaste kiss on the lips.

"Mmmm. Now that's how I like to start my morning." He said, kissing me softly before heading into the bathroom.

The shower turned on a few seconds later. I glanced at the clock realizing that I had a little over forty-five minutes until I needed to be at work. Hmmmm. I decided to rest my eyes for just a few seconds more.

I woke up for real the second time, with a hand clamped around my ankle with an unbreakable hold, dragging me down the bed. Asshole. I only wanted fifteen more minutes.

"I'm up!" I screamed into my pillow, which I'd managed to hold onto through my rough treatment.

"We need to leave in ten. You need to get your ass in gear. I've got a ton of shit to get done today, and I need to drop you off on my way; let's get going." Gabe stated, while giving my ass a smack and leaving the room.

Heaving an exasperated sigh, I rolled out of bed, and took a quick shower. I threw my hair up into my usual messy bun, swiped on some mascara and deodorant, and then went in search of clothes. Finding some clean ones at the end of the bed, I pulled on a pair of fold-over capri yoga pants, an ancient shirt from my junior year volleyball team, and my hot pink tennis shoes. Perfect.

Being an athletic trainer really worked well for my style of dress. I wasn't expected to dress up, and tennis shoes were a required accessory when you needed to get places in a hurry.

When I was in high school, I was at a volleyball summer camp, prior to my senior year, when I tore my ACL. It was a horrific experience. I still remember trying to put weight on my bad leg and walk off the court when the top of my leg went one way and the bottom went another. After about six months of recovery and therapy, I found my calling. It also didn't hurt that I could wear what I wanted to. With the help of the trainer from my high school, I started down a path that found me where I was today. I graduated from a local Baptist college, ETBU, four years after I graduated high school. Then I found my dream job in the town that I grew up, and close to my only family, Max. Now Gabe was here too, and that made my life all the better.

There was that bothersome gang that kept putting a damper on things, but I knew that Gabe and Max would figure this out. As long as I was safe and did what I was told, I knew that I would be okay.

Rushing outside of the room, Gabe was nowhere to be found. Assuming he was outside, I grabbed my bag and phone and ran out the door. There he was, on his death machine. Today, he was wearing dark washed jeans with a red plain cotton t-shirt. Ray-Bans covered his eyes, his black hair was pulled back with a bandana, and he was just reaching for my helmet when he spotted me. He grinned broadly and patted the bitch seat behind him. Smiling inwardly with glee at his beautiful smile, I dashed towards the motorcycle and hopped on the back, wrapping my arms around him tightly.

"Ready!" I cried excitedly.

I love this bike; it makes my day when I get to ride on the back of it. The ride was so free and exhilarating. I loved how my hair became a tangled mess around my face. I loved the way my stomach would turn and flip when we went around a tight curve. I also loved when Gabe revved the motor it would make my whole body feel like I touched a live wire. Gabe loved to do that. He thought it was hilarious that I would squeal in excitement.

We were just about to take off when I saw Max come out of his place and turn to walk towards his bike. I tapped Gabe on the shoulder and got off sprinting in the direction of Max. When I got close enough, I launched myself onto his back, wrapping my legs around his waist and my arms around his neck. Max started to flip me off his back almost instantaneously, but I held strong, clinging like a monkey and started giving him big smacking kisses on his cheek. I made sure to put extra drool into them for good effect.

"You're such a fucking weirdo. I swear I don't know how we're related." Max said shaking his head in exasperation.

Laughing lightly, I dropped my legs and arms and took off running towards Gabe. He had his head back laughing when he noticed Max wiping the slobber off his cheek. Taking in his expression made my heart feel light. It wasn't often that I got to see him smiling and carefree. He was always in such a dark mood, and it made me wonder about his past and secrets. I knew he would tell me in time, but, for now, it still bugged the crap out of me not to know.

"He's gonna repay you one of these days, and don't come hide behind me when he does. I don't want my ass kicked, please." Gabe said to me.

He handed my helmet back to me, then gunned the engine, taking off into the early morning air.

We arrived at the campus in record time. He pulled right up to the back doors of the gym, and got off. He pulled his helmet off, hooked it on the handle, and then extended his hand to me. Grabbing it, I climbed off and did the same with my helmet. There were a few students milling around, and they'd all stopped and stared at Gabe. The girls were all glassy eyed, while the boys were all looking at him with envious eyes. Guess riding a motorcycle made you popular with the jocks.

Gabe was oblivious to the stares. He was taking in the new security system, walking around watching, while the cameras moved to different angles every thirty seconds. Grabbing my hand, he walked with me up to the gym door that now had a scanner you needed to use to get in. He held out his hand and I gave him my lanyard, which had my school ID attached to it. He slid my card and the little light beside the panel glowed green. The door clicked open and we went inside.

"My office is –" I started to say when he interrupted me,

"I know where your office is, Em. I was the one who installed a lot of the security. There's a camera in your office, by the way, so don't do anything I wouldn't do. On the other hand, if you do want to do something like that, let me know so I can pull up the feed. I have this all hooked into my phone; it's also fed back to the compound." Gabe said as we arrived at my office door.

He used a code to get me into the door and closed it behind us. Surveying the office with critical eyes, he walked up to the window and peered out. Then walked back to the desk and pulled the desk drawer open.

"Your panic button is right here. If you even think you need to use this, use it. If you have a feeling that something is wrong, then use it. It'll notify all of us, but it also sends a direct phone call to the KPD. Remember what we talked about last night. You do not, under any circumstance, go outside. You stay in your office or the training room. Don't wander around. There're plenty of students around here who would give a left nut to do something for you. Use the button. Call me if you need anything. I'll be back around four to pick you up." He said quickly before kissing me.

Shit.

The day started on a good note, but by the end of it my head was pounding, my back was aching, and I was in a foul mood. I still had two hours to go when I decided to stop for the day. I was tired of whiny kids not doing what they were told. They treated this as a teen hangout, and that was not what this place was. This was a place for healing and relaxing. One certain jock wasn't taking the hint, and I finally called campus security remove him. Closing and locking the doors of the training room, I made my way slowly back to the office.

Pulling out my phone, I started to text Gabe for a ride, when I bumped into something solid. Looking up I spotted one of my favorite students. I started to smile at him when I noticed the deep regret in his eyes.

"What's wrong, Kale?" I asked him.

Kale was of Native American descent. He had coal black eyes, long black hair, and a wiry lean body. He would be gorgeous in another couple of years.

Kale took so long to answer that I started worrying that something was really wrong. Now he was looking down at his feet. Reaching my hand out, I grabbed his hand and gave a small tug.

"Kale?" I asked again.

His look told me he was agonized about something. Finally, he seemed to come to a decision, reached into his pocket, and pulled out a white envelope and handed it to me. He pulled out a blue bandana and walked away. What.The.Fuck? Opening the letter, I read it and then re-read it again.

Ember,
I know you trust me, and I wish I could've been worthy of that trust. I'm the one who told the Blue Skulls about you. I didn't know what else to do. They have my little brother; he's only ten. Last week they made him beat an old lady. I can't get him out without getting back in myself. I never would've believed when I left them that they would recruit him. I got to get him out. I'm gonna watch out for you as best I can. I'll give you information when it's safe. Forgive me.
Kale

My breathing turned sporadic, and tears stung my eyes. That poor kid. Poor baby. Oh god. Reaching for my phone, I whipped it out and dialed Gabe's phone number. It rang three times before he picked up.

"I'm outside, come to me." Gabe answered, before hanging up.

Hands shaking, I made my way outside; the sun blinded me as I pushed the door open. Gabe was there straddling his bike, but was quickly by my side as soon as he registered the look on my face. Gabe's hands went around me, and I buried my face into the muscles of his chest. His dog tags dug into my forehead, but the pain wasn't registering. I was numb.

"What happened?" he asked.

"Kale sold me out!" I cried.

Taking my head in his hands, he pulled my face out of his chest and wiped my tears with his thumbs.

"One more time." He said.

"Kale, my most beautiful and promising student, joined that gang. And he sold me out!" I said handing him the note.

He took the note out of my hand, and scanned it. He reread it and then folded the note up, shoving it in his back pocket.

"This could be a good thing, Ember. I know you don't like that he did that to you, and I sure as fuck don't like it either, but we could use this to our advantage. We can get some information next time I corner him. He could've kept this from us; I think he wants to help, because if this got back to the Skulls, he would be dead. It wouldn't be a nice death, either. These gangs are crazy as fuck." He said to me gently.

"I know. I just can't believe that this was who started this for me. I brought him food, I gave him rides home, and I picked up his brother and him when their car broke down. I even took his little brother to his pediatric appointment when he broke his arm!" I said.

"We'll figure this out, bebê." He whispered into my hair.

When he said things like that to me, in Portuguese, it made me all tingly inside. My heart lightened a little from its heavy feel. Gabe made me feel things, things that I haven't felt since I was a teenager, when my parents died.

"You make me feel alive and whole again; I haven't been right since my parents died. I feel like I'm slowly getting back to my old self. I can put on a good front, smile and act happy, but it's been a long time since I have truly *felt* happy. I know we're in a shitty situation, but you being here makes it all okay." I whispered to him, while burying my face into his neck.

"I want you to tell me more, but not until we get you home. Being out here in the open makes me twitchy." Gabe explained.

He grabbed my hand and hauled me over to his bike. The ride took no time at all. As soon as we made it through the front door, I made a beeline for the fridge and grabbed us both a beer. If I was going to spill my guts, I needed some liquid courage. Handing him his beer, once I was back in the living room, I plopped down into the Lazy Boy that sat directly across the fireplace, where Gabe had parked himself.

'Okay, here goes nothin'' I think to myself. I hadn't spoken about this to anyone since the week after it happened. I'd spilled my guts to Cheyenne, and we never spoke of it again.

"It's been a little over nine years now, and, at twenty five, it feels just as raw now as it did then. I can still remember when Max came to get me from school to tell me. It was during lunch, I was sitting at my usual table with Cheyenne, and our closest friends. We were having a great time laughing and playing around when I glanced up and saw Max there, dressed in his fatigues, wearing a grim expression. The lunchroom had gone quiet, and all eyes watched as Max scanned the lunchroom for me. My stomach had fallen to my knees, and I stood up slowly. Max found me then, and started walking towards me."

I closed my eyes and took a deep breath, and then started again.

"I hadn't seen Max in a little over six months. He'd joined the army right after high school, and when he left for boot camp, it was the hardest thing I've ever done. Max was my rock, my confidant. He knew my hopes and dreams; he beat up anyone that looked at me funny. I'd never been away from him for more than a weekend since I was born. When he deployed, I was lost. But seeing him right then, I knew something had to be horribly wrong since he was supposed to be thousands of miles away in Iraq. He didn't waste any time. Once he reached me, he grabbed me by one hand and Cheyenne by the other and led us out into the hallway. He didn't stop until we reached his old Blazer in the front visitor's lot."

Gabe must have felt I needed the support because, suddenly, I found myself sitting in his lap, my head tucked up under his chin.

"Keep goin'." He said.

"Anyway, once we came to a stop beside the truck, Max took me into his arms and nearly broke me with a bear hug. He told me that our parents had died on their way back home from visiting my grandmother. Their plane crashed while it was landing. The landing equipment never engaged. They didn't die right away either. They burned to death. They were wrapped around each other when they were extracted from the burning remains of the plane. We had a whirlwind the next two days. The funeral was planned for the day after, and Max was shipped back to Iraq before we could even take a full breath. I was left alone in a huge empty house. Cheyenne's mom had guardianship of me, but I didn't stay with them. My parent's life insurance policies were doled out; we had plenty to pay off the house, cars, bills, funeral costs; I invested the rest. I had to go from partying carefree Ember, to responsible Ember in less than two days. When I needed my brother the most, he wasn't there. I didn't see him unless he was on leave. The only good thing in my life was Cheyenne."

"Sounds like we could be soul mates. I've had one shitty thing happen to me after another too." He said to me forlornly.

"I think, since I shared my shit life story with you, you should share yours." I said seriously.

This was my chance. If I had known that was all it took, I would have spilled these crappy memories from the get go. I'd been wondering what made Gabe tick since I met him. He was always the 'sit in the back of the room and watch' type of guy. He would join in reluctantly, but never of his own volition.

He was also the type of man whose presence you couldn't ignore. My eyes were always drawn to him; I itched to be near him. However, he always came off unapproachable. It was as if one damaged soul was drawn to another. His story had to be hard, in order to bring down a man whose presence seemed bigger than life.

"Not really much to tell. I just have shit luck. My dad died when I was young, my mom remarried a piece of shit who made me feel like I wasn't good enough to do anything. Then my mom died of the same disease that took my dad. A year later, my girlfriend aborted my kid without my knowledge. Since then, two of my closest friends have died. I'm just not that lucky. That is, until I met you. When I met you, I started to feel different. I was happy when I was around you." He said.

I sat up straight in his lap, then turned to look into his eyes. They gave nothing away. When he gave that speech, it was all monotone. Like he didn't feel any emotion anymore.

"Okay. Do you mind if I ask you questions?" I said while looking deeply into his eyes.

"You can ask, but I don't know that I'll answer. Some of it's still too raw." He said.

I didn't know where to even start. Therefore, I started with the one that irritated me the most.

"So ... who's the bitch I need to kill, and where does she live?" I asked seriously.

Gabe burst out laughing, making my heart go a pitter-patter. I didn't say anything else, though; I was completely serious. If I knew where she lived, I would give her a piece of my mind. I had a strong pro-life stance, and felt that every human being deserved a fighting chance.

I knew there were some circumstances where abortion was the only option, but in Gabe's case, I felt like there was something more to the story. She didn't have that excuse. Once his laughter died down, he started speaking.

"I met Sidney when I was home on leave. We hit it off, and

dated for about a year when we found out she was pregnant. I was over the moon. I was confused on how it happened, since I never once forgot the condom and, supposedly, she was on the pill. That's neither here nor there. I was a guarded happy. I wanted the baby, but wasn't too sure about her. The circumstances seemed a little fishy, but there was nothing I could do about it. She found out the day before I was to deploy for six months, and I didn't have enough time to process that she was pregnant. She made a doctor's appointment, and sent me a picture about four weeks in to my deployment. Three months in, she sent me a "Dear John" letter. It said that she was no longer in love with me, that she found someone else. She was kind enough to tell me in a P.S. that she wasn't pregnant anymore; she took care of it the day after I was deployed."

I was stunned into silence. I honestly didn't know what the fuck to say to that. Who in the hell would write that in a letter? This man was fighting for our freedom. He was in a danger zone that could've killed him if his whole mind wasn't on the task at hand. Anyone who was anyone would have known that you didn't tell someone that. Hell, if that woman had any morals what-so-ever, she wouldn't have aborted his baby in the first place. What kind of God-awful person did this?

"I don't even know what to say to that." I said quietly.

Leaning down, I gave him a soft kiss on the lips.

"Nothing to say. I just hope I never see her again. I had the landlord kick her out of the house. Apparently, the new love interest had moved in. I closed the account that had our name on it. I also called movers to move all my shit into storage. I didn't leave her with a thing. I was so disgusted with her that I cut all ties with her. I never went back to that town. I moved here when I retired from the army." He said.

The more he told me about this woman, the more upset I got. If I'd been a cartoon character, I would be blowing steam out of my nostrils and ears right about now. My eyes would also be shooting laser beams. What. A. Bitch.

"What a bitch!" I fumed.

One of Gabe's rare smiles flashed across his face. It was a good thing to see right about now. No wonder he always seemed moody. He's had a tough lot given to him in life.

"How long ago was this?" I asked cautiously.

"I got out of the army a year and three months ago." He said quietly. "If the baby had lived, he would be a year and a half."

Oh Jesus. Tears were running down my face.

"Your mom?" I sniffled out.

"She died while I was on deployment. She didn't even tell me. I never knew until they told me she had gone. My stepfather had the funeral before I could even get home on emergency leave. Didn't even bury her where she wanted to be buried; next to my dad. He had her buried in some tomb in Grand Rapids, Michigan. She hated it there. Dad was buried in Detroit." He said easily.

A little too easily. His face was closed off now, and I knew that I had pushed him farther than he wanted to go. Deciding to change the subject, I started telling him a funny story about Max, James, Cheyenne and me.

"So this one time at band camp." I said, while pausing for

effect.

He rolled his eyes, exasperated at my attempt at lightheartedness. I small smile crooked the corner of his lip up.

"Okay, it wasn't at band camp. Cheyenne and I were having a sleepover and found out that Max and James were going on a double date that night. So, we did what any thirteen year old would do, we hid in the back of the car while they went to pick up their dates. Things were moving along nicely until around ten that evening. We thought they would just go to a movie, but they didn't. They went to some party, and we were stuck in the car for hours. Luckily, we planned ahead and brought snacks and drinks. Here we were hanging out in the back seat eating some trail mix when the cops show up. The car was boxed in pretty good, and there was utter chaos going on outside our doors. Deciding that it was best for us to get out of there, I hotwired the car-" I was saying before he interrupted me.

"What do you mean, you hotwired the car?" He asked.

"I learned that useful skill on YouTube. I also know how to get out of zip ties, and pick a lock. Cheyenne and I practiced." I said proudly.

"Why would you need to know how to do this?" he asked.

"Duh. Because it is useful information. Especially in that situation. Anyway, I started the car, and only hit the car in front of me twice before I managed to get us turned around and headed out of there. About that time, James and Max come barreling out of the house. Their dates were nowhere to be seen. They're running full tilt towards us and hop in the back seat just as I peeled out of the driveway, skirting the cops as I went. I was one of many cars, though, and managed to get out of there before being questioned. Max and James were drunk as skunks in the back seat, and passed out before we even made it home. I parked outside of Cheyenne's house and we left there asses there on the front lawn. We went back to my house. The next morning we went out to the car and realized that more damage was done to the car than we'd originally thought. Cheyenne's mom came out around that time and found us staring at the car. You should have seen how pissed she got. To this day, they don't remember how they got home, and think that one of them wrecked the car and drove drunk."

"You can't be serious." He said to me. "You were only thirteen. How did you know how to drive?"

"I used to borrow Max's car all the time. I was a little bit of a delinquent." I explained.

"A little bit of a delinquent. Are you still this way?" he asked.

"I'm a tad impulsive, but I would never endanger myself."

"Well, thank God for small things"

Chapter 5

I wake up in the morning and I piss excellence.
-Talladega Nights

Gabe

"I think we can use this kid. He doesn't want to be in this situation, and if we help get the brother out, he won't have a reason to be entering the gang anymore."

I was in the down room with Sam, Max and Jack. Elliott was at home with Blaine, who was perilously close to dropping her kid out on the pavement at any moment. Cheyenne and Ember decided to help Blaine around the house. James was delivering a bird to her new cage in South Louisiana.

"What does Luke think?" Sam asked.

I turned my head and looked Sam in the eyes. He had his feet propped up on the edge of the desk, while grease covered him from head to toe, and a Heineken dangled from his fingers.

"He tried to make contact, but the kid's like a ghost. Knows his shit. I've only been able to tail him twice in the past two days. Once to school, and the other on his way home from school. He gave me the slip though, because when I knocked on the door the grandma said he wasn't home, and she didn't look like the type to take any shit. I haven't seen any Skulls near him at all." I answered him.

Sam nodded and seemed to lose himself in thought. Max

was staring at me with scrutinizing eyes. He'd been doing this ever since Ember started staying with me. He knew that I was sleeping with his sister and didn't seem too happy about it. He could go fuck himself.

My phone rang, interrupting the quiet. Ember's bright idea of putting "*The Bad In Me*" by Jake Owen, shifted the mood from serious and somber to playful. Sam chuckled, and Max faced cracked into a semblance of a smile. Apparently, he understood his sister's sense of humor. I would have sworn he'd kick my ass when he heard the part about having nothin' on.

For the life of me I couldn't figure out how she found this song, let alone how she managed to get the shit on the phone. I haven't changed it yet. It's something she would do to me, calling me at work when she knew I couldn't come to her. Teasing me, and making me want her for the rest of the day.

Ember's name and picture of her foot flashed across the screen, and I smiled wide as I picked it up.

"Yeah?" I asked.

"Can you take Blaine, Cheyenne, and me to Baby's R Us? Elliott needs to go check on his mom, and Cheyenne's mom has the twins. We need to get her the rest of the shit she needs before the baby gets here. She's being induced in a week."

Oh didn't this just sound like a shit load of fun. It was nice that she at least asked me to go with her, instead of just going, as I knew she wanted to do.

"Yeah, I'll be there in about ten minutes. Is that enough time?" I asked.

"Perfect. We'll be waiting outside Blaine's." she stated before hanging up.

Sighing loudly, I touched the end button and shoved the phone back into my pocket. Walking over to the desk, I grabbed my spare Colt out of the desk drawer, pulled the slide back to check the chamber, then shoved it into the back of my jeans. Normally I only carried my Glock on my ankle, but today I felt the need for some extra firepower just in case I needed to shoot myself in the middle of the baby food aisle. Just kidding. Maybe.

"Gotta go take the girls to a fuckin' baby store." I grumbled. "Let me know what Jack can pull up, I'm sure I could use some distraction while going to baby land."

Sam and Max chuckled.

"Better you than me, my man." Sam said.

"It'll be you again in a couple months." I shot back as I walked out of the room.

Sam's cell started ringing just as I made it through the bay door. I bypassed my bike and decided to walk since I wouldn't be using it. Turning to the side of the garage, I saw Ember with her arm around Blaine's waist. She was whispering in Blaine's ear, but her eyes locked on me. It was obvious they were talking about me. The giggling cut off once I was close enough to distinguish clear sounds.

Ember was in a pair of tight white jean shorts and a Ranger's shirt. Blaine was wearing her usual long dress that brushed the top of her feet, stomach bulging out from her tiny frame. She looked like she would pop at any moment; not that I would dare tell her that. She was a little fire cracker, and I'll be damned if I lit her fuse.

Both women wore blinding smiles, which, if I was being truthful, made me a tad nervous. I always found that when women wore smiles like that, things didn't end well for me.

"Where's Cheyenne?" I asked.

"She and Sam are going to have a little alone time since her mom has the twins for the night."

I nodded. Must have been the call he got as I was leaving.

"Y'all ready to go?" I drawled.

I loved teasing Ember about her accent. *'Y'all'* was never in my vocabulary before I moved here. Ember decided to broaden my horizons, and started teaching me a few slang terms. I still couldn't figure out how they worked *'might could'* into a sentence. That one might never stick. *'Fixin' to'* was definitely easier to accommodate her with.

"Sure am. Blaine, here, is gonna need a lift into that monster truck of yours." She said.

I rolled my eyes. It wasn't that big. I just had thirty-five inch tires, and a four-inch lift put onto my Chevy the day before. Cheyenne and Ember absolutely adored it, or so they said; not like I cared what the girls thought. This was the dream truck I wanted since I was a little kid. My dad always used to talk about the kind of vehicle he would get if he could afford it; this was the one. I got it for him.

"Let's roll." I said, while walking to my truck.

I hoisted Blaine into the front seat, and did the same for Ember in the back.

Pulling out of Free, I hooked a left and started down Main Street. Just as I was about to turn onto Grand, a blue Impala zipped around me and cut me off. I'd clocked him as soon as I pulled out of Free, but I wasn't sure he belonged to the Skulls. Now I was. These kids in the front seat were wearing their signature blue bandanas and sitting low in their seats, practically laying down. They hit the brakes suddenly, but I expecting it and adjusted accordingly.

"Call your brother." I said, while breaking and putting some distance in between their car and my truck.

The little pricks were trying their hardest to get me to hit their vehicle, but this was nothing. I dodged IEDs in Afghanistan while driving an armored Humvee. Avoiding these shit heads was a piece of cake.

They weren't very skilled. They looked to be around fifteen or so, with just enough balls to think they could handle playing with the big boys. They most likely didn't have a learner's permit yet.

Ember was speaking quietly with Max, while Blaine sat tensely in the passenger seat, chewing her thumbnail. Flashing lights appeared in my rear view mirror, and the Impala took off. Two police cruisers passed us with a roar. The air that came off their car when they passed shook the truck, rocking it from side to side. Ember hung up with Max, and Blaine took a deep breath.

"Okay?" I asked them both.

"Okay." They replied.

Letting my grip loosen on the wheel slightly, I headed into the direction of the store. Ten silent minutes later, we arrived. Crisis averted.

"You have to park in the expectant mother's spot so Blaine doesn't have to hoof it too far." Ember said.

Blaine silently agreed with a nod of her head. Fuck me. Giving up the fight I knew was inevitable, I swung the truck into the spot that had a stork carrying a baby on the sign. Feeling like a dolt, I got out and rounded the car. Ember was sliding out of truck, while I went to the front door and helped Blaine down.

"Jesus Christ. My vagina bone is fucking killing me. I swear it feels like this kid is sitting in my vagina and pushing my pelvic bone to impossible proportions." Blaine said to Ember.

Ember made accommodating noises while I ignored them. Over the past year, I've gotten really good at tuning out their chatter. After listening to them talk about their periods, I concluded that it would be easier to ignore them. That wasn't something I liked to hear about, and Blaine's vagina bone was completely off limits.

The store itself was worse than I thought. It looked like a baby factory puked up its contents and arranged them in order. Bottles, beds, torturing devices disguised as breast pumps; clothes were scattered everywhere. There was even a second floor of more crap that I'm sure a baby would never use. We spent an hour on the bottom level of the store. In that time, a bitch of a storm rolled in and shook the building with the intensity of its thunder. Blaine also used the john no less than four times.

They decided that it was time to tackle the second floor, so we took our cart full of baby crap and made our way onto the elevator. The doors closed with a whoosh. The lights flickered once, and I had a horrifying thought that we shouldn't have taken the elevator; the lights went out completely and we were stranded in between the floors. Cursing silently, I made my way towards the numbers panel when the emergency lights came on. I pressed the big red emergency button, and a disembodied voice said that they were aware of the problem, and would get us out as soon as possible.

I hung my head and groaned. "Well doesn't that just fucking figure?"

"Blaine?" Ember cried shrilly.

Whirling around, I took in the figure of Blaine, hunched down over her big stomach. She was slightly panting, and her coloring was as white as a sheet.

Years' worth of medical training kicked in and I went to Blaine's stooped figure. My boots slipped slightly in a puddle on the floor and I knew, without asking, what it was; Blaine's water broke, in a stranded fucking elevator … with the fucking lights out. Panic came over me, but I shoved it down where it belonged. Panic had no place here right now. Just because I've never dealt with anything of this caliber before, didn't mean I couldn't handle it. Blaine probably wouldn't be in danger of having her baby before the lights were fixed anyway; first babies always took hours and hours to deliver. We were good.

Boy was I wrong.

Ω

Ah hour and a half later.

"Goddamn you, Elliott. You're never getting near my lady lumps again. No more hiding the salami. You had better cherish this baby, because *never* will you get another one. I really want to chop your dick off right now for doing this to me! Why'd you have to go and see your mother anyway? You should have been here with me. How could you do this to me?" Blaine was wailing to Elliott, who was on speakerphone. He was outside the elevator with medical crews standing by.

A tractor-trailer hydroplaned and took out a whole city block of power poles before it came to a stop. The Swepco crews were working frantically to get the power back on, but it wasn't going to be fast enough. Ember had Blaine's head in her lap, wiping sweat off her forehead with one of the baby washcloths from the buggy. I was in prime view of the newest Master barreling its way into the world.

I'd taken my paramedic classes, and finished my degree. Only once have I seen a baby born, because, in the ten years that I have been a medic, never once was one born on the front lines of Afghanistan where I was stationed. The only birth I'd seen was in the video they'd shown in class during the week we covered birthing. My knowledge was true though, and my instincts took over. The baby's head was now crowning.

Looking into her pain-filled eyes, I said, "Okay Blaine, this is how it's going to go. When I tell you to, I want you to grab your legs and push with all you have. When I tell you to stop, you stop. Understand?"

She nodded, and I glanced at Ember, letting her know, silently, that she could do it. She must have known I was scared, because she nodded and reassured me with a smile.

Going back to the task at hand, I directed Blaine to push on her next contraction.

Twenty minutes of pushing later, baby boy Masters was born kicking and screaming.

"It's a boy!" I exclaimed loudly so Elliott could hear.

A loud whoop sounded from the doors behind me, and followed closely by the loud whoop over the phone line.

While I was working, the doors were finally propped open a mere four inches. A metal pipe was wedged into the space to hold the doors open. Elliott stuck his arm inside and slapped me on the back, giving me a thankful squeeze. I could hear Sam and Max clearly now, giving orders to the fire fighters who were on scene. A medical kit was squeezed through the opening, and dropped onto the floor at our feet. Ember set Blaine's head down gently and reached for the kit.

"I need the nose bulb, two clamps, and the scissors." I said to her.

Blaine was smiling, sleepily, at the baby I placed on her chest. Reaching over Ember's head, I grabbed the baby blanket they'd picked out only hours before, and ripped the tags off, tossing them down beside me. Unfolding it, I covered the baby. Ember handed me the bulb, and I sucked the baby's nose and mouth out quickly. Once done, I went to clamping the cord, and then cutting it. I started an IV and hung the bag off the cart's handle.

The placenta was delivered a short time later, and I tossed it unceremoniously into the corner away from us. We were a fucking mess of blood and other things I didn't care to think about. I was just about to reach for the towels Elliott was handing me from above, when I noticed blood starting to pour from Blaine.

"Take the baby, and place him to Blaine's breast. Get him to feed. She's hemorrhaging." I said to Ember.

Blaine was quickly losing consciousness though. She put up no fight when Ember took the baby from her. Ember started feeding the baby, while I started massaging Blaine's uterus. Blood was still pouring out of her at an alarming rate.

"I need some Pitocin, now!" I boomed to the paramedics that were waiting for instructions. I could hear Elliott calling to Blaine, but tuned it out to focus on what I was doing. A syringe and small vial of Pitocin dropped down to me, and I quickly administered a dose straight into the line of her IV. I continued massaging her uterus for the next minute, and slowly the bleeding came to a stop. Thank fuck.

"It's stopped. We're going to need a pint of O negative. She's lost a lot of blood, but it's stopped for now." I explained to the medic who was peeking in through the cracks in the door. He nodded his head and disappeared.

Ember was still holding the baby to Blaine's breast, but he wasn't sucking anymore. He'd finished, and was dozing contentedly, unaware that he nearly lost his mother. Ember was rubbing his cheeks to try to get him to continue, but he was out. I turned and eyed the opening of the door again. We were in between the first and second floor. The bar that was holding the doors open looked solid and I came to a decision.

"Elliott!" I called.

Elliott appeared at the opening seconds later. I moved into his line of sight so he couldn't make out the huge mess of blood that covered the floor.

"I'm going to need to pass the baby to you. He'll fit easily through the gap. He's tiny." I informed him.

A smile graced his face, and he looked so eager, yet sad at the same time.

"Is Blaine okay?" he asked.

"The bleeding's stopped. She's still unconscious though. I think it'll be best to hand the baby out to you because I need Ember to help me get Blaine situated. She's going to need some blood." I said back.

He nodded, and held out his hand. I clasped it with mine, and then turned to take the baby gently from Ember's arms. She was smiling down at the baby, and gave me a huge smile when she saw how my large hands engulfed his tiny little baby.

"What's his name, Elliott?" I asked while turning back to him.

Elliott's eyes trained on his son. Bright, with unshed tears.

"Justin Douglas Masters." Elliott whispered.

My throat clogged up a little bit, and my eyes started to sting. Must have been from sweat dripping into my eyes or something.

"Welcome to the world, Justin Douglas." I said to him.

Carefully maneuvering towards the doors, I held the tiny infant up to the crack in the door, and handed him off to his father's capable hands with no problem. I could see Max, Cheyenne, and Sam crowd around the bundled infant, and head off towards the waiting paramedics. Another paramedic arrived with a bag of blood and handed it off to me. Turning back around to my other patient, I now saw that she was making her way back to consciousness. Starting another IV in her opposite arm, I hooked the blood bag up, and started transfusing.

"Where's the baby?" Blaine asked groggily.

I leaned down and cradled Blaine's face in the palm of my hand. "His over the moon daddy has him. He's off spouting his mouth about how he made a boy to Sam and Cheyenne."

"Sounds exactly like him." She laughed weakly.

I was in the process of cleaning Blaine up the best I could on one side, while Ember kept her company on the other, when the lights turned on. The elevator lights blinded us as they came back on. The floor beneath us jolted, and hummed as the elevator made its way up to the second floor, only an hour and a half too late.

Elliott met us at the door with his new son bundled in his arms. I picked up Blaine, while Ember grabbed the IV and blood bags. I placed Blaine on a stretcher, gently, and backed off as the paramedics made sure I didn't fuck anything up.

Ember curled into my side; I dropped and buried my head in the crook of her neck. I let out a breath that I didn't realize I'd been holding. Blaine, Elliott and little Justin were carted off downstairs to the ambulance. The storm was still booming overhead, but it was the first time I'd heard it in nearly an hour.

Grabbing Ember's hand, I made my way down the stairs and didn't look back. This was one experience I didn't wish to have again. It really shook me to see someone I cared about nearly die. Never again would be too soon.

Little did I know that I would be experiencing it twice more in the oncoming months. Moreover, it wouldn't just strike someone I cared about; it would strike someone that was my reason for breathing.

Chapter 6

I do like killing the messenger. Know why? Because it sends a message.
-T-shirt

Ember

"Gabe." I said.

"What?" He said distractedly.

"Gabe."

"What?"

"Gabriel."

"Huh?" He said.

His eyes were still glued to the TV. I glared daggers at his back, and there he was still ignoring me. I'm surprised he could even hear me. He had these big chunky earphones on, and I could hear the gunshots ringing out even with them planted firmly over his ears. Max and he were playing this stupid game called *Modern Warfare Three*. They'd been playing it for over three hours now. I was beyond bored, and I was really getting annoyed that he was ignoring me. I was used to Max ignoring me, but not Gabe. All I had to do was say something and bam, there he was. He'd been practically up my ass this past week, since Blaine delivered her son.

He seemed different. He was a lot more alert. Almost like he was hyperaware of our surroundings, even at Free. I wasn't allowed to even go take a tinkle without him knowing where I was going and how long I planned to be gone. I mean, I've never timed my bathroom breaks before, but as of my last one, I was down to one minute and eighteen seconds; that was with washing my hands, too.

We weren't at the stage in our relationship where I could do all those bodily functions in front of him, let alone even speak openly about them. So, instead of answering him, I would roll my eyes and leave without saying anything. Yes, I'd let out a discreet burp here and there, but nothing like the nice long belches that sounded like they came from a four hundred pound man, like I was used to doing.

"You have got to be fucking kidding me." Max said. "I shot that fucker in the head with a shotgun. His face would be gone, he wouldn't be able to get up and shoot me."

"Good thing you don't have those slow reflexes in real life." Gabe chuckled. "We wouldn't be here today otherwise."

"Fuck off, Ponch." Max shot back.

"I do *not* look like that guy off of Chips!" Gabe said, while shooting an assailant who tried to sneak up behind him and won the match.

"You totally do. You're the perfect match. You could be his twin." Max said while tossing his controller onto the couch in a sign of defeat.

"Just because I have dark, luscious hair and beautiful, darkly tanned mocha skin doesn't make me look like him." He volleyed back. "Don't be jealous."

To tell you the truth, he kind of reminded me of Uncle Jesse from *Full House*, but bulked up with muscle, and a few tattoos and scars to boot. He had that beautiful smile with perfect white teeth. He also had a great head of hair, pitch black and straight. Even his skin color was nearly the same.

"Jesus, get over yourself. Want to go again?" Max asked.

Gabe took his controller back from its perch on the coffee table. "Sure."

Men. If that were me, I would've been pulling hair by now. He'd yet to acknowledge that I was standing there waiting to ask him a question. I know he heard me, but he was doing his best to ignore the fact that I wanted to go do something, and he didn't want to. Well screw that. Just because I couldn't leave the compound didn't mean that I couldn't find something to do. He should know better by now. Just a couple of days ago, I got myself stuck on the lift in the garage for over an hour.

Ω
Three days before

Cheyenne and I had a bright idea. Since we were bored, and the girls were napping in their car seats in the back of Sam's truck, we moved the truck into the garage and stayed close in case they woke up.

I'd been playing with the nifty little levers that they used to hoist the cars up into the air when Cheyenne dared me to get up and ride it to the top. Never one to turn down a challenge, I'd gotten all the way to the top before we realized we had no clue how to get the thing back on the ground.

Cheyenne had spent the next forty-five minutes looking for a way to get me down.

89

You'd think being in a garage that they would have a ladder of some sort; but no, not in this garage. So, there I sat when Max and James walked through the door.

It could've been anyone else, and it would've been fine.

When those two got together, I always ended up hurt, crying, or worse. It took them fifteen minutes of laughing and making fun of me before they finally made a move toward letting me down. Regrettably, before they got me down, Gabe and Sam walked in. They took in the scene in three seconds, and immediately joined in on the teasing Ember parade. I was getting pissed. I'd been up there for nearly an hour, I had to piss, and I was yearning for a Snickers.

I'd told them I was going to jump down if they didn't get me down. Cheyenne immediately started to come let me down when James grabbed her from behind and wouldn't let her come. She knew I wasn't bluffing. Gabe was still having a laughing fit. They were all less than a foot away, so I pretty much said, "Screw it" and jumped towards Max and Gabe. I knew one of them would catch me. One of them did. Gabe.

One second he was doubled over, the next, I was in his arms. Air had rushed out of me in a whoosh when my body slammed into his. I made sure to smack Max with my elbow *accidentally* too.

"Don't ever do that again." Gabe said angrily. "What would have happened to you if I hadn't caught you?"

"Owww. I think you broke my nose." Max whined nasally.

I ignored Gabe as he lectured me not to do anything stupid anymore, but I couldn't help it. I had an innate ability to get into trouble. I was also plagued with being curious. That's why I've had seven broken bones and twenty-seven stitches in total, in my lifetime. I should know better, but never once did I stop to think that this was a stupid idea until I was already in the throes of doing said stupid idea.

Ω
Present

Walking out of Gabe's door, I headed into the direction of Cheyenne's house. Sam was outside washing his truck. He was shirtless in jeans, a ball cap, and boots. His stomach rippled, and his arm flexed as he pulled a Mr. Miagi with his "*wax on, wax off*" motions. I would've drooled a little if he wasn't my best friend's man. Didn't mean I couldn't look though. I knew he clocked me as soon as I walked out of the door, but he didn't say anything until I got right next to him.

"She's in the garage. Something about putting a new sticker on a truck and needing a razor blade." He answered my question without me even asking it.

"Thanks." I acknowledged before turning and walking into the garage.

Cheyenne was in the back of James' truck using a razor blade to scrape off an old sticker off the back glass of his brand new Ford F-350.

"What are you putting on there now?" I asked her.

"A '*piss on Ford*' sticker." Cheyenne said nonchalantly.

"Jesus Christ. Don't you two ever stop?" I queried.

"I think it's gonna be hilarious when he sees it. He's the one who let all the air out of my tires the other day, and put a broken down sign on it. Sam didn't question me at all, didn't even ask what kind of sticker it was. He just told me where

91

the razor blades were." She laughed wickedly.

Cheyenne and James had a fight once a week about what make was better. She was a Chevy girl, all the way, and he was a Ford. They tried to one up the other, and it turned into a sibling war, which might possibly start World War 3.

"Here, put this back in that tool box right there." She said, as she handed the razor to me.

She gestured with her head at mammoth toolbox in the corner, "I got it out of that black one right there."

I walked over to it and opened the first drawer, then the next, and the next. Wrenches. Sockets. Screw drivers. Air wrenches. All meticulously lined in a certain order that made no sense to me. Why couldn't they line these up in order of size? What it looked like was one side had one set that went from small to large, and the other side did the same thing. Seems to me that they should combine the two and then line them all up in order of size.

"Whose toolbox is this?" I asked her.

"Gabe's." she answered.

A smile split my face. A smile so wide that my face kind of hurt.

Feeling devious, I rearranged the first drawer that had the wrenches in it. Then moved on to the next and did the same thing there. Then when I got to the socket drawer, I took them all out of their little holders and lined them up the way I felt they should go. He was probably going to have a shit fit, but it serves him right for ignoring me. Maybe next time he'll have a little sympathy.

It was in the fourth drawer that I found a hammer, and a box of metal rods that had a letter on the end. Curious, I took one out, inspecting it. Then it dawned on me what they were for, and I went about spelling, "*I LOVE EMBER*" on the top of Gabe's toolbox. It looked pretty nifty if I did say so myself.

Feeling like I'd accomplished something, I wrote a note on a pad that he had sitting on top of the tool box, and set it on top of the rearranged wrenches in the first drawer. Cheyenne and I were just about to leave when a little white Honda pulled up to the gate and pressed the call button. Jack came out of the office and walked to the gate. A little bottled blonde stepped out of the car, all long legs and ass. Her hair was perfectly placed. She was wearing a white sundress and white sandals on her feet.

Immediately, I recognized her as the slut-bag who I saw Gabe having lunch with a few months before when he was supposed to be having lunch with me. He'd called and canceled about fifteen minutes before, and I didn't pack my lunch, so I made a run to The Back Porch for a quick burger, where I saw the two of them together, walking out with his hand on the small of her back, guiding her like a fragile flower. I knew instantly that I didn't like the bitch. She smiled up at him like the fake she was and laughed the most annoying laugh I'd ever heard.

They walked to Free's work truck and got in together. He'd made sure to hold the door open for her and help her inside. I saw a flash of her white panties, and knew that he'd gotten a prime view as well.

I was hot. I went ahead and ordered my lunch, but then decided that I was going to go ahead and give him a piece of my mind. So I drove to Free, getting more and more upset as I drove. When I got there, Gabe still hadn't arrived. Once I was done talking with Cheyenne, I knew I had to leave before I made a complete fool of myself. I'd managed to ignore him completely until I'd gotten attacked. It never even registered, in my mind, that I was mad at him that night. I knew I needed him, and I knew he would come. So I called him, never doubting for a second that he wouldn't be able to help me in some way.

Now here that woman was. She and Jack spoke for another minute before he punched the code in the panel at the gate. She fell into her car, pulled it up to the front of the garage, and turned it off. My eyes never left her. She sat in the car for another minute before her gaze found what she was looking for, and that was my Gabe.

I didn't realize that Jack called Gabe until I saw him rounding the corner of the garage. He saw me and froze. I could see his mind working. We hadn't discussed the fight we'd had over this woman. Although it was inevitable now.

Of course, he was able to put the mother fucking X-Box controller down for her. I was totally going to kick his ass. Maybe even hide his controllers. He was going to be frozen out tonight if I had anything to say about it.

The woman stepped out of her car and called out a greeting to Gabe, but it fell on deaf ears. He ignored her and walked straight up to me. He grabbed me and pulled me into a scorching hot kiss. My arms and legs automatically circled his body; fingers forked their way into his hair and held on for dear life. His kiss ravaged me. I was seriously on the verge of the Big 'O' when he pulled away. I didn't drop my arms or legs though. If he put me down right now, I would land on my ass. My legs felt like Jell-O.

Leaning forward for another quick kiss, he leaned forward and my butt found the tailgate of James' truck. Letting go of my death grip on his hair, he backed slowly away from me and turned to regard the woman. She had a scrunched up face, as if she'd sucked on a sour lemon. I smirked at her and her glare got even more intense. She looked ready to claw my eyes out, and if she even took one threatening step towards me, I was going to kick her ass. Not that she had any ground to stand on. Gabe was mine, and she wasn't going to take him away from me.

"What can I help you with, ma'am?" he asked.

I found that funny. He only used ma'am when he couldn't remember names. A small laugh escaped me, and he turned with a raised eyebrow. I shook my head at him, and he turned back to her.

"My car is having a few more problems, and I wanted to see if you could fix them for me." Whore said.

"I've got a huge project I'm working on right now, but Jack here could fix you right up."

He was so getting a blowjob tonight. He had totally erased my pissiness from his earlier treatment. The whore pouted when Gabe told her he couldn't help her. Not that I totally understood why she was turning her lip at Jack. He was nothing to sneeze at either. The army seemed to hire hot men. Every man I knew that was in the army was unbearably hot. Jack was tall, built, and handsome. The complete package. That is, if you didn't take in the air of remoteness that seemed to repel you if he didn't want you anywhere near him.

Gabe turned and regarded me. I tried not to squirm or look guilty, and must have succeeded, because he gave me a slow wet kiss and left the garage. I'm sure he was going to play that stupid game again, but I didn't mind as much now.

Cheyenne and I watched and listened quietly, while Jack spoke with Story. What the hell kind of name is that anyway? A stripper name? Okay, if I was honest, it was kind of cool, but she was a whore in my book, so it became a stripper name by default. Story and Jack worked out a few details, and then an Audi pulled up to the gate: Story's ride. I wondered if she had a man, because it'd make me feel better if she did. Jack opened the gate for the Audi and it became clear that she was a very rich woman. The woman got out of her car and helped Story transfer the contents of her car into the Audi.

I wasn't paying close attention until a car seat caught my eye. There was a little girl. A year and a half at most. She was beautiful. Her hair fell to just about armpit level in loose black ringlets. Her complexion was the same bronze that Gabe had. The little girl was asleep with her head leaned to the side of the car seat. Something kicked in my heart. Gabe's baby would look like this.

I've always wanted babies, but I didn't think they'd be in my cards. Losing my parents so young made me realize how suddenly life could take a drastic turn for the worse. My ovaries started crying out for Gabe's little soldiers to fertilize their eggs.

So I could get a closer look at the little girl, I made my way to the car to ask if they needed any help. "Y'all need any help?"

I wasn't looking at them though; I was looking at the little girl in the back seat. Nor did I expect an answer since I didn't really want to help. The girl was waking up now that she was hearing voices. She was turning her head from side to side in annoyance at being woken before she wanted to. Now that I was closer, I could tell that she probably was one and a half. It was eerie how much this baby looked like

Gabe. If I'd seen her with Gabe, I would have said they were father and daughter without any hesitation. A body slid into my vision, blocking the baby. The mom of the girl had a look on her face that could kill. Not that I understood why. I hadn't done anything but admire her baby.

"She's beautiful." I said to her.

Jesus. This kid even had the same bone structure as Gabe.

"Thanks." She snorted.

I didn't see any of the mom in the baby. The mom had red hair that was styled in a do that probably cost hundreds of dollars to be done. She was wearing designer dark linen pants and a cream shirt. She didn't look like she belonged in a garage, let alone in the freaking parking lot.

The woman was looking around, as if she was waiting for someone to pop out and come after her. Not that anyone here would ever think about hurting her. Just the opposite in fact.

Story put the last of her stuff into the woman's car and got in without even saying a word to us. Taking the hint, I nodded and told the woman to have a good day. She acknowledged my statement with a nod, and then got back into the car and slammed the door.

Just as she was closing the door, I heard Story say "Thanks, Sid."

I looked at Cheyenne questioningly, and then transferred my gaze to Jack who had the same puzzled expression as me. They both wondered what was going on, but didn't say anything. Story gave her number to Jack through a crack of the window, and then closed it immediately. The woman tore out of Free as if her ass was on fire, burning rubber smelled in her wake.

I made a note of the license plate, and jotted it down into my notes on my phone before I forgot it. Something seemed very fishy there. Why was that woman so nervous?

Cheyenne joined me in the middle of the parking lot as we watched the car pull away, practically burning rubber to get out of there.

"Did you see the little girl in the back seat?" I asked them both.

"She looked tiny, but I bet she was the same age as Pru and Piper." Cheyenne stated.

"I got her license plate. I think we should run it. Will you run it Jack? That woman seemed like she was jumpy." I asked.

"I got it already. Woman did seem jumpy, so to be on the safe side I was going to run the plates. It would've been done anyhow though. Just in case the car owner doesn't show for non-payment. We have an alternative number and contact just in case." He said.

I felt better that I wasn't the only one who sensed something weird. I said goodbye to them both, but that little girl never strayed far from my thoughts. Made me think of futures and shit. I headed to the house where I found Gabe at the stove, stirring something that smelled heavenly.

Grabbing the can of biscuits that was sitting next to a cookie sheet, I tore the paper off and banged it on the counter. After two good thuds, it burst open in a flourish, scaring the bejesus out of me in the process.

"Fuck!" I exclaimed, hand going to my thundering heart.

"You're such a dork." Gabe laughed. "You knew it was gonna happen, why'd it surprise you?"

"Name me one person who doesn't jump when they open biscuits!" I grumped.

"Me."

"You aren't human." I said in rebuttal, all while throwing biscuits down one by one onto the cookie sheet. He stopped stirring the gravy and came up behind me, wrapping me up tightly from behind. He rested his chin on the top of my head for a moment before diving in.

"What's really bothering you, Em?"

I really shouldn't tell him that I saw a kid today that looked exactly like him, that made me want to have his babies. I really shouldn't, but before I could stop myself, my mouth opened and I started word vomiting all over the place.

"When you left that girl at the shop, her friend showed up and gave her a ride. There was a baby in the back seat. I swear to God, she could've totally been your kid. Do you want kids?"

He froze behind me.

Then I felt like a complete loser when I realized how insensitive I'd sounded. He'd just told me about his ex-girlfriend aborting his child. I knew it was still a painful subject, and I brought it up anyway with my big mouth.

"I haven't had sex since Sidney. I never really wanted kids with her; she was just a person to pass the time with. It got to be routine. I wasn't in love with her, but having someone to come home to made me keep her around. I've always wanted kids. Just hadn't found the right person who I wanted to have them with. What did this lady look like that had the baby?"

"She was around my height. She had dark red hair, blue eyes, and expensive designer clothes. The baby didn't really look like hers. The dad must look kind of like you since she had the dark tanned skin and deep black hair."

As I was describing the woman to him, a dark look came over his face, and then passed in an instant. If I wasn't paying such close attention, I would have missed it.

A timer pinged behind him, and the moment was broken. He finished his preparations and then set it all out on the table.

Dinner was amazing. He cooked fried chicken, mashed potatoes, and green beans. I didn't usually get the treat of eating a nice meal unless I went over to Cheyenne's or went out to dinner.

I stood to clear the dishes. It's amazing how a military man can be so unorderly.

Seriously, it was as if he dropped trash wherever he might have been at the time. He could be standing next to the damn trashcan as he opened his beer, but does he throw the cap in the trash? Fuck no. He sets it on the counter, next to the trash.

The nightstand next to the bed has five half-filled water glasses. Does he take them out in the morning when he's through with them? No. He just brings a new glass to bed every night instead. As a result, I just started cleaning up after him, because there was no way I could live in this filth.

He was almost as bad as Cheyenne.

Turning around, I found myself face to chest with Gabe. One second I was staring at his t-shirt covered chest, the next I was licking his bare nipples after he whipped his shirt off. His nipple pebbled in my mouth, and I switched to the other. Then I ran my tongue up his chest and started following the tattoos. He has a gorgeous one that spans his entire back, shoulder and his waist. It peeks around his front above his shoulder, and under his left arm, curling around his pectoral. At first glance, it looked like your normal tribal tattoo. However, once I was able to examine it, I started finding words in the design.

"What does this mean?" I asked quietly.

I didn't stop tracing the tattoo; I continued to follow it with my tongue.

Groaning in defeat, he snatched me up and tossed me over his shoulder like a sack of grain. He bypassed the living room, and headed straight for his bed. Once he reached the edge, he gave his shoulder a little kick and threw me on the bed. I bounced twice before coming to a stop on my back.

I looked up into his eyes and pleaded with him. He seemed to understand, and nodded his head once. He stepped back from me and turned around. From this angle, I could see it all a lot better.

"They're a bunch of things my mom and dad used to say to me." He started. "From the first memory I can remember, my dad started giving me words of wisdom. When he stopped, my mom picked up the slack. The week of her funeral, I started on this."

I got up on my knees and started tracing the curves and

lines.

"What language are they in?"

"Portuguese." He said. "My dad was from Brazil. He felt we should know both languages, so I grew up listening to him tell stories in his native tongue. When he died, my mother tried to pick up the slack; she would tell me stories of my father in Portuguese. She really sucked, but it was the thought that counted. Some of these quotes are inked exactly the way she said them. Whether they were right or wrong."

"That's the sweetest thing I think I've ever heard." I whispered.

Aside from the Ranger emblem he had on his right forearm, that was the only other tattoo he had. Although, the pure massiveness of it should count as more than one. Maybe like eight. I started tracing the tattoo again, but this time with kisses. His back started to break out in goose bumps; he turned rapidly and pinned me to the bed with his body. My breathing turned harsh when I felt his erection press into my core. Neediness swamped me, and I came to the sudden realization that if I didn't have him right then, I just might die.

I broke contact with his body to shimmy my shirt up and over my head. I wasn't wearing a bra; my nipples puckered, and poked into Gabe's chest. His dog tags rested in the middle of my breasts, and were a cool weight against my chest. My hands smoothed down his chest and found their way to his jeans. He sucked in his stomach to allow me access to his cock without unbuttoning his jeans. I slipped my hand in, and went straight for the prize.

His cock was a solid weight in my hand. He was hard as stone. The vein that ran up the underside of his cock absolutely fascinated me; I ran the tip of my finger along the underside, following it all the way down to the base and up again. Smoothing my thumb over the mushroom shaped head, he jerked in reaction. He must have been closer to the edge than I realized, because in the blink of an eye I found myself divested of my jeans and panties. He made short work of his jeans and underwear, and was back on top of me. However, he didn't stay that way for long.

Ever so slowly, he made his way down to my core. His tongue snaked out and gave a long lick from my opening all the way up to my clit. My body bowed up off the bed as zings shot through my clit. He worked my clit with the ultimate precision, and I was just about to peak when he thrust two fingers inside me. I shot into orbit.

"Gabriel!" I whimpered.

He continued to work his fingers in and out of me until my climax slowed. Pulling his fingers free, slowly, he stuck them into his mouth and licked my orgasm off his fingers. Moaning, I grabbed him by the hair and pulled him down on top of me. He wasted no time before slamming himself home. This was how it was with us. Hot, hard and furious. We always tried to go slow, but never finished slow. Something made it where we couldn't control ourselves. Repeatedly, he slammed inside of me. It shouldn't be possible, but I was already working up to my second orgasm. He pounded relentlessly into me. Over and over again, he hit so deep that a little jolt of pain shot through me. But I loved it.

Gabe changed positions, slightly, for me. I was gone again. Distantly, I heard him grunt out his own climax, but I was too focused on mine. Waves of delight were traveling through my vagina, and he kept hitting the perfect spot with each thrust of his cock. Finally, the waves subsided and I opened my eyes to find Gabe's eyes locked on my face, studying me. He leaned down and gave me a chaste kiss on the lips before pulling back.

"I love you." I whispered to him.

A brilliant smile broke out over his face.

"I've loved you for over a year now. I've just been waiting for you to realize you love me back." He said gruffly.

Something heavy seemed to lift off my chest. Knowing that he returned my feelings went a long way in making me feel more secure in our relationship.

Chapter 7

Alcohol, Tobacco, and Firearms. Who's bringing the chips?
-T-shirt

Ember

"That woman who wants Gabe works here now!" I whisper yelled into the receiver.
I watched the woman out of the corner of my eye as she went from trashcan to trashcan, emptying each one into her larger trashcan that was part of a big yellow cart.

"The brunette or the one that has the hots for Gabe?" Cheyenne asked.

"I already said the one who has the hot's for Gabe, dummy!" I answered.

I watched her a little more and noticed that she kept glancing in my direction, but then would turn away hoping that she wasn't caught staring. She finished up with the trash, then made her way out of the training room. I got up and walked to the door, and looked both ways. She was gone. Good.

"What the fuck!" I cried. "This's fucking nuts!"

"Dude, call Gabe and tell him. Better yet, just send him a text. He is in the middle of painting Dougie's bike, but I've seen him check his phone five times in the last hour. I'm guessing it's because of you." Cheyenne said.

"Will do." I agreed and hung up.

I didn't text Gabe though. The bike was too important. After Dougie's death last year, a pall seemed to hang over the group. There was still joy, but all the lightheartedness that Dougie brought with him when he entered the room was gone. The construction of the bike seemed to bring Dougie back to us, if only by bringing his friends back together, laughing and telling old stories that involved him. Pulling those memories to the forefront, and painting or constructing them into the bike.

Instead of interrupting, I got busy. A football player came in with what looked like heat stroke and a concussion. He must have passed out, and then been tackled once unconscious.

In the Texas sun, it was a very real thing to have heat stroke, even when all you were doing was a little gardening in the shade. It could get up to one hundred and ten on a summer day, and with the humidity added to that, we could possibly have a head index of one hundred and twenty. This was no laughing matter, and I lectured the coaches daily on giving multiple water breaks every hour. Being in full pads only ratchets up the possibility of heat stroke. Every year athletes died of heat exposure, and I would be damned if I had that happen to me.

The paramedics were called, and I explained the situation to them just before they carted him off in the ambulance. I watched them exit the college parking lot, and start to Longview with their lights and sirens going. I took a few deep slow breaths before I marched over to the football field to give the coach a piece of my mind. I failed to notice that I was no longer alone. It never crossed my mind to not go outside and say something to that little shit head of a coach.

I marched through the practice field, interrupting the plays that were being ran. Each and every player gave me a wide birth. They must've seen the look on my face, because I was livid. Spying the little prick across the field, I made a beeline straight for him. He saw me coming and called a halt to practice.

"Water break!" he yelled.

All the players jogged over to the opposite side of the field and crowded the two coolers full of water.

"How many times do I have to tell you water breaks once an hour? And I know for certain it's over 104 out here. You're supposed to call practice when it reaches over one hundred! I'm going to have your job for this. That boy is lucky to be alive, and it's no thanks to you!" I yelled, getting right up in his face.

Coach Martin was forty-five, and thought he was God's gift to everyone. He was a slimy bastard and didn't care about anything but making himself look good. I wasn't bluffing when I told him I would have his job. The athletic trainer had a lot of pull, and I was good friends with my boss. He would know that I would never lie about something so serious.

"I'll call practice when I feel like calling practice, and not a second sooner. So how about you trot your tight ass back to the gym where you belong, and leave this to the big boys who actually know what they're doing?" he said snidely.

"Know what you're doing? What a joke. You don't know your ass from your face. You're only looking out for yourself out here. These boys look up to you for guidance, and when you push them this hard, they *will* break. What will you do when you have no players to play because you were too stupid to call practice when you were supposed to?" I seethed.

Coach Martin didn't take too kindly to my belittling him in front of his assistant coaches and the players. He started to step into me when he was halted by a very low and dangerous voice.

"Do not touch her. If you even think about it, I'll rip the jokes you call nuts off and feed them to you." A familiar voice said directly behind me.

I whirled around and saw Gabe standing directly behind me. He was in a pair of worn jeans that had grease stains all over them, and a black t-shirt that I'm sure had more of the same. He had on a Texas Ranger's ball cap pulled low on his head and a pair of Ray Ban's covering those eyes I loved so much.

His mouth was set in a grim line, and I knew that this was going to escalate if I didn't do something to avert his attention. Tearing my eyes away from him, I focused on the other forty people standing behind me, as well was the entire football defensive line; they looked pissed at the coach. Jesus. How was this coach not bawling in his own puddle of tinkle? If I'd seen the crew that I had at my back, standing against me, I'd be hauling ass in the opposite direction.

"Alright boys, it's time to call it a day." I said to them. "You know better. Y'all should have said something to him. There's a thermometer right by the water coolers. I fully expect one of y'all to come see me if this ever happens again. The next time it could be you who has a heat stroke, and you might not be as lucky as Jason was today."

Walking towards Gabriel, I stood up on my tiptoes, gave him a peck on the cheek, and started back across the football field. As the head athletic trainer at the college, I had other obligations besides the football team. I had two other trainers under me, as well as three assistants.

One of said'assistants, June, was at the gym door hopping from foot to foot looking quite anxious. She was one of my prized pupils as well. She was also in love with Kale. I'm not sure where they stood now that he was back in the gang, but I knew a love like that doesn't just quit because the person you love is doing something stupid.

"What's up, sweet cheeks?" I asked.

"I need to talk to you, like bad."

"Let's go to my office."

Swiping my card at the gym door, I held the door open for June, and then made sure the door latched behind us. I weaved through the maze of hallways until I got to my office. Since no one was in the hallway, I left the door open and motioned with my hand for her to have a seat. Choosing to forgo the seat, I grabbed a coke from the fridge and propped my hips up against the counter, and looked at her expectantly.

If anything, she looked even worse now. It was going on five minutes of silence before she finally opened her mouth, only to snap it back closed. Loosing what little patience I had, I motioned with my hand to get her talking.

"Kale isn't seeing me anymore. He said last night that it was getting too dangerous for us to be together. He told me when he got his brother out that he would come back to me." She said sadly as a few tears dropped from her eyes, spilling onto her cheeks.

"Well that's understandable. He doesn't want to get you hurt. I know it's hard, but what exactly do you expect him to do here? He's making a bad decision, but it's commendable that he doesn't want to bring you down with him."

Taking a deep breath, she finally got the courage to say, "He said that they were going to make him kill you. If he wanted his brother out, he was going to have to do that before they would let him go. He told me because he knew I would relay that information to you. He also said you had a man following you around, and that it would all turn out okay. I'm not sure if that means he won't actually shoot you, or if he'll be stopped before it goes that far. Ember ... I'm four months pregnant with Kale's baby."

"Tell me more about this shooting business. Does he have death-"

"No one is going to be shooting you. It'll be over my dead body. What the fuck is going on?" A very angry Gabe said from the doorway.

I jumped about three feet in the air and dropped my coke on the ground. Brown fizz spewed into the air and drenched my thighs. My hand automatically covered my racing heart. Whirling around so I could see the doorway, I lost my balance and went down. I would've busted my ass if Gabe weren't there to catch me. His callused hands took a firm grip on my hips, and steadied me until I had my balance.

June was sitting there in utter amazement. One, because she just spilled her guts in front of some man she didn't know, and two because he was hot.

"June this is my, uh, Gabe. Gabe this is my assistant trainer, June. June here is seeing Kale, or she was until he broke up with her today." I explained.

"Nice to meet you. Now tell me what's going on." He said shortly.

His tone booked no room for argument. Therefore, I started to explain what June had told me. I wasn't sure at what point he started listening in, so I started at the very beginning, which was when June met Kale at the beginning of last year.

"June became an assistant at the end of volleyball season last year. She's now two years into her degree. She met Kale during a football game. They've been dating ever since. He got out of the gang when he was younger and since his brother-"

"I know all of that. Get to the part about him killing you." He said testily.

"Well, I don't know very much. Only that he was tasked in shooting me. We hadn't gotten very far before you walked in."

Nodding he said, "Okay. Let's get out of here. You won't be coming back here by yourself until this is finished. Nice to meet you, June."

"Wait!" June said, as Gabe took my hand. "You're the only one here. Mack and Trammel went home with the stomach bug. If you leave, we have no one else. There're two injuries on tables in the training room."

"Fuck." Gabe said dejectedly.

Taking that as permission to go about my work, I left my office and went to the training room. June wasn't kidding about there being no one here, which was unusual at the beginning of the year. I checked each of the three kids that were in the room. One was a senior football player needing an ice bath, one was a sophomore who had shin splints from the cross-country boys' team, and the last was a freshman girl with a knee injury from volleyball drills.

Deeming that the knee injury was the worst, I started with her. I saw June come in and start the ice bath for the football player, but I focused on the nasty swelling going on around the young girl's right knee. It was about three times the size of her other knee, and was already bruising.

"Did you try to walk?" I asked her.

"N-no. It hurt too much, I d-didn't e-even try to." She stammered out.

Understandable. I did try to walk after my knee injury, and it is something that will be forever burned into my brain. To this day, the teammate that was helping me still says it was the grossest thing she'd ever seen.

"Alrighty then. Let's get you in a brace, and then we're going to get you to the ER." I said to her, while taking a leg brace that wouldn't allow the knee to bed out from one of the cabinets underneath the table. I strapped her into the brace, and then retrieved some ice for her to place on the knee while we waited for her ride. The volleyball coach arrived a few minutes later to take her in to the emergency room.

While this was going on, I didn't fail to notice the silent presence of Gabe at my back. I retrieved some crutches, gave the coach some instructions, and then sent them on their way. Gabe watched the entire time. Eyes never stopped scanning. To tell you the truth, it kind of gave me the willies. He really didn't want me to be here, and if his posture and demeanor was anything to go by, he wanted me to know it.

I finished up with both athletes in a little over an hour. It was now four thirty in the afternoon, and it was time to be going. Sending June home, I replenished supplies and made out an order form of what all we would need to order from our suppliers within the next week. Wiping down all of the tables, I finally deemed the room ready, and turned to Gabe. Two hours later, he was still scanning the area. Granted, it was a large space, but not much could surprise you since we were down a long ass hallway in the boonies of the college campus. But what did I know?

"Ready." I said to him, bending over one of the tables to reach for my sweatshirt.

Once my tummy hit the table though, I felt a presence at my back, pinning my hips to the table. Gabe's hips were up snug against my hips. He ground his erection into me, and I swear if the table wasn't underneath me, I'd have fallen to my knees. Which, to be honest, might not have been a bad thing.

I peeked over my shoulder to notice that the training room door was closed. When that happened, I don't know.

"We can't do this right now. I work here Gabe."

"Seeing you strutting around in these tight little pants drives me nuts. What the hell are these anyway?" He asked.

This was not a discussion I wished to have. How do you tell your boyfriend that you're wearing Spanxx? What do you say that they're for fat people who want to suck their fat in?

"Ummm, uhhh, I don't really want to tell you to be honest."

His hands tightened on my hips as he said, "I don't really give a fuck what they are, just keep wearing them. They drive me fucking crazy. Do you wear underwear with these things?"

"Yes. Not wearing underwear would give me a camel toe. No one wants to be seen with a camel toe. Those are so not cool."

A brief laugh escaped him, but didn't deter him. He grabbed the waist of my pants and yanked both pants and panties down to my thighs. These babies were so tight that I wouldn't be able to move my thighs but a few inches apart. That didn't seem to bother him though, because his seeking fingers had already found my sweet spot.

My back arched off the table, while my eyes rolled back into my head as he curled his two fingers and worked me. It wasn't long before I was pushing back against his fingers, trying to get him deeper inside of me. I was seconds away from coming when he pulled out. One second his fingers were inside of me, and the next he was slamming his cock into me.

"Jesus!" I gasped.

He froze and said, "Too much?"

"No, it was just a surprise. Keep going." I pleaded, as I pushed back against him.

He did it slowly though. Gabe and I drifted more towards fast and furious when it came to sex. It felt the best that way for us. Today, however, with my pants keeping my knees close together, and him moving in and out of me slowly, it felt abso-fucking-lutely amazing.

I could feel every ridge and vein on his cock as he pumped it in and out slowly, over and over again, until I was ready to shout at him to go harder; just as I was about to demand that of him the doorknob jiggled.

My body tensed, ready to push him away, but Gabe didn't stop in his ministrations, only ramped up his efforts. He gave a little twist at the end of each thrust that had me seeing stars.

"The guy's bike who brought her this morning is still parked in her spot. So where is she at?" I heard someone ask.

Holding on to the edge of the table with one hand, I buried my head into the crook of my elbow, willing myself not to scream. This was torture in its truest form. I was working up to one hell of an orgasm, and I needed to be quiet. This could get me fired in a heartbeat. I loved this job, but nothing short of death could stop me right at the moment. Any second I would blow, and I knew I wouldn't be able to hold in my scream.

I could still hear the two people speaking only ten feet away, with a flimsy door between us, but in the next instant, they weren't even on my radar. Gabe must have sensed that my orgasm was imminent because he reached his hand around and covered my mouth, trapping the scream before it poured out.

Once my orgasm made itself known, Gabe started to slam inside of me, just how we both liked it. Again and again, he pounded into me, spurring my orgasm to continue. Gabe grunted and slammed into me one final time, planting himself deep inside of me, before pouring his come deep.

He let go of my mouth; my face dropped onto the leather of the training table beneath me. Gabe slid slowly out of my body, and tucked himself back into his jeans, zipping and belting them up.

I watched with my face still planted on the table. That was exhausting, and I could really go for a teensy tiny nap right now, but it was not in our cards. He gave my ass a good slap before backing away and heading to the door. I squeaked and hauled my undies and pants back over my ass.

"I wasn't going to open it; I just wanted to hear if they were still out there or not. You were pretty loud there towards the end, I wouldn't be surprised if they heard you." Gabe teased.

"It wasn't my fault! It was your fault. None of this was my idea!"

"I didn't see any fight on your part!" Gabe chuckled.

I'd rather forgotten about the messiness that comes with sex, and now I could feel all the wetness leaking out of me, onto my pants. I'm sure there was a nice little wet spot on the crotch of my Spanxx.

"Let's get out of here so I can go change my pants. I'm leaking." I said before heading to the door.

Gabe's arm hooked around my waist before I could get it open and I was hauled back into his arms. His lips skimmed down my exposed neck and goose bumps puckered up all down my right side.

"Are you saying you feel dirty?" he asked quietly.

"No, not dirty. Just squishy." I laughed out.

"I happen to like it there; I like knowing I was inside you." He whispered into my hair, and then gave me a three tap on the butt that meant it was time go.

Gabe did the three tap a lot. When he was leaving, he would tap my butt three times before he let go of me and left. In addition, when I was sitting on his lap, he would tap me three times to let me know he wanted up.

Disentangling myself from him, we walked hand and hand down the corridor, and out into the scorching heat of the Texas sun. If you think you've experienced heat, you haven't. Yes, there are those places that reache higher than Texas' one hundred and ten degrees, but that's dry heat. Here, you have humidity on top of it. All you had to do was walk outside and you were drenched in sweat.

We walked to the Death machine, and Gabe swung his leg over, mounting the bike. He kick started the engine and that familiar vibration rocked my body. Adrenaline poured through my veins, and I hopped on, wrapping my body around his. He handed me my helmet, and we both strapped them on before he took off.

He took the turns low, and my body swayed as one with his. I loved being on the back of his bike, with my arms wrapped around him. It felt like everything was okay. There were no death threats from gangs, no coaches trying to push my kids too hard, and no crazy chicks making nutty eyes at my man. Pure perfection. But, of course, my dear Gabriel did ruin my high.

We got to Free and pulled up into the main garage area. He hauled me off the bike, walked me over to the toolbox, dropped my hand and said, "Fix it." Before he turned around and left me standing there. I did get a good laugh though.

Chapter 8

Losers all whine about their best. Winners go home and
fuck the prom queen.
-The Rock

Ember

While cruising the aisles at the super Walmart, I was at a loss on what to have for dinner. I hated cooking, and I only knew how to do so many things. I pulled my phone out and texted Gabe without looking. My eyes were on the cupcake display that was directly in front of me.

Me: *Chicken vaginas okay for dinner tonight?*

I piled in two six packs of cupcakes, one vanilla with whipped icing and one vanilla with buttercream icing. I couldn't decide which sounded better, so I got both. This was also why I wore Spanxx. I enjoyed Chick-Fil-A and cupcakes too much. I also didn't work out as I used to.

"Jesus, are you eating for two there, Ember?" Cheyenne teased, as she bumped my cart with hers.

"Nope. I know how to use contraception. No babies until I want them; unlike someone I know." I said, giving her a meaningful glance.

She blew a raspberry at me and made sure to add some spit to it.

"Sicko." I said as I wiped my face with my sleeve.

The phone chimed in my hand and I slid my finger over the screen to unlock it.

Gabe: *Yuck*

Feeling baffled, I was about to reply asking him why when I re-read my first message and then burst out laughing.

Cheyenne took the phone out of my hand, read the messages and then burst out laughing herself.

"Chicken Vaginas? Is that a new recipe?" She asked, while snickering.

"Yep. I saw it on Pinterest." I stated.

"What did you mean to say?" Max said from behind me, making me jump only a little bit.

"Jesus. This was an A and B conversation. C your way out of it." I answered rudely.

I wasn't really upset that he listened to our conversation though. I just liked giving him hell. That's what a little sister is for, right?

"It could've only been one of three things. That's all she cooks: spaghetti, chicken fajitas, or sausage casserole." Cheyenne supplied helpfully.

Ignoring them, I made my way to the produce section, trying to escape the twin terrors that were following in my wake. I didn't succeed though. They still found me in front of the bananas. Watching them out of the corner of my eye, I chose a bundle of bananas, and then texted Gabe back.

Me: *I meant chicken fajitas. Does that sound okay? LOL.*

My phone immediately pinged with his reply.

Gabe: *Good I only want one and it's yours.*

Feeling my face flush, I shoved the phone back into my bra and turned towards the twins in time to see them each grab a kiwi from the bottom of the pile. Of course, you can guess what happened next. Yep, the whole fricking thing came tumbling down, and they each found it hilarious.

"Cheyenne! Your kids just dropped all the kiwis on the floor." I whisper yelled to her, when she rounded the corner.

She stood there, wondering what the hell she was supposed to do. There were literally hundreds of kiwis spread throughout the produce section. Max fixed it all by scooping up the girls, depositing one in each of our buggies, and then taking said buggies and guiding them out of the produce section. Cheyenne and I both looked at each other, and then sprinted after him.

Yes, it was wrong, but it was an accident, and I really didn't want to get down on my knees and pick all those bastards up. Just as we were leaving the Walmart, my phone dinged again. I didn't look at it until we loaded sixty-seven bags of shit into the back of Sam's Suburban. Yes, that was sixty-seven bags. I counted.

Gabe: *Won't be home until late. Got some shit to take care of. Leaving now.*

A man of few words. What the hell was that? We'd spent every night together for the last two and a half months. It'd been quite a few weeks since the football player had had heat stroke. I'd practically moved in. Nearly all of my clothes were at Gabe's place. Everyone referred to Gabe's as '*Our Place*' but he'd yet to ask me to move in.

Deciding not to make too big of a deal of it, I gave him the space he seemed to want tonight. I didn't text him back. Thinking about it now it would be somewhat nice to get in some girl time.

"Cheyenne?" I called to her.

She turned her head and regarded me with a raised eyebrow.

"Do you want to go into Longview tonight? Catch a movie, have a cookie monster?" I asked.

"Perfect! I've been craving one of those like crazy. What do you want to go see?" she asked.

"I hear Magic Mike is still at the dollar theater. How about that?"

"For the love of all that's holy, please, anything but that. I don't want to see that shit." Max grumped from the driver's seat.

"That sounds perfect! Max. Go to moms and let's drop off the girls. Then we can go drop the groceries off, get dressed and head out." Cheyenne demanded.

Perfect. Maybe a little Channing Tatum and his hot ripped abs would go a long way to ignoring the fact that I'd rather be with Gabe tonight.

Ω

An hour and a half later, we found ourselves in Gabe's room getting ready. At least I was anyway. Cheyenne was practically dressed.

"Does this look okay?" I asked Cheyenne, while checking out my ass in the floor to ceiling mirror.

I didn't want to look like I had a muffin top or anything. I had on a new pair of Wrangler Rock 47's that I'd bought just last week, paired with a white wife beater. My bra was a bright neon yellow, and was definitely noticeable under my tank top, but I didn't really care. It was the only one I owned, and I wasn't going to go out and buy a new one when what I really wanted was to lose the bra all together. My hair was down in loose waves. No makeup though. I didn't like the way it made my face feel greasy.

"Yea, your ass looks great in those. Where'd you get those?"

"I went to Baskin's last week. The pants were forty percent off. Good thing too, because I wasn't going to drop a hundred bucks on a pair of jeans. I had to lay on the bed to get them buttoned though." I answered.

"They're awesome. My pants already don't fit." She said, while gesturing to her jeans that only had three of the five buttons done up.

"Funny. I seem to be losing weight. I've been the same weight since high school, but ever since I started staying with Gabe I seem to fit into my clothes a lot better." I said cheerfully.

It really was awesome. When I'd hurt my knee, I'd lost all my muscle and gained a ton of weight. Not working out and sitting on your ass would do that to a person. Especially when I ate like shit.

"You're such a hoe bag. Why would you rub that in my

face? Just look at this!" She said pulling up her shirt to expose her belly. Not that I hadn't already seen it; with the tight shirt she was wearing, you could make out the bump of the baby inside of her. The bottom two buttons on her jeans were undone, and her belly seemed to bulge out from between the gap in the jeans. Studying her predicament for a moment, I went to the bathroom, and grabbed two black hair ties and came back.

Going down on my knees, I bent close to her pants and looped a hair tie through the buttonhole, then stretched it across the opening and fit it around the button. I repeated the process for the other hole and was about to sit back up when I was interrupted.

"Should I come back?" Sam queried from the doorway.

Willing my heart to stop trying to pop out of my chest, I said "Yeah. Just need a couple more minutes. It's my turn next."

Cheyenne laughed, and then turned her body so Sam could see what I was actually doing down on my knees.

"Ember's a fucking genius! Look what she did to my pants." Cheyenne demanded, thrusting her stomach out.

She looked like a goober, but who was I to say anything? I was a nut too. That's why we're best friends.

"Looks good." Sam said as he rubbed Cheyenne's belly.

I walked into the living room, giving them a few moments of alone time. I grabbed the purse Cheyenne let me borrow and shoved my keys, a tube of Chapstick, and some of the candy that I'd bought at Walmart that day, along with a coke.

Cheyenne came up behind me and shoved her own drink in.

Apparently, she wasn't bothering with a purse since I was carrying one. Sam hooked an arm around both of our necks and pulled us in to his chest giving us each side hugs.

"Don't leave Max tonight, got it?" He asked.

"Aye Aye, Captain." I saluted.

Rolling his eyes, he let us go, and walked us out to Max's Blazer. I hoisted myself up into the front, then crawled to the back since the seat no longer slid forward; all the while, praying I didn't rip my pants. It was about ten minutes into our drive when Max nearly killed us.

"Titties!" I screamed out at the top of my lungs.

Max gripped the steering wheel tight.

"Jesus Christ! Was that fucking necessary?" He fumed.

"Max, I really don't know why that surprised you. We say it every single time. Every. Single. Time. I'm not sure why you ever whine about it; we've been doing this for forever."

The 'titties' in question were actually known as the Texas Titties to the locals. LeTourneau Technologies used to produce bombs in the dome shaped buildings. From the air, they looked like boobs. Nipples and all.

"Y'all know better. Now seriously, shut up and leave me along for ten more minutes. Y'all are already making me go see a man stripper movie. Don't make me kill myself beforehand."

We gave him the peace he was looking for, but it was only about three minutes or so before we lost the desire to make him happy.

The movie was beyond our expectations. I don't think I'll ever listen to *'Pony'* by Ginuwine, ever again without picturing Channing Tatum stripping to it. I might've had to take off my sweater because I got a little hot.

Max, on the other hand, did *not* like it. He thought it was trash. He said it had no story line, and was practically porn - minus the penises and boobs.

"It would have been better if they'd have shown some boobs at least. This was like a really bad porno. They had the bad storyline, and forgot to show dicks and tits." Max stated.

That was my brother: crass and blunt. I loved him anyway.

"Let's go to Cheddar's now. It's heading towards eleven, and I'm about to keel over. Gabe doesn't let me get much sleep." I stated, mostly to rile Max a little bit.

"Oh my God! My ears! For the love of all that's holy, please never speak of that with me around again. I just can't deal with that shit." He pleaded.

We kept right on talking though.

"Sam does that to me too. It's as if I go to sleep, after just having some of him, and I wake up with his hands-" Cheyenne said before Max interrupted her.

"Shut up!" Max barked. "Fuck."

We both laughed. Payback was a bitch unfortunately. He got us good in the car.

"I have a feeling something bad is gonna happen." Max stated.

Immediately, Cheyenne and I both covered our noses with our shirts. When we were younger, we watched a movie called *Stick It*. One of the main characters said the same thing right before he'd farted in the car. This was a running thing for James and Max to do to us since we were fifteen. This time was no different.

We arrived at Cheddar's minutes later, and then poured out of the Blazer gagging with tears in our eyes. Max's booming laugh proceeded us, and I slammed the door in annoyance. He was a mutant!

I hooked arms with Cheyenne, and we were weaving through the cars when I saw him. Stopping so fast, I rocked back on my heels and collided with Max's chest. My eyes locked with Gabe's and I saw immediate understanding flare in his eyes. My heart felt like it was being ripped from my chest.

A large bubble sat at the base of my throat, making it hard to swallow. My eyes stung with tears, and I turned and ran in the opposite direction, weaving through the cars as if the devil was on my heels.

I knew I wouldn't get far though. He'd seen me. He knew I'd seen him with another woman, his arm around her shoulders laughing with her. How could he do this to me? Never did I see this coming. Never.

Ω
Gabe

"Alright. You've got your new information memorized, right?" I asked.

"Yep. Thank you so much for helping me. I feel like I can finally breathe again. You sure he won't find me here?"

Lark asked.

"As sure as I can be. We've practically deleted you. When Lark was born, Libby became non-existent. All of her old life, her job, her credit cards, her bills, everything is gone. Even if you wanted to go back, you couldn't. It's easier when there's no family to remember you. In your case, since you had no family, you pretty much ceased to exist. There're plenty of fail-safes just in case your husband ever tries to come looking for you though. Try not to worry." I said to her, giving her a one armed squeeze.

Lark was definitely a survivor. She was married to a very abusive man for ten years. She'd had two kids, and he killed both of them in front of her, threatening to do the same to her and anyone else, if she told. He was a sick man, but extremely powerful. This is why Free existed, to get these individuals out before they were killed, hurt or worse than they already were.

"Whew. Now if I could just get used to the weather!" Lark cried as she fanned herself.

I laughed. It's been over a year since I'd moved to East Texas, and I still wasn't used to it; it was a long way from Michigan. I gave her shoulder a pat. I was just dropping my hand from around her shoulder when movement caught my eye.

Turning my head, my eyes met the beautiful ones I love so much. Ember. Bone deep pain showed in her eyes. Seeing that there made me sick to my stomach; Ember was my world. Seeing her in pain killed something inside of me.

Cursing under my breath, I took off in a sprint. It was obvious that she'd misunderstood what she saw. I hadn't told her what we do yet, it just never came up; but I was about to let her in on that detail, as soon as I caught her that is. Max started to go after her, but stopped himself when he saw I was going myself. I made sure to yell to Max to take care of Lark, but I didn't really care if he heard me. She'd be all right; Ember might not.

Ember rounded the edge of the building before I caught up to her. She probably would have gotten further if she wasn't wearing such ridiculously tight pants.

"Ember! Stop!" I grounded out before hooking my arm around her waist and dragging her up against my chest.

"Fuck off, douche bag." She spit. "I don't have to do shit."

"Would you just give me a fucking second to explain?" I questioned.

Twisting and turning in my hold, I readjusted my grip to where I hopefully wasn't hurting her.

"Why would I need to have you explain? Your arm around another woman was enough explanation for me." She said, wriggling in my hold.

She was kicking and scratching now. She was like a little hell cat trying to get away.

"It's my fucking job, Ember! Ask anyone. Your brother. Cheyenne. Call Sam and ask him what I'm doing tonight. Go ahead and call him. Never mind. I'll call him for you."

Figuring restraining her was the best way to go about calling Sam, but wanting to keep her where she was, I tossed her over my shoulder in a firefighter's carry, before digging out my phone. Tiny fists beat into the small of my back, her nails trying to grasp the limited fat that was back there.

Smacking her ass to get her to quiet down, I hit Sam's name and waited two rings before he picked up.

"Get Lark all settled in her new place?" Sam asked.

"Yea, about that. Will you tell my hardheaded woman exactly what I was doing with Lark so she'll stop trying to rip my balls off?" I asked him.

Sam's short bark of laughter didn't appease any of my anger. I was still mad. Not necessarily at Ember, but at the situation.

"Oh, God. Is she really trying? That sounds like something she'd do. Hand her the phone." Max laughed.

"It's on speaker phone, asshole." I growled.

"Ember, honey, listen to Gabe. Lark is one of our Freebirds. She just relocated tonight. I told him not to give out too much information yet because she'd be living here. Sorry, Ember, you can let his balls go now."

Ember slowly retracted her claws from my back; then her whole body seemed to lose its tension before she fell limply like dead weight. Hanging up with Sam, I shoved my phone back into my pocket before I set her back down on her feet. Her head hung, refusing to meet my eyes.

"Talk to me, minha garota louca."

"You just called me a crazy bitch, didnt you?"

"Uhhh, no. Not exactly."

"You did, didnt you?" She said, before finally meeting my eyes.

I saw fear there. She looked terrified.

"I called you my crazy girl. What's wrong?"

"I fucked up. I'm sorry for jumping to conclusions. I didn't mean to, but seeing you there with someone else, your arm wrapped around her, it hurt. A lot. You're making me crazy."

"I know what it looked like, sweetheart. I would have felt the same thing. Although, I'd have fucked the guy up first, asked questions later." I said, before kissing her nose, and then her mouth.

She exhaled loudly and wrapped her arms around my body, burying her head into my chest. Her nose skimmed over my nipple, and it hardened underneath the light touch. It was then that I remembered that her jeans looked like they'd been painted on. My hand slowy inched down her back until it cupped her ass. The rhinestones were rough against the palm of my hand. I growled, unintentionally, at the way her ass fit so perfectly in the palm of my hand.

A shrill shrieking siren pierced the still night air behind the resturant. My phone was wedged between our two bodies so I had to lose some of the closeness that we'd aquired in the last few minutes. Reaching into my pocket for my phone, I answered it without looking at the display.

"Hello?"

"We're heading out, I assume you've got her under control. I sent Lark home. Made sure she had all her stuff together. Catch you in the AM." Max said before hanging up, leaving me no room to reply before he was gone.

Shoving the phone back into my pocket, I yanked Ember's body back where I wanted it. Where I wanted her stay. Forever. I wouldn't tell her that yet, though. She was like a feral cat at times. Startle her, or get too close when she doesnt want you to, and you better watch out for your eyes, because she was about to be gouging them out with her fingernails.

I took possession of her mouth. My tongue entered her mouth, her lips parting, sucking my tongue, giving erotic flicks as she does when she flicks the head of my dick with her tongue. Just thinking about having her mouth on my cock put my body into overdrive.

Growling, I shifted us to where her back was up against the building and her legs were around my waist. I ground my cock into her mound, wishing I could feel her hot slick skin wrapped around my cock. Reaching in between us, I took hold of the edge of her jeans and pulled, making sure to pop every button open. Wasting no time, my fingers dove inside her pants and underwear. Delving into her folds, I found her entrance with my fingers and drove three fingers all the way in to the webbing. Crooking them slightly towards the front of her body, I worked my fingers in and out of her, over and over again. I could hear the slick sound of her sex in the quiet of the night. The sound was turning me on beyond belief.

Ember's head fell to my shoulder; her teeth sank in to the cord of my neck, likely leaving imprints of all her teeth. A faint noise of shuffling feet sounded to our right, and I turned my head and watched one of the waiters walking to his car. He didn't notice us though. Moving deeper into the shadows, I continued my ministrations, but kept an eye out to make sure we stayed unnoticed.

"Gabe." She whispered.

Her head lifted up off my shoulders when the couple started talking beside a later model Ford Mustang. Finally noticing we were no longer alone, I could feel her start to get wetter. She liked the possibility of being caught. Good to know that she was as into this as I was, because it was about to go a lot further if she didn't do something to stop me.

"Tell me to stop." I whispered against her lips.

She flicked her eyes up to me, and then returned them to the couple a few car lengths away from us. They were standing under the bright light of a street lamp, where we were cocooned in the shadow of the building. Shielded on one side by a cinder block wall, and on the other side by a large power pole about three feet in diameter. The duo was laughing and carrying on about some customers that had just eaten there. Not that I could give a fuck at that moment.

"I want your cock inside me; I don't want you to stop." She stated quietly.

"Baby, these pants are so tight I don't think we'd be able to get them down. You'd be practically naked if we did this here." I explained reluctantly, while starting to pull away.

Her vaginal muscles clamped down on my fingers, and her legs tightened around my back, keeping me exactly where I was. I knew I didn't have much control left, and if she didn't let me go quick, she was going to be pant less, with me in her in no time at all.

"Ember." I said gruffly, looking into her lust filled eyes.

"Please."

"Let me take you somewhere else. I promise we won't drive

far, just far enough to give us a little more privacy; where I don't have to worry about someone catching us with our pants down."

"Okay, but hurry. God, I need you inside of me. I'm so close. Just go over there, behind those trees."

It was at this point that I didn't give a fuck where we went. Dropping her legs from around my waist, she buttoned her jeans and took my hand. I led her to my bike, passing the couple as we left. They looked startled to see us come out of nowhere, but I didn't give them much to process since I was on a mission. I handed her her helmet that was now a permanent fixture on my bike now. She fit the helmet onto her head, and climbed onto the bike. Doing the same, I started the bike up with a deafening roar.

Gunning the engine, I made for the back of the buildings and the woods that proceeded it. Pulling into an alcove that was lined on two sides with woods, and one with a brick building, I aimed the bike for the deepest part of the shadows. I wasted no time shutting off the engine and then getting Ember to her feet. I made quick work of the buttons, shoving her jeans down to her ankles, effectively hobbling her to where she couldn't move.

I pushed her chest first over my bike, making her ass rise in the air, permitting me the perfect view of her delectable backside and wet channel. Losing all the control I'd managed to hold onto, I yanked the buttons on my own jeans, freeing my cock. One second I was in my jeans, the next I was buried to the hilt inside her, bumping her cervix with the head of my cock as I pounded deep. I ground my cock deeper, feeling her body tremor.

"God, Gabe. Stop jacking around and fuck me already. I want it hard." Ember said.

That's my girl.

Pulling back my hips, I pulled free of her all together and she moaned despair. Wriggling her ass, she tried to get me back inside, but I had different plans. I wasn't going to last much longer, and I wanted to make sure she got off before I did.

Dropping down to my knees, her ass and pussy were at eye level. I leaned forward and licked her clit. Repeatedly, giving her those teasing licks. She ground her ass back into my mouth, and I reached up and shoved two thick fingers inside of her. I continuously pumped them inside her, all the while sucking and licking her clit.

It didn't take long and I could feel her body clenching and unclenching around my fingers. Finally, she started to come, and I could wait no longer. Standing, I slammed inside of her, continually, grunting with my effort. I could still feel her insides contracting, and it sent me over the edge myself. I poured my come inside of her, spurt after spurt, drenching her insides.

Panting, I pulled out of her slowly. My cock popped free with a soft plop, and Ember moaned at the sudden emptiness. Her head rested on the seat of the bike, her beautiful hair lay scattered over the seat, and falling down the other side.

"You're so beautiful." I said to her.

She gave a soft laugh, and then leaned up. She reached down and pulled her jeans up, but didn't button them.

"Alright, I'll suck in, you button." Ember said sheepishly.

Rolling my eyes, I reached down to button her pants. Why she wore pants that she couldn't button without laying down, was beyond me. Must be a woman thing.

Once they were buttoned, she wrapped her hands around me and gave me a soft kiss on the lips.

"Take me home, babe."

"Gladly." I said.

We were on the back road to Kilgore when the car came out of nowhere. One second I was staring at a dark road ahead and behind me, and the next headlights came right up to my back tire.

Fearing he would clip my tire and send us flying, I gunned the throttle and took off, going at least twice the speed limit. Luckily, the car didn't have the same get up and go that my bike did. They'd also never tried to catch a bike either. When I was sixteen and got my first motorcycle, I made it a priority to know my bike inside and out. I knew this beast like the back of my hand. I knew how it handled, how it rode, and what it could do. Right then, I knew it could take a corner a lot faster than that car could, and I was going to prove it to them.

Seeing the nearly 90 degree turn up ahead, I heard Ember's panic emanating from behind me. I just prayed that she trusted me enough to hold on and not let go. The car was gaining on us quick, and I knew I needed to do something. Pressing the clutch in, I decelerated at an alarming rate, but I had complete control and saw how I was going to take this turn, and then accelerate through it. I knew that beyond this turn was a straight patch for nearly a mile and a half. I was going to lose these fuckers there, and then join them at their own game.

I did just that too. One second they were nearly on me, and

the next I was going through all of my gears. The headlights were behind me a good distance now, and I knew they wouldn't be able to catch me if I didn't want them to. I was up to 120 before I started looking for a place to pull off. Spotting a good spot, I braked hard and pulled off the side of the road, hitting the lights.

I stopped behind an old rotted pine, and tapped Ember's leg three times.

"Get off, I'm going to go catch them, and then come back for you. In the meantime I want you to take this," I said, handing her my spare Glock, "and hide right here. Call Sam and tell him what's going on."

During that time, she nodded in understanding, and then hid down behind the pine. Slipping her phone out of her shirt, I heard her make a call to Sam and explain what was going on. The car passed us with a blast of air, and I started the bike back up and tore after them, leaving my light off as not to alert them that I was there. I caught up with them a minute or so later.

Luckily, they were going a lot slower now, thinking they'd lost me, or this wouldn't have worked so well. Taking the .45 out of the pancake holster at my back, I took aim with my right arm, and shot out their left rear tire. It didn't take long and they lost control. The car pulled hard to the right, and then flipped several times, brutally, before coming to a stop in a ditch that ran along the side of the road wheels up in the air.

I stopped about twenty feet away and waited to see if they would emerge. They didn't, and I wasn't stupid enough to go to them, so I waited too. It didn't take long and until I could hear bikes roaring in the distance; I knew the cavalry had shown. We were maybe ten minutes from Free, and I knew they would be hauling ass to get here fast.

I watched and waited for whoever was in the car to emerge; they didn't disappoint. Slowly, one fell out and then the other. Both were coughing and moaning, but I felt not one iota of remorse. These crazy fucks could've killed my woman, and I'd be damned if I felt sorry for nearly killing them when they almost took everything from me.

Getting off my bike with my .45 still in my hand, I walked up to them slowly. They noticed me at the same time and raised their hands into the air. Now that I was closer, I could tell that they were still very young. Fifteen or sixteen, at most.

"Face down on the ground, keep your hands behind your head. No sudden movements or you'll be sportin' a new hole. Don't test me; if you do, I won't hesitate. I don't relish shooting a kid, but damned if I won't do it."

Jack was the first to arrive, followed, shortly by James. They pulled up beside my bike, and walked up cautiously. This wasn't their first rodeo. They were coming blind into a situation, and they were being careful, taking in the situation and their surroundings in seconds. It was clear what was going on, but one could never be too careful.

"See you have a situation here, where's Ember?" James asked.

"She's about a half a mile back that way." I said, while pointing back behind me.

James nodded, then got on his bike to go get her. She was probably scared shitless waiting for me. I loved a smart woman who knew how to deal with a scary situation. Ember was cool under fire, knew when to argue, and knew when to just sit back and listen. She wasn't one of those silly girls who went charging head first into a situation she knew she couldn't handle.

Sirens could be heard in the distance and I cursed. Someone must have heard the accident and called them. I wanted to question them, and it looked like I wouldn't have the chance to unless I made it quick.

Crouching down, I grabbed the first one by the head, and stuck the pistol against his temple. The boy had blood running from his nose and mouth, but that didn't sway me from my course.

"Tell me what your orders were. Who is giving them?"

"Fuck you." Man boy number one said.

"No, that'll be you in a very short time if you don't start talking. Do you know what kind of connections I have? Do you want to watch your ass every time you bend over while you're in lockup?" I asked monotonously.

I could make these kids life a living hell, and I would, if they didn't give me what I wanted. They'd talk eventually.

"You ain't got that type of pull." Man boy number two said.

"Do you want to find out? I can get back to you in a couple of days; see what you have to say then. Personally, I hope you choose that option. I bet you both would enjoy it after a while."

"You ain't got nothin'." Man boy number one said.

"Alright, I'll come visit in a few days, we'll see then." I said before backing away.

The sirens were right on us now, lights bathing the black night red and blue. Two Rusk County Sherriff cars pulled up about two seconds after I put my .45 away. Wouldn't be good for them to see an armed man standing over two individuals that clearly just got in a wreck.

One was a heavy set, and the other one, who was a little older in years, looked like he'd seen it all. The young black man was still wet behind the ears. They both took in the situation, noting the two parked mammoth Harleys, the two huge men in black, and a couple of kids with their hands on their heads, it didn't look like it would be a fun explanation; especially, when the cops immediately stiffened and moved their hands closer to their guns. Not placing them on them, but close enough to get to them if needed. That was a sign of a good cop, always ready for what could happen, whether it good or bad.

"Officer." I said and nodded my head to them both.

"What's going on here?"

Before they could receive their answer, James pulled up behind their cars, Ember on the back. Not wearing a helmet, I might add.

"Where's your fuckin' helmet?" I asked, distracted from the original question posed by the officer.

"Well, I took it off to sit on it, but when I heard James I took off towards the road, and kind of left it behind." She said sheepishly.

"You don't get on a bike without a helmet. Never. Too many things could happen, even in that short stretch of highway. The highway doesn't care. It doesn't care that you were only going to be riding for a couple of seconds. The highway is an unforgiving bitch."

"Jesus, Gabe. He didn't even get up over twenty miles an hour."

I had this conversation a lot. The guys were used to it. Unfortunately, I witnessed two motorcycle wrecks in my time, and neither one ended well for the individuals that were on them.

"You see that guardrail right there?" I asked her.

She turned, and looked at the guardrail. In addition, I noted that Jack, James, and each of the officers did as well.

"I witnessed a wreck one time with one of those. Want to know what happened? The guy was going just over thirty miles an hour and hit an oil spot. His bike went one way and his body went towards the guardrail. The side of his head hit the guardrail. Split his head open like a watermelon falling to the ground."

"Not that this isn't interesting, but shouldn't you be doing something with those two?" She motioned towards to the two boys on the ground.

When Ember pulled up with James, both officer's attentions had immediately zeroed in on her. She looked like she'd just been fucked, which she had been). Her hair was windblown, cheeks flushed. Her shirt had ridden up exposing some of the smooth skin at her belly. Now that she'd brought up their inappropriate behavior, they were all business.

"They seriously hurt?" the young officer asked.

"No, just a little banged up. These little assholes deserve this and more, they almost ran my girl and me off the road. I had to use some creative driving to get away from them before they made road kill out of us. We're lucky to be alive right now." I said and then started in on my explanation.

The officers listened to the whole explanation, took the kid's explanation as well, and then gave them a seat in the back of the police cars. Each one in a separate car. With handcuffs.

Tomorrow was going to be a busy day for them; I'd be making sure of it.

Chapter 9

"Yippie-ki-yay, motherfucker."
- Die Hard

Ember

"Get that out of my face." Cheyenne said to me.

"It's not in your face, it's in my hand."

"Get what's in your hand out of my face."

Both of us burst out laughing.

"Do you both ever stop? That's all I fucking hear. If I have to hear penis, penis, penis, vagina, vagina, vagina one more time, I'll shoot myself." James said petulantly.

Sherlock Holmes and Varsity Blues were only two of the movies that we constantly quoted. We were both goody two shoes in high school. All we did was watch movies and eat in front of the television. We didn't party, we didn't stay out late, and we didn't do anything illegal. Well maybe not too illegal, but still. They were lucky we watched movies; we could've been having sex with half of Kilgore's population like the rest of our senior class.

"Penis, penis, penis." Janie yelled.

James whipped his head around and glared at us as if it was our fault. Not once today had we even said anything from Varsity Blues! He's the one who said it. Sticking my tongue out right back, I turned my head back to the computer and started pointing out the bike helmets that I liked.

I'd gone back the next day to find it, but when I did there wasn't much left but a shell. The straps had chew marks, and no padding was left where your head went. I still haven't heard the end of that one.

"She's three, James. What exactly do you expect when you say something that's so easy and catchy for her to say?" Cheyenne asked.

He'd been with her for a year now, and he still found himself flabbergasted at the stuff she said and did. Just last month she'd tried to take a shit on the potty at Lowe's. While Cheyenne and I were busy laughing our asses off, James was running in the opposite direction. We'd calmly taken her down once we'd gotten ourselves under control, and then took her to the actual potty. She still never figured out why you couldn't go since there was a potty right there that she could use.

"I like that one. The one with the skull. Do you think he would let me wear it?" I asked the group in general.

"He'll be happy as long as you have a helmet, dimwit." James grumped.

Throwing my ruler at him blindly I said, "Order it."

Cheyenne one clicked it, and that was that.

"You know, he said to pick one up at the Harley shop today." James said helpfully.

"I didn't like any of those, loser. Plus, this will be here tomorrow by one in the afternoon, guaranteed." I replied.

"Doesn't help the fact that he will want you to have it for tonight when we do that rally for the local schools."

"I'll wear Cheyenne's. Since she's not allowed on the bike anymore."

"I'm so going on the bike. Get your own helmet." Cheyenne said.

"No you're not. Sam said so, and we both agree. No more bike for the pregnant chick." I said, nodding to James with my head.

"Harrumph." She grouched.

"Speaking of which, we need to go ahead and get some hotel rooms. Gabe left me his card so we could charge them on the company account. Let's go ahead and get that over with since we're already here." I advised.

Thirty minutes, four websites, and six hundred dollars later, we had six rooms for two nights. The town of Tulsa was going to be insanely busy, so we booked our hotels about forty-five minutes from there, in a small town called Bixby. We probably weren't the only ones to think staying an hour drive away would be easier in the end, but it would have to do.

"Alrighty then. I have myself a date at Shogun's tonight, with Gabe, after the rally. What should I wear?" I asked Cheyenne.

For the next couple of hours we listened to the soundtrack for Pitch Perfect and searched for some clothes that would be appropriate for a biker babe, and a hot date at Shogun's, one of the nicest restaurants in three towns.

Ω

"Shouldn't we be getting to the rally?" I asked.

"We are. I just wanted to take you here first." Gabe said as he pulled up in front of a plain brick building.

The black door sported a gun decal with Doc underneath of it.

"What is this place?" I asked.

"This is the Gun Doctor." He said as if I knew what he was talking about, which I didn't.

Why would you need a gun doctor?

"Umm, why?" I asked confused.

"So we can get you a pistol that's more comfortable for you, and fits your hand better." Gabe said simply.

Well, didn't that just explain everything? He held the door for me; the smell of gun oil immediately assaulted my senses, making me sneeze.

There were glass cases encircling the room. Any and every type of gun adorned the cases. On the walls hung some rifles and shotguns. Immediately, my eye snagged a purple shotgun, and I fell in love.

"I want that one." I said pointing to it.

"That one won't fit into your purse." He said dryly.

"Okay, but when we come back I'm getting that one." I said before starting to look into all the cases.

145

"Can I help y'all?" a young sales associate asked.

"You the Gun Doctor?" I asked him.

"Nope. Just an employee. Can I show you anything?" The sales associate asked.

"This one." I said pointing towards a black gun with hot pink grips.

"Jesus, I should have known you'd pick that one. That one is a .40 caliber. Not too bad of a gun either. It's a Ruger SR40. We can get you some lithium sites for it too." Gabe said.

"Damn. I guess you don't really even need me." The sales associate stated.

"We want to take it into the range and try it out. We'll need a box of ammo too. Some of those disposable ear plugs also." Gabe said.

The associate didn't hop to very fast though. He was busy checking out my tits. I knew I should have worn a bra, but Cheyenne guaranteed me that I didn't need one.

"Now would be nice." Gabe barked.

Rolling my eyes, I began to wander the room while they discussed the details. This place would be the place you would want to be if you were ever attacked by someone, or something. Every type of gun imaginable was here. Some even looked like they were from the future. One of the guns had a rounded tip at the end of the barrel; I studied it wondering what it was.

"Laser sights." Gabe said from behind me, making me jump three feet in the air.

"Jesus. Don't you ever stop doing that? You're like a fricking cat!" I gasped.

Gabe's smile was beautiful; I always felt my heart flutter when he gave me one as he was giving me now.

Wandering around some more, I came to a stop in front of the shotgun again.

"Can I help you?" A young woman asked.

She was probably a year or two older than my twenty-six. She had short blonde hair that came to just under her chin. She was tiny, maybe five feet at the most. The more I looked at her, the more she seemed familiar to me. She seemed to be studying me as well. Her head tilted slightly to the side. I'd seen her before. Then suddenly it hit me.

"Jolie!" I squealed.

"Ember?" She asked.

"When did you move back?" I asked excitedly.

She smiled sadly before saying, "My mom passed away a few months ago. This is the first time I've been back, ya' know, since that happened."

I nodded sadly. Jolie's dad killed James' best friend in high school. Something terrible had happened to her, and I haven't seen her since she left in the middle of senior year. James was always sticking up for her, watching over her. They'd started spending a ton of time together. Cheyenne and I had been in junior high when all of that went down.

147

Though we heard about it, we never experienced it firsthand.

James did, and he did *not* like it. There was a huge fight during their senior year picnic; James left with a suspension, and Jolie never came back. Apparently, it was something bad, because never once did we hear exactly what happened from our brothers. James was pretty close to her, but he never opened his mouth. He was in a sort of depression for a while after Jolie left. I think she was the reason that he went into the army, and Max, being his best friend, followed him.

Jolie hadn't changed much in thirteen years. She looked as great at 32. Her hair was a tad shorter but other than that, she was still the tiny, spunky girl that she used to be. I wonder how long it would take James to figure out she was back. He had ways of knowing things. That, or I might tell him; he deserves to know.

"What are you doing working here?"

"There're guns here. I figure it's the best place for me. I'm not going to tell you why. I'd rather not tell you in here anyway. Maybe we can meet for drinks sometime." She said quietly.

A sick feeling lodged in my throat, and I knew it was something bad. I felt two strong arms wrap around my waist and pull me up against a hard chest. Jolie's eyes had widened until nearly all the white was showing. She also seemed to shrink into herself, as if she was scared of a big man like Gabe.

"Got a lane. Let's go, we have to be at the rally in about forty five minutes, and I want to see if you like this before we buy it."

"That sounds great, Jolie. Call me whenever is good for you." I said with a sincere smile.

Giving Jolie a meaningful look, we headed into the back of the store. We came to a metal door, and the young man who helped us, opened it and walked through. It led into a room that was roughly the size of a small gym. At the far end, targets hung. In front of each target stood a metal table and chair. There was plexi-glass sectioning off each table for flying shells.

The young man showed us how to use the mechanical target mover, and then left us to it. Gabe gave me a set of earplugs, and I hung them around my neck when he started to explain.

"Alright, this doesn't have a safety you click on and off, it's got a trigger safety. You have to depress both the little lever on the trigger and the trigger at the same time to shoot it. Don't put your finger on the trigger unless you intend to shoot something. If you point this at someone, you had better intend to shoot him, or her, with it. Don't bluff, because they might call you on it."

He then went on to show me how to load the clip, inject a bullet into the chamber, unload it, and then, finally, how to aim and fire. He then unloaded it, and then handed it to me. My guess was this was a test to make sure I knew what I was doing.

I smiled, grabbed the earplugs from around my neck, and then put the them into my ears.

I did know what I was doing. Expertly, I loaded the clip, then the gun, and then aimed and fired at the target. Firing rapidly, I unloaded the clip as fast as I could. Then, I set the pistol down and studied the target. Center mass on all but one, and that was the one where I aimed for the head.

Still got it.

"Jesus. You didn't tell me you could shoot like that. I think I just came in my pants a little. That was hot." Gabe hollered, while he studied the target as well.

"Cheyenne and I used to compete in high school. My dad was big into competition shooting, and I was daddy's little girl. I can shoot skeet too. We had a blast, and I continued shooting after dad died. I knew he'd want me to."

He levered the target up to the front and replaced the target with a new one. This one had nearly an entire body.

"I'm gonna move it, you shoot for the 5s."

The fives were located at the main artery points. Carotid, subclavian, brachial, femoral, and popliteal. Supposedly, these were designed as kill shots when you couldn't shoot center mass to bring your target down. If you wanted them down for good and didn't have a good center mass shot, you would aim for these areas. I loaded my clip, chambered it, and then got ready.

"Go." Gabe said and then moved the target sharply to the right.

I took aim and got within an inch of the femoral artery on the right leg. He moved it sharply backwards and slightly to the left.

"Go."

We continued this pattern until I fired all nine shots. He

pulled the target and studied it silently for a couple seconds. Then he turned to me and regarded me.

"Mother fucker. You're a crackshot!" Gabe stated, grinning.

"I guess so. Can we go now?" I asked.

I didn't like how shooting made me feel anymore. I didn't enjoy it like I used to, and ever since my dad died I didn't feel like having anything to do with it. I'd made it through to my senior year before I stopped competing. It brought up too many memories. They were bittersweet, and reminded me of what I was missing

Left a huge gaping hole in my heart.

Gabe must have made the connection, because the next thing I knew I was wrapped in his arms, fighting back tears.

"You're not alone anymore, Em. I'll always be here. I love you, sweetheart. Cheyenne, the girls, Sam, Blaine. Everyone loves you. You're not alone." He said as he kissed my forehead.

We left shortly after. Gabe was also the proud new owner of a .40 caliber Ruger something or another. I'm sure there's a name for it. I'm also sure he told me, but, like always, it went in one ear and out the other. You would think after six years of competition shooting that I would know what kind of weapons I'd used. I didn't. That was my dad's job, and I refused to take it over.

"So, where exactly are we supposed to meet for this Biker's Rule for School?" I yelled into Gabe's ear.

We were driving down Highway 42, and it seemed to me we were more riding than getting to a destination. We passed over the Sabine River, and I noticed that it was getting quite low. We'd had one hell of a summer, and we were lucky it was as high as it was. Sometimes, during a bad summer, the river slowed down to little more than a creek in some spots.

"You'll see." Gabe said cryptically.

We rode for another ten minutes or so when I saw the first bike. Then it wasn't just one, it was hundreds. We waved, spoke, joked around, and rode. What the Bikers Rule for School was, was a bunch of bikers entering their bikes in the rally. You didn't even have to be a bad ass like Gabe and the rest of the guys; you could be an old man going through his midlife crisis. The money that you paid to enter your bike then went to buying the local kids school supplies. This was my first year riding in it, but it sure wouldn't be the last.

We rode for six hours straight. By the end of the day, I was ready to drop. We've ridden on long rides before, but never one where I spent the entire six hours riding straight. By the time we pulled up in front of Shogun's, I was ready to burst; bathroom breaks were essential, and after riding for forever and a day, I was in major need of one

Gabe managed a front row parking spot, and I thanked God for answering my prayers before I pissed my pants.

Running into the bathroom, I barely slammed and locked the door before I dropped my pants. Sighing in intense relief, my eyes rolled back in my head, and I listened to the door slam and two cackling women enter the bathroom. They sounded snobby, and I was glad I was in the stall and didn't have to see their faces. I might have to bitch slap them.

Finishing up, I was buttoning my jeans when what they were saying penetrated my brain. Then I started fuming.

"Did you see that trash that came with that hot hunk of man?" Snotty bitch one asked.

"Yes. He could do much better. Did you see what she was wearing? You don't wear that type of outfit out to a nice restaurant. You wear a dress." Snotty bitch number two countered.

"Oh my God. For real! She must have a golden vagina to keep him. She didn't even have boobs. I wonder if I gave him my number if he'd call me." Snotty bitch number one quipped.

Motherfucking son of a bitch.

The lock made a sharp clicking sound as I slid it out of the locked position and slammed the door open. Both girls turned at the sharp sound of the stall door slamming against the wall. Then both of their eyes widened as they saw me walk out.

Busted.

"For your information, I give really good head. He keeps me around for when he wants me to give him the business." I said sweetly.

I washed my hands while glaring daggers at them.

Both girls were frozen, unsure of what to do or say. They came unstuck when I walked out of the bathroom, swinging the door open so hard that it slammed against the wall also. I stomped my way back into the main part of the restaurant. Gabe saw me coming, and instantly took in my expression. Alarm came over his face, but then settled when he saw the women exiting behind me. Shaking his head, he looked down to his feet and contemplated his boots.

I walked up to stand beside him and watched the two women walk to their prospective dates, and immediately commenced talking shit about me. I could see the faces of the dates, and each ones showed clear disgust. Their faces became more and more animated before the beefier of the two broke off from the group. He marched over and tried to stick his finger in my face. Except that, he got nowhere close.

One second he was marching towards me, and the next he found himself face down on the floor.

"I don't really care what those ladies told you. You do not come up to my woman threateningly. If you have a problem, you come to me. I better not find out you did this to some other woman. Have some respect man." Gabe spit, as he pushed off him.

He did make sure he kneed him in the kidney first though.

Right as he stood up, our buzzer started going off; I grabbed Gabe's hand and pulled him towards the hostess station. The hostess gave us a wide berth as she seated us in their most secluded place. Apparently, she felt a little uncomfortable having us with general population.

Dinner was a success though. Our first date went off without too many hitches.

"I really enjoyed our cook. He was pretty awesome with his spatula." I said to Gabe as we made our way outside.

"Yeah, that's cause he thought you were hot, and he gave you more attention than he did anyone else."

Shogun's was your typical Japanese restaurant. They seat you around a large flat grilling surface, where the cook takes the orders for everyone that surrounds his station. He'll cook everything to your specifications, and entertain you in the process. My favorite is the onion volcano.

"Yea, I'm pretty sure this scoop neck t-shirt and jeans really did it for him."

He stopped abruptly and turned to look into my eyes.

"You are a very beautiful woman. Those women were just jealous of you. You don't have to dress up to be the classiest person in a room. You can pull that off with some yoga pants and a t-shirt. They're just jealous bitches who have no place in our thoughts." Gabe said, before giving me a quick kiss and resuming our trek across the parking lot.

As usual, Gabe moved the bike even though he had a front row parking spot. He did this for two reasons: One being he doesn't like to be too close to other cars in case he needs to get out of an area fast; the other being that he doesn't want anyone touching his bike.

There was one rule among bikers, and that was that the bike was sacred: you don't mess with other bikes. Bikers know this, regular people do not.

I enjoyed the heck out of our date, snotty bitches or not. I just wish I'd had someone take a picture of us. I'd yet to get a picture of the two of us together, mostly because Gabe wasn't the picture type of person. Apparently, bad asses were allergic to pictures. The only ones I ever got were the shots where he wasn't paying attention. Also, the ones that he accidentally was flipping off the camera. It was amazing how often that happened.

155

I was pulled from my thoughts with a jolt, as Gabe sent me careening to the ground. Gravel dug into the palms of my hands; I looked up just in time to see Gabe plant his booted foot in a man's face. Gabe's foot landed on his jaw with a sickening thud, and the person was down for the count. That wasn't the case with the other person. He'd jumped on Gabe's back and tried to subdue him with his arm around his neck.

Adrenaline was coursing through my veins as I watched Gabe drop his right shoulder and use the attacker's momentum against him. Over Gabe's shoulder he went, and slammed him into the ground. Gabe went Stone Cold Steve Austin on his ass and power slammed him onto the ground, making his head bounce off the gravel. One punch to the jaw and the other attacker was down for the count as well.

It took all of fifteen seconds from start to finish; which was pretty fucking scary if you asked me. The amount of strength he had in one hand could probably kill me with one blow like the one he'd just given to the man lying on the ground. Not that he would ever use that kind of force with me. Anything he ever did would be a total accident; never would he intentionally hurt me.

Gabe scanned his surroundings once more before coming to me.

"You okay?" He asked.

He wasn't winded in the slightest. His hair was a little out of place, but other than that you would never be able to tell that he just kicked two guy's asses.

I nodded my head, and regarded him.

"That. Was. Awesome." I said to him enthusiastically. "Will

you teach me how to do all of that?"

"I'll teach you whatever you want, honey. Let me see your hands. Fuck, I'm sorry. I didn't mean for you to hurt your hands, but it was the fastest way I could get you down. The little fucker had a fucking tire iron." He said while inspecting my bloody palms.

A groan sounded from one of the morons on the ground, and Gabe went to them while I called the cops.

Gabe was persuasive with his fists, and the man let us in on why he thought it'd be a good idea to hurt us. Turns out the women from the restaurant told their men that I threatened to 'hurt them in the worst way' while we were in the bathroom. Therefore, the dates decided to take it upon themselves before getting all of the facts. Now they would be going on a trip to the local slammer, all because they trusted their dates instead of collecting more information. Pretty sure that was worth it … Not.

Flashing lights poured over the shadowed parking lot and my favorite cop was there to check on us.

"Everything alright?" Luke asked as he walked up.

"Yeah. These morons here thought they could sneak up on Terminator here. Little did they know Gabe was going to pull out his bad ass and show it to them. Gabe did a couple of fancy moves, and, all of a sudden, they were just lying there - out cold. I think I should have videoed it. This could've been one of those YouTube videos that went viral. Maybe if we could-" I answered but laughing interrupted me.

Both men were looking at me as if I was crazy.

Shaking his head, Gabe asked, "What are you doing here,

anyway? Aren't you a detective or something?"

"Something like that. They let me do what I want. I heard on the scanner that it was Ember so I came. Wasn't too far away. Got someone watching my girl, and figured I could stop by real quick to check on you both before heading home."

"Luke, if you ever need anyone to watch her, I'm more than happy to do it." I threw out there.

He smiled in appreciation, and then turned back to Gabe. They spoke for a few more minutes. Statements were made, and then we headed home.

Ω

Studying what I had to wear, I settled for some of my old comfy volleyball shorts that were so tight you couldn't wear anything but a thong with them, and a camisole. I didn't like wearing bras, and this was one of my ways around wearing one. I grabbed one of Gabe's flannel shirts out of the closet and shrugged it on too. Gabe kept it like a meat locker in here. Not one time was the AC set on anything above sixty-eight. I wasn't one to complain, so I made sure I always had a blanket or shirt nearby.

I walked out of the room and towards the kitchen. It was time for something to eat. Grabbing a bag of Chex Mix Muddy Buddies and a coke, I left the room, but instantly turned around when I heard Gabe yell for a beer. I found myself doing this a lot.

Walking in to the living room, I was immediately assaulted by the sound of gunfire. Rolling my eyes, I set everything down and sat at the edge of the couch with my ads and my coupon binder.

"What the fuck is that?" Gabe asked.

Looking up I met Gabe's eyes.

"What's what?"

"That." He said gesturing to my binder.

"This little gem is my coupon binder."

"Why would you need a coupon binder? Don't you have a good job?"

"Well yeah, now I do, but I didn't used to. I had to save any way I could. I don't like to touch my inheritance, makes me feel like I exchanged money for their lives. Anyway, I became engrossed in saving money where I could. Which, then, turned into an obsession. I don't buy anything that's not on sale. I price match, and I never pay full price for anything. Nobody will go to the store with me anymore. They get embarrassed when I pull out my coupons and ads.

"Thanks for the heads up." Gabe said, "Give me some of those."

I reached for the bag, but found them empty. Oops. I've been doing that a lot lately. I'm eating like a cow, but still managing to lose weight. Aces.

"Um, no can do. I ate them." I said holding up the empty bag.

"Wanna play?"

"Nah. I have about three hundred more coupons to cut out. Thanks for the offer."

"Sniper is behind you, James." Gabe half yelled.

I looked up and saw he was wearing his earphones, and then rolled my eyes. Whomever they were playing against didn't stand a chance when the guys teamed up. Then again, they were probably playing against twelve year olds.

I was starting to get hot, which wasn't that surprising since the flat screen put off so much heat, and I was working my arms out by cutting out all of my coupons. You wouldn't think that it would be that hard, but once you hit the hundred mark, your arms start burning. I pulled the shirt over my head, and tossed it behind me on the couch. A while later I had all the coupons cut and stacked in neat little piles when Gabe's voice interrupted me.

"Would you get mad if I scattered all of those coupons when I fuck you on the coffee table?" Gabe asked.

Glancing up at Gabe, I noticed that the game was still being played, but Gabe had lost focus. He was staring at me with an intense expression.

"Why do you need to do it on the coffee table? There's a perfectly good floor, a recliner, a couch, and a wall just right there." I noted.

He ditched the headphones and controller, and wrestled me to the ground, softly, beneath him, between the coffee table and the couch.

"These shorts sure make your ass look great, and this shirt doesn't cover your nipples very well. I can see every bump and the outline of your nipple through the white. You don't wear this out in public do you?" He asked, while leaning down and sucking my nipple through the camisole.

I didn't answer. His erection was grinding against me and I'd lost all cognitive ability; except for the direct line that led from my hoo-ha to my brain. I moaned long and loud when Gabe shifted onto his back, taking me with him, and then thrust up while pulling me down onto him. I threw my head back and savored the feelings that this man always made me feel.

Distantly, I became aware of yelling in the background, and the sounds of gunshots from Gabe's game, but paid it no mind as his body did delicious things to my own.

Gabe's hands pulled the camisole down until my breasts popped free, and then sprang up to his forearms and devoured my nipples with his mouth. I was arching against him, rubbing myself hard against him when he suddenly stopped.

I cried out. However I was instantly appeased when my legs were raised practically over my head, and my shorts torn off. Gabe's hands were between his legs, working himself free from his tight jeans.

"I need to be inside you, now." Gabe said before slamming into me.

"Yes." I moaned out long and loud.

This position wasn't giving Gabe the penetration he wished for, because one second I was on top of him, and the next I was back against the couch with Gabe on his knees pounding inside of me. I watched as his slick flesh penetrated me in and out. Each stroke of his cock took me higher and higher. Watching was making me closer and closer to another orgasm, and I reached up and pinched my nipples, adding to the already swirling sensations happening inside of me.

"Oh, God. Touch yourself - I'm not gonna last when you play with your nipples like that."

Complying with his wishes, I left one hand on my nipple while the other snaked down to my clit. The first touch of my finger, added to the effect of his cock pounding inside of me, started the upward spiral of my orgasm. Flicking my clit faster, I worked myself quickly.

Gabe's cock hit my cervix with each rough thrust, and I returned my gaze to where we were connected, and lost it.

Sensations built inside of me and burst, hurdling me into another mind-blowing climax. Gabe's followed shortly after mine, as I continued to watch our connection.

"Like what you see?" Gabe asked.

My eyes flicked to his stare, and then went immediately back to where we were still connected. Gabe's erection was still hard, not losing any of its hardness after his climax. I let my hand travel down from my clit and feel around our connection. It was amazing that he fit inside of me. He was so huge, bigger than any man I'd ever seen. Not that I had much to compare it with, only the porn magazines Cheyenne and I used to sneak out of our brother's room when we were younger and curious.

"What are you thinking about?" Gabe asked.

"I was wondering if your cock was bigger than most. I don't really have anything to compare it to, and I was curious. I was just trying to remember when Cheyenne and I were fifteen and looking at James' porn magazines. There weren't that many penises, because it was a magazine for men, but there were still some in there."

Gabe laughed and gave a little thrust of his hips, sending his cock a little deeper inside of me.

"I don't really know. Never was the type to compare my dick with friends." He laughed out.

Smiling at him, I said, "I have a ruler in the other room. Maybe we can measure it real quick."

"Nah. I have some different plans for you at the moment."

Then he showed me those plans. In great detail.

Chapter 10

Sometimes I wake up grumpy; other times I let her sleep.
-T-shirt

Ember

I'd just woken from my afternoon nap.

It was Sunday; I was allowed to be lazy. I woke up to an empty house, and took the opportunity to try on my new workout compression shorts that had a holster for my pistol built in. I was admiring how great the compression part sucked in the fat when I decided I needed to show this puppy off, but first I had to find the gun.

I went to the closet and started to search for my firearm when I came across a small box on the top shelf of the closet. Curious by nature, I slipped the lid off and looked inside. The box was full of pictures. Grabbing the box, I took it with me to the bed and had a seat. I dumped the entire thing out onto the bed. Some of the photos were old, and some were much newer.

Starting at the bottom, I looked through and found a family photo of a young Gabe, a handsome older man that looked like a slightly older version of Gabe now, and a beautiful woman with shining brown hair. They looked like the perfect little family. It's hard to imagine that Gabe lost such beauty in his life. Setting the photo on the nightstand, I went about sorting through the pictures. Some were of old army buddies, others were of a much more tired looking version of his mom. Even a few of him in high school.

I smiled when I saw the one of a group of men in the desert. I spied Gabe first. He had his shirt off and tucked into the front of his pants. His rifle slung cross ways across his chest, and he was smiling big for the camera. His dog tags hung between his well-defined pecs, and he was wearing a pair of Oakley's covering his eyes. He had both of his arms slung around two men. They were shirtless as well, shirts tucked into their pants in nearly the same way. Their guns were resting on their shoulders, and both were laughing full out. This one made me happy, so I decided to keep this one out as well, and placed it on top of the family photo.

Closer to the front was when the pictures started getting annoying. That was where all the women were.

One photo in particular caught my eye. The picture was of Gabe in his dress uniform, and a young woman who looked vaguely familiar. Not sure why, but something about her stood out to me. Gabe looked so handsome in his uniform. Metals were pinned to his coat, colors of all kinds stood out starkly on his left breast. The woman clashed with him in the looks department. She was wearing a form fitting green dress that looked entirely inappropriate for what looked like an army function. Her hair was up in a tight do that made her face looked pinched. She wasn't smiling, but neither was Gabe. This must be Sydney.

Feeling a little killer like, I decided maybe I should put the pictures up before I went to the backyard and started offering burned pictures as a sacrifice. Or, seeing if I could make a voodoo doll. I felt a little hostile right now, and would probably jump her sorry ass if I had her in the same room with me.

Standing up, I gathered the pictures and shoved them back into the box, making sure to grab the two that were on the nightstand and placing them onto the dresser where I could get them later. I put the box back where I found it, and then went in search of my new gun.

I found it in the kitchen. Why? I don't know, but hey, who am I to question a man's way of thinking?

Sliding my new Ruger into the holster, I did a few jumping jacks to see how the fit was.

Kinda annoying, but definitely doable. It was definitely a heavy presence at my back.

Slipping my bare feet into a pair of old Nike's, I changed my shirt into an old volleyball one from high school, and walked out the front door. There was no answer at Cheyenne's place, so I tried Blaine's, but had the same response. Then I went searching and found them all in the bay area of the garage.

All eyes turned to me as I walked into the bay area of the garage. Everyone was there. Gabe, Blaine and Elliot, Sam and Cheyenne, James, Jack and Max. All the boys had beers in their hands, and the girls were drinking what looked like sweet tea.

"So, how did he measure up?" Elliott asked when he saw me walk through the back door.

Cheyenne and Blaine snickered and my stomach sank. Why would they ask that? Looking to Gabe for a clue as to what was going on, I found him giving Elliott the look. You know, the one where if it were possible, he'd be slicing you in half with his death ray stare.

"How did what measure up?" I asked confused.

"You know...the package." Jack chimed in, glancing at Gabe then back to me.

Glancing around, I tried to figure out what the hell they were talking about, but found nothing.

"I'm confused. What are y'all talking about?"

"Well, apparently, Ember dear, your man over here forgot to turn off the sound on his microphone. Your sexcapades were heard over the airwaves. Unlucky for you, everyone was playing at the time. So, how big was he best friend?" Cheyenne teased.

My face flamed, and I was stunned speechless.

They'd heard the entire thing!

Turning my own death ray stare towards Gabe, I found him contemplating the rafter's in the ceiling. I let my eyes travel down his t-shirt covered chest, down to his jean-clad package. This was one of those times where I was supposed to let it go. Unfortunately, my mouth didn't agree with my mind.

"Well." I drawled, "I never got him out of me long enough to measure him. My Gabe has some stamina. I did measure him with my fists and mouth though. How big would that make him if he takes up both fists and all of my mouth?"

They all looked thunderstruck.

Poor Max's face was bright red, eyes squeezed tightly shut. Blaine's mouth was hanging open, and Gabe was close to crying he was laughing so hard. Albeit silently. It was the type of laugh when you were laughing so hard no sound came out.

Cheyenne came unstuck first.

"You've got to be kidding me. Come on, let's go measure." She said grabbing onto my arm.

I shook her off, and turned back to Gabe.

I slapped him on the arm and said, "Knock it off, you big galoot."

He straightened and wiped the tears that were running down his cheek.

"What do you think of these?" I asked Gabe as I turned around and lifted up my shirt.

"That's fucking sweet!" Blaine yelled.

"I thought so, but does the gun look noticeable? I don't really want anyone to know I'm carrying it."

I felt Gabe's hand on my back as he traced the outline of the gun.

"Pretty nifty little contraption. How does it feel?" Gabe asked.

"Can you run around in it without it falling out?" Max asked.

"Do a couple of rounds of the parking lot and come back." Sam said.

Rolling my eyes, I took off across the lot, did two loops, and then came back to the garage. All the while, the gun stayed in the correct position at the small of my back.

"Feels good. No slipping or anything." I noted.

I tried my best to conceal that I was winded just from two loops around the lot. Must get to gym more.

All the men were studying my back as I looked over my shoulder.

"Where did you find these?" Cheyenne asked, "Do they make them in maternity sizes?"

"Amazon, and no, probably not." They were stretchy though. "Try them on later and see if you like them." I said to her.

Nodding, she made a loop around me, and I decided I'd had enough attention for the moment. Clapping my hands and turning around, all eyes went to my face.

"Now, what's for dinner?" I asked.

"We could go out. We haven't done that in a long time." Blaine suggested.

Nodding my head, I concurred.

"Sounds like a plan. As long as we go somewhere that will let me wear these shorts, we're good."

Everyone had something to say about the shorts again, but I went to Gabe and gave him a soft kiss on the cheek.

"Love you." I whispered into his ear.

He leaned back and took my face into his hands.

"Love you more." Was his gruff reply.

Ω

We were all sitting around a table at Bodacious, a local BBQ joint, when the woman in the photo finally clicked on where I'd seen her.

"Motherfucker!" I shouted when it finally registered.

Turning to Gabe I asked him, "What does Sidney look like?"

"Tall, brown hair, skinny. Dresses like a high society princess. Why?" He asked perplexed.

"Cheyenne, do you remember the lady that came and picked Story up?" I asked.

"Tall, brown hair, stuck up." Cheyenne supplied.

It was all starting to fit together. Story thanking "Sid" for the lift as the door closed. Why the woman looked so freaked to be at Free. Then another sinking feeling started seeping into my chest, and burrowing in until I couldn't get the thought out of my head.

Jesus Christ. That woman had a baby. Oh my God. No.

"Can I talk to you a minute?" I whispered to him.

His eyes studied me for a moment, and noted the change that had come over me. Standing up, he grabbed my hand and lifted me out of my chair. Guiding me outside, he took me to the bench that ran along the front and side of the building. Taking a seat, he pulled me down next to him, and waited for me to tell him what was wrong.

"Gabe." I said and swallowed thickly.

How do you tell someone you think he has a kid out there that he's never met?

"What?" He asked evenly.

He could sense something was wrong, but he had no clue. This was going to be one hell of a bombshell.

"Last month, when Story was picked up, it was by a woman named "Sid" who, I swear on my life, looks like the woman who was in the Army Ball photo of you that I saw in the closet. She looks exactly like her, just a tad older." I said.

His mouth opened and then closed.

"But she lives in Michigan. Why would she be here?" he asked.

"I don't know, but that's not all. She also had a baby with her. It looked to be about a year and a half old. She looked just like you, and seeing her was what made me ask you about kids later that day. She made me want to have one that would look just like you. Just like that little girl." I whispered brokenly.

Gabe sat in stunned silence.

He sat there so long, that I was beginning to get worried.

That is until he exploded. I watched the seat where he had been sitting not even seconds before, and then turned and watched him as he stalked to his bike, started it with a roar, and tore out of the parking lot. Without his helmet even strapped to his head, I might add.

Going back into the front door, I made my way back to the tables that we'd pushed together. My food still sat half eaten

171

on my plate, but I had no appetite what-so-ever. Even looking at it made me want to puke. Looking around at the curious faces, I finally settled on Max.

"I'm gonna need a ride. Gabe needed a minute." I said to him.

Nodding, he said, "Lucky for you that I had a bitch seat put on. Didn't want to have to deny any rides if I wanted to pick someone up at a bar or somethin'." Max said bawdily.

Curling my lip, I started to explain what was going on, and what I thought might be going on.

"So let me get this straight. Gabe was seeing someone during his last deployment, got her pregnant, and went off to war only to be dropped like a hot potato and told she'd aborted his baby and ran off with another man. Then she lied, or possibly lied, about it all, and actually had Gabe's baby? Do I have all this straight?" Blaine summarized.

"That's what I'm thinking. I saw that little girl; she's the spitting image of Gabe in the looks department. I remember thinking that she could totally pass for his kid. Except, I think that really was his baby. There're just too many coincidences here." I said.

"Let's get out of here. I'll call Luke and see if he can find her last address. We can run a check on her at the shop. Jack, go see if you can find Gabe." Sam demanded.

Time to find the underlying cause of this monster clusterfuck.

Ω

"I'm coming with you, and I'm not arguing with you. If you don't take me with you, I will just go myself." I said to Max and Sam.

172

Sighing in defeat, we all made our way out to Sam's Suburban and piled in. We were going to go stake out Sidney's house, and see if we could collect any more information. I'd grabbed my Canon in case I was able to get a photo. I wanted to prove to Gabe that this was his child. I didn't want there to be any doubt.

Thirty minutes later, we were parked three houses down in one of the nicer subdivisions in Longview. The Moran household looked like one of the nicer ones on the block. According to the background check Elliott ran, and the information from Luke, Sidney was now Mrs. Logan Moran. They'd married about a year ago, and had a one and a half year old daughter. Mr. Moran was an engineer at LeTourneau industries. Sidney was a stay at home mom, and didn't have a record.

We watched the house for over an hour before we got our first break. Sidney pulled up in her Audi and parked outside the garage. She went to the back door and started unbuckling the child that was in the back seat.

Using this excellent opportunity, I leapt out of the car with my camera ready, and started snapping photos of Sidney and the little girl. Sidney set the girl down and walked up to the house, calling out behind her for the girl to follow, and getting upset when the girl stopped to grab a flower that was growing in a flowerbed on the side of the driveway.

I stayed out of sight, but zoomed in as far as I could go, getting some excellent shots of the little girl with the flower up to her face. I took picture after picture, and only stopped when Sidney was fed up with the little girl. She hauled her into the house by her arm, and slammed the door with a loud bang.

My heart was pounding. That was Gabe's little girl. I just knew it.

Getting back into the Suburban, I clicked my seatbelt into place, and waited patiently for Sam and Max to get over their shock.

"How could a person do that, man?" Max asked.

Nobody answered. We didn't know.

The ride back to the compound was a silent one. Arriving at Free, we all headed into the office where everyone else was residing. Checks were being run on the Moran family. Cheyenne was on the phone with the hospital setting up a DNA test. Blaine was on the phone with a judge. Elliott was on the phone with a lawyer explaining what was going on. All these people loved Gabe, and this proved it.

A thundering roar pulled up outside of the shop, and I knew that Jack finally convinced Gabe to come home. I sat and waited, camera still in hand, for him to come through the door. He didn't disappoint.

He looked ravaged.

Ω
Gabe

"I need to get in contact with a lawyer." I said to no one in particular.

"We've already got the ball rolling. All we are waiting on now is paperwork, which can't be filed until tomorrow morning. Your lawyer will be filing a custody suit at eight AM. She'll be served with papers shortly after. Blaine, here, called in some favors and the Judge moved the case to the front of the list. As soon as they're served, a trial date will be set.

The lawyer recommends not having any contact with the Moran's until you have him present. He doesn't want to leave anything to chance." Elliott explained to me.

I was dumbstruck. All this had been done in the two hours since leaving the barbeque joint. A little bit of hope took life in my chest.

Finally making eye contact with Ember, I noticed the camera she had clutched in her fingers.

"What's going on?" I asked her.

She didn't answer, but instead showed me.

Picture after picture was of a beautiful black haired, olive skinned girl. The girl was wearing a yellow top with flowered shorts. The shoes she was wearing were bright yellow. Her hair was in pig tales, ringlets flying in the wind. One picture was of Sidney, herself, taking the little girl out of the car seat. Another was of the little girl bent over picking a flower. Another of her smelling the flower. The final one was of a mean faced Sidney dragging her by the arm. The last one set my gut back to churning.

"Jesus Christ. What've I done?" I asked roughly.

"Gabriel, you didn't do anything. You did what anyone would have done when presented with that situation. Why would you think she would lie about something like that? That's just not something a good person lies about. Take this in, and then let it go, because you're about to be in the fight of your life." Ember said softly.

She always knew just what to say to get my mind in the right place. She knew if I needed a laugh, if I needed some love, and when I needed it to be real. She just knew me, and I was never more grateful for her presence than now.

"Alright, tell me what I can do. I just can't sit here. This is driving me fucking nuts."

"Actually I finished my part of the bike. It's all yours. You have a week to get it painted." Jack said to me.

Nodding my head, I contemplated what to do. My head wasn't in the right place to do anything that had to do with Sidney, I didn't want anything to go wrong; painting the bike was probably the best option I had right now. I also knew that the intricacies of painting the bike in memorial of Dougie would put everything in perspective for me. This was when I thought my best, made my best decisions.

I left the room without another word and went to work.

I buffed, primed, taped, and painted for hours. I didn't stop until my vision started to get blurry from lack of sleep. The clock on the wall told me it was a quarter after three in the morning, and that I'd been doing this for way too long. I was surprised that Ember let me be on my own for this long; but since she knew me so well, she probably knew that I needed to think. Being the woman that she was, she knew that if she interrupted me, then I wouldn't be able to think like I needed to.

I'd worked it all out in my mind; how I wanted tomorrow's meeting with Sidney to go. I knew what I was going to say to her, I knew what I was going to offer her, and I knew I was about to be in one hell of a fight. That woman didn't have one reasonable bone in her body when I was with her, and I was sure she hadn't changed much in the year and a half since I'd last seen her.

Putting all my tools and equipment away, I quietly made my

way around the shop and to my front door. No noise came from inside; I knew Ember was sleeping already.

I unlocked the door as quietly as I could and was bombarded with the smell of baked goods. Following the scent into the kitchen, I found a pan of brownies and a note that read:

Everything always looks brighter when you have something sweet to eat. I love you.
Em.

Damn. I love that woman.

Tomorrow I was going to stop by a ring store and find a ring that was perfect for her finger, and I was going to put it there for the rest of her life. If anything else, today proved how much she meant to me. How well she supported me. How much she loved me.

I ate three brownies with a large glass of milk, and then went to the bedroom and took a shower. I dried off, and then climbed, naked, onto the bed behind Ember. I needed her.

I made love to her slowly, and when we were finished, I held her close throughout the rest of the night, feeling her heartbeat against the palm of my hand. I was one lucky SOB.

Ω

The next morning

"Do you still have this letter?" Martin, my lawyer asked.

It took me a minute to decide where I'd left it, but decided I never moved it from its original location. "Yeah. It's in my rucksack at the bottom of my closet. I felt damn near homicidal after reading it and I wanted to be able to read it later when I was in a calmer state of mind. I never touched it again though. I just stashed it in a book she'd gotten me and left it there."

"Good. We need to have that letter on file, and then I want you to put it in a safe deposit box for safekeeping. Now, on to the main event; do you want to have full custody, or do you want to have joint?"

"Full." I said without hesitation.

"Alright. With everything that's been discussed today, I will go over it with my junior attorney. We will get these papers filed ASAP. She'll probably be served with them later this afternoon. Most likely, the trial will be held in a month's time. Until then, I can assure you we will work out some sort of visitation schedule so you can meet your child. The DNA test will have to be done later this week, as per court order. You'll have to go provide a sample at your convenience. I'll have my secretary give you the information on where it's located. I highly advise you to go ahead and start making plans as if she will be coming to live with you. The more you show that you want her, the better it will look in the judge's eyes." Martin explained.

We made our way to the door, and shook hands, when I glanced over and spotted Ember in one of the lobby chairs. She came; I didn't even ask her to. She smiled when she saw me, and made her way to me, wrapping her arms around my waist and resting her head against my chest.

"Ember, this is Martin Barnes, Martin, this is my girlfriend Ember Tremaine." I said.
"It's a pleasure to meet you Ms. Tremaine. Gabe here tells me you're the one who made the connection." Martin said.

Ember nodded, but didn't say anything. Pleasantries were

exchanged, before we made our way out of the building.

"How'd you get here?" I asked.

"Drove."

"Alone?"

"Yep."

I stopped her with a hand on her shoulder, turning her to face me.

"Let me get this straight. You drove over here, with a hit on you, by yourself? At least tell me that someone knows you came."

She looked at me guiltily, and I immediately knew that no one was privy to her whereabouts.

"Don't do that again, Ember. I can't lose you. Promise me that you won't go out by yourself until we get this gang situation figured out."

"How long exactly should I have an escort? It's been four fucking months, and I'm tired of this shit. I want to be able to go somewhere by myself. I can't even take a shit without one of you knowing it." She fumed.

"Honey, if you want to take a shit in private, all you have to do is ask, and I'll leave the house."

"This is not a joking matter. I'm sick and tired of it. Figure it out. Do something, but get it done, because I'm *not* going to deal with this much longer."

"You will deal with it as long as it needs to be dealt with.

This has never been put on the back burner. We've been working on it for months now. The police are working a sting operation, and, hopefully, with that in the works, you'll be taken off the hot seat. They might forget about you. The reason we haven't used force yet is because we don't want to bring you to their attention any more than you already are."

"You've got two more months. That's it. I can't do this anymore. Now, let's go get breakfast, and then I want to go watch Sidney get served."

Laughing, I led her to my motorcycle, handed her her helmet, strapped mine on, and we rode to the Ihop.

"I want two sausages, not the breakfast sausage, but the Eckrich sausage type. I want three eggs, hash browns, and three buttermilk pancakes. Oh, and a Dr. Pepper." Ember told the server before she even had a chance to say hello.

"Jesus, are you hungry?" I asked.

"Yeah, I don't know what it is, but I have the weirdest cravings for sausages lately. What are you getting?" She asked me.

"I'll have the breakfast sampler. Sausage and Bacon. Coffee." I said to the server.

"O-okay. C-can I get you an appetizer or anything?" She questioned sweetly, while batting her eyelashes so hard that she looked like she had something in her eye.

"No. That's it." Ember said tersely.

The server turned and sashayed away, but I looked at Ember with raised eyebrows in silent question.

"She was flirting with you. She never even looked at me. The entire time she was here she never even acknowledged me. Now, tell me how it went today."

I recapped what happened during the meeting, and what my expectations were. Also, how he planned to put those plans into effect.

"He really thinks this will only take a month?"

"That's what he said. Now, whether that will actually be the case is a completely different story. Sidney was always a difficult woman to deal with, and I don't expect this to be any different. In fact, I feel like it'll be even more of a fight than she usually gives. I still can't believe that I have a kid out there. How could she have lied to me about this?" I asked her.

"Not a clue, y'all just better make sure I'm never alone with her. I'd seriously kick her ass."

Really, she wouldn't, because she didn't want to jeopardize my ability in getting my child. We both knew that, but she was in need of a vent. I'm surprised she's lasted as long as she has. She had dark circles under her eyes, and I worried that maybe I shouldn't have worked my frustrations out on her for so long the night before.

"You doin' okay?" I asked her.

"Yeah. I guess so. I guess I'm just in shock. I'll be less worried when we have a little more to go on."

My phone buzzed in my pocket, so I reached in and then answered it, noting that it was Sam.

"Ember's gone." Sam said briskly.

"Yeah. Sorry, she's with me."

"Okay." Sam said and then hung up.

"Sam seemed a little upset that you forgot to tell everyone that you were leaving." I said to her.

The inevitable argument was delayed by the arrival of our food and drinks. My food was placed down first, followed by my drink, the ketchup, but I stopped her when she tried to place the napkin in my lap.

"If you don't put my food down and get out of here, I'll make sure you don't work here anymore." Ember said through clenched teeth.

The server didn't look too concerned, but still placed Ember's food and drink down.

"Can I get you anything else, sir?" The server asked.

"No." Ember said tersely.

"Okay, well here are a few extra napkins then. Holler if you need anything." She said while placing a napkin next to my plate.

The napkin wasn't clean, however. It had the server's name and number, which I made sure to crumple up in a ball and toss to the floor, all while Ember watched with her nostrils flaring.

"It wasn't my fault." I said to her while holding my hands up in a placating gesture.

Rolling her eyes, Ember went on to devour her food. Where she hid it all, I didn't know.

"Do you want anything else, ma'am." The server asked on the way past our table while eyeing Ember's empty plate with a look of disgust.

"The check." I said while staring at my own plate, not giving the woman the benefit of making eye contact, but also unable to keep the smile off my face at the hostile look reflected on Ember's none too happy face.

"I'll be back." Ember snapped.

Nodding, I watched her walk to the bathroom. She came out a few minutes later, but made sure to stop by the checkout table and speak with a manager, just like I knew she would. Ember couldn't help but give her opinion on things, which is what I loved about her. She wasn't afraid to speak her mind, and let other people know how she felt. I always knew where I stood with her. She wasn't the type of woman who gave the silent treatment. Nor was she the type who played games.

The server dropped the check off a few seconds later, but didn't stay because the manager called her to the front. Taking that as the cue to get out, I grabbed the check and paid at the register. The server and the manager disappeared through the kitchen door, but that didn't mean we couldn't hear the reaming she was receiving from the manager. She's lucky that was all Ember did. Things could've been worse, like the time I saw her pull a pregnant woman out of a bar by the hair.

We rode in silence to Wildwood Subdivision where Sidney lived. Parking three houses down, we didn't have long to wait when a Lincoln Town Car pulled up, and an older gentleman stepped out. In his hand, he had a file folder with the words 'Confidential' written in bold black letters. My heart started beating wildly, and my palms started sweating. This was really going to happen, and it honestly scared the fuck out of me to know that in a few weeks, I might have custody of my child, and her life would be in my hands.

The older man knocked on the door, and it wasn't but minutes later when the object of my disgust answered the door. I guess, somewhere deep inside, I'd hoped that Sydney wasn't truly that evil; that I hadn't spent years of my life with a woman who would keep something so important from me. That she would lie about something that would have changed my life.

Sidney look confused when she took the papers. Once the papers exchanged hands, the older man started walking to his car. Sydney opened the package, and we both watched as her eyes widened, and a look of fear crossed over her features. Then she started after the old man.

"What in the hell is this?" She shrieked.

"I don't know ma'am. I only deliver the papers. I don't know what's in them." He said before getting in his car and driving off.

Sidney's hand went to her hair as she pushed it out of her eyes. This used to be a sign that she was nervous at being caught lying about something. When I saw this sign, I always knew she was lying, and, seeing it today, I knew that that little girl was mine. What I did wonder is whether she had tried to pass the little girl off as the other man's, or whether the other man knew what she'd done. I was very interested, and I vowed that I wouldn't stop until I knew exactly what she'd done and why.

184

"Let's go." I said.

Ember nodded against my back, and then settled the helmet back over her head and wrapped her hands around my waist.

Something deep in me had caught fire, and I knew things would never be the same. One thing I was certain of; Ember was going to be mine forever.

Ω

I swallowed hard. Saliva was pooling in my mouth. My palms were clammy, but I wouldn't let him see my weakness. This really wasn't going to be that bad, I just needed to suck it up and get it done. He wouldn't have a problem. He would be happy for us. Wouldn't he?

Deciding to grow a pair, I opened the door with a bang and walked inside. I'd asked Max to meet me at The Sport's Page. I needed his acceptance to marry his sister; when he said yes, I would go directly to the jewelry store to buy her ring.

Spotting Max with his back to the room, in a back corner booth, I weaved my way through the tables and sat down across from him. This was not my favorite position to be in, and the bastard damn well knew it. With many years of caution ingrained in me to be prepared and aware of my surroundings, I hated having my back to a door, but since I was about to ask the man across from me if I could marry his sister, I decided to leave it alone.

"Thanks." I said to Max for being considerate enough to order my beer.

"Yeah. Welcome." Max mumbled.

His eyes were on my face. He was studying it, learning all of my secrets.

During our military days, Max was the one who could make anyone talk, and I do mean anyone. He was one scary motherfucker. You did *not* want to be found guilty of something and not confess. He had ways of getting you to talk. Where and how he learned them, I don't know, but he was good at what he did.

I distinctly remember our first mission together. We were all new to the group. The only ones who knew each other were James and Max. Even though we were all part of the army, we still didn't trust each other with our lives. We didn't have a reason to.

Our first mission was to get some intel on a leader that was collecting young soldiers, as young as nine and ten, and introducing them into a local rebel group that branched off of Al Qaeda. It was our sixth day into the mission when everything went FUBAR.

We'd been boxed in on all four sides, and they were just waiting for us to try to get out. That, or call for help. Not that we would've known that if it weren't for Max. Dougie had caught a man sneaking in. At the time, we hadn't known that anything was wrong. We were under a black out, no communication in or out. We'd thought we were in a safe house. We hadn't been.

When Dougie brought that little bastard into the room, everyone was stunned speechless. Yes, we did have a patrol, and that very reason was why Dougie found him, but we were running off of a mission that was supposedly handed down to us by The President himself. We never thought that our position would be leaked. Maybe we were green around the gills, but after that mission, we never relied on anything but each other. We still took missions, but we didn't take them blindly. We did our own recon on top of what was given to us.

Max was the only one who spoke the boy's language, and was the logical choice to interrogate him. What we didn't know was just how brutal an interrogator he was. Not one single thing could've prepared me for the force that was Max. Listening to that interrogation had given me chills; not much scared me those days. I was living on borrowed time, and I went balls to the wall every single time I stepped into my combat boots.

That day changed things for me. Max somehow has a sixth sense about things , and, at that moment, sitting across from him about to ask for his sister's hand in marriage, I was worried that he wouldn't give me permission. Taking a deep breath, I opened my mouth and started in with my speech.

"I know I'm not good enough for her, and I know she deserves the world. I never believed in forever, until I met her. These last few weeks have proved to me that I need her in my life. She's the good in me, and pushes away the demons that never seemed to give me a break. I haven't had a nightmare since she started sleeping over. I used to dream about my dad, I used to dream about Iraq, and Afghanistan. My mom and dad dying. I swear to God, my brain used that time to make me remember since I never allowed myself to do it in waking hours. I need her." I said.

Max just stared, and I started to feel the impulse to squirm in my seat. I haven't felt the urge to do that since my dad caught me trying to sneak some Twinkies out of the kitchen in my pants.

"My mom wanted her to have our grandmother's ring when she was proposed to by the man of her dreams. I can get that for you on the way home. We have a safety deposit box at Kilgore Bank and Trust." He said simply.

A huge weight lifted from my shoulders that I hadn't realized was there.

"Fuck." I said simply letting my head droop in relief.

I hand clasped my shoulder and I looked up and stared into Max's eyes.

"You aren't good enough. Don't disappoint me." He said, upended his beer, and then took off.

I sat in the booth for another hour before making my way back home. Tonight was Ember's turn to cook. I grimaced and prayed that she didn't find another recipe off Pinterest. They may look good on the sight, but that didn't mean she could reproduce the same thing in our kitchen.

Paying the tab that Max conveniently left me, I walked out into the muggy afternoon. The sun was behind some dark ugly clouds, and I double-timed it to my bike. I'd just pulled up in front of the house when the skies opened up. You weren't truly a biker if you didn't ride in the rain. I enjoyed riding in the rain, but today, I had other plans.

Rain poured down, and drenched me to the bone within seconds. Luckily, I had my phone stashed in its Life Proof case; otherwise, it'd have been toast. I pounded up to the porch and stopped once I reached the door. Reaching behind my head, I tugged the collar of my shirt and yanked it over my head. Next, I did my boots and socks. Right when I was about to start on my jeans a piercing whistle sounded next door.

I knew she was there, which was precisely the reason I

started stripping in the first place. Looking up, I spotted Ember and Cheyenne two houses down.

"Don't you dare, Ponch."

Rolling my eyes skyward, I counted down from ten. I hated when Max called me that, and here his little sister was, doing the same thing. I'd beat the bastard, but it might be frowned upon to kick your wife's brother's ass. Turning my back to the women, I noticed Ember was wearing my favorite yoga pants. A niggling of want popped into my head, and once it was there it amplified into full-blown need.

Crooking my finger at her, I waited for her to come to me. She shook her head, so I decided to play dirty. Popping the first button on my jeans, I saw her eyes widen. She started to take a step towards me but then stopped herself when she realized what'd she'd just done. She was calling my bluff. Turning my back to her, I quickly popped the other four buttons and started to lower my jeans just to the curve of my ass. Glancing over my shoulder, I saw Ember charging towards me through the rain.

She hit our porch and promptly leapt onto my back. Her wet, hot, slick skin warmed my back, and I growled at the heat emanating from her. Taking her by the arm, I slung her around to where her front was plastered to my front, and her legs were wrapped around my waist.

Her warm lips traveled up the side of my neck and she hummed. "Now we both have to get nakie."

Leaning her against the side of the house, I placed a soft kiss on her lips. One tiny, soft touch.

"Precisely." I whispered against her mouth, and then kissed her for real.

She moaned and started moving her hips against mine. I pinned her harder against the wall with my body, but then had to make a mad grab to keep my pants from exposing anything to Cheyenne who I knew still stood there watching us. Looking to my left, I confirmed my suspicions when I saw her and Sam leaning against the wall watching us with smiles on their faces.

"You know," Sam yelled. "We do have little kids here now. You might want to take that inside."

"É bebê fazendo tempo." I yelled back at Sam.

Sam burst out laughing and then hooked an arm around Cheyenne's neck, dragging her to the door with him.

"I don't need the weather!" He yelled before slamming the door.

If I wasn't wrong, they were about to be doing the same thing I was about to do. There was just something about a good thunderstorm that brought out the bad in me.

"What does that mean, what you just yelled at him?" She asked me.

"Look it up in the morning." I growled against her neck.

She might flip if I told her what it meant.

"Tell me now." She whispered against my neck.

Thunder boomed overhead, making us both jump at the suddenness of it. My body held Ember's up against the brick of the house. Both of our breathing was heavy. Ember's hair lay plastered to her head. Her white shirt was

190

transparent now. I could see her hard nipples poking through, and immediately knew she wasn't wearing a bra.

"You're not wearing a bra." I growled against her lips.

"No. That suckers gone as soon as I get home," She laughed. "And, besides, it's not like I need one anyway. All it does is stop my nipples from being seen."

"That it does. But seeing your nipples drives me crazy." I informed her, all the while grinding my cock into her mound.

Lightening rented the now dark sky, followed by thunder. I slipped my hand up Ember's waist and then grabbed hold of her waistband and yanked them down her legs, forcing her legs to let go of my waist. I divested her of her panties a second later.

"We can't do this out here, Gabe." Ember said, while licking a path up my neck to the line of my jaw.

That didn't stop her from winding her legs around my waist again though. Reaching between us, I freed my cock from my jeans and positioned myself at her entrance. With one thrust, I was inside of her tight wet heat.

Ember threw her head back and cried out.

"No one can see us. It's too dark out here, and with the rain it makes it nearly impossible to see." I said gruffly.

"What are you an exhibitionist or something?" She asked.

I pulled out of her nearly all the way and then thrust back in to the hilt. My cock head bumped her cervix, and I immediately pulled back out and thrust forward again. I wasn't going to last very long. There was just something so right when I was with her.

Snaking my hands in between our bodies I found her clit with my thumb and started massaging it in slow circles. Ember's hips bucked at the contact. Her fingernails dug into my shoulders so hard I knew I'd have marks in the morning. Her head was still thrown back and the long column of her throat was exposed. I sucked on her neck, then trailed my lips downward until I got to her pebbled nipple. Sucking her shirt and all into my mouth, I gave a strong pull and she shot off like a rocket.

Her walls started constricting around me and that was all it took. I detonated and started shooting deep inside her. A long deep moan escaped from my mouth that was now hovering above her nipple.

Once we were both spent, I gave her an easy kiss on the mouth.

"I'm not an exhibitionist, or, at least, I wasn't until I met you. Now, I can't seem to get enough of you. I don't think it was physically possible for me to take those three steps into the house." I said to her.

Her eyes twinkled and then went round as saucers when thunder boomed overhead.

"Will you tell me now what that meant? What you said to Sam?" She asked.

Laughing, I pulled out of her and dropped her legs to the ground. Making sure she was steady, I let go of her completely and then shucked my jeans completely. My boxers were dry, so I left them on until I could get inside and change. I bent down and scooped up our clothes, and then opened the front door.

"Come on." I said to her.

"You aren't going to tell me, are you?"

"Not yet."

"Soon?"

"Maybe." I said.

When, in actuality, I wouldn't say a word. Ever. That is, until I accomplished it.

Chapter 11

If a woman is upset, hold her and tell her how much you love her. If she starts to growl, retreat and throw chocolate at her.
-Bumper Sticker

Ember

"Where are you, hoe?" I yelled as I entered Cheyenne's house.

"In here." She called back from somewhere in the back bedrooms.

I went to the kitchen first to grab a Dr. Pepper, and then decided to grab the box of iced oatmeal cookies while I was at it. Cheyenne always had the good stuff. She went to the store once a week, compared to me, when I realized I didn't have any more cheese.

Shoving a cookie into my mouth, I walked towards the back of the house, checking first into the girl's room, then the spare room, and finally going to the master. I found her laying on the bed looking quite exhausted.

Plopping down beside her I asked, "What's wrong with you?"

"I have an ultrasound appointment today. Want to go with me?" She asked, avoiding my question.

"Sure. Your mom have the hellions?"

"Yeah, Sam dropped them off on the way to Dallas today. He has to go pick some parts up at Dunnam's."

"They should really start delivering. It's ridiculous that they have to drive three hours."

"They also charge about twenty percent less for an engine than their competitors. Give me one of those cookies." She demanded.

I reached into the box but came back empty handed.

"Um, that's not going to happen. It's empty." I said shaking the empty box at her so she could hear the crumbs rattling inside.

She gave me a look of disgust and then her gaze zeroed in on my left hand that was holding the box up for inspection. Her eyes went wide and then she gasped.

"Hey, I'm sorry. We'll go buy you some more before your appointment. I just need to go put on some tennis shoes." I mollified.

I didn't wear tennis shoes, or any shoes for that matter, when I was at home. That's why the bottom of my feet resembled alligator skin.

"What the fuck is that?" She yelled.

"What the fuck is what? I told you I was sorry! Jesus, I'll buy you more!"

"Not the box, you dumbass. I don't care if you ate my cookies. What the fuck is that rock on your finger?"

Glancing down, my heart nearly stopped. On my finger was

my grandmother's diamond engagement ring. It was a very simple design. White gold band with a large princess cut diamond centered in the middle. I used to try it on when I was younger. I even made my mom promise that she would give it to my future husband. Max and I had a knockdown, testicle kicking, hair pulling, hurt each other until we booth cried fight over it. Neither one of us won, and then mom had died, and I never thought about it again.

Until this moment, with it shining on my finger.

"Oh. My. God. " I whispered as tears rushed to my eyes.

"Wait a minute, you didn't know?"

"No. He never asked me. Not that this surprises me any. It's perfectly Gabe. Just put the damn thing on my finger while I'm sleeping with no explanation, and expect me to just accept it." I said, crying full out now.

"Iiiyyeeeee! This is awesome!" She squealed and then hugged me.

All my breath whooshed out of me with the amount of pressure she was squeezing me with, and I couldn't help but laugh. I didn't care though. This was perfect.

"Let's go find him. Let me borrow some shoes first though. My feet aren't touching that nasty floor in the garage." I said as I pulled a pair of flip-flops from the floor of the closet.

"We've got about fifteen minutes before we need to leave, are you dressed in what you're going to wear?" She called from the bathroom.

I looked down at myself. It was my usual of yoga pants and t-shirt. Works for me.

"Yep. Let's go."

We were out the door shortly after, and then entered through the open bay door of the garage. I let my eyes adjust and saw Max, James, and Jack, but no Gabe.

"Where the hell is he?" I called to them.

Max smiled his knowing smile, and I was about to go in search of him when he walked through the door that connected the office to the garage. He had a donut in his hand, and a bottle of water in the other. Today, he was wearing some seriously dirty jeans that looked like they would forever be stained with grease and dirt. The shirt looked clean, however. It was taut across his abs and biceps. His dog tags were resting on his chest, and they stood out starkly against the red of his shirt. I took this in for all of fifteen seconds before my feet propelled me forward and I was running full throttle towards him.

A smile lit up his face as he shoved the donut in his mouth to hold it, and caught me in midair, his free hand wrapping around my ass to hold me to him as I leapt up to him. My arms wrapped around his neck, my legs around his waist, and I leaned in and took a bite of his donut. Chewing thoroughly, I watched as his eyes sparkled with humor. He didn't have anywhere to go with his hands full of an opened water and me.

He walked forward and placed the bottle on the nearest toolbox, and then grabbed the donut out of his mouth.

"So, is that a yes?"

"Depends."

"On what?"

"Can I have that donut?"

He threw his head back, laughed, and graciously handed me the donut. Taking it from him I took a big bite, chewed, swallowed, and then gave him a peck on the lips.

"Best trade ever." Gabe laughed out.

A cheer went up through the garage and we both turned to see everyone watching us. I let my legs go from around Gabe's hips, and then ran full out for Max who was leaning against the car lift. He caught me with a grunt, and I wrapped my arms around his neck and kissed his cheek.

He smiled sadly at me and said, "She would want you to have that. I love you, you little booger."

I laughed at the use of my old nickname. Using that name used to put Max in a world of hurt, but today it just made everything perfect.
"I love you too, Maximillian." I said, as I squeezed his neck as hard as I could.

He made a gurgling laugh sound before forcefully removing my arms from his neck. Letting him go, I walked back to Gabe and gave him a quick kiss on the neck, took my last bite of donut, and waved goodbye to him.

"Where are you going?" He yelled when he saw Cheyenne pull her car keys out of her pocket.

"I've got a doctor's appointment. Ember has graciously agreed to go with me." Cheyenne informed him.

"Aren't you forgetting that you have a gang after you, Ember?" Gabe called to me.

Oh yeah, that.

I turned around and waited for the instructions that I knew were about to come.

"I'll take them. I have to go pick Janie up early for a Doctor's appointment in the same building anyway. Let's go." James said to us both.

Nodding in approval, Gabe returned to the office and I watched his backside go until it disappeared from my line of sight.

Yum.

"Hurry the fuck up! I'm going to be late!" Cheyenne yelled from the front passenger seat of James' truck.

Rolling my eyes, I used the driver's side and crawled up into the truck.

"Won't you catch fire if you're in a Ford, Cheyenne? Isn't it against your religion or something?" I asked sarcastically.

"Screw you and your cat, too."

"Thems fightin' words." James' muttered under his breath.

"I hope she finds twins." I sneered at Cheyenne. "And don't talk about my cat; he's worth two of your ugly dog any day."

"Yeah? Well I bet Gabe got you pregnant last night. He told Sam it was baby making weather. And then y'all did it on the porch."

"What?" I shouted.

She smiled evilly at me and then laughed when she saw the expression on my face.

"You heard me. That's what he yelled at us right before you showed your whore tendencies on the front porch."

My mind was reeling, not because of the fact that she knew I'd had sex on the front porch, but because of what Gabe had said.

"How do you know that's what he said?" I asked.

"I asked Sam. He said Gabe used to say that all the time. Something his dad used to say to his mom when it stormed." Cheyenne said with a brilliant smile on her face.

I glared at her and then turned to James.

"Is that true?" I asked him.

"Is what true?"

"Did he used to say it was baby making weather?"

"Yeah."

"How do you say it?"

"É bebê fazendo tempo," He said butchering it compared to Gabe. "Or something to that effect."

That sounded about right, and that's when I started to get worried.

"I swear to God, if I'm pregnant I'm gonna neuter him when I find out."

Not that I was really that worried. I had an IUD. It wasn't as if we were doing anything unprotected. That wasn't the point though; the point was that he should have discussed this with me.

"He won't need his boys anymore if he's got you pregnant, dumbass. The deed will already be done." Cheyenne said helpfully.

I brooded in the backseat the entire way. James walked us up to the doctor's office, waited for us to get inside, and then left us there to go get Janie for her appointment. We waited for a good hour before the nurse called Cheyenne's name. What the fuck took so long, I don't know, but we both headed back, following the nurse. She was a cute little thing, beanpole thin, and her scrubs swallowing her even though they were probably already the smallest size they made.
"If you'll just step up here, Cheyenne, we'll get your weight, and then send you to the ultrasound room." The nurse said with a smile in her voice.

Cheyenne grumbled but stepped up on to the scare.

"Holy Shit!" I said playfully when the nurse said her weight.

"Go fuck a duck." Cheyenne growled under her breath.

I laughed aloud and weighed myself as the nurse took Cheyenne's blood pressure. I'd lost seven pounds in the four months I'd been seeing Gabe, and I was ecstatic. When I had my knee surgery, I'd struggled to lose the weight I'd gained; I've been fighting a losing battle ever since. I thought the weight was there to stay, but something was helping me now because I haven't been at one forty five since high school.

"I've lost seven pounds!" I cheered.

Cheyenne gave me a nasty look and the nurse laughed as she led us to the ultrasound room.

"She'll be right in." The nurse said as she left the room.

"You're such a bitch. How could you rub something like this in my face?"

"Cheyenne, you're pregnant. Take a chill pill." I said.

To pass the time I started braiding Cheyenne's hair. We did this from time to time. Acted like little girls, when, in reality, we were twenty-six. The ultrasound tech came in a few minutes later.

"Hello Cheyenne, is this your partner?" She asked.

I could see how she thought we were a couple. I was holding the braid I'd just finished in the palm of my hand while Cheyenne searched in her bag for a hair tie. She handed me one and then replied flippantly.

"Yes, this will be our third love child together."

"That's so wonderful. Did you do in-vitro?" The tech questioned.

"No, we used turkey basters. Worked like a charm." I answered cheerfully.

"That's so lovely! We don't see enough of that here." She admitted.

She laughed as if we'd told a joke, then got her machine

turned on and Cheyenne ready to go. Just as she was setting the wand on her stomach, her pager went off. She took it off her waistband, glanced at it, and let out a squeak.

"I'll be right back." She said hastily as she hustled out of the room.

We both watched her exit the room in a rush. Then we looked at the door, Cheyenne's goo slicked stomach, and then back to the door.

"I bet I could do that." I informed her.

"Sure you could." She agreed.

Taking the wand, I ran it over Cheyenne's stomach about belly button height. On the computer screen, a black blur and it looked like a bunch of nothin to me.

"Lower." Cheyenne said to me.

"If I get any lower I'll be shoving it up your hoo hoo." I said to her.

"Ya know, they do make those. I had one with the twins. I was too late in the pregnancy for one this time. It won't pick up your baby yet, since you just made it last night." She teased.

I playfully lifted up my shirt and ran the wand over the lower part of my stomach just above my pubic bone. What I saw nearly made me faint. However, I did drop the wand. It swung in an arc and slammed up against the side of the ultrasound machine. Cheyenne leaned up and placed it back where the tech had left it. We both sat there silently going over the momentous discovery we'd just uncovered.

Minutes passed before the tech came back in the room, she went over Cheyenne's belly and the baby came into view.

"The baby's moving right along for 22 weeks. Would you like to know the sex?" She asked.

"Yes." Cheyenne whispered.

"It's a girl; see those three lines? That's the labia. Looks like a little hamburger. Congratulations." She said excitedly.

"Yes, congratulations, snookums." I said to Cheyenne trying to move around the elephant in the room.

Once done, she guided us to the room where Cheyenne was to be examined, and left us there alone.
"So ..." Cheyenne started.

"I have an IUD. How could this have happened?" I cried.

"Honey, just the other day you told me babies were miracles, and that I should feel blessed to have one on the way." She said sarcastically.

"I meant it was good for you, not for me!" I whisper-yelled.

"Well that's a little hypocritical, don't you think?"

"Screw you."

"What's the big deal here? I mean, you're engaged. You've graduated college, have a good job, and you're in love with the father. What's the problem?"

"I don't want to poop on the table when I'm giving birth." I explained.

"That's it?"

"Well, no, not all of it. I guess I'm just scared. When you put it the way you just did, I should really have nothing to worry about here. How do I tell him this? That me and you were fucking around with the ultrasound machine and I just happened to fall on it and saw that I had a baby in here?" I asked gesturing to my stomach.

My mind was whirling with all the possibilities. I knew he wouldn't be upset, but with Gabe, just finding out he was a father to a baby he's never met, and us getting married, a gang putting a bounty on my head, and the fact that I was pregnant, was some serious shit going on all at once. Then another thought hit me, and it was awful.

"Cheyenne, I have an IUD. I've had one for three years. Aren't those dangerous things to have when you're pregnant?"

A look of fear flashed through her eyes before she squelched it and answered, "Let's ask the doctor when he comes in."

Someone knocked on the door two raps, and entered a few minutes later. It was Cheyenne's doctor, and a man I knew.

"Dr. Robinson!" I called out before giving him a big hug.

"You two know each other?" Cheyenne asked.

"Yep. His wife had a climbing accident when I was in school. She was my first solo patient during clinicals. He'd said he was a doctor, but I never knew what kind. How is your wife?" I asked.
"She's doing well. She doesn't climb anymore, and that chaps her ass, but she's still very active outdoors. How're

you doing today, Mrs. Mackenzie?" Dr. Robertson asked.

"I'm doing okay. No morning sickness this time." She answered.

"That's good. The heartbeat was strong, and from what I saw on the ultrasound, the baby looked great. Measuring in right at 22 weeks. You're looking good. This is the time when you get your second wind … blah blah blah blah."

He lost me after that. My mind had slipped back into freak out mode. Part of it was excitement, but the other part was fear. I didn't know how to handle a baby. I wasn't married. I had an IUD somewhere in me that could possibly kill the baby, and I had to tell Gabe.

Worst of all, I wanted my mother, and that was the one thing I couldn't have.

Ω

"Thanks for coming, James." I said to him as we walked into the training room.

He parked himself to the side of the door and took in the chaos. The room was a flippin' mess. A table was over turned; gauze strewn all over the floor and a bucket of ice sat leaking all over the floor at the center of the room. I don't think I've ever seen this many people in the training room at once. The rest of the tables were occupied, as well as two of the chairs that lined the back wall.

"What the hell is going on, June?" I asked.

"That would be our lovely football coach. He got upset when they called practice on him. One of the players came up here to talk to you, but the only one here was Adrian and I. I called the athletic director while Adrian went to speak with the coach. The coach then came here looking for the player, but I'd already sent him home before he got here. Adrian went to the ER with a broken nose thanks to the lovely coach, and here I am by myself with a shitload to do, hints why I called you."

"Alright, let's get started."

We worked in companionable silence for the next hour wrapping sprains, splinting arms, and giving one boy an ice bath. James watched from his perch. His eyes never stopped scanning the area. He looked like he was lazily leaning against a wall, but I knew he could be lethal instantaneously if need be.

"Alright, anyone need some ice?" I asked.

Five hands went up, and I went to the far wall and filled up five ice bags. Just as I slammed the ice door down a commotion started up in the hall. I sighed, thinking, at first, it was just another fight that had broken out, but then there was the sound of gunfire and my blood ran cold. My eyes sought out James, but he was already gone, closing the door silently behind him.

My heart was pounding, but a sudden rush of calm washed over me and I knew what I had to do. I heard another two bursts and cringed at the thought of James being out there by himself. I knew if I'd had gone out there that I would have just been a distraction.

"Everyone, I need you to get into the storage closet. I'll be right behind you."

How we fit five injured people, June and I into that 6X6 storage closet, I don't know. There was tons of junk piled into the corners, but I left it there because I didn't want anybody to see the stuff lying outside and know that we had people in the closet. Once situated, I locked the door from the outside and closed myself in with the rest of the group.

Pulling out my phone, I dialed 911.

"911, what's your emergency." A brisk woman answered.

"I'm at Kilgore College. I'm an athletic trainer, and in the training room. There have been shots fired, but I have no clue how many are out there nor what's going on. Five students, my assistant and I are locked in the supply closet in the training room." I informed her.

"Okay, stay where you are."

Duh. I wasn't a dumbass.

"My friend is in the gym. He just got out of the army, so he knows what he's doing. I don't know what he's doing either, I just know that he was in here when the shooting started and isn't now. His name is James Allen."

"Okay ma'am. Stay on the line." I agreed but didn't mean it.

Ignoring her while hanging up, I quickly dialed Gabe's number and listened to it ring three times before he answered.

"Hey, baby."

"Gabe, someone's shooting in the gym." I said without preamble.

"Get into that supply closet-" He demanded before I interrupted him.
"I'm already there. I have six other people with me. James

went out the door and I haven't seen him since. I've heard a total of four shots so far. It's been seven minutes."

"Okay. I'll be there as soon as I can. Stay where you are. Turn your phones on silent. Don't come out no matter what; I'll let you know when it's safe."

"Okay. I love you." I whispered.

"Love you too, baby." He replied gruffly.

I had a bad feeling about this. Super bad. Nothing good was going to come out of this, I just knew it.

Ω
Gabe

"Listen to me!" I roared at the dumbasses who were about to go into the gym without having the first clue on how to handle it. "I've been in that gym hundreds of times. There're over ten hallways. It's a fucking maze. You won't be able to just bust in there like bulls in a china shop. You need more of a plan than what you have. I have a man inside; I also have my fiancé inside. This is not going to happen." I fumed.

"I don't really care who or what you are. You have no authority here. None. Now go back behind the yellow tape before I arrest you." The cocky little cop said.

I wanted to smash his head in with my foot. He was the first on scene, and if I hadn't gotten here as quick as I had, the little fucker was going to go in with his little band of commando cops and get everyone in that gym killed. He had no experience. He was twenty-two at most. His attitude sucked, and he wasn't listening to me. It wasn't often that I lost my temper, but right then I would have gladly put my fist through his face if it would get me to where I needed to go.

"Listen to me. You have no clue what you are doing. I've done this hundreds of time. Longview SWAT is still forty minutes away, and unless you can pull a trained SWAT team out of your ass in the next five minutes we will not be going in." I seethed.

It had been twenty excruciating minutes since Ember called me. Twenty minutes of no communication. I know I told her not to talk, but it was still no less concerning. Sam was nearly here from his Dallas parts trip, he'd just taken the exit for Kilgore off the interstate when I'd last spoken to him. It was as if he had a sixth sense because he didn't stay in Dallas like he'd originally planned. He came straight home, not even taking his usual stop off half way home.

The other members of our team were scattered around the campus looking for possible entry and exit points. They'd each arrived here on the heels of me; going in different directions disappearing as if they'd never even been there.

"Gabe." Sam's commanding voice said from behind me.

Instantly I calmed. I wasn't alone anymore. Having the man that saved my life on a daily basis at my back, now, cooled my temper down to a slow boil instead of that erupting volcano feeling I'd previously been sporting. I turned my back on the little prick and turned my attention to Sam.

"For the love of all that's holy, please tell me you have good news." I asked Sam.

"Yep. Luke here is taking over." He said gesturing to his left.

Luke was in black cargo pants, a black shirt, black boots, and a black gun vest. He was carrying a tactical shotgun in

210

his right hand, and in his left, a microphone dangled. He gave me a steely nod and then turned his attention to Officer Prick.

"Listen up, Gibbs. These men have taken shits longer than you've been a police officer. I'll tolerate none of the bullshit I just heard you spitting. Go work the police tape. I don't want anyone past it. Move." He barked.

Hiding a smirk, I regarded Luke and Sam.

"I told her to hold off cell communication until it was absolutely necessary, or if she thought her life was in danger. Here's a map of the hallways. I have eyes on the inside; I just have to get Jack to pull the feed up on his phone. The only place I don't have them is the restrooms." I informed them both.

Sensing his need, or maybe just overhearing, Jack materialized at my right side. He handed over his cell phone that had the video feed on it and nodded briskly at Sam and Luke. There was no movement in any of the rooms. Not one single person was milling around, which meant that they'd moved them into either the girl's or the boy's locker room, which is what I thought they would do.

The locker rooms had no windows, it was large enough to fit a large group in, and there were two exits if needed. Obviously, the shooters did their homework. James appeared at the end of one hallway in clear view of the camera that he knew was there. He held up three fingers, flashed them down low, showed a fist, and then disappeared in the next instant.

"There're three shooters. Boy's locker room. Multiple hostages." Sam informed Luke.

Luke nodded, not arguing or questioning how Sam knew since we'd all seen the same sign. Luke may not have been able to decipher it, but since he was a smart fellow, he knew that we could. We spent the next fifteen minutes discussing how we would go into the building. Luckily, Elliott remembered to bring the earpieces, because now we would be able to hear and communicate what was going on once we entered.

"Alright boys, you know what to do." Sam said.

We spread out to different entrances and entered the building soundlessly. Jack was my partner, and would help me clear each room, as well as watch my back, as we made our way to the boy's locker room.

With our guns in hand, we set out. The first hall we came to was the one that led to the gym. Once in the gym, Jack went low and I went high. With the bleachers stacked against the wall, the gym was one big open area, and it was immediately apparent that it was empty. If the bleachers were out this would have been a different ballgame.

"Lock it." I instructed Jack.

He immediately used the lock on the top of the door, turned the key, and then slid the key into his pocket once he was done. Hugging the wall, we made our way to the other door at the far side of the gym. Once there, we opened the door slowly. Lucky for us, it swung in instead of out.

"You're clear for the next hallway, Gabe." Luke said into our ears.

"Copy." I confirmed softly, barely a whisper of sound.

Easing cautiously into the hall, we locked the gym door

behind us too.

We were locking the doors behind us, because we didn't want to lose the shooters in the maze of rooms in the athletic wing. With the gates closed off that connected the athletic department from the rest of the school, we made it to where the shooters only had one-way out. If the shooters did run, we wanted to make it to where they couldn't escape.

"Alright, boys. Still no movement on any camera. I can see the boy's room crack open every now and then, but nothing besides that." Luke said into my ear.

"Copy." Sam said.

"Copy." I said.

"Copy." Elliott said.

"I've got James coming up to your right, Sam. Try not to shoot him. Looks like he's waiting for you." Luke's voice broke the silence.

"Got him." Sam said.

We continued to make our way down the maze of hallways and finally stopped once we were at the training room door. Planting myself in front of the door, I watched the hallway as Jack entered the room using the key I'd made when all the gang business started. Not that I'd thought I would be using it for this.

"Clear." Jack said.

Easing into the room, I closed and relocked the door and headed for the supply closet. Lowering my weapon, I unlocked the closet door and swung it open while Jack covered my back. I wasn't sure of what I would find, but never in a million years did this possibility cross my mind.

I honestly thought that Ember would be just fine. I thought I'd get in here, and she would jump in my arms when she saw me. Seeing this young girl with the wide brown eyes standing behind Ember with a knife to her throat was the last thing I would've expected.

"She fell for it perfectly. I was told if I came in here acting hurt, that I could be backup in case the others couldn't get to her. Looks like they were smart to have a plan B, huh?" The little girl said.

"Mari. You don't have to do this. Drop the knife; I don't want you to get hurt." Ember's voice quivered in fear.

The little girl looked like she was standing on her tippy toes to see over Ember's shoulder. She looked barely old enough to graduate high school, let alone be in college.

"What about your kids?" Ember asked. "Don't you want them to have a mommy in the morning?"

"Shut up, bitch. I'll be there for them in the morning, but you won't be." The girl snarled.

"You've got about two seconds to get that knife away from her throat or I'm going to put a bullet in your brain. I don't care how old you are, or how many kids you have." I voiced with a deadly calm.

I felt anything but calm though. Here I was, watching, while the woman I loved had a knife up to her throat.

The other kids in the closet huddled in on themselves. Each had their head down with their ankles and hands tied

214

together with tape. How this girl managed to do this by herself and hold Ember hostage was nearly impossible.

I also wasn't stupid.

"Sleeper." I mouthed to Jack.

He must've been under the same frame of mind though, because his eyes were already moving over the rest of the group.

"Let the hostages go. You can keep me. Just don't hurt my June bug." Ember said pleadingly.

June's head snapped up and her eyes furrowed. She looked completely confused. I wasn't though. She was saying bug because of the girl who was sporting a ladybug tattoo on her foot. Jack and I knew each other so well that when I shifted my gun from the one who had the knife on Ember, to the ladybug girl, he never even questioned, just stayed constant with his sights trained on the girl's forehead.

Ladybug tattoo girl's eyes went glacial once she realized we were on to her. The next instant was a complete blur. Knife girl went low with the knife. Ladybug lunged forward, gun in hand, and two things happened at once. Jack's weapon and my weapon discharged simultaneously.

Two barks of our firearms discharging split the still air. One went into the heart of ladybug girl. The other went into the left side of knife girls head. Ember went down with startled cry, and everything returned to real time.

Jack kept his weapon trained on knife girl who was still moving, and I went to Ember and lifted her up into my arms. One glance and I knew she was in pain. Standing her on her feet, I scanned her body and found the knife protruding from her left side just to the right of her kidney.

"Stay still, baby. I know it hurts. It's gotta stay there though, I don't want to risk pulling it out without knowing if it hit anything vital." I said to her.

"Locker room cleared. Looks like the boys cut a fucking hole in the fucking ceiling and went out that way." James said into our earpieces.

"Need a couple of ambulances. Ember has a knife wound to the left side, I think it's just in some fat, but I won't be able to tell until someone can bring me a kit in." I relayed.

"Copy." Luke said.

"I don't have any fat. You're a butthead." Ember declared weakly.

"That was pathetic, my dear." I whispered into her hair.

"Gabe, I have to tell you something. Don't freak out. Okay?"

Conversations that started with 'don't freak out' normally didn't turn out well. For Ember's sake, I would try not to freak out though.

"What, baby."

"I'm premmmmt." She mumbled into my shirt.

"What?" I asked confused.

She lifted her face from my chest before whispering "Pregnant."

Seconds passed before it finally sank in.

Sweet Jesus.

"Did you just say what I think you said?" I clarified.

"Yes."

"How do you know this?"

Before she could answer, the door opened and the boys filed in, along with the rest of the Kilgore PD, two firefighters, four paramedics, and Ember's boss. One set of medics came to Ember, and another went to the girl on the ground. The other girl was most definitely dead. They only glanced at her. No other reason to stop. Her blood was lying in a pool under her body. It was slowly spreading outward, creeping bigger and bigger by the second.

That, and the left side of her head was missing.

"No casualties. I don't know what the fuck the show was for, but I'd kill to find out. I feel like we're missing something here." James said, clearly confused.

"We probably are." I agreed.

"If that one lives." Jack gestured to the girl writhing on the floor under the care of the medics. "She'll know more."

Ember's boss, Mr. Dean, chose that minute to come up to Ember and see how she was feeling.

"Ember, are you all right?"

"Yes. It's only a knife wound. I'm sure it's not that bad. I think it only went in three or four inches." Ember said with sarcasm dripping from every word.

Mr. Dean was oblivious though. He gave Ember another once over and then said what he needed to say.

"I hate to be the one to do this, but you're a liability at this moment in time. Until this is no longer a problem, you'll be on unpaid administrative leave effective immediately. Your job will be held open for six months. Please get this figured out and come back as soon as you can, I really don't want to lose you."

"I understand, Mr. Dean." Ember whispered pain clear in her voice.

Tightening my arms around her, I let the day's events start to seep through, the ones that I've been holding in check since I'd first gotten Ember's call.

I felt tired. Tired of my soon to be wife, and mother of my child, being in danger. Tired of all the drama. Tired of the shittiness in the world as a whole. Just plain tired. I needed a break. Sadly, that wasn't in the cards for me right now. I needed to grow a pair and get my shit together. It was going to stop soon; I would make sure of it.

Ω
Ember

"He hasn't said a word to me, Chey Chey." I cried.

"Honey, just give him a few minutes. Being held at knifepoint by a psycho bitch, while he watched, is a little nerve wracking. I think he's allowed to be a little scared." Cheyenne said comfortingly.

"What the fuck do they do around here, grow them virile?" Payton asked.

218

Payton was a friend of Cheyenne's; they'd met during clinicals nearly three years ago. She was a little ball of spunk. She had a larger than life personality, which made up for her four foot and eleven inch frame. Her brown hair was a riot of jagged edges that hung to just below her shoulders in the longest spots. Every few pieces she had highlighted it with neon pink and jet blue. She was solid muscle despite her midgetness.

Payton and Cheyenne still ended up being in the same graduating class, even though both of them took a year off. Cheyenne's excuse was because of the twins. Payton's was a lot more in depth.

Payton was on a date with her boyfriend when a couple of men attacked them. Said boyfriend took off, leaving the attacker there to do what he wished with Payton. It took her nearly a year to come back from the attack physically. Mentally was a different story.

"Must be something in the air." I drolled.

"Yeah, y'all's legs." Payton quipped.

I burst out laughing. Pain made itself apparent despite the good medication they had me on, and then I sobered when I started thinking about why I currently in a hospital bed in the first place.

Both Payton and Cheyenne were on shift on the OB floor, which was where I was. Once in the ER, a doctor removed the knife that, luckily, only went through the fat of my back, just as Gabe predicted. They transferred me to the OB floor for monitoring since learning I was pregnant.

This's where I met Cheyenne and Payton. Cheyenne was furious that I hadn't called her, but really what did she expect?

"I can't believe I'm pregnant. Again." Cheyenne sighed miserably.

Fortunately, Cheyenne got over it quickly, and then we went about monitoring the baby.

Gabe followed me up here but left soon after without a word. This was the point we were at now. Two hours later and still no Gabe.

"He's going to fucking kill me. I did everything right, Cheyenne!" I wailed.

I really was wailing. My emotions were all over the place, and without Gabe here with me, I felt oddly empty and alone. Cheyenne and Payton were doing their best to be here for me, but they did have work to do and couldn't stay with me every minute.

"Alright, chick. Got a few more rounds to do. See you in a few." Payton said as she flounced out of the room ponytail bobbing behind her.

"You have the weirdest friends." I hiccoughed.

"Yes, I do. Gotta go too. I'll be back in thirty. I'm gonna ask if they'll do an ultrasound on you." Cheyenne said.

She gave me a slobbery kiss on the forehead, patted my ass, turned the lights out, and left the room.

I was plunged into darkness, and then my head started spinning. I'd gone through a lot in the past four months. My mind was whirling. How would I pay for an apartment if I didn't have a job? How would I pay for a baby? Would

Gabe even be there? I knew he loved me, but he had a lot going on too. He already had one kid that he was worrying about, and I'd just added another in the span of a week! The rhythmic 'lubb dubb' of the baby's heartbeat calmed me enough for a fitful doze. I was still crying, and would wake myself up choking on snot and the likes, but still managed somehow.

"Are you in pain, baby?" Gabe whispered into my ear.

I came out of my doze to find myself on my side, my back to the door. Gabe was at my back leaning over my body wiping my tears away with the back of his hand. I could smell him. It was a mixture of Irish Springs soap and a faint hint of burnt motor oil.

Didn't matter how many times he washed his hands or his clothes; he always smelled as if he'd just come from the garage. Which he did.

"No. They gave me some good shit." I said into the darkness, while cringing away from his touch a bit.

I didn't really want him to touch me. It made me want things I wasn't sure he wanted to give at that moment in time. He felt my withdrawal and got up to come to the other side of the bed so he could see my face.

"What is it? Is it the baby?"

"Do you care?"

"What the fuck kind of question is that? Of course, I care. How could you ask me that?" He whispered heatedly.

"You didn't seem too excited when I told you. You freakin' left me here by myself. I'm scared shitless here. You haven't said one single word to me since we left the college."

"Ember, I was pissed. Not about the baby. Not at you. In fact, pissed isn't even the word here. More like irate. How would you feel if your fiancé was held at knifepoint, and, to top it off, she was pregnant?"

"Well I don't lean towards that side of the fence. So, if my fiancé was pregnant it would be a miracle."

"Ember." He growled, exasperated.

"Okay, I'll give you that. But why were you gone so long?"

"I was questioning the girl that Jack shot. She was lucky. Only skimmed her face."

"What'd you get out of her?"

"She was high on the painkillers too. What I got was there was some tension in this branch of the gang. Some of the main people don't agree with what the gang leader is doing to you." He said, while running one long finger along the belts at my stomach.

"That good?"

"Could be, we'll see." He said as he bent his head and kissed my cheek.

The sound of a large thump on the other side of the door had Gabe tensing in wariness. He didn't need to worry though because Cheyenne's clipped, "Motherfucker" soon followed the thump.

I let out a watery laugh when I heard that. Even her being at work couldn't curb her mouth.

Standing and walking to the door, Gabe opened it for Cheyenne.

"Thanks." She said as she pushed the ultrasound machine in.

"What's going on?" Gabe questioned.

"We get to look at the baby!" Cheyenne squealed while jumping up and down clapping her hands.

Gabe watched her as if she was on crack.

"If it's a girl, you have to name her Cheyenne." Cheyenne said.

"Fuck that. You wouldn't name either one of your girls after me! What makes you think we'll name mine after you?"

"Ember's a weirdo name. I didn't want to stick my kid with a weirdo name."

"Ember is not a weirdo name! What the heck is Cheyenne? That's like white-trash redneck."

"Take it back." Cheyenne fumed.

"You first."

"Seriously? Would you two shut the fuck up?" James barked, as he, Sam, Max, Jack, Elliott and Blaine walked into the room.

"Make me." Cheyenne and I said at the same time.

"What are y'all, two?" Max asked.

"Do you still keep those porn magazines in your bathroom?" I asked Max sweetly.

His faced reddened and I burst out laughing.

"You do!" I squealed.

"I do not. I was fifteen! Tell me what fifteen year old boy didn't have a fuckin' porn magazine."

I looked at Gabe who was wearing a sheepish expression. I laughed and then groaned when my side pinched.

"Where did you keep yours?" Blaine asked Elliott.

"Mattress." He answered.

"What about you?" Cheyenne asked Sam.

"My car."

"Wow. Y'all are a bunch of pervs." Cheyenne exclaimed.

"Hello, group. I'm Dr. Robinson. Can everyone but the father and the bed ridden give us a moment, please." Dr. Robinson instructed.

Everyone filed out of the room leaving only Gabe and I alone. Dr. Robinson walked to the side of the ultrasound machine, turned it on, and then around. Gabe made his way back to my side and regarded the doctor.

"You've had an exciting day, haven't you Ember?" Dr. Robinson asked me.

"You could say that." I answered dryly.

"I'm assuming you've not had a chance to tell this young man over here what we discussed earlier, correct?" Dr. Robinson queried.

"Not yet. I wanted to do it face to face, and we haven't had that chance yet."

"Okay, I'll lay it all out again." He nodded and then turned his attention to Gabe. "We discussed the risks of an IUD pregnancy. We have two options here. We can leave the IUD in, or we can remove it. If Ms. Tremaine is at 12 weeks or less, removing the IUD is the better option. Once the IUD is removed it will have the same risks as a normal pregnancy."

Heart in my throat, I glanced at Gabe's face. It was completely blank and I couldn't read anything off his facial expression as to what he was feeling.

Nodding my consent, he got started.

"What we are looking for is gestation first. Then we will look for IUD placement."

The doctor squirted a clear gel on my stomach that was colder than a witch's tit. He rubbed it in with the alien probe and our little alien face lit up the screen. He did some clicking with the mouse and moved the wand again.

"Looks to be about sixteen weeks. Due date should be around February 7th."

A small inhalation from Gabe had me looking his way with raised brows.

"That was my mom's birthday."

"Alright, the IUD doesn't even look like it's there anymore. At least it's not in the correct place. My guess would be that it is somewhere in the uterus, most likely behind the baby since we can't see it. It's also possible that it isn't there at all anymore. When was the last time you felt the strings?"

My face flamed. To feel the strings you had to stick your finger's up your vagina. Who the hell wanted to admit the last time their fingers were up there? The last time I had my finger up my vagina was months ago, before Gabe and I were officially seeing each other. I'd also been getting off to thoughts of Gabe, but now that I think about it, I didn't feel them then either.

"Uhh, well I haven't felt them in a while." I stuttered out.

"I haven't noticed them either. So it's been four months, at least." Gabe said with a shit-eating grin on his face.

Dr. Robinson laughed quietly under his breath.

"We'll monitor you once a week. I still want you to come in tomorrow, and then every other Tuesday until you deliver. We'll probably move you up to twice a week once you get closer. Any other questions?" Dr. Robinson asked.

"No." I answered quietly.

I wasn't sure what to feel. I couldn't get too excited, what if I lost the baby?

Seeming to read my thoughts Gabe asked, "What's the likelihood of this pregnancy going all the way?"

"There's no way to tell. This could be just a perfectly normal pregnancy. If the IUD is still in there, I have hopes that it will

226

just float around on the outside of the amniotic sac. As I said, it's also possible that the IUD fell out and you never noticed it was gone. This is one of those wait and see type things. I have no guarantees right now."

"Is it too early to tell the sex?" I asked him.

"This isn't normally my forte, but I will definitely give it the try. The ultrasound techs have taken over this job for me and it's been many years since I've gotten to do it. Let's see." He said as he moved the wand around. "This is a leg. This is a foot. This, right here, is a penis. Nope, no mistaking that one, he just let it all hang out there."

Everyone chuckled at the lack of modesty of our little guy. Like father like son.

"Here are a few pictures. Careful of that side there. I'll get the nurses to bring your discharge papers. See you in the AM." Dr. Robinson said, as he walked briskly out the door.

"I'm scared." I whispered.

"I know, baby, me too."

"Who wants hotdogs?" Cheyenne said as she burst into the room.

"You interrupted my moment. I was about to get hospital sex." I whined.

"Don't lie. Gabe would never let you do that." Cheyenne argued.

"How do you know? Do you have superpowers now?" I asked her.

"Gabe's a good guy. He would never do it anywhere where it was possible to get caught." Cheyenne said confidently.

At that, I laughed my ass off. Of course he wouldn't.

"Hello, all. Ember, dear, these are your discharge papers. Come in if you experience any bleeding or contractions. Your follow up appointment is tomorrow at 9:30 A.M. Sign here." Nurse Wilma said.

I didn't know if she was actually named Wilma. She did, however, resemble Wilma off The Flintstone's.

Just like that, I was released from the hospital. Gabe helped me downstairs with an arm around my waist. I felt like I'd been run over by a Mack Truck. I ached in places I didn't even know had muscles.

"I want to go to Cancun Dave's." I announced to the group.

Everyone groaned, but we loaded up into Sam's suburban and James's truck and headed over.

Cancun Dave's was one of those restaurants that you either loved or hated. My mother used to describe it as a hole in the wall, mom and pop place. It used to be located right beside its current location, but it burned to the ground from an unexplained kitchen fire. Then they bought the old pawnshop next store and converted it. They'd plowed down the old one and now used it for extra parking.

I was devastated when I'd found out that it burned down. I spent months in a state of depression because I couldn't get my queso fix like I was used to every Thursday. However, it was back now and better than ever. The whole place was done up in Retro 50's diner.

Entering in through the main door, I walked up to the host and said, "Nine please."

The young teenybopper's eyes widened when she got a gander at the sexy man flesh at my back. Then again, who wouldn't? They were all over six feet, scary, muscled, and menacing. None of them looked to be in the mood to go out to eat, but they would for the poor girl that was held hostage and stabbed in the fat.

I was practically bouncing on my feet I was so excited to eat here, but as I rounded the corner, I stopped dead at what I saw in front of me.

"Motherfucker." I said under my breath.

"What?" Cheyenne asked.

"Look." I said.

By this time, the rest of the group had caught up with us, immediately catching on to what I was seeing, it was too late. There, sitting in front of us, one table over from the one we were about to sit at, was Sidney, her husband, and the baby. Sidney looked up, and her eyes widened when they connected with what I expected were Gabe's over my shoulder. I could feel the fury vibrating at my back as he put his arm on my hip and pulled my back to his front.

This hurt, but I dealt with it because I knew he needed something to ground him, or he'd blow.

Getting tired of the staring match, I made my way to the table and sat at the far end. Gabe sat at the head so he had a clear view of the table where his baby sat, eating beans and rice. Both Sidney and her husband were arguing. Something likely heated, if their body language was any indication.

It didn't take long for the baby to notice the tension, and she started to whimper. Big huge tears welled in her eyes and started spilling over her cheeks. Gabe's body went rigid when he saw the baby silently crying. It was as if she knew crying would get her nowhere, so she held it inside, crying silently while her parents ignored her.

Gabe's control snapped, and he was out of his seat, fists clenched in unhappiness. Max was nearly on his heels when I grabbed his hand and refused to let him go. Sidney and her husband noticed, instantaneously, that this was going nowhere fast, so they yanked the baby out of her high chair and headed out the door seconds later, tossing a $100 bill down before they left.

Gabe followed them out, and I gave Max a shove to make him follow just in case Gabe needed a hand. Yes, it was obvious that he was going to go anyway, but what are little sisters for if not to annoy the crap out of you?

"Sam. Sam. Sam. Sam." I said repeatedly until his eyes turned to me. "Go stand at the window and tell us what's going on."

"No. Just leave it. They don't need an audience. He'll tell us or he won't. That's that." Sam scolded.

I looked at him and understood he wasn't going to budge, so I did the next best thing, which was turn to Cheyenne. Cheyenne was twelve steps ahead of me though, because she was already up and walking towards the window. Fortunately, we were the only ones on this side of the restaurant because Cheyenne started yelling out the play by play.

"Gabe is standing there all badass silent like. The husband is yelling at the wife, the wife is strapping the baby into the car. She doesn't look happy at all. Kinda like she swallowed something sour. The baby's still crying, loud now. Gabe just said something that made both of their heads whip around as if he'd slapped them. Must have been something to do with the baby because Sidney slammed the door and is now standing in front of it, so is the husband. Uh oh. Now they're pissed. Hubby is gesturing with his hands. Sidney's face is turning purplish. Uh-oh. Now he's done. Coming back to us now. He has a look on his face that could strip paint off a car. Spit nails with his teeth. Beat someone until he shit his pants. Until they're lying in their own puddle of tinkle. Like he could shove a longhorn up the guy's a-" She narrated.

"Stop. Come sit down, dammit." Sam scolded.

"My name's not dammit, it's Cheyenne."

"Cheyenne, dammit, that's not what I meant and you know it."

"Name's not Cheyenne Dammit either, by the way." I pointed out.

Annoyance registered on his face as he said, "Oh my God. Would you two quit?"

"Quit what?" Gabe asked as he took his seat at the table.

No Max though. He was still outside. That, or taking a piss, because he did that, too.

Cheyenne ignored the question and asked, "Where's Max?"

Gabe knew a diversion when he heard one but let it go and

answered, "Either Sidney drove him to drink, or he needed to take a piss."

"I ordered you the enchiladas." I announced, but what I meant was tell me what happened.

"Is that a girl's way of asking me what happened?" He asked.

I fluttered my eyelashes at him and waited.

Heaving a sigh he said, "Not much happened. I wanted to make sure my girl was all right. They have to submit to a DNA test tomorrow morning. They said as much, or the husband did. He flat out said that he would prove it tomorrow morning. I don't know what the fuck he's thinking though; how a baby with that coloring comes from two blonde haired, blue-eyed people is beyond me. She must've snowed him good."

The rest of the evening was spent at home, with us alone. Gabe must have felt sorry for me because he let me watch Twilight and didn't complain once. Just sat there and occasionally rolled his eyes. One time I think he muttered something about 'sparkling douches' under his breath, but I could've been mistaken. He must have known I needed comforting though, because when I put on the third twilight he didn't mutter a sound. Only took it like the man he was.

It was going great until we were lying in bed. Gabe was on his side, I was on mine. Tonight wasn't a cuddling night. Seems being stabbed didn't allow that to happen easily. He brought up my plans for the next day.

"Well, after the doctor, I thought I would come back here and hang with Cheyenne since she's off. What are you doing tomorrow?" I asked sleepily.

"I'm going to finish the paint on the auction bike tomorrow. I'll go with you to the appointment, and then bring you back. I want you to stay here. Clean the house. Fold the clothes. Watch TV on your ass all day. I want you to stay inside, away from the workers. If you go see Cheyenne, I want you to stay there. It would be better if you had her come here so nobody saw you. We're going to have a crew out here tomorrow. They have to level the ground towards the back of the shop. We're adding on a building for the custom bikes we plan to make in the future. More to the point, it's going to be a security hub. We're going to start monitoring a few places, and we need something more secure to store our Freebirds documents, computer equipment, and security paraphernalia. Things are getting bigger than we'd originally intended, and having higher security will make it safer for all involved."

Vaguely I heard him finish his discussion, but I was stuck on 'fold laundry' and 'clean the house.' It wasn't often that my feministic side came out, but when it did, I could be a right bitch. Whew, boy. Gird your loins. Getting up to my knees in bed, I reached over and turned on the light, and then turned to face Gabe.

"Did you just tell me to clean the house? What am I, your maid?"

Gabe's brows lowered in confusion when my rant started.

"I was just giving you ideas to..."

"No. Just no. You can do your own laundry. You can pick up your coke cans. You can put your own socks into the laundry room. You can wash your own dishes."

He interrupted me by taking my mouth in a heated kiss. He

stopped before it could get too far, because, hey, I was injured.

"Would you shut the fuck up? I wasn't telling you to do anything. I was telling you that you needed to stay inside while the crew's here, that's all. Turn the bitch off."

I might have been a tiny bit of a bitch, but I also didn't need him to tell me I was. Glaring at him, I turned the light off and laid down on my uninjured side again. He gave me a soft kiss on the side of my head and went to his own side; I fumed for a whole 2.3 seconds and then promptly fell asleep.

My last thought, however, was, *'doesn't he know better by now then to tell me not to do something?'*

Chapter 12

*I eat pieces of shit like you for breakfast. You eat pieces of
shit for breakfast?!*
-Happy Gilmore

Ember

"Do my thighs look like they touch in these pants?" I asked
Gabe as he was walking out to the living room to start the
coffee.

He stopped and turned, regarding my cautiously. I was
standing with my back to him in my new Rock Revival jeans.
They were a little tight in the thighs since I'd ordered a size
smaller than I normally wear, especially in the thighs. I'm
sure he was trying to decide if he should answer honestly or
not.

He still had the streak marks from the pillow creased on his
face, and I had to try hard not to laugh. He was wearing
boxer briefs and a pair of socks. He did weird things like
this. He said he didn't like the feel of the sheets on his feet,
so he always wore socks to bed. His dog tags were
dangling between his solid pecs. His hair was an absolute
mess. My man could definitely pull off the sleepy look.

Reaching into my shirt, I pulled out my iPhone and snapped
a quick picture. He didn't say anything though. He must be
thinking hard on what to say.

"Honestly, I could give a fuck if your thighs touch or not.
Mostly, I just care about your thighs when my head's
between them sucking you, or when my thighs are wedged

235

between them and my cock is inside you."

Holy. Shit.

I think I just had a mini orgasm.

"Good answer, baby." I said to him.

He smiled and exited the room, going for the coffee that was his life force in the mornings. I went ahead and finished getting ready, putting on shoes, a shirt, and throwing my hair up in a messy ponytail at the top of my head. That was about all I could expend today. My side was throbbing in tune with my heartbeats, and I really had no desire to put any more effort in than jeans and a t-shirt. It was a deodorant only kind of day.

"How're you feeling?" Gabe asked from directly behind me, making me jump and then cringe.

"Sorry, baby." He said before kissing the side of my head and shuffling to the bathroom.

I followed him in and watched him strip. His backside looked like it was sculpted out of granite. Smooth hard lines ran down his back, ass, and thighs. He bent over to take his underwear off and I had a clear view of his balls hanging between his legs and his half-hard cock.

My mouth watered. Damn the fact that I had such an early appointment time. I was running late as it was, otherwise I would join him in the shower.

I watched as the muscles in his forearm, bicep, and shoulder flexed and relaxed with each forward and back motion as he brushed his teeth. His eyes watched me in the mirror as I watched him. Spitting and rinsing, he turned the shower on and stepped in without checking the temperature.

I shivered, but not because he didn't check the temperature, but because of the water running down his defined chest and abs. He was beautiful.

"If you don't knock it the fuck off, I'm gonna have you on your knees with my cock in your mouth." Gabe ground out.

My eyes went wide, but not in indignation. I actually wanted to do it.

He finished washing the soap out of his hair and off his body, turned off the water, and then stepped out. All the while, his eyes were on me. He was no longer half-hard. No, he was completely hard. His skin stretched over his cock tightly. The veins that ran along his penis stood out starkly. The head was slightly purple in color, and I longed to have him in my mouth.

He stalked towards me and took my mouth in a rough kiss. His large hand curled around the bottom of my jaw, cupping my chin, and held my face in place while he devoured my mouth. He backed me up against the wall, and I took that as my cue and dropped to my knees in front of him.

Reaching up with my hand, I gently cupped his balls. His sharp indrawn breath made me smile right before I took him in my mouth. I went as deep as I could go before withdrawing. I worked him like an ice-cream cone. Traced the veins on his cock with my tongue. He lost the struggle with his hands and one went to the ponytail that gathered my hair, and the other went to the wall behind me.

Guiding his cock back into my mouth, he used his grip on my hair to set the pace that would get him off the quickest. In and out, he thrust, trying to keep it shallow so he didn't gag me. I was having none of that though. Grabbing a hold of his thighs, I pulled him forward, harder, until he hit the back of my throat. I swallowed, and heard him hiss. This was turning me on beyond belief, so I unsnapped the buttons of my jeans and snuck my hands into my panties.

Finding my clit, I started rubbing it in circles. I looked up and caught Gabe watching my progress down below. His eyes were like blue fire as he watched me rub my clit, as well as his cock tunneling into my mouth. His eyes made contact with mine and I lost it.

My orgasm burst forth and I moaned around his cock, which set him off too. Come splashed into my mouth, and I swallowed convulsively. He eased from my mouth with a soft pop, and I licked my lips and smiled at him.

"Fuck that was hot." Gabe panted.

I smiled, and reached my hands out for him to help me up. He obliged, and then buttoned my pants for me.

"I've got to go, I'm super late. Max is taking me, right?" I asked him as I wrapped my arms around his neck.

"Yeah, baby. I'm sorry I'm not going, but we have a small amount of time left to finish this bike and get it registered, or the bike won't make it to auction. Call me when you're leaving, I love you, Em." He said before letting me go.

"Love you, more." I said and then walked quickly out the door.

Max was on his cell phone, but quickly hung up when he saw me. Helping me into the truck, he started it up and then took off towards the doctor's office. We parked in the parking garage and walked at a fast clip to the office, all the while not saying a word. He hooked an arm around me once we reached the elevator doors and kissed me on the forehead.

"We're lucky you made all the lights or we would've been late." I said idly.

"That's 'cause I'm the man."

"I'm sure that's it." I said, dryly, as I opened the doors to the office.

"I wasn't here but a year ago with Cheyenne. These nurses probably think I get around a lot." Max whispered beside me.

"Don't you?" I asked sweetly.

"Well, yeah, but I don't leave any evidence behind."

"Ewww. That's just nasty."

"You know what's nasty? Hearing your sister have sex while you were innocently trying to play a war game. That's nasty."

My face flamed and the receptionist watched us with curiosity after overhearing Max's comment.

Rolling my eyes at her, we went to sit down. Max being the ass he is sat two seats away from me. He liked his elbowroom, and we'd played this game before, many times. There was a TLC program on about giving birth, and I watched Max watch it with revulsion in his eyes.

His horror-filled eyes turned to me and said, "Don't expect me to be in there with you."

"Of course I do. You're my only family. I need you." I stated simply.

I didn't really, but there was no way I was letting him know that. Terrorizing him was my favorite past time. When he was in Iraq, I missed teasing him like crazy. I felt empty without him, and very alone.

When he was hurt, I went to pieces. I cried for three days straight. I couldn't even go see him because they couldn't tell me where they took him. They didn't know if he was all right, they only knew that the Humvee tripped an IED, and that Max sustained injuries. It was truly the worst experience of my life.

Watching him now, you would never know he was ever even hurt. He looked perfect. Although, he'd go into his zones where he'd draw into himself. Those times were hard because he would never tell me what was wrong. We told each other everything, and it was tough when he didn't trust me with those aspects of his life.

"I really do need you, you know." I whispered, so only he could hear.

His eyes went soft, and he moved to the seat beside me. "I owe you an apology. I know you've had it hard since mom and dad died. I wanted to apologize for leaving you, and then for making you feel like shit after I came home."

His words made my heart swell. I hadn't let myself contemplate it, but I needed to hear that he was sorry. Sorry for leaving me alone when I our parents died. Sorry for making me grow up so fast when I needed him so much. He'd left me broken, and I'd never healed.

"That was a shitty thing to do. Why'd you leave me when I needed you so much?"

"I was hurting, too. I didn't even think about you, to be honest. I was in so much pain myself, that I buried myself in my career. Took all that pain out on the enemies. I should've come back, but I couldn't forgive myself after I'd realized what I'd done. Gabe succeeded where I couldn't. It was only after I got hurt in that Humvee that I let myself think about what I was doing. I love you, Emmie. Please forgive me."

Everything he said was true, and who was I to judge for how he coped with losing our parents? Everyone grieves a different way.

Tears pricked my eyes, and I blinked rapidly to dislodge them. "I know, Maxie. I never held it against you. I forgive you. Will you buy me a new car to make up for it?"

He laughed, and the spell of sadness was broken.

Thirty minutes later, I found myself on the scale. I was two pounds lighter since yesterday. Which didn't surprise me since I ran on adrenaline and a prayer for a few hours yesterday afternoon. The nurse showed us to a room, and I sat on the table while Max took the only available chair. He surveyed the room, and quickly turned away from the model that showed a baby passing through a birth canal.

"I can't wait for you to have a kid of your own. You're gonna end up having to deliver the baby all by yourself. You'll have to watch your wife's vag stretch to the size of a melon. It's gonna be awesome. I'll video your reaction."

"That's absolutely disgusting."

The appointment went about as expected. We talked about risks, can-dos and can't-dos. He told me I wasn't allowed to have sex in water. No more than two cokes a day (this was one of the worsts), and limited amounts of mercury. While I listened with half an ear, Max looked like he was taking everything the doctor said to heart, memorizing it, and then storing it in the vault he called a mind. Some of the things were so obvious that I wondered what type of person wouldn't know that you shouldn't chain smoke or drink whiskey. Um, duh?

"Any questions?" Dr. Robinson questioned.

"Nope." I answered.

We were out the door by ten o'clock, which meant I could still make it to McDonald's before they stopped serving breakfast. Score!

"I want an Egg McMuffin." I informed Max.

He nodded but didn't answer, just pulled up into the nearest McDonald's. He ordered me a number one with a sweet tea, and himself a number one with two extra sandwiches. The boy probably could down about two more, but he had a rule that he didn't eat unhealthy if he could help it. I, on the other hand, had a rule that I didn't eat healthy if I could help it.

We'd just pulled up in front of the car when I noticed the Audi. It seemed vaguely familiar, but didn't register who exactly it was until I heard her obnoxious voice. It reminded me of nails on a chalkboard. Just one of those voices that made you want to cringe. She was standing toe to toe with Gabe, while Sam, James, and Elliott looked on. It was apparent she'd been going at it for a while because all of the guys had beers in their hands that were half full.

Did I mention it was ten o'clock?

"You need to withdraw the suit. Cora may be yours by blood, but you're not her father. Never were."

Uh-oh. Them's fighting words.

Gabe's face remained blank, but his words were anything but because they shot out of him like a whip.

"You better pray that your lawyer's good. I guaran-damn-tee you I'll get her. If you're nice, you'll still get to see her. Have a nice day, Mrs. Moran." Gabe said coldly.

Her face paled, and I was glad he'd never spoken to me like that or I would have broken down and cried. Pulling my Egg McMuffin out of the bag, I sat down at Sam's desk, propped my feet up, and started eating my food. I watched, head turning back and forth like a cartoon listening to Gabe and Sidney argue.

"You can't do this!" She screeched.

"I can and will. You cost me a year and a half of her life. I don't even know her fucking birthday. I missed her first steps. Her first tooth. Her first time crawling. I've missed everything thanks to you. How do you even live with yourself?" He seethed.

"You were never even home. How was I supposed to know you'd want her?"

"I bought a fucking cradle for her before I even deployed the last time! How does that say that I'm not interested?" He yelled.

"You're going to ruin everything if you pursue this. He'll

leave me, and I won't have any way to put a roof over your baby's head." She sneered.

"Good, because I have a roof. She won't need you anymore. She's gonna have my wife. You're gonna be nothing to her. Do you hear me? Nothing."

"You can't take her away from me! I'll leave the country before I allow you to have her."

"Try it. I dare you."

Chills slithered like a snake down my spine when I heard Gabe's tone of voice. He was one scary motherfucker when he wanted to be. She took two large steps back, so she was closer to my chair, and I heard what she probably meant for nobody to hear.

"I fucking told him this wouldn't work. You have ways of ruining everything. That stupid prick." Sidney muttered under her breath.

My brows slashed down in question. What they heck did she mean that? Who was this, her husband, or someone else?

"I think it's time for you to leave. We're supposed to have the results from the DNA test in a few hours. My lawyer's drawn up papers to put into motion my visitation rights. I'll be having Cora with me by the weekend."

That was news to me, but it also excited me. I did feel that maybe he needed to spend some alone time with her, and I went through my plans for the weekend in my head. I didn't have anything planned. Maybe Max and I could go and stay at the cabin.

The cabin was my parent's favorite getaway. When they needed some time to unwind, they would all go up to Hainseville, and stay in the cabin. It was primitive. There was no running water, nor working lights unless you had the generator running. There were some 4-wheelers there last time I checked, but I hadn't been on them in well over eight years. The weekend before my parents died.

Deciding that would be a good plan, I typed up a text on my phone asking Max if he would go with me.

Me: *Can we go to the cabin and stay for the weekend?*

Max: *Sure. I just got some lights and indoor plumbing installed.*

Me: *Since when?*

Max: *Why are we talking like this when we are sitting next to each other?*

Me: *Because we're awesome.*

Me: *You aren't talking.*

I saw Max glance at his phone, roll his eyes, and then lay the phone back in his lap.

Me: *Max*

Me: *Maxie Poo.*

Me: *Maximillian Horatio Tremaine.*

Max: *Where did you get Horatio? That's not my middle name.*

Me: *This is getting good. What do you think he's gonna do?*

It was getting good too. So good, I decided to tape it. Good thing I did too, because she used that moment in time to slap the shit out of Gabe. I was so stunned that she'd done it that it took me a few seconds to react. One second I was leaning back in the chair and watching the drama unfold, and the next, I was grabbing the bitch by the hair. I pulled my arm back, and propelled it forward, knocking her square in the eye. She crumpled to the ground on her hands and knees.

Yanking her by the hair, I very nearly dragged her until she got back on her feet and followed me out the door. I let my grip on her hair loosen as I got to her car. Leaning away from her, I watched as she straightened.

"I don't care how upset you are. You do *not* hit him again. EVER. I swear to God, if I see or hear that you did that again you won't eat solid food for a month. Got it?"

She opened her mouth to say something, but then thought better of it. Yanking open her door, she folded inside and slammed it behind her. She did a pretty impressive burn out once she was in the street, and I wondered if I could ever do one of those in my POS car. Probably not.

I turned around, startled to see the men of Free lined up behind me. Every last one of them was wearing a shit-eating grin on their face.

"Excuse me while I finish my hash brown." I said squeezing in between James and Sam.

Sam ruffled my hair as I walked past. Everyone came back in except for Gabe, who I saw walk into the direction of his house. I'd go check on him in a few minutes, but my guess was that he needed a few minutes to calm down.

"I gotta say, Ember, it's completely awesome when you do that hair-dragging thing. Last year with Sam's psycho, and then again with Gabe's; it's just truly a pleasure to witness." Elliott said delightfully.

We shot the breeze for another twenty minutes before I deemed it safe to go in search of my soon to be hubby. Ditching the boys, I walked into the garage and stopped dead when I saw the bike that was going up for auction. It was absolutely stunning. The motorcycle was polished. The wheels gleamed. The paint job was an American flag. It looked like it'd been through one hell of a war with tatters swaying in the wind. A hand reached up from beneath the ground as if seeking the flag to lie with him in his final resting place. Written on the side in a beautiful script the words: For Kayla.

My heart squeezed.

At the one-year mark to Dougie's death, we went to the Arlington cemetery and decorated his headstone with flowers and flags. Kayla drew a picture of her daddy in the sky with a stick figure Kayla blowing kisses at him. She was a very intelligent at the age of four, although, very quiet when you compared her to Janie. We had a memorial service/wake for him at a local pub since that's what he would have wanted.

Everyone was having a good time when the idea to make a bike and auction it off at one of the biggest motorcycle rallies in the South came about. Although, never in my wildest dreams would I have guessed it would look like this! It was magnificent. Fat tears splashed down my eyes when I thought about the reason this bike was made in the first place.

At first, I was skeptical that a bike would be able to portray a person as fine as Dougie, but this bike resembled everything that he believed in and more.

Two strong arms wrapped around my waist, and I sank back against the chest of the man I loved.

"It's beautiful." I told him.

"I think it turned out nice. No one knew what we all planned. Everyone just built off the previous man's work. When I got it, it was already a piece of art. I just polished it up a bit." Gabe whispered against my hair.

We stood like that for a long while. We stopped only when my side started to protest.

"I think I'm gonna go take a nap. I'm exhausted. I'm not going to do any laundry today, by the way." I supplied before blowing him a kiss and walking towards the back door.

His laughter followed me out the door.

Cheyenne intercepted me on the way to Gabe's, and she ended up coming over to keep me company. Nevertheless, what we really did was both fall asleep in Gabe's bed, and sleep the afternoon and evening away.

I woke disoriented. I heard the murmur of men's voices, but was too comfy to move. I had my arms wrapped around Gabe's pillow, and my face buried in it breathing deep before I felt movement at my back. Looking down I noticed a skinny arm wrapped around my stomach, and snoring happening right behind my head.

"This is hilarious." Gabe whispered.

A soft chuckle followed this statement and Sam snorted, "Cheyenne's drooling on Ember's hair."

That wasn't the first time it'd happened, and probably wouldn't be the last. I slept over at Cheyenne's place, at least once a week, since we were sixteen. Only recently had that slowed down. Every single one of those times, I would wake up in this position.

"It's like the snoring wars, Texas edition."

Indignation flooded my body and I raised my finger and flipped both of them the bird. Chuckles escaped them as I untangled myself from Cheyenne's death clutch. Gabe reached down and hefted me to my feet, and I made my way, groggily, into the bathroom. I made quick work and zombie walked into the living room to find them both playing Call of Duty. Rolling my eyes, I walked up beside Gabe and plopped down next to him. I curled into his body, making it hard for him to work the controller.

He didn't shrug me off though. I stayed like this for ten minutes before they set the controllers down and started talking about dinner.

"Pizza." I muttered into Gabe's arm.

Just then, Cheyenne walked into the room and made herself comfortable in Sam's lap.

I must've fallen asleep again but I woke when the front door closed quietly, and the lovely aroma of Italian spices and pizza sauce filled the air.

Sitting up, I rubbed the sleep from my eyes and glanced at the clock. Yikes. It was already eight at night. We'd slept the day away. Cheyenne was knocked out on the couch so I threw a pillow at her and hit her in the face.

Grinning when she threw the pillow back at me blindly I said, "Wake up, homie. Pizza's here."

Walking into the kitchen, I sat at the table and started eating pizza directly from the box. I had no clue where Sam and Gabe were, but it wasn't long before Cheyenne joined me. She grabbed us both a coke and we devoured an entire pizza between the two of us. I let out a large belch that was followed shortly by Cheyenne's slightly shorter one. I beat her by at least three points.

"That was attractive." Sam grunted as he walked in the door.

Her answer was to let another one rip, and I laughed. Gabe followed behind Sam and started laughing when he heard her burp.

"I'm good as long as she doesn't fart. Then I might be a little grossed out."

"What, you haven't farted in front of each other yet?" Cheyenne asked.

Gabe glanced at me and said, "Not intentionally."

"What's 'not intentionally' supposed to mean?" I asked quizzically.

"Nothing." He muttered and opened the pizza box.

I decided to let this slide for now. It struck me as being one of those things you don't want to hear in front of others.

"What happened to all the pizza? Did y'all already put it in the fridge?" Gabe asked.

"What do you mean? We ate it all. Wasn't it ours?" Cheyenne asked.

I concurred by nodding my head.

"No. That was an extra-large! How could y'all eat all that? We only went outside for more beer. Are y'all being serious?" Sam asked.

"What did you want us to do? We thought y'all took the other box outside, or wherever y'all went!" Cheyenne squirmed uncomfortably.

"Oops." I said.

Rolling their eyes, they sat back and drank their beers. They were much better sports than we would have been.

"What time are we leaving this weekend?" I asked them.

The rally in Tulsa started this weekend, and I couldn't wait. We'd never been to a rally before; we were excited to experience something new that our men loved so much.

"Probably Friday morning. It's going to take a while to haul the bike on the trailer. So we're gonna just go early so we're not trying to rush." Gabe explained.

Nodding my head, I made a note to myself to call the hotel to see if they could add one more day on to our stay.

Standing up, I went about making them a sandwich. If I thought about it, I might feel somewhat bad that we ate an entire extra-large that could've fed two full-grown men. Who was I kidding? Why would they think an extra-large would be enough for four people? Then again, it's not their fault Cheyenne and I could eat like men. Cheyenne got up and helped, seeing as I didn't know what Sam liked.

I wasn't sure what Gabe liked either, but I took a wild guess that he would eat anything. Therefore, I made him two huge sandwiches with turkey, ham, two kinds of cheeses, lettuce, tomatoes, pickles, mustard, and finally mayo. My mouth watered as I looked at the finish product, how I could still eat was beyond me, but I've always been like this. I can eat a full meal, and two hours later eat another. My family called me a bottomless pit, and I had a feeling this pregnancy wasn't going to be good for my figure.

I did pretty well on the sandwich. The only thing he took off was the tomatoes. Good to know. Just as the last bite cleared his mouth, his phone rang. Chewing quickly, he reached into his pocket and dug it out. His expression tensed as he saw who was calling, and we all held our breath as we waited for the news.

"Hello?" Gabe answered, licking the tips of his fingers free of mayonnaise.

He listened for a few minutes as expressions came and went on his face. Nervousness, indecision, anticipation, hope, and finally savage joy. A bright smile lit his face as he heard what I was assuming the lawyer, told him.

"That sounds wonderful. When do I get to pick her up?" He asked.

Nodding his head he said, "Okay. Neutral is probably better. How long do I get to keep her?"

"Okay, thanks for everything. I'll see you tomorrow

morning."

We all watched him as he processed the information he was given.

Making eye contact with me he said, "She's mine. Not that we had any doubt. We have to go pick her up Friday evening at her daycare parking lot. They feel it's best that we meet somewhere neutral for the first time. I'll get her until Monday morning, and then I'll take her to her daycare."

A smile broke out on my face when I jumped up and clapped my hands. "That's fucking great! Cheyenne, we need to go shopping. Like now. That's two days away. WAIT! We're going to a bike rally on Friday! Can we take a baby to a bike rally?"

We all sat silently thinking when Cheyenne said, "Well, we're taking the twins. They're the same age, so what's the problem here?"

That was true. We were planning to ride there, but that would be out of the question when there was a baby involved.

"Cheyenne and I can ride in the car with the kids."

"Y'all don't know how to drive a trailer. James was going to drive it with the kids. One more kid won't make a difference. I bet he'll enjoy the shit out of this trip." Gabe grinned evilly.

I ran into the bedroom, grabbed my tennis shoes, and then came back out.
"Alright, let's get going. We have two hours until Target closes."

Sam decided it was in his best interest to stay here.

Something about being allergic to Target. On impulse, I grabbed my coupon binder before I headed out the door. I wasn't sure I would need it, but I brought it anyway. Who could go to target just for what you came for?

I think Gabe was secretly excited. He didn't out-right say it, but you could tell he was eager to buy something for her. He didn't let out one argument about not wanting to go shopping. He was silent on the trip there, and only said something when asked a question. When we actually got to the baby section, it was a different story. He started piling crap in by the bucket load.

"Gabe! Why are you getting newborn? We don't even know what size she is. Let's focus on the main essentials like a bed, car seat, and some accessories."

He gave me an "are you kidding me" look and continued to toss anything he liked in the buggy. I didn't interrupt him. He looked like he was on a mission. Not that he ever lost sight of me or let me get more than four feet away from him. While he was busy buying junk, I was getting baby wash, towels, diapers, blankets, wipes, and on and on. By the time we were finished and I pried the shopinator away from the baby section, we had two buggies full of baby stuff. As well as tickets to get a crib and changing table, dressers, and a jungle gym.

We got up to the checkout and I started pulling out the coupons, my Cartwheel app, and bringing up my mobile coupons. There was a line behind us, and they were all gawking at the price and the mass amount of shit we got. Cheyenne walked off, because she hated being with me when I started arguing with the cashiers.

The total rang up to nearly three thousand, and then I handed her the coupons. One and two dollar coupons don't seem like they would add up, but they most certainly do. Especially when you combine them with store coupons. The total went down nearly two hundred bucks. Then I went to the mobile coupons, which brought it down another thirty dollars. By this time, we had a crowd watching to see how much I could bring it down.

Gabe stood by fascinated. Once all the manufacturer and store coupons and Cartwheel coupons were subtracted, the total was brought down by nearly five hundred dollars. Now, tell me again, why does everyone bitch and complain when I just saved five hundred bucks just by being a couponer?

There were a shit load of people behind us watching; they even clapped as we left. It was wonderful to have someone be aware of my awesomeness.

"That was pretty fuckin' awesome. Do you do that all the time?" Gabe asked as we made our way out to his truck.

Cheyenne was knocked back in the front seat reading on her phone. We started putting the junk into the truck, and I'd just loaded the last box of diapers when a Blue older model Chevy turned slowly into the parking lot. The bass on the truck was thumping so hard the entire car was shaking. It sounded awful, and I would've loved to make a comment to them but I was sure Gabe wouldn't like that too much.

It was when I was getting into the truck that Gabe's body covered my own. He'd stepped in front of me and backed me up hard against the truck. The car passed us though without incident. My heart was pounding so hard I thought it was going to pop out of my chest. Gabe herded me to the backseat and got me in without any further ado. He took off out of the parking lot and we were on the highway in no time.

Gabe clenched the steering wheel with one fist. His knuckles were white; the veins pulsed on his arm and neck. He was severely pissed, but I didn't really understand why. Nothing happened, and it seemed like a coincidence that they were even in the same parking lot as us.

"Gabe, what's the big deal?" I asked.

He ignored me, so I tried again.

"They didn't even see me. Nothing happened."

Still no answer, so I shut up.

We drove home in silence. Cheyenne must have sensed the tension in the air, because she didn't say a word either. Gabe stopped in front of Cheyenne's door and helped her out, walking her to the front door. I decided to go drop in on Max. I was thinking that Gabe needed a minute, so I'd let him unload all the shit since he decided to ignore me the entire way home.

Walking in Max's front door, I closed it with a bang, not looking back to see if Gabe noticed or not. Max was on the floor, back up against the couch. He had the remote in one hand and a beer in the other. In front of him on the coffee table was a slice of cake. My mouth watered, and I looked at him. He didn't acknowledge me, but he knew who it was. Plopping down next to him, I grabbed the fork and ate half of his cake.

I longed for the other half, but I wasn't going to eat all of his cake. I knew how much he loved his sweets.

"What's wrong, babydoll?" Max asked finally.

"Gabe's mad about seeing a skull in the parking lot of

Target. He ignored me all the way home, so I'm gonna ignore him for a while. I'm letting him unload the truck while I sit here and ignore him."

Giving me a sideways glance he said, "Sounds like a solid plan. Let me know how it works out for you."

It ended up working out better than I anticipated. I sat there for three hours before falling asleep around one in the morning. Max covered me up at some point, and I slept the rest of the night on the couch before waking up somewhere around five in the morning, with a bladder that was about to burst. Once taking care of the awkward morning moments, I walked out into the cool morning air and headed to Gabe's place.

Something must be wrong for him not to come get me. I twisted the front knob and opened the door. I found him sitting on the couch. He was staring at the dark flat screen that hung on the wall. His head turned and watched me cross the floor until I took up a seat across from him. He stared into my eyes for long moments before he spoke.

"This isn't going to work. How do I do this with my little girl? How do I put her into danger? There's no way to protect her with all this shit swirling around her. Something's got to give." He said quietly.

My stomach sank as his meaning filtered through my brain. He wanted me to leave.

"I understand. You do what you have to do." My voice quivered.

He stood and stared down at me for a few long moments.

Walking towards the door he said, "I will. I'm going for a ride to clear my head. I'll see you when I get back."

He didn't even give me a kiss.

The roar of his bike broke the silence of the morning. He rode out of the back lot, and then around to the front. I could track him in my mind. In my mind's eye, I saw him turn into the parking lot of the garage. Stop at the front gate and put the code in. Then he roared off down the street, taking my heart with him.

I knew what I had to do.

Going to his bedroom, I packed all my things and loaded them into the car. If I weren't here anymore, he wouldn't have to worry about his baby. If I weren't here, she wouldn't be in danger. Gone would be the danger swirling around her.

I decided the best thing to do was to go to the cabin. Once I got there, I would figure out my next move. I knew I had to get out of Kilgore though. This wasn't going to work anymore, and I would have to pick somewhere that the Blue Skulls didn't have any affiliation with, maybe somewhere up North.

Once all my stuff was loaded, I gave a last glance around the living room. I took the ring off my finger, laid it down on the coffee table, and wrote a quick note.

After the note was written, I tucked the ring on top of it, and stared for a few seconds. A lone tear rolled out of my eyes and dropped to the paper, splashing onto it and making a small watermark. That was my cue to go before I was crying too hard to see.

I got into my car, started her up, and took off out of the

driveway. Luckily, Free had an automatic gate for those who had the tag reader in the window. If not, I might have ran the thing down in my haste to leave. I drove for nearly an hour before I pulled up into the old driveway. The last time I'd seen it, the road was nearly washed out where the creek ran under. Max must have had it fixed recently because a brand new road was poured, and a shiny huge pipe ran under the road to allow the creek to flow through it without causing any damage.

I drove up and passed the pond, wondering if there were any fish after all these years. Most likely there wasn't. Years ago, we used the pond as a shooting range. Daddy would toss bottles and cans and we would practice shooting, or just shoot for fun. Mom would sit back and take pictures while I shot to my heart's desire. That had to be the thing I missed the most about them.

I spent more time with my dad. It wasn't that I didn't get along with my mom; it was because my father did the things that I loved doing. Hunting, fishing, riding 4-wheelers, and shooting guns were my hobbies back then. When he died, all of that was a distant memory, along with my parents.

Seeing this cabin brought back bittersweet memories. As I made it up the steps, a smile crossed my face as I remembered the time my uncle fell through the railing when he was drunk. Then I passed the window that my dad's best friend shot a hole in while he was cleaning his gun. Using the key on my keychain, I breathed a sigh of relief when it opened the door. It never occurred to me, until right then, that Max might have changed the locks.

The cabin still had the smell of the old wood burning stove that took up the majority of the living room. The kitchen and living room had an open floor plan with vaulted ceilings. Two bedrooms sat across from each other, and a bathroom in the middle of the two. A small, quaint retreat held many loving memories. Today was a good day to remember those loving times, because, if I didn't have those to think about, I would be remembering the smell of Gabe's skin, or the deep timber of his voice.

The longing for Gabe was too powerful to ignore, unfortunately, because it wasn't two seconds later that I started bawling and didn't stop. Laying down in my parent's old bedroom, I saw that Max hadn't changed a thing since they left. The candle still sat at the bedside. The same comforter adorned their bed. My dad had had an old green plaid one for years before he met my mother, and they brought it out here as soon as they bought the cabin. It'd been washed so many times that it was smooth and soft just like a t-shirt that had been worn a million times.

Burying my face into the comforter, I cried. I cried for my parents, for Gabe, for Gabe's situation, and, finally, for the baby that I was carrying, because I had no clue whether the baby would live or die. This has turned out to be one hell of a week, and I didn't think I could handle anymore. I just wanted to lay here and sleep forever. Sleep didn't come easily; I must have cried for nearly two hours before it finally caught up to me.

Maybe everything would look better after a nap.

Chapter 13

I promise to treat you as good as my leather, and ride you as much as my Harley.
-Sons of Anarchy

Gabe

I knocked on Cheyenne's door looking for Ember. I'd ridden my bike for three hours before I decided I was being an ass and needed to apologize.

I'd seen the way she looked at me when I told her I couldn't do this anymore. I knew she was worried, but something had to give with those assholes. I couldn't keep putting my future wife and children's lives at stake. Luke said all they needed was a little more information on a crime ring that the gang was involved in, and nearly the whole East Texas chapter of the gang would go down. If that didn't work out, then I would turn to the more drastic measures of taking care of the problem myself. My family couldn't live in fear for the rest of their lives.

I'd stopped in the office and had a sit-down with Sam and Max. We agreed that something needed to be done, and we would have a meeting with everyone at the shop later that night. I left them shortly after to go find Ember and apologize for not going to get her last night. I knew she was upset, but after I unloaded all the junk front the truck, I'd sat down and gone over what I could possibly do to fix this situation. I hadn't even realized it was so late until the sun peaked over the horizon and stabbed through a crack in the blinds.

Ember walked in a few moments later, and I seemed to spit out my thoughts before ever thinking about how they would come across. She probably thought I blamed her, but I didn't. This wasn't her fault in the slightest.

She wasn't in the house when I got to the back, so I went in search of her at Cheyenne's place.

Cheyenne opened the door with a child attached to both legs screaming.

I looked down and reached for Pru who had big crocodile tears rolling down her cheeks.

"What's wrong?" I asked.

"They had their shots today. The shots make them run fevers and feel bad for 48 hours. So here we are." Cheyenne said dryly.

I gave Pru a kiss on the forehead when she laid her head down on my chest, wiping tears and God knows what else on my shirt.

"Where's Ember?" I asked.

"I haven't seen her; like I said, we just got back. I was about to run up to the shop. Could you carry Pru for me? That's probably where she is. Sam just said everyone was there."

Nodding in agreement, I walked with Pru while Cheyenne picked up Piper. Pru was fast asleep by the time we got to the shop. Pizza had been ordered sometime in the fifteen minutes I'd been gone, and everyone started chowing down.

Everyone, that is, except Ember.

Turning towards Max I asked, "Is Ember asleep at your place or something?"

"No, I thought she was with you." He replied.

It was then that it sunk in. She left. She heard what I said this morning, and left. Passing Pru to Blaine, I ran out the door and slammed into the house. Glancing around the living room, I noticed what was missing. Her blanket was gone; her shoes that were normally strewn half-hazardly in the corner were gone.

I went into the bedroom and it was the same. All her clothes were gone. Her toiletries that covered the counter were no longer there.

My hands went to my hair as I yanked on it. Of course, she would do this. She didn't want my child to be in danger; she left thinking she was doing the right thing.

I walked into the living room and finally noticed the note on the coffee table and on top was her ring.

Gabe,
I'll let you know where I end up. Don't worry about me, worry about your sweet girl for now. I'll give Max updates when I can.
Ember.

The tearstain at the bottom of the note was what broke my heart. Oh God, she'd better be all right or I was going to do something this world had never seen before. I balled the hand not holding the note into a fist so hard that my knuckles cracked.

Max walked through the door taking one look at my ravaged

face and nodded his head that he knew she was gone.

He handed me a paper and key, then said, "She went to the cabin. I have sensors set up. The whole place is wired. The code is on this paper. No one will get in without me knowing. She's laying on the bed right now sleeping. Here are directions. Pack a bag and stay a few days, I think y'all need it right now. I would have known earlier, but my phone was dead."

I ran to the room and packed a small overnight bag, and then back into the living room. Max was gone, which wasn't surprising. Walking at a fast clip out the door, I straddled my bike, glanced at the directions, and took off. I rode hard and arrived in forty minutes. The gate at the bottom was locked so I pulled the bike over in front of the gate and shut it off.

Swinging my leg over and off, I hopped the fence and walked up the long driveway. It was a sweet spread. Trees lined both sides of the driveway and about a third of the way from the gate a creek ran underneath through a large drain.

I walked about half a mile when I saw a pond. No fish jumped from what I could tell, but that didn't mean they weren't there. Around the bend of the pond, the cabin came into view. I couldn't see Ember's car, which meant that she parked behind the cabin itself.

Pulling the key out of my pocket, I unlocked the door. The main room looked neat and tidy. A wood burning stove dominated the entire left side of the room. Large cedar beams lined the vaulted ceilings. The cabinets were cedar as well. Overall, this looked beautiful, and had a ton of potential.

I walked quietly to the hallway where I assumed the bedrooms were. The bedrooms split one on each side, and I stood in the middle of the hallway to look into both rooms. Ember was asleep in the one on the left.

Her face was tear stained, and every other breath caught in her throat. It was my undoing. I dropped to my knees and ran my hand over her hair, smoothing it down. She slowly opened her eyes, blinking away the sleep.

I moved my face closer to hers, and then ran the tip of my nose along her face. I kissed her nose before leaning back on my heels and regarding her slowly. Her eyes filled with tears, and then spilled over.

"Alright, crazy girl. I know I said something that set you off, and I can guess how it sounded and what you think I meant. Let me tell you what I really meant. This gang has to go; I don't want you, or my kids getting hurt. Either I'm going to help bust them, or I'm going to take them out. I don't really care what it takes, but it's going to happen. I don't want to fear for your safety when we go buy shit for our kids."

Her mouth dropped open about halfway through my explanation; by the end of it, her tears dried up.

Rolling herself onto her back, she threw her arm over her eyes and muttered, "I'm a dumbass."

"You're not a dumbass. I can see where you got that I wanted you to leave, but how could you think I'd just want you to leave like that?"

She didn't answer, but she didn't need to. She thought she would lose me eventually, and she was waiting for the other shoe to drop.

"You're not getting away from me. You're mine now. Forever. In fact, I have a few calls to make. Be back in a few."

She still had her arm over her eyes, and used her left hand to give me a thumb up as I left the room.

I dialed Max and let it ring.

"I need a few favors." I said when he answered.

I went on to explain what I wanted, and he said he'd have it done by Thursday. Which meant we had two and a half days here by ourselves before I had to get her home for our surprise.

The next few hours were spent exploring the property.

"This is where I got stuck. When we first moved here, this was all flooded. The swamp from the next land over flooded and it extended to the back of our property. I was riding through here one day, by myself, on the 4-wheeler, when I got high centered on a rut. I had no clue why I'd been stuck, and I needed help. I had to walk back to the cabin from here, and about half of it was in calf high swamp."

"What'd your dad have to say?" I asked while glancing over the area, trying to pretend that I wasn't terrified for the little twelve year old that was in the middle of a fucking swamp.

"He was pissed at first. He told us never to go back there without one of them. That I was lucky an alligator didn't eat me. When he saw the 4-wheeler, he knew immediately that I was high centered. We spent nearly two hours getting it unstuck, and by the time we got back, we were both covered from head to toe in mud. It's one of my greatest memories."

We continued to walk, and, finally, circled back around to the cabin where we went into the AC to cool down.

"This is the room that reminds me of him the most. I remember him cooking us bacon and eggs. He would cook the eggs in the bacon grease, and it would taste amazing. No one else cooks eggs like that, and I have yet to find a restaurant that does it either. He also used to make some breakfast sandwiches that were similar to Egg McMuffins. The only difference was that he made them with over easy eggs; as soon as you took a bite, you'd have the yolk everywhere." She smiled.

I watched the expressions flit over her face and asked, "You don't talk about them much. Where was your mom?"

"She didn't come over until later in the afternoons, and then would drive home later that night. She wasn't into ruffing it, but when she was here, she had a camera in her hand and a smile on her face."

"I'd love to see the pictures sometime. So, Max fixed the place up since you were last here?"

She glanced around before saying, "Yeah. He's done a lot. I haven't been here since my parents died. It was always too difficult to think about coming here when I knew they wouldn't be. Hence, why I've stayed away. Max, obviously, didn't have the same problem. He put in indoor plumbing, and electric. The rest of the cabin still looks the same though."

I loved the way she lit up when she spoke about her family. It seemed to me that she kept this part of herself hidden; if she spoke of it, she would feel the pain of losing them even more. So, instead, she ignored it all together. Except here, she couldn't, because everything she saw reminded her of them.

Her expression turned sad so I distracted her with food, as any good man would do.

"I'm getting pretty hungry, Em. What do you say we go get something to eat?"

"That sounds pretty good, actually. I haven't eaten since last night's pizza."

I glanced at my watch, noting it was two in the afternoon. It'd been over eighteen hours since she'd eaten, and I felt a sharp ache in my chest when I realized it was my fault.

"Em, you know you can't do that anymore. You have to make sure you eat for the baby." I admonished.

Her expression went from sad to desolate, and I curled her into my chest when I noted it.

"What is it?"

"What if he doesn't make it?" She cried.

"Our boy is a fighter. If he's anything like me, he'll come out swinging. Try not to worry so much. There's nothing we can do about it right now, and we need to make sure we keep our attitudes positive." I said as I kissed her forehead.

Getting her emotions back under control she said, "The closest place is Mineola. It's about a thirty minute drive."

"Then that's where we'll go. By the way, do you want this back?" I asked holding out her ring.

I was rewarded with her sweet smile. She held out her hand and I slipped it back onto her finger. Lifting her hand, I gave it a kiss before I wrapped my arm around her neck and led her to the bike. Our hips bumped as we walked, and she giggled the entire time.

The drive was a scenic one, and I promised myself we would come out here more often. She enjoyed the ride, as well as the familiar landmarks that she hadn't seen in so long.

We agreed that Mineola would be the place to go and spent the afternoon walking around downtown. We ate in a small restaurant called Armadillo Willie's. It was definitely a redneck establishment. They were very proud of their tin cups and plates, as well as their eclectic menu.

They offered "Armadillo Eggs" which were nice ways of saying 'bull balls.' They also offered squirrel, possum, gator, and venison. I decided to go wild and try some of the gator while Ember stuck with the old-fashioned hamburger. Apparently, she had her first bout of queasiness, and just thinking about anything other than a burger made her stomach churn.

The ride back to the cabin was beautiful with the sun setting in front of us, and the love of my life at my back. I pointed out deer every couple of miles, and laughed at the squeal of happiness she would let out when she saw them.

The next two days were spent reading, exploring, and making love. Our nights were spent playing cards, laughing, talking, and making love. Tomorrow was back to the real world. Too bad we weren't aware that, very soon, something so terrible was going to happen that would make us long for those two days back. Darkness was about to ascend on our world, and we needed something pure to hold on to.

Chapter 14

Why would you want to marry me anyhow?
So I can kiss you anytime I want.
-Sweet Home Alabama

Ember

We pulled up to Free, him on his bike, and me in my car. Instead of pulling around the garage to the houses in back, he pulled up to the bay door and shut the bike off. I pulled up next to him, and got out with brows raised.

He took my hand and led me into the office, and then out into the garage. All the lights were off, which was exceptionally unusual because, normally, at this time of day, air wrenches were singing, tools were being dropped, hammers were banging, and a loud blaring of rock music played in the background.

None of that was happening today, which was downright freaky for three in the afternoon.

"What's going on?" I asked curiously.

"Ember Leigh Tremaine, will you marry me?" Gabe asked into the darkness.

"I already said yes, weirdo. Why do you think I'm still wearing the ring?"

His laugh vibrated off the skin of my neck when he said, "I mean today; right now, as a matter of fact."

At that statement, the lights flipped on blaringly bright, and I was presented with our friends and family in the shop. It was decorated in skulls, red and black, just like I'd always wanted.

I turned from all of our friends staring, expectantly at me. Then back to Gabe, before I threw my arms around his neck.

"Of course, you didn't even need to ask." I said right before I kissed him.

"You're supposed to kiss after you say, '*I do!*'" Jack yelled from across the room.

"Let's go." He said against my lips.

And so, we were married. By Elliott at that. Apparently, Dougie had dared him at one point to get licensed to be an ordained minister, and Elliott wasn't one to pass up a challenge. Max had somehow pulled off getting a marriage license without the both of us present, which was illegal since blood tests were involved, as well as both of our signatures; but hey, who was I to say anything here?

I got married in jeans and a t-shirt. The only thing missing were my parents, but I knew they were watching me with smiles on their faces.

Max walked me down the aisle. He held on to me tight, and gave me a bear hug before releasing me to Gabe's arms. I ignored the "fuck up and die" look he gifted Gabe with, and smiled at Elliott who winked at me.

The ceremony was short and sweet. Everyone cracked up each time Elliott said something minister like. Cheyenne and Blaine were at my side crying their eyes out. Not sure why though, because there was nothing to cry about here. I was almost as happy as I could be.

We spent the afternoon eating, dancing, laughing, and carrying on. Kids ran around at our feet laughing and playing. I'd shared a dance with my husband, brother, and then every member of Free after that. I also might have slow danced with Cheyenne and Blaine. By that night, I was so tired that Gabe ended up giving me a piggyback ride back to our place. He dropped me on my feet right at the door, and then picked me up bridal style.

I looked into Gabe's eyes as he carried me through the door to his house. They were soft and warm, full of love, and I never wanted to look anywhere else.

"I love you, Gabriel. This was the best day of my life."

"It was a pretty perfect one for me, too. Thank you for saying yes." He grinned.

"Anything for you. Anything."

Unlike a normal wedding night, we spent the next few hours sorting through the enormous amount of baby paraphernalia. Gabe installed the car seat with only a little guidance from Sam. I sorted out the spare room, shoving all of my belongings out the door and into our room to sort through later.

"What's in that box?" Gabe asked as he came into the room.

"All the newborn stuff you had to have."

"I can't wait for the baby to wear it. We're gonna have to add on to the house like Sam did so we can have another room. There's not enough room in this place."

"Gabe, honey, Cora won't be able to fit into any of this stuff.

You bought it for no reason, and some of this is even for a boy!"

His gaze looked at me until the confusion that was on my face registered with him.

"You do realize that we're having another baby, right?" He asked carefully.

The light bulb went off in my head and I started laughing. My brain was stuck in Cora mode, not on our own baby.

"Gotcha. Sorry, not sure why that didn't register with me."

We spent the rest of the night unloading, putting away, and organizing. This wasn't the ideal wedding night, but it was perfect for us.

Ω

Gabe was looking a little green as we pulled into the daycare Cora attended. His face was a little pale, and his breathing a tad fast. The hand that I held was clammy.

"Gabe, it'll be just fine. Take a deep breath. Don't let them see your nervousness or they'll think you can't handle her."

Nodding, he visibly toned down the terrified look, and a blank mask replaced it. We pulled up to the Audi that The Moran's were standing beside, and shut the truck off. From their faces, I knew this wasn't going to go down easy.

We both got out and walked to the front of the truck.

Sidney spewed acid first, "You can't have your whores around Cora. According to Texas law, you have to take her by yourself if I'm uncomfortable with the girlfriend, or I can refuse to give her to you."

273

"Actually, Ember is now my wife; that law wouldn't apply in this situation. Anything else? Is she already inside, or what?" Gabe asked calmly.

She looked ready to chew nails when she heard that juicy tidbit. I tried looking into their Audi, but the windows were newly tinted, and so dark that I wasn't able to see in anymore.

"I'll pay you a million to sign your rights away." Mr. Moran spoke evenly.

"No. Now where is she?" Gabe replied.

I watched them volley back and forth until finally I couldn't handle it anymore. Pulling out my phone, I sent a text to Cheyenne who would send in backup. We knew they were going to try something, so it came as no surprise when they started with bargaining, and then turned to threats.

"You'll never find business in this town again. I could put that biker club of yours underwater in two seconds flat. Are you sure you want to do this?" Mr. Moran seethed.

Gabe visibly got his temper under control before he replied, "Listen, I just want my daughter, nothing else."

They didn't get a chance to reply before two police cruisers pulled up alongside our cars and got out. Luke stepped out of one, and a handsome red head stepped out of the other. Both of them were drool worthy in their KPD shirts and black cargo pants. They looked like total badasses.

The redhead flashed a blinding smile in my directions, and two twin dimples popped out on each cheek. He looked too cute! He was stocky, about Gabe's height, and had muscles bulging. What was with all the men in my life lately? They all looked like they competed in body building competitions.

The red head surveyed the situation before asking, "What seems to me the problem here, gentlemen?"

Apparently, the women didn't count. But, then again, I wasn't the one in a hostile position. Gabe and Mr. Moran were. Sidney stood at the door to the Audi like she was a sentry sent to guard the gates of hell.

"This, this vagrant is trying to take our daughter." Sidney spit as she curled her nose in distaste.

"Gabe, didn't realize you were a vagrant. When did that happen?" Luke queried.

"I'm just trying to pick my daughter up. We just got visitation scheduled, and this is the first day that I'm supposed to get her for the weekend. I have the papers right here if you need to see them." Gabe said as he handed over the papers.

The red head took them, read over them quickly, and then passed them to Luke. Luke read over them quickly, and then handed them back to Gabe.

"Looks like he has the law on his side, Mrs. Moran. Where is the baby? According to the papers, he gets her until Monday morning." Luke said evenly.

"He can't have her. According to the law, if I feel uncomfortable with his girlfriend here, I don't have to let him have her." Sidney said rudely.

She was really quite dumb. There was no such law, but I wasn't about to get into the middle of this. I didn't want it to look like I was trying to hurt this situation. I wanted to be the silent support that Gabe needed. Every instinct in my body was telling me to open my mouth and let this woman have it, but I held my tongue, because I wanted that little girl just as much as Gabe did.

"Actually, Mrs. Moran, there's no law against a girlfriend living with him. Although, they were married yesterday, so it's a moot point anyway. Now, this is a court order, so if you refuse to give the child over then we will be forced to arrest you." Red head said.

I really liked this guy. I've never met him before, but I knew I would like him just by that little speech alone. It also didn't hurt that he was hot.

"This is outrageous. He wasn't even there for her birth or the last year and a half of her life. She doesn't even know him." Mr. Moran said.

At that comment, I lost my will to stay quiet.

"Listen here buddy. That wife of yours," I said, pointing at Sidney accusingly. "Told Gabe, while he was deployed, that she aborted his baby. Then she broke up with him. How was it his fault that he's not spent the first year of his child's life with her? He's done everything he could in the last week to gain the right to see her. He's known for a week. Does that sound like someone that doesn't want to be in his child's life? He was devastated when he learned she'd aborted his child. Shattered."

By the time I was done, I was in tears. Fucking hormones.

Mr. Moran stood there in shock, as if he wasn't aware that was what really had happened. Which he probably wasn't. Sidney was a devious bitch; by the look on his face, the light finally came on, and he wasn't too happy with that dear of wifey of his.

"Cora's in the daycare right now. We'll be back Monday morning. Please call if you have need of anything." He said stiffly, and then got into his Audi.
I didn't miss the look he passed his wife, which had her scrambling to get into the car before he took off.

A smile broke out over my face, and I jumped up and down while clapping my hands. Then I threw my hands around Gabe's neck and jumped up and down while hugging him hard. Then repeated to Luke. I might have done it to the red head, too.

"Let's go get her!" I screeched.

I was to the door and inside by the time Gabe caught up with me. The woman at the counter smiled warmly, and then asked for our ID's to verify our identity.

"She's in the toddler room eating her morning snack. It's down this hallway, second to last door on your right. Would you like me to take you to her, or do you think you can find it?" The worker asked.

I gave her a bright smile and shook my head. "No, I think we can find it. Thank you!"

We opened the door to the toddler room and saw two tables with chairs built into them, filled with toddlers. They were all eating what looked like toast, but it was all chewed and slimy, so it could've been anything at that point.

I immediately found Cora. She was the only girl who had black curly hair and olive-toned skin. She was dressed in a pink solid shirt with black leggings. No shoes. Her face had remnants of her snack sticking to it, and she was drinking from a green plastic sippy cup.

I smiled at the teacher who came to greet us. The teacher was in a bright blue t-shirt that had "Primary Colors" across the boobs, and blue jeans. She was young, brown-haired, and blue eyed. She was also giving my man googly eyes.

"You must be Cora's dad. You look just like her." The teacher surmised.

"Yes, I am. Did Sidney tell you the situation?" Gabe asked.

She looked confused when she said, "What situation?"

"I'm filing for joint custody. I'll be picking Cora up every other Friday, as well as every Wednesday until we have it settled." Gabe explained.

"How awful, I'm sorry to hear that you and Mrs. Moran are separating." Blondie said.

Gabe didn't answer, but went to stand to the side of the table that Cora was at, and squatted down to Cora's level. He regarded her for a second, and then reached out and ran his finger down the side of her cheek.

Cora giggled, and immediately held her hands out for him to pick her up. My heart soared when I witnessed this. One of my fears drifted away. I was so worried that Cora would be scared of Gabe since she'd never met him; but, apparently, she didn't have that "stranger danger" mentality yet.

Gabe leaned over and picked her up out of the chair. He put one forearm under her tiny little bottom, and the other circled around her back to hug her to him. His eyes closed, and my heart melted. This was perfect. I couldn't have asked for this to go any better.

We exited the daycare and hustled to the truck where I strapped Cora into her new car seat. Gabe watched on since he didn't have a clue how to do it. We stopped by Subway to pick up lunch, and then headed back to Free.

Everyone and their brother, literally, because Max came too, poured out of the front office to welcome us home. I got out and unbuckled her from her seat. She was dead to the world, so I did it as carefully as I could so I didn't wake her. Cora's head fell limply to my shoulder, and I closed the door quietly before turning to the gathering.

They all looked on with adoration in their eyes, and gathered close to get a better look at her. Cheyenne raised up on her tiptoes to give her a kiss on the forehead before backing off. Blaine repeated the process as well.

"She's beautiful, Gabe." Jack said gruffly.

"Thanks, man." Gabe said, before smacking him on the back.

Walking to Gabe, I passed Cora over. He didn't out and out say it, but you could tell that he wanted to have her in his arms again. She transferred smoothly, and I grabbed the lunch out of the front seat before walking in to the office. I picked the chair next to the desk so I could have somewhere to sit my lunch.

Everyone followed, and took seats where they could. Gabe stayed standing, swaying back and forth. Max snuck up behind me and tried to grab a chip.

I smacked his hand away and mumbled, "Back off, bitch."

Cheyenne laughed and informed me that I wasn't allowed to say bad words anymore.

Yeah, right. We'll see how that goes. I tried quitting once; it was the worst seven minutes of my life.

Ten minutes later Cheyenne's mom rolled up with her twins and Janie. Her girls weren't quiet little creatures. They were loud, obnoxious, disrespectful, and awesome. I taught them everything I knew. Janie was also my little creation. I taught her how to belch, give Wet Willies, and how to play Candy Land. When the twins were old enough, and the same went for Cora now, I would teach them the same things.
Cheyenne's mom looked about ready to pull her hair out as she walked in.

"I tried to shoot for nap time, but I just couldn't handle it anymore. Janie watched the VMA's last night, and she keeps getting her teddy bear and dancing crazy like that Miley girl. The twins were copying her, and I just couldn't handle it anymore. She doesn't stop."

I burst out laughing. "So, she was twerking?"

"If that's what you young kids call it these days. I remember when you and Cheyenne used to sing and dance to those boy bands. At least they didn't do a bunch of butt shakes. Lord knows I heard and saw enough of them to last me a lifetime." Cheyenne's mom said.

N'Sync and Backstreet Boys were the bomb when we were younger. I used to have a picture of Justin Timberlake above my bed. Cheyenne had a picture of Nick from the Backstreet Boys over hers. We constantly fought over who was better. To this day, we still argued over it.

"N'Sync!" I yelled, just as Cheyenne screamed, "Backstreet

Boys!"

Out of the corner of my eye, I saw James roll his eyes in exasperation. "They both blew, if you want my honest opinion." He said.

I turned and glared into his direction. "Well no one asked you, Jamie. Keep your opinion to yourself."

Cora chose that moment to blink her eyes open, smiling happily at Gabe as she lifted her head from his shoulder. There was a circle of drool where her head had rested. Although, he didn't seem to mind.

Sam interrupted the festivities and cleared his throat for everyone's attention. "Alright, we need to start getting ready. How about we take the kids out back, we can let them play while we load. Jack, why don't you bring the auction bike around to the trailer? The trailer's hooked up to the Suburban already."

The next few hours were spent getting ready and loading the Suburban with all the essentials that we needed to take. Okay, well maybe the guys loaded everything, and the girls all sat inside and watched Pitch Perfect for the thousandth time. Fat Amy sure was a trip; everything that came out of that girl's mouth was hilarious.

We were also given the privilege of seeing Janie "twerk." Really, it was more of a bending of the legs more rather than actual ass shaking and grinding that Miley had going on at the VMA's.

We sent Hoochie home with Cheyenne's mom for the weekend. She already had Cheyenne's Mastiff for the same reason; it would be interesting to see how the two got along.

The car seat for Cora was installed, and James, of course, didn't have a problem with one extra in the car with him. Pack and plays were loaded for three children. Bags, snacks, diapers, and finally the kids. I've concluded that kids require a ton of shit, and next time we should just rent a U-Haul; and, possibly, some movers.

We'd just loaded the kids into the car, and I was heading to Gabe's bike, when he stopped me. He grabbed me by the waistband of my jeans to stop my forward movement.

I looked at him curiously over my shoulder, and then lifted a brow in question. "What?"

"I think you should ride in the Suburban." He said warily.

"Why?"

He watched me warily for a moment. "You're pregnant with my child, and I don't want to put you at risk. I would feel better if you rode in a vehicle from now on."

Seeing the intensity in his eyes, I decided not to argue. Instead, I gave him a small nod and a kiss on the lips before heading back to the Suburban. I glanced over my shoulder before I got in and saw him standing there flabbergasted.

I gave him a small smile and blew him a kiss.

He caught it with his hand and brought it to his mouth before turning and straddling his bike. He started it up with a roar, and pulled up next to Sam to discuss something. I buckled in next to Cora's seat and smiled down at her.

She sure was a gorgeous baby. She was a perfect little version of Gabe, and she was going to grow into a stunning woman.

We were rolling out of the parking lot by two in the afternoon. Sam was in front, with Gabe a little back and slightly to his right. James was behind Gabe, and Blaine and Elliott followed behind us in their own car. Jack, James, and Max followed up in the rear.

"I think it's time for some tunes." I called up to the front seat.

Cheyenne smiled at me conspiratorially and reached for her iPhone. We used to do this a lot when we were younger. With us being the youngest in both of our families, we always got our way. Especially if they had to listen to us whine while on a long car trip.

As Backstreet Boys filled the car, James beat his head onto the steering wheel. "Oh, Jesus H. Christ. Please don't do this to me."

Cheyenne thumbed her nose at him. "You know how car trips go, Jamie boy. Just suck it up and be a man."

The next hour we listened to our favorite songs from our childhood.

It was going on an hour of driving time when I finally couldn't take it any longer. "I have to take a wee."

"Are you serious? Janie's still holding it, there's no reason you can't hold it a little longer too." James said sounding disgusted.

"Actually, I need to go also. Let's stop at the next rest station." Cheyenne declared.

James gave up with only a little fight, and flashed his lights to gain Sam and Gabe's attention. Gabe slowed down to see what James needed, and nodded in agreement with some signal that James had relayed that told him we needed to pee.

We took the next exit, and barely stopped when I bailed out of the car. I was on the ground and running towards the bathroom, because I honestly had to go much worse than I thought I did.

You know that feeling where you have to go, and once you get close to your destination, it suddenly hits you like a ton of bricks? Yes, that's exactly what happened, and apparently, pregnancy exacerbates the issue.

I moaned as my bladder released itself of its minuscule contents. "Fuck that feels good."

"You sound like you're having sex in that stall. You should try to control yourself a little better." Cheyenne said as she followed suit.

I was just buttoning my pants when a small fart escaped from the next stall over.

"Oops," Cheyenne said sheepishly.

I laughed and washed my hands. I was inspecting my stomach in the mirror, trying to see if I could define a baby bump when a loud wet fart echoed off the walls of the bathroom.

My jaw fell open and I turned to Cheyenne's stall to stare in surprise when her door opened and her eyes met mine. They were sparkling with mirth.

"It wasn't me!" She mouthed silently.

We both turned to the only other stall with a closed door. Just then another more disgusting sounding fart broadcast, reverberating the stall doors with its intensity. Okay, well maybe it wasn't that bad, but it was still enough to hear it from outside the doors.

A knock came on the outside when we heard laughing outside the doors, as well as a muffled voice asking if we were both all right. The farts were coming long and loud now, and we both doubled over clutching our stomachs as we laughed.

Cheyenne grabbed my hand. We exited the door just as a small explosion sounded behind us, and it had nothing to do with fire, if you know what I mean. We both gagged and gasped. Tears were rolling out of our eyes as we laughed silently.

All eyes were on us as we went down to our hands and knees laughing hysterically at what'd just occurred. James and Max were both laughing as well. Sam, Jack, and Gabe were still by the bikes, but watching us as we laughed on the ground.

I rolled over onto my back and stared up at the blue sky. "That was sick."

I also felt somewhat sorry for the poor woman who was in there. We'd all had those days where it couldn't be helped. It's just one of those things that you hope never hits you, but if it does you want it to be at home.

A pair of motorcycle boots came into my vision, and I followed them all the way up the strong thick thighs, past the oh so beautiful package, past the sculpted abs, beautifully defined chest, and finally to the face that starred in my dreams.

Gabe was staring down at me with an amused expression on his beautiful face. "Are you ready? We kinda want to get there before dark."

I held my hand up to him and he hauled me to my feet. Just as I was about to reply, a dark haired beauty came exiting out of the bathroom. She didn't make eye contact with any of us, but instead walked past as fast as her three-inch heels would carry her.

Cheyenne watched as she got into a BMW with an older man at the wheel. They took off shortly after, and we made it about three seconds after that before we started out laughing again.

Gabe just watched us all laughing with a bemused expression on his face. He helped me to the car before straddling his bike and taking off.

The next three hours consisted of two potty breaks, three diaper changes, and a food stop. We pulled into the hotel just as the sun was setting. We unloaded all of our various items, and settled into our rooms for the night; all exhausted from a day of travel.

I'd just laid Cora down in the far corner of the room when I slipped into the shower with Gabe. He gave a satisfied grunt as I wrapped my arms around his waist from behind.

I rubbed my face along the muscles of his back. "She goes down really easily. I read her a book and rocked her for all of two minutes before she fell asleep."

His voice vibrated his back as he spoke. "She's a good baby, but there're a few things about her that have me puzzled. Like when I hold her, she holds on as if she never wants me to put her down. Or when I give her a kiss, she looks startled like she's never gotten one before."

"Gabe, honey. I don't want to start anything, but it occurs to me that Sidney isn't the best parent in the world. Just from what I've seen before, she doesn't look like she actually cares about her, only that she has her as a trophy. She wasn't even torn up about letting us have her; she was pissed. Seems to me like she may not actually care for her, only tolerates her."

"That's possible. Makes me never want to give her back. I'd feel horrible if anything ever happened to her. It's like the moment I saw her, she became a part of me. Like a part of my heart is walking around outside my body."

I nodded in agreement, and kissed his back. I got a little distracted by the clenching and unclenching of his muscles as he shaved his bearded stubble. I don't know why he bothered since it grew back so quickly. By morning, it would look like a 5 o'clock shadow all over again, and he hadn't even started his day.

He must have sensed my shift in moods because he turned around and had me pinned to the wall in three seconds flat. His big body pinning mine against the wall. I watched as a droplet of water slid down his chest to curl around a tightened nipple before falling off.

My mouth watered.

He raked his gaze over me, pausing at my nipples, and then continuing down to my mound. He ran the hand not holding his razor down my stomach, and then clenched my pubic hair with his fingers, tugging softly.

I opened my legs a little wider to give him easier access, and he took advantage, running his long fingers through my folds. Taking the razor from his hand, I finished the few parts he missed on the underside of his chin before placing it on the shower ledge.

He just started thrumming my clit with his expert finger when a shrill cry rent the air. Cora was crying from the next room, and nothing could've been more effective at cooling us down. It was as if a bucket of ice water was thrown over the both of us. Leaning forward he gave me a peck on the lips in apology before rinsing the rest of the shaving cream from his face, and stepped out of the shower.

I washed my hair with Gabe's shampoo, and then used his razor to shave my legs before exiting the shower as well. I dried off, and went into the room to find Gabe on his back in the bed, with Cora laying on his chest. Both were sound asleep.

Deciding to leave them as they were, I dressed, turned off the lights, and curled onto my side next to him. My heart swelled in my chest, and I didn't think I've ever felt so full. Now if we could only get our other little one here, happy and healthy, everything would be perfect.

Ω

The joke was on us. Cheyenne and I had never been to a bike rally before. It rather reminded me of a rock concert. There was a large open area, and every square inch of that area is a mass of people, bikes, booths, food, tents, and porta-potties.

It took only one look for Cheyenne, Blaine, Janie, the twins, Cora and I to get right back into the Suburban and head back the way we came. There was no way that was a small child friendly place. You would have to have eyes on them 24/7. Otherwise, you could look away for a mere second and they'd be gone.

Gabe didn't understand why we refused to go, but after Sam explained the problem in man terms, he conceded the point. Once the bike was off loaded, we were off, trailer and all. Cheyenne drove, and we only ran over four curbs by the time we made it back to the hotel.

The weekend ended on a high note with Free raising $98,000 from the chopper they'd made for Dougie. Tears sprung to my eyes when I heard the news. College was an expensive endeavor, and we wanted Kayla to get her life started right when she came to be an adult. Dougie would be so proud of these men. Just as I was.

Chapter 15

Ever notice how sometimes you come across someone you shouldn't have fucked with? That's me.
-Gran Torino

Ember

"Are you sure?"

Gabe was speaking to someone on the phone while he twirled a piece of my hair around his finger. His arm rested across my stomach that was still quite small for my seventh month of pregnancy. Really, it only looked like I'd gained weight, and was packing around a muffin top. I could still fit into all of my jeans, as well as still wear all of my t-shirts; I just looked fatter in them.

I was told that some women just don't show the same way as other's do. Our boy was growing well, and exceeded all expectations at each sonogram.

If Cheyenne and I stood next to each other, you'd never be able to tell that I was pregnant, and just a month behind her.

Gabe's tone of voice had gone from lazy happiness to tense readiness when he heard what the person on the other end of the line had to say.

He eased my head off his lap before standing up. "We'll be there in ten. Is she alright?"

I got off the couch and hurried to our bedroom to get some shoes on. I was in my usual yoga pants and t-shirt, and was ready as soon as Gabe hung up the phone.

"That was Sidney. Cora was at daycare when she fell and hit her head on a metal toy. They think she needs stitches, and she can't go pick her up. We've got to go get her and take her to the ER." Gabe said as he jammed his feet down into his boots.

"Not that I'm complaining about this, because I'm actually really happy she called us instead of someone else, but isn't this a little out of left field? I mean, in the last three months since you found out about Cora, when has she ever done anything to help us?" I questioned.

"She must really be in a bind to call me. I'm just glad I know beforehand, and not this weekend when I go pick her up from school and see the cut."

I nodded in agreement, and waited for him to finish lacing his boots.

We were out the door minutes later and headed to Cora's school. Pulling out of Free, we were minutes from Cora's daycare, just about to pass an intersecting street when the blue car pulled out in front of us. We didn't have enough time to stop.

When you hit someone, time seems to slow. You know you're going to hit them. You know that it's going to hurt. You have just enough time to brace yourself before the collision happens.

Gabe's truck hit the blue car with the ferociousness of a train barreling into a stalled car on the tracks. He had no time to brake, only enough time to throw his arm out, pushing me back against the seat.

The sound of crunching metal, popping and hissing filled my ears. The airbag blew out, cushioning my head and chest. The powder burned my eyes and face, but that was the least of my injuries. My legs were numb, and everything hurt so bad that I passed out from the pain.

I woke some time later with the sound of voices filling my ear. Tuning my head, I got my first good look at Gabe. He was still in his seat, head slumped forward, chin resting on his chest. He had a thin line of blood running down his temple. I looked for signs of breathing, and saw his chest rise and fall in a steady rhythm.

Some of the tightness eased from my chest, but not all of it. It returned the next second as I watched Gabe's door get pulled open, followed by a man with tattoos on his face, neck, arms, and hands cut his seatbelt with a knife and yank him out of the car. He fell to the pavement with a hard thump

My door was yanked open the next second, and they did the same to my seatbelt. They were able to hold me up though. The jostling of my body sent pain radiating up my right leg and left arm. Nausea rolled over me and I threw up all down the shirt of whoever had a hold of me.

A blow to my face knocked me back into unconsciousness. Just as I passed out, I heard the OnStar come on and ask if we were all right.

Fuck no. Nothing was even remotely all right.

Ω

Water poured down my face, blindingly cold. "Wake up, bitch."

My eyes open slowly, and met the eyes of a young Hispanic

male who looked to be all of thirteen. I took stock of my body: I was sore, bleeding somewhere on my leg if the blood on my pants was any indication, and I was tied to the chair with my arms behind my back.

I closed my eyes slowly, trying to see if I could feel the baby kick, but couldn't feel even the slightest movement. Horror consumed me, and a tear leaked out of my closed eyelids.

My eyes snapped open as his taunting voice filled the air. "Awww, look at the little woman, such a pussy."

Looking past him at my surroundings, I found Gabe in a similar situation as the one I was in. However, his arms and legs were bound to the chair, as well as a gag stuffed into his mouth. His eyes were blazing with a scary light that sent a shiver down my spine.

When he got loose, he was going to kill them all. There was no doubt in my mind. They would be lucky to be in one piece when he was through with them. They'd still be dead though.

Gabe had blood drying on his neck, and blood dotting his face where shards of glass hit his cheeks and forehead. His nose had a trickle of blood leaking out of it as well. He was wearing no shirt, just his jeans and boots.

We looked to be in a large warehouse. There were hooks on the ceiling, kind of like what they'd use for a meat packing plant to transfer slabs of beef around. It looked dusty, and worn. Trash decorated the floor. Discarded beer cans stood in a pyramid tower in the far corner.

A younger man, with dark brown hair, dark eyes, and olive skin walked through the door and stood in the middle of Gabe and me. He regarded us slowly, and I wondered if he was the head honcho. He was in a nice pair of slacks, and a black polo shirt; I assumed he wasn't just some random gang banger. His brown hair was slicked back on the top of his head, giving him have a greasy look.

He smiled a creepy smile. "It's so very nice to finally make your acquaintance. You both have been at the top of my list for over seven months now. Well, not anymore, because we're going to kill you both. I will save you, bitch, for last because I want to enjoy you first."

Gabe strained at his bonds, muscles bulging, veins standing out against his arms and neck. The bonds didn't budge though. However, if looks could kill, the man would be dead right now.

"Now, I would like you to sit very still. Although, if you feel like fighting, just remember I haven't had a woman in a few days. She's a little fat, but I could just flip her over and do her from behind; that way I wouldn't have to see her." The man sneered.

My heart skipped a beat, but I tried to keep a neutral expression on my face. Gabe was anything but neutral. He was livid.

Two other men walked into the room, each carrying a length of chain. My heart pounded as I watched them both walk up to Gabe and wrap it around each of his arms. He sat calmly, and stared into my eyes as they attached the two chains with a nut and bolt, and then hauled him to his feet.

Gabe's ankles were bound together, so they had to carry him backwards until they were directly underneath one of the hooks in the ceiling. Looping the chain onto the hook, one went to the wall and raised him up until only his tiptoes touched the concrete floor.

I was crying silently at this point. I wasn't sure what they were going to do, but I could guess. They were going to beat him, maybe even kill him, and I was going to have to sit here and watch.

Once Gabe was secured, the two men left the room, and Greasy walked up to Gabe. Slipping his hand into his pocket, he withdrew a pair of brass knuckles, and slipped them into place on his right hand. My breath caught in my throat at the first strike of the brass knuckles meeting flesh.

Gabe didn't cry out though. He watched my eyes with an inner calm that I wouldn't have believed if I hadn't seen it. Time after time, he was hit in the face, chest, stomach, and back. I didn't let my eyes stray from Gabe's. It was the only thing I had to offer, and I would do that for him, because I could do no less.

Leaning over as far as I could, I emptied the contents in my stomach onto the floor.

"I had hoped to hear you scream. Perhaps you would scream if I went lower." Greasy mused.

Crouching down, he used a pocketknife to free the bonds from Gabe's legs. He was standing from his crouch when he smiled.

Except, he made a fatal mistake.

He took his eyes off his target, and got too close. Gabe's legs flashed out lightening quick, and wrapped them around the Greasy's neck and face. He thrashed for a good thirty seconds, trying to pry Gabe's legs from around his neck, but his body gave up the fight and he went limp.

Gabe didn't release him for a while though. Mainly, I'm assuming, because he wanted to make sure he was actually gone and not faking it. Greasy's body hit the floor like a brick. Gabe did a stomach curl and lifted his legs up and over his body. Wrapping his hands around the hook with his hands, his legs curled over the chain at the top.

I stared, amazed, at Gabe as his muscles worked and bunched. Using an unbelievable amount of strength, he gave one good heft and disengaged the chain from the hook. He dropped down to his feet with a clink of chains, and hustled to me.

Just as Gabe crouched down, a young gang banger with his pants around his ankles walked into the room trash talking to someone behind him. The other young man followed behind, and they laughed about whatever they were saying.

They got about six feet from me before noticing that something wasn't right. Seeing Greasy's body on the floor and no Gabe, they went into a flurry of motion. One threw himself towards the door, but a length of chain hitting him square in the face and silenced him. Moaning, he went down hard, clutching his face in his hands.

The other boy tried to swing a punch at him, but Gabe was just too good. With one well-placed punch, he took the kid down. The kid's body hit the chair Gabe had previously occupied, and crushed it to pieces. Walking over to his prone body, he bent down and twisted the kid's neck, breaking it swiftly.

"Gabe, watch out!" I croaked, when I noticed the first boy.

The first boy stood on shaky feet to come after Gabe, but he was on a rampage. He took the kid out with two hits, one to the kidneys and one to the temple. I closed my eyes as I

296

saw him bend down next to the kid's fallen form.

Another audible crack filled the air, but I wasn't upset. Far from it, actually. Opening my eyes, I watched as Gabe's chest heaved. He dropped down to his knees beside me and started untying my hands. The chain clinked against the side of my chair, but he got me loose quickly, and I threw myself into his arms.

Tears streamed down my face, and I shook as I sobbed into his chest.

"Come on, we've got to go. There're more, and I don't want to be here when they find out." Gabe said as he eased me slowly to my feet.

Gabe went to Greasy's body, dug into his pockets. He produced a pair of keys, and a brand new iPhone. Pushing him onto his stomach, he wrenched the pistol out of the waistband of his jeans, and palmed it expertly. He checked the clip and slide making sure it had bullets, and was loaded before we moved. We went to the very edge of the room, hugging the wall. He put my hand to the waistband of his jeans, and started our progress forward.

"Call Sam." He whispered.

Taking the phone, I dialed the number for Free since I didn't know Sam's number.

Jack's terse voice filled my air. "Hello?"

"Jack." I whispered.

"Ember. Is Gabe with you? Where're you at?"

"We're at some sort of meat packing plant. We were in an

accident, and a few of the gang members took us. Gabe says there're more, but we don't see any as of yet." I explained.

"I'm running a track on this phone. Put it in your pocket, but leave it on the line with me. Be careful." Jack demanded.

I did as I was told, and followed Gabe. Once at the door, he paused, listening to the sounds of voices coming from the left of the door. He pushed me back flat against the wall and stepped to the other side just before they entered.

There were two men dressed in jeans that were around their knees and oversize blue t-shirts. They never saw it coming either. Two quick chops to the neck and both men went down hard. I'd really have to learn this trick. The next trick I didn't want to learn though.

He placed his big booted foot on each man's neck and pushed down, a loud crunching noise was the result; I was nearly hurling by the time he finished with them both.

I knew why he was killing them, he didn't want them to come up behind us or sound the alarm. It didn't make it any better to stomach though. He turned left once he was satisfied with the look of the hallway, and we hurried along, following the glare of sunlight shining through a window.

He took stock of our surroundings as we went; his eyes never still. We got to the window, and he hoisted me out after making sure all was clear. We went to the back of the lot where there were trees, and hauled ass.

He made me run. I haven't ran in seven months, and you would think that being in somewhat decent shape before I got pregnant that I'd have some sort of stamina, but I didn't. I was panting and gagging by the time we made it half a mile into the woods. Stopping at a nearby tree, I rested my forearm against it, heaving breath in and out, holding my vomit at bay.

Reaching behind me, Gabe took the phone out of my pocket and started talking to whoever was on the line. In the back of my mind, I discerned pickup, Jefferson's, and hurt, but I was so sick, sore, and tired that I just couldn't concentrate anymore.

I fell down to my knees, and then rolled over onto my back, hoping to alleviate some of the throbbing. I placed my hand on my stomach, probing. I was rewarded with a sharp kick where my fingers were poking, and I smiled hugely.

Thank God, he was okay. I don't know what I would have done if I went through all of the agonizing weeks of my second trimester, worrying whether I'd miscarry or not, just to get him taken away from me once I didn't have to worry anymore.

Gabe dropped down to his knees beside me, placing his hand over my stomach, giving me a concerned look. The baby kicked his hand, and his lip curled up at the side once he felt the baby move.

"Can you walk another mile? I have Sam picking us up on Sixth Street. It's just through those woods over there." Gabe gestured to the woods behind me.

Groaning, I rolled partially to my stomach and pushed up on hands and knees before getting to my feet. A hiss sounded from behind me, and I looked over my shoulder as Gabe watched me get to my feet. He traced his fingers down my neck, and I flinched.

"That's gonna need stitches. Let's go, baby."

We walked for a little over fifteen minutes before Sixth came into view. We stayed to the side of a Laundromat, and waited. Gabe wrapped his arms around me, holding me tight. I let my weight sag against him. I was truly exhausted, close to tears, and I wanted a coke.

Gabe didn't say a word the entire ten minutes we stood behind the Laundromat. Tires crunched on pavement, and a black Nissan Titan came into view. The breath whooshed out of my lungs, and I let out a relieved breath as Jack pulled up beside us. Jack hopped out, and he and Gabe gently eased me up into the truck.

The interior of the truck still had that new car smell, and I worried about getting blood on his seats. "Jack, do you have a blanket?"

"Sweetheart, I don't give a fuck about my seats. Get comfortable any way you can. Buckle up; we're going to the hospital." He said softly.

The entire trip to the hospital Gabe and Jack discussed the accident and subsequent kidnapping; how he got out and all the other details that I'd rather tune out.

Luke was at the ER entrance when we got there, waiting to take our statements.

"Hey man, just let me get Ember and the baby checked out, and we can come talk to you." Gabe said absently walking past him.

Luke gave a stiff nod and continued to keep watch. My guess was he was hoping some of the gang members would be stupid enough to follow us here. I was hoping for the exact opposite.

I hoped they all would go die somewhere. I felt lower than dog shit for getting everyone into this. It was entirely my fault that Gabe had been hurt. My fault now that our entire group was now locked down at Free. My fault that I'd nearly gotten   our   baby   killed.

"Whatever you're thinking, knock it the fuck off. This wasn't your fault." Gabe said as a nurse showed us to a room.

I nodded absently, but knew I didn't believe him. He wouldn't see any of this as my fault. Nevertheless, I did.

"Ember, honey, what the heck happened?" Cheyenne's mom bustled in.

"I'm okay, Daina. I just want to make sure the baby's okay. Gabe says I also have a cut on the back of my neck. I think I may have one on my leg right too." I gestured.

She tossed a gown at Gabe. "Alright, Gabe. Help her into this. Use the scissors to help her get the pants off if you need to. They look beyond saving anyway. Call me if you need help."

Once the door closed, he helped me out of my t-shirt, carefully easing it over my head. The bra went next; this one he cut as so he wouldn't put me into any further pain. One shoe, and then the other. The yoga pants were cut too, and then he slipped the panties off next.

He studied my bruised and battered body. Noting the bruise where the seatbelt ran across my chest and lower abdomen. My leg had a deep slash in it, most likely from a piece of glass. He slipped the gown over my shoulders, and tied it at the back of my neck.

He sat down on the bed, and then drew me down into his lap, cradling me like a sick child. A thought popped into my head, and it flared into alarm

"Jesus Christ, Gabe. Cora!" I jack knifed out of his lap.

His eyes flared, and he reached for his phone that was no longer in his pocket. I went out to the hallway, closing the gown at my back, to find Cheyenne's mom again. She was standing at the nursing station, speaking with a doctor.

"Daina. I need to use your phone." I whisper yelled to her.

She handed the phone over without comment, and continued her conversation with the doctor. His eyes flicked to me, running a catalog of my injuries, and then went back to the conversation as well.

I handed the phone to Gabe who started dialing as soon as he got it into his hands.

"I'm calling to make sure Sidney was able to get Cora to the ER alright." He said gruffly. His stance stiffened. "What?"

Uh oh. I knew that what. That what meant someone was about to be in trouble.

"Thank you. I appreciate it." He said as he hung up.

His intense stare did nothing to relieve the hot knot of fear that lodged into the pit of my stomach. "She was never hurt."

His words dropped like a bomb between us, and I started getting light headed. I wasn't stupid. How convenient that we go to pick her up, and never actually make it there.

We watched each other. Neither one of us knew what to say to the other. Daina rolling an ultrasound machine into the room broke our silence. The doctor she was speaking to earlier followed her.

"Hello. I'm Dr. Stephens. I'm here to look at you. Your chart says that you're twenty-nine weeks pregnant. Have you had any problems during this pregnancy?" He asked.

Gabe explained all of the problems we'd had so far, and some of the concerns we were still dealing with.

"I understand. Your doctor is actually on his way down here now. You were in luck, he was delivering a baby, or he'd be at his practice right now. Let's go ahead and check the baby out. I'm going to have a PA come in and check your other injuries. They'll sew you up if needed."

I laid on the bed, and held Gabe's hand as the doctor ran the wand over my stomach.

"You sure don't look like you're so far along. It's odd to see someone so small this far into their pregnancy, although it does happen. Normally, those are the ones that never even knew they're pregnant." The doctor mused as he looked at the screen.

I didn't answer him. Same old story, different person.

"The placenta looks fine. The baby's heart rate is great. Its 143 beats per minute. Looking good. I'm not seeing any other signs of bleeding. We'll wait for your doctor to do the internal exam to be sure you're not dilating. Little guy here looks really healthy. Chubby."

I smiled at that, and squeezed Gabe's hand. He squeezed back, and we watched as the doctor left it in place so we could see his face and upper torso.

Ω

I was released from the hospital two hours later. Gabe left after he knew the baby was all right to go speak with Luke. Cheyenne had shown up, and was walking out with me now. I'd yet to see Gabe since he left, and I was getting worried that he went back to the warehouse himself and killed the rest of the people he could find.

He was right outside the entrance, though, talking with the redhead that I now knew as Downy, and Luke. At some point, he must have changed his clothes and had his cuts cleaned, because there were a few white strips on his face and neck. Both officers looked relaxed. However, Gabe did not. His shoulders were tense, and he was nodding his head to whatever Luke was saying to him.

They stopped when they saw us, of course, and turned towards me to watch my progression. Once there, I curled around Gabe and hugged him with everything I had at that moment.

"Let's go home. I don't want to be here anymore." I pleaded.

"I can't. Apparently, I'm needed for questioning. I have to go down to the station. You can go home with Cheyenne though. The cops arrested everyone else that was left at the warehouse. They questioned a few of them, and they squealed on their friends when they were faced with the charges that were set against them. No one is left to hurt you anymore." He said softly.

Relief poured through me. It'd been a long seven months, and I was finally free to go to the fucking grocery store by myself again. No more listening to Max whine about how embarrassed he was by my couponing. No more bodyguards following me around while I buy my granny panties. I was so relieved; I almost forgot what else he said.

"What do you mean, you're being questioned?" I hissed.

Not giving him time to answer, I turned to Luke and Downy and glared at each of them. "What's the meaning of this?"

"Down, Mama Bear. It's only routine. We need to get his account down, and the easiest way to do that's down at the station." Downy explained with his hands up.

"Well then that means I can come with him. Don't you need mine as well?" I said sweetly.

Gabe laughed and gave me a soft kiss on the forehead. "Go rest, sweet cheeks. I'm gonna go. I'll be back as soon as I can."

"You better. You've got until three. That's four hours, before I come down there myself. Trust me; you don't want me to come down there." I said, giving each man a good glare before turning and walking to Cheyenne's truck.

Ω

The bed dipped behind me, and soft lips ran up the side of my face. Gabe smelled freshly showered, which reminded me I needed one too.

"Why didn't you wake me? I need a shower too." I said to Gabe.

"Sorry baby, I'll take another one with you."

He helped me up, and stripped off his boxers before helping me out of my clothes and into the shower.

"So, what happened?" I asked.

He soaped up my hair, being careful to avoid the stitches on the back of my neck.

"Apparently, killing four people causes a lot of paperwork. They wanted to make sure it was a righteous kill. Which it was. They dropped all charges that were against me."

"What?" I screeched. "You had charges brought up against you?"

"Uh, yeah. Sorry for not explaining that earlier. I didn't want to worry you."

I rolled my eyes at his attempt levity. Of course, he would keep the fact that he was being arrested from me. Max had stopped by and stayed with me until I got tired and fell asleep on him. Literally on him. I used him as a pillow, and he let me because he was worried about me.

He wasn't the most touchy feely kind of person, but he'd do anything for his baby sister.

"Max went home?"

"Yeah, he was here until I got in. Then went home. Said you had a rough couple of hours."

I had. I cried on and off for the rest of the afternoon, and then fell asleep. I'd wake up screaming, and then Max would soothe me back into sleep again.

"I almost got you and our baby killed. I almost lost two of the most important people in my life." I whispered.

"Oh, Em. It's all right. It wasn't your fault, and you know it. All you were responsible for was making friends with a stupid kid." He said gruffly into my hair.

I believed him, too. For the first time in hours, I felt like I could breathe again.

"I love you, Gabriel."

"I love you, too."

Chapter 16

Four wheels move the body. Two wheels move the soul.
-Biker Truth

Ember

"Are you ready?" I asked Gabe.

We were at the courthouse. It'd been one month since the accident. One long month of drama. One long month of hair pulling, scratching your eyes out fun, battling it out with a lawyer that Gabe's ex employed.

She'd tried everything under the sun to undermine my abilities as a step-parent. Today was the day the judge would rule over our case.

I was scared shitless. This was the day Cora would come home. For good. We'd been in deliberation for nearly five hours now. We were on a lunch break, and I was about to die of starvation. I was going on my eighth month of pregnancy, and I was still no bigger now than I was five months ago.

Not that you could tell from my appetite though.

I turned and studied Gabe's beautiful face. "I'm gonna go to the car and get my Lunchable."

He nodded, absently, and I left without looking back at him. He was in a mood. His ex was a total bitch, and kept bringing up things that "supposedly" made him a bad father. Like the fact that he killed four men months ago. Not that saving the life of his wife, unborn child, and himself was worth it.

We'd never been able to prove that Sidney set up the ambush that we drove into. We all had our suspicions, but without proof, the cops could do nothing about it.

I passed Sidney on the way out the door, heading to the women's room, and I even managed the keep the disgust off my face.

Bitch.

Once out in the parking lot, I shivered at the bite in the wind. Today was cold for Texas, at twenty-seven degrees. With the wind blowing made it feel more like twenty. It was positively frigid compared to yesterday's seventy.

I was weaving through the cars to get to Gabe's new truck when I happened to see Sidney's Audi three spaces over from ours. I glanced at it quickly, but looked away again because I thought about keying it. Something made me look at it again, though. Veering off toward her car, I was nearly to the front bumper when it finally hit me.

Cora was strapped into her car seat. She wasn't moving. It was colder than fuck, and she wasn't even wearing a fucking coat.

Oh, Jesus help me.

"GABRIEL!" I screamed.

I put everything I had into that scream. It felt like a hot fire poker was shoved down my throat, but I didn't stop screaming. I tried all four doors, but they were locked. I looked around frantically for something to break the windows with, but could find nothing. Somehow, I found myself up on the roof of the SUV, and I was kicking the windshield with the heel of my dress shoes. I kicked it over and over again. On the sixth kick, the windshield cracked, but still didn't break.

I found myself hauled down by a pair of unfamiliar arms, and I started kicking and screaming to get back to what I was doing, but stilled when I saw that Gabe had his Glock out prepared to break the window with the butt of the gun. He had the door open in seconds, and was in the backseat with Cora moments after that. Gabe worked diligently, getting the baby out of the car seat in short order. Cradling her in his arms, he ran for the door to the courthouse steps. I could hear sirens in the distance, but disregarded them.

I ran after Gabe, and found him on his knees on the floor of the lobby. Cora was cradled tightly to his chest. His shirt was off, and he was wrapping his jacket around her back. I ran and dropped down to my knees. Mashing myself against her other side, trying to use the heat of my body to get her back with us.

The baby still wasn't moving. She was so motionless, I feared Cora was dead, and bile crept up my throat. Gabe had a haunted look in his eyes, and I knew how he was feeling. Over the last four months of knowing Cora, I've grown to love her as my own. She even slept with us when she was staying the weekends at our house.

The paramedics arrived, and Gabe rode with the baby to the hospital. Seeing the two of them together made my heart kick. They looked so much alike it was uncanny. Once the stretcher was loaded into the ambulance, they took off out of the lot. Feeling like a zombie, I turned to head back into the courthouse and came face to face with Sidney.

Not one ounce of remorse showed on her face. She didn't even look at all affected. She had a small smile on her face even.

"I saw this happening a different way, but this works. For two years, I've resented him for what he did to me. Seeing that just made it all worth it. His stupid stepfather didn't make it worth it." She sneered, before leaving through the maze of hallways that led deeper into the courthouse.

Max came bursting through the door not a minute after the Sidney left, and came straight up to me, pulling me into a tight embrace. Once his arms closed around me I lost it. I cried for that poor baby. I cried until I had nothing left to cry. Deep ugly sobs poured out of me. Snot, snorts, the whole nine yards. I prayed, repeatedly, that she would survive. Hoping beyond hope.

Her lips and face were blue. Her limp little body showed none of the signs of life.

"Max." I said gruffly.

"Yeah, honey?" He asked.

I told him what happened in the hallway, and what Sidney had said only moments before he showed up. A veil came over Max's eyes, shielding something. I didn't know what, but whatever it was, it wasn't going to be good. If he wasn't my brother, I would've been scared of him in that instant. He pulled his phone out and called Sam, telling him everything that'd happened in the last hour. Grabbing my hand, he took me to his bike, and we climbed on. The ride to the hospital was torture. I knew that our lives were about to change, and I hoped that little girl would be there as a part of it.

Ω
Gabe

I've gone through many things. I watched my father waste away from cancer. I've patched up men with their limbs blown off. Stuck my bare hands in wounds to stop bleeding. Witnessed one of my greatest friends die. Saved the life of a woman that meant the world to one of the people I loved. Killed four men while my wife was tied to the chair, scared shitless that she was about to die. Nothing, and I mean nothing, compares to this. Seeing someone you love so deeply near the brink of death was heart wrenching.

My Cora was fighting a losing battle.

I was in the back of the ambulance, close to the door. I was doing my best to stay out of the way, so the medics could do their jobs. They'd intubated her, and then started IVs in both forearms. They started her on heated drips to help bring her temperature up to a more stable level. Then they took her vitals, and monitored her levels. Nothing much they could do but drive to the hospital as fast as they could. The wail of the siren, the sharp honk of the horn, and the beeping of the monitors were nearly overwhelming. I wasn't prepared for this.

I was so goddamn mad at Sidney. During the trial, she'd brought up every bad thing I'd ever done. The time I smoked pot when I was sixteen. When I took a joyride in my neighbor's '64 Ford Mustang. The time I had sex with her in front of an open window, even going as far as saying that I'd forced her. Everything she had on me was seriously stupid shit that I hadn't done in over ten years.

When Ember left me sitting on the bench, I knew she was a little miffed with my attitude, but I just couldn't help the deep-seated hatred I felt for Sidney. Every time I saw her, I wanted to choke the life out of her. I was trying my hardest not to take my annoyance out on Ember, so I kept my mouth shut and waited for the judge to call us back in to his chambers.

I was about to get up and head after her when Ember's piercing scream tore through me. My heart dropped down to my toes, and I ran faster than I've ever ran. I slammed the doors open and bounded down the steps. I saw her on top of a car, kicking for all she was worth. Taking in every little detail, I saw the form of a small child in the backseat, and knew exactly what she was trying to do. Extracting the gun from the small of my back, I used the butt to break the passenger window.

The next few minutes flew by as I tried my best to bring Cora's temperature up. The paramedics arrived, and I decided to ride with them. I rode with her, and left Ember on the courthouse steps looking devastated. I sent Max a quick text telling him to get to the courthouse ASAP, and shoved it back into my pocket.

We arrived at the hospital, and I stayed out of the medic's and doctor's way, as they brought Cora to the trauma room. One of the emergency room nurses told me to have a seat in the waiting area, and I did so reluctantly. It was the hardest thing I'd ever done, walking away from her.

I was in the rickety waiting room chairs for a little over ten minutes when Ember burst through the doors. Her hair was wild. What was once a braid now resembled a rat's nest. She had bruises forming up and down each of her arms. Her face was a tear-streaked mess. Her mascara was running down her cheeks in little black streaks. She looked horrible.

She saw me and ran full tilt towards me. She barreled into me and wrapped her arms around my neck.

"Oh God, Gabe. Is she okay?" She rasped.

Just as I was about to answer, a hysterically screaming Sidney entered through the doors of the main entrance.

"My baby, my baby!" The deceitful bitch screamed.

My blood ran cold. That fucking bitch.

Ω
Ember

"You have got to be fucking kidding me!" I screeched.

I sounded like I'd just chain smoked twelve packages of cigarettes. My throat burned with each word I said, but that woman made me see red.

I made it two steps before Max was able to catch me. I struggled to get away from him while security went over to the horrid woman. Two cops that were inside the trauma room came out into the lobby at the sound of the commotion. One split off and came in our direction, and the other went off towards Gabe's ex.

"What's going on here?" The cop asked.

"That woman was the one who left her child in the car to die. I saw her in the hallway when the ambulance pulled out. She said she resented Gabe, and seeing all that happened with her baby made it all worth it. She also said something about Gabe's stepfather, but didn't elaborate." I managed to get out.

Gabe passed me like a shot. One second he was behind me, and the next he was shoving the cop out of the way to get to Sidney. Max cursed and let me go, heading to intercept the fight that was inevitably about to break out.

That was the last thing that Gabe needed right now.

Coughing to get my voice to come out a little stronger, I listened as the officer addressed the one trying to get Gabe away from Sidney.

"Murphy. Give it a second." The uniform yelled.

Murphy backed up, and let the train wreck play out. Max had his arms banded tight around Gabe's chest from behind. Muscles were bulging on both of their bodies. Gabe looked like he was about to choke the life out of her.

"How could you forget our baby in the mother fucking car?" He roared.

"You're nothing to her. Where were you when I had to give birth to that little rat? That's right; you were deployed. I needed you and you weren't even there. So, I did what I had to do." She sneered.

"Sidney! You told me you aborted her! How was I supposed to be there with you when you told me you aborted her, and then wanted to break up?" he said with deadly calm.

She must have sensed that she was in serious danger because she retreated two steps back and bumped into the wall.

"That kid ruined my life. My husband left me when he found out that kid wasn't his. He was skeptical in the beginning when he saw the black fucking hair and the dark skin and he left me, but I managed to convince him to come back. All was fucking great until that bitch came along and ruined everything. I lived for the day that I got to rub her in your face. Today turned out a little differently than I'd planned, but it all worked out well in the end. Too bad your step

315

daddy wasn't here to witness this." She snickered.

The bitch was not only crazy, but she was suicidal. Max strained, but his grip held true. Time for me to intervene. I walked up slowly and placed myself in between Gabe and Sidney. I was plastered right up against Gabe so I didn't touch Sidney at all. He was looking over my shoulder, not acknowledging me in the slightest. I got up on my tiptoes to look him in the eyes.

"Gabriel." I said to him.

Still, he didn't look down at me.

"Gabriel Luca Maldonado Junior, look at me." I demanded.

My throat felt as if I was rubbing a barbed spike up and down my throat, but I ignored it and concentrated on Gabe.

His eyes snapped to mine so fast that my head spun. He looked scary.

Swallowing past a lump in my throat, I held his eyes and grated. "This isn't accomplishing anything. Let's go see how your daughter is doing."

Giving a sharp nod, he shrugged off Max's arms as if they were tiny irritants, and walked towards the nurse's station. I nodded at Max to follow, and he walked off abruptly with a scowl in Sidney's direction. Turning slowly, I regarded Sidney. She was wearing a cat ate the canary smile. As the officer's closed in, having heard enough, I asked her a question.

"Are you stupid?"

She only thought she accomplished something, but, really,

she'd just made this all the more easy. Turning in disgust, I didn't wait for her response. Gabe and Max had disappeared.

Great.

Ω

I was sitting on a gurney in the minor ER when Cheyenne came through the room.

"What the hell is going on?" She yelled at me.

She knew everyone here, so no one questioned her when she picked up my chart and started scanning it. She was in her last few months of nursing school, and knew what she was doing. She was also massively pregnant.

"A vocal hemorrhage? Really Ember?" She asked.

I shrugged my shoulders. It wasn't as if I planned to do this. I didn't know that such a thing was even possible.

"Alright, they released you. Where did they move Cora to?" She asked.

I shrugged. I had no clue. I hadn't seen Gabe in a little over two hours. I didn't even think he knew that anything was wrong with me. Not that I would've told him right now. He needed to be with his daughter. Not down here worrying about me, too.
Cheyenne went to the nearest computer and started typing.

"Third floor. That's not the ICU floor; it looks like she's more stable than we originally thought. Let's go." She said.

Gathering my strength, I walked with Cheyenne to the elevators, and then rode them up to the third floor. My throat was throbbing like a son of a bitch.

Sam arrived about twenty minutes after Gabe and Max went to see Cora. I was telling him what was going on in more detail when blood started to leak out of my mouth after I coughed. I didn't even realize that it was happening until Sam's face went sheet white and he called for a doctor.

That's when I was told I'd had a vocal cord hemorrhage. Sam settled down once he found out it wasn't life threatening, and I sent him off to make sure Gabe was doing okay. I also threatened his manhood if he told Gabe about my voice before I did. He must've taken it to heart because Gabriel hadn't made an appearance yet.

We arrived on the floor, and walked up silently to the nursing station. Cheyenne must've been on this floor during her schooling too because she started talking about the woman's cats; I was getting very impatient. Walking away, I wandered around until I heard low murmured voices. Peeking around the corner, I saw Gabe, Max, and Sam talking in low quiet tones. I leaned my face against the cool tile and listened.

"What do you want us to do?" Sam asked.

"Take her home with you. I think I need to be alone for a while." Gabe said.

I knew immediately he was talking about me. Fuck that. I marched right on up to Gabe's back, and saw Sam and Max's mouths twitch.

"I will not go home and leave you here. I will stay here, with you!" I ground out.

Oops. Too late, I forgot about my throat. Shards of agony

shot through my throat again; I started coughing, and everyone knows once you start it doesn't stop until it wants to stop. Gabe was staring at me waiting for me to get myself under control when suddenly his eyes widened. He snatched me up into his arms so fast that my neck whipped back with the force. Blood dribbled out of the corner of my mouth, and that's when I realized why he'd reacted badly. I pinched my eyes closed, and counted down from twenty to get my mind off the feeling of fire ants biting my throat. Slowly it dialed down to a more manageable notch, and I opened my eyes.

Gabe's eyes were panic filled.

"She's not supposed to be talking. Dammit Ember. You could lose your voice permanently if you keep that up. Is that what you want? All you need are a few days of vocal relaxation, and it'll all be fine. Shut the fuck up already. How many times do I have to tell you this?" Cheyenne grumped.

I gave her a sheepish look and turned my gaze back towards Gabe.

Understanding flashed over his face, and he gave me a soft kiss on the throat. Tears threatened to spill over my eyes, but I reined them in.

"Did she tell you what's wrong?" Gabe asked Cheyenne.

"Vocal hemorrhage. Apparently, when she was screaming for you, a blood vessel blew in her vocal cords." Sam said.

"You really should go home. I think you need some rest. I'll be fine here by myself." Gabe said.

Shaking my head, I opened my mouth to tell him how it was

when the glare he shot my way snapped it shut.

"You're not going to give in, are you?" He asked quietly.

Shaking my head, I leaned into him, wrapping my arms around his waist. Once I got my tears sucked back in, I peaked around his big body into the room that housed Gabe's daughter. Following my line of sight, Gabe started in on what was going on with her.

"Cora's stable. Apparently, she was in there since they'd arrived at the courthouse at eight this morning. They're not sure there will be any lasting brain damage. Her brain shows activity, but, really, we won't know until she wakes up. They're keeping her sedated for another twelve hours to make sure everything's back to normal before they start waking her up." Gabe said with a pain filled voice.

"I checked in with Luke. He was outside when I got to the ER. The little bitch tried to get you in contempt of court when you didn't show. Your lawyer was off site for lunch, so when he got back he didn't know what happened. The freakin court reporter and half the courtroom started yelling at the same time, all trying to tell them what happened. The dumbass thought she could get away with it, too. They also have her in custody for child endangerment. They think it'll stick, too. Luke was a fountain of information, not that he was telling me this. He was talking to another officer. He may have more; I just don't know what it is yet." Cheyenne supplied cheekily.

All the men stared at her as if she'd grown a second head. I was impressed myself. Sneaking up on a man of Luke's caliber was freakin' awesome!

"I'm fucking dead on my feet. My vagina bone feels like it's been pummeled to death. Can we go sit down?" Cheyenne asked Gabe.

Nodding my head in understanding, I untangled myself from Gabe and walked into Cora's room. She was hooked up to multiple wires, and machines. Her body looked swallowed in the large hospital bed. The monitors beeped with each beat of her heart. The lights were turned down low for her comfort. Her hair was a beautiful riot of curls, and her little body was covered under mounds of blankets. One of Cora's arms was thrown up above her head, and it reminded me of Gabe. This was the sweetest thing I'd ever seen.

Reaching forward, I ran my fingers lightly through her hair. It was so soft. Gabe came up behind me and wrapped me up in his arms.

"I feel like a failure. She could've killed her." He said brokenly.

I stretched my arm up and cupped his face with the palm of my hand, patting it consolingly. I let my hand drop and then reached into my pocket for my phone. I had a lot of stuff to tell him, and since I couldn't speak, this was the next best thing. Sitting down in the chair that was next to the bed, I started explaining about what I thought of Gabe, and how he was a wonderful person.

Gabriel,
You are the most wonderful person in the world. You have a tender heart, whether you choose to acknowledge it or not. You care about others. You save people's lives. Never once, have I feared what would happen to me since I met you; I feel safe and loved. You are the type of person that your father would be proud of. It breaks my heart that Cora wasn't with you for the last year, but she has you now. You will always have her, and she will always have you. Don't beat yourself up over this. Everything will be okay. I love

you.

Once I had it all typed out, I handed him my phone. He was sitting on the edge of the bed, holding Cora's hand. He took the phone in his other hand, and started reading. Once he was finished, he let out a breath and hung his head. A few minutes passed like this, until finally he raised his head. His eyes were shimmering with emotion. Taking the phone back, I started a new note. This one was simple.

I need ice cream.

I turned the phone around so he could read it, and he busted out with a deep belly laugh.

Smiling, I rested my head on the back of the chair and let myself drift off to sleep. This had been one hell of a day.

Ω
Gabe

It'd been two days now. Cora still wasn't awake. They stopped giving her the meds that kept her from waking up, nearly twenty-four hours ago. Everyone had been here on and off for the past two days, hoping to lend a supporting hand. There was food brought every time someone entered the door. Blaine visited quite often with Justin since he didn't move much. Cheyenne dropped in during her clinical shifts. Sam and the rest of the guys came in after work, or during lunch. All were hoping to see Cora open her eyes, but it hadn't happened yet. They removed her intubation tube; now we were playing the waiting game.

Ember was laying down next to Cora on the hospital bed, running her fingers through her springy curls. I could tell when she fell asleep. Her passes through Cora's hair got slower and slower until it stopped completely resting with her palm curling around the apple of her cheek. She was cradling Cora's head to her chest, and their breathing seemed to be in harmony. Turning my attention to the Ranger's game, I watched another three innings before I noticed something different.

Slowly turning my head in Cora and Ember's direction, cerulean blue eyes met mine. They watched me carefully. My heart started beating a mile a minute. Joy surged through me.

"Hey, sweet girl." I whispered to her.

She continued to study me. Reaching out, I took her small hand in mine and rubbed it with my thumb. Her hand with the IV in it had a death grip on Ember's braid, and she brought it up to her mouth and started sucking on it.

"Uh oh, big girl. Better stop doing that before she finds out." I said to her.

"Too late. She's already found out, but she doesn't really care." Ember said sleepily.

I flicked up my eyes to find Ember's on mine. Tears were shimmering in her eyes, threatening to spill over. I gave her a huge smile, and continued to talk to Cora.

The doctor came in a short time later to give her a thorough exam. He was very optimistic that since she was responding well to us, and interacting, and that she would recover fully. He ensured us that if all went well the next day or so that we should be home by the weekend.

Sidney was officially charged with child endangerment, and the custody case was thrown out. The judge formally awarded me full custody of Cora, and didn't approve supervised visits with Sidney. I would maintain full custody until the trial was over and her sentence was served.

Ember's cell rang on the bedside table. I knew it was Cheyenne by the ringtone, but I was too confused as to why she would be calling since she was supposed to be taking her nursing boards today.

"Cheyenne? Did you finish already?" Ember answered on speakerphone.

"Sure did. Sat in a puddle of amniotic fluid the whole time, but I got that bitch knocked out!" Cheyenne said panting.

Ember's startled eyes met mine. "Does Sam know your water broke?"

Her voice quivered for a second, but came back stronger after a few panting breaths. "I can't get a hold of him. My mom isn't answering either, but she has the girls today, so she might be taking a nap with them. Could you come get me? I'm not sure I can drive."

Gabe was on his feet with phone in hand. "I'm gonna send Gabe. He's on his way to come get you. It's the college, right?"

"Yes. Hurry." She panted.

"She's at UT Tyler Longview Campus. She's probably waiting for you outside. Hurry." Ember pleaded.

Ω
Ember

A quick peck on the lips and he was gone. I looked over at Cora who was playing with her bed remote; she smiled at me when she caught my eyes on her.

A nurse entered the room, the one that knew Cheyenne so well, and checked Cora's fluids, as well as her temperature. I learned over the past two days that her name was Jacie, and she was retiring later on this year after thirty-five years as a nurse.

"She's looking great. It's amazing how well kids bounce back from these kinds of things." Jacie announced.

I grabbed her hand to stop her advance to the bathroom to pour out the pitcher of water.

"Jacie? Do you think it'll be okay to take Cora down a flight to see Cheyenne? She's in labor, and I want to go see her, but I don't want to leave Cora alone."

"Well, let me see what I can do. I'll speak with her doctor, and we'll figure something out. If anything else, I'll stay in here with her." She said as she bustled out of the room, taking the water pitcher with her.

I started the round of phone calls, and was finally able to get a hold of Sam.

"Yeah?" Sam answered.

"Sam! Where are you? Why aren't you answering your phone?" I demanded.

"I was underneath a car, we were trying to get the timing right. Why?" Sam asked.

"Cheyenne's water broke during her test. Gabe's gone to her and he's bringing her to the hospital. You need to hurry up and get here."

Cursing was heard, and a bunch of commotion as he said,

"Okay. I'll be there."

"Cheyenne's in labor?" Blaine said from behind me.

I whirled around to find her standing with Justin propped up on her shoulder sleeping.

I laughed out and told her exactly what Cheyenne had just told me. "Yeah. Can you believe that?"

Blaine was laughing, and we both sat to wait for some news.

Jacie hurried in with a bright smile on her face. "It's a go. You can take Cora; just have to leave the IV in just in case. I'll come down to check on her during my next rounds.

It was going on an hour later when Gabe called me to tell me he was on the Maternity floor. We gathered up Cora, Justin, and the IV pole, and made our way down one floor. When we stepped off the elevator, I was rewarded with the sight of Gabe, except he had crazy eyes going on.

Speed walking up to him. "What's going on, Gabe? Is Cheyenne okay?"

"She's fine. I swear to God, if you make me deliver our baby, I will never forgive you. I can't handle that stress. First Blaine, and now Cheyenne. Why the hell is everyone always making me deliver babies? Sam knows some medical too! He should've been the one to deliver his own kid. Not me!" Gabe gestured wildly.

From what I was gathering, Gabe had to deliver Cheyenne's baby. I snickered. His eyes blazed when he caught the smile on my face.

"You saw Cheyenne's vagina?" I snickered.

His eyes narrowed, and I decided to shut up while I still could.

"That's not even the least bit funny, little girl. You're lucky you have Cora or I'd spank the shit out of you right now." Gabe threatened.

I rolled my eyes at that comment. He was all bark and no bite. He wouldn't even have rough sex with me anymore. Just because I was eight months pregnant didn't mean I was fragile.

I couldn't help it. I'm a glutton for punishment. "Did she poop?"

"This is not even remotely funny. Would you knock it off?" He growled.

"I didn't poop, Ember. You probably will though. Everyone and their brother will probably witness it, too." Blaine piped in.

I gave her the stink eye, and returned my attention to my husband. "Did Sam make it?"

He smiled wide. "Yeah. He made it just as the head came out. He almost passed out, too. He saw all the blood, and would have taken a nosedive if he hadn't sat down. It was great; I'll be able to remind him of it for years."

"Suck my dick, Maldonado." Sam said from behind us.

We all burst out laughing at Sam's pale complexion, and jittering hands. He really was a big ol' softie. I walked up to him, and gave him a huge hug. Well as good of a hug, one could give with a toddler asleep in my arms.

"Let's go see her, I'm dying here." I said, snapping my fingers at them.

We walked to Cheyenne's room where the party had started. Everyone was there. Even an uncomfortable Jack was sitting in the very corner. Cheyenne was sitting up, crossed legged in bed, laughing at the girls as they sat with James; he had the baby in his arms, and was showing Pru and Piper their new baby sister.

"You just had to have my husband see your vag, didn't you?" I announced loudly.

Cheyenne's laughter filled the room. "It was an accident, I swear."

After transferring a sleeping Cora to Gabe's arms, I stole the baby from James, smiling widely when she scrunched her nose at the jostling. "What's her name, oh holy name hider?"

"Phoebe Elise Mackenzie. She was seven pounds twelve ounces." Sam said proudly.

Looking down at Phoebe, I couldn't help but long for my own baby in my arms. This would do for now though.

Chapter 17

Why do people say, "Grow some balls"? Balls are weak and sensitive. If you wanna be tough, grow a vagina. Those things can take a pounding.
-Betty White

Ember

"Thank you, thank you." Cheyenne chanted repeatedly.

"Take a chill pill already. Go do your last meeting. It'll all be okay. We'll call you if we need anything. Now go."

We all banded together the last two weeks, and today was Cheyenne's last ever class. She'd passed her nursing boards with excellence, and I was dropping her off at the hospital now so she could finish her last class meeting and graduate on time.

Blaine had baby Phoebe. Gabe had Cora, and I had the twins. I was going to make a grocery run if Cheyenne would get the fuck out of my car.

"Love you, Em." She said before making her way into the hospital.

Pulling out, I merged with traffic, and saw a motorcycle pull out behind me. The motorcycle caught my eye because it was so mean looking it had these crazy wheels on it that looked like they'd cut someone in half if they got too close. A shiver went through me, but I pushed it down and concentrated on driving.

Pulling into the Sam's Club parking lot, I parked next to a buggie return, and got both babies seated in the buggy. This was going to be my last shopping experience before the baby came, and I was ready to do some serious overhauling. Coupons didn't work at Sam's, but their prices were so good that I didn't need the coupons to feel that I got a good deal.

I passed two cars before the motorcycle registered. It was following behind me, and, at first, I didn't pay it any mind. That is, until it stopped in front of me at an angle, cutting off my advancement. The same bike that had pulled out behind me at the hospital.

The man was older. He had a long beard that had six rubber bands holding it in place at a point. His hair was long and slicked back, tied in a leather thong at the base of his neck.

He was wearing a black leather vest with the word *Bold* in thick white letters above his heart. There wasn't a shirt on underneath the vest; you could see a lot of dark tanned skin. He was actually quite attractive, especially someone older like he was.

Pru and Piper startled at the sudden sound of a motorcycle, but quickly got over it since they were so used to being around them. Pulling them both out of their seats, I hugged them close to my chest and regarded the man.

"Can I help you?" I asked with as much authority as I could muster, given the situation.

"Those are my grandbabies. I just wanted to get a good look at them." The man growled.

I backed up until my back hit the car behind me. From what I was told, this man wasn't a good man. He'd been a horrible father to Sam his entire life, and here I was with his grandkids and no way to protect them.

"I don't know if you are who you say you are. I also have no right to let you see them. If you're interested in having a relationship with them, you need to go through Sam." I said with a quivery voice.

He smiled a tight smile, and then started his bike back up. "I know, darlin', I just wanted to get a message to him. He'll know what it is; you don't have to tell it to him or anything. You can tell him I'm going to be calling in my marker soon, though."

Then he was gone the same way as he came.

My arms were trembling, and I could barely move. I turned around abruptly, leaving the buggy where it was, and hoofed it back to the car as fast as I could. I left them both in the front seat, and locked the doors before I called Sam and Gabe.

Deciding the landline at Free was the best option; I dialed the number and waited. It rang twice before Sam answered.

"Free."

"Sam. I, um, well; I think I just met your dad."

Silence greeted me at the end of the line.

"Where are you?" He rumbled.

"Sam's parking lot. I'm in my car with the doors locked. Do you want me to drive home?" I asked.

"No, stay where you are. I'll come on my bike and escort

you home." He said and then hung up.

It wasn't but ten minutes later, when Sam's bike pulled up behind me. I'd already strapped the girl's in, and waited to see if he wanted to talk. He didn't. He let me know this by gesturing with his hand in a shooing motion.

The trip back to Free was uneventful. No strange motorcycles. No traffic. I didn't even catch a light. I pulled into Free, and drove around to the back to park, since I noticed the girls were asleep, and it was time for their nap anyway.

Sam got one girl, and I got the other so we could put them to bed. He gave both a kiss before shutting their door, and grabbing my hand to drag me back outside.

"How do you know it was my dad?" He asked finally.

"He said he was here to see his granddaughters. Said he wanted to give you a message, but wouldn't tell me what it was. Also said he'd be calling in his marker soon."

His face got stony and cold, but once he registered how uncomfortable I was, he cursed and grabbed me into a tight hug.

"I don't like that he was able to find me so easily. I owe him one, and he wants me to know he hasn't forgotten."

"Okay. Well, if you don't mind. Could you go get Gabe for me? I need him. Like now."

I said just before my water gushed down my legs full force, drenching my legs, and Sam's, in the same instant. He looked from my eyes, to his feet, and then let me go slowly. Once he made sure I was steady on my feet, he took off at a run towards the back door into the garage. It was obvious he was uncomfortable, and I'm sure it didn't help matters that had my body fluids practically drenched his bottom half.

Thank God, I wasn't at the supermarket. How embarrassing would that have been? Imagine being in the Freezer isle and that happening. Clean up on aisle ten!

I walked into our house, and exchanged my wet pants for a loose pair of knit shorts. Then I started to gather my crap that I've been procrastinating on packing. Being only thirty-five and a half weeks, I didn't think I'd need to pack this early. Luckily, the baby's bag was packed ever since the baby shower two weeks ago.

I threw my toothbrush and toothpaste into my bag just as Gabe came barreling through the door. His hair looked somewhat wild, and Cora was attached to his hip. She was giggling profusely, and I couldn't help but smile with her.

I studied him for a moment longer. "Relax, Gabe. I'm not even feeling contractions yet. I'm not going to have this baby on you. Have you called Max to come get Cora yet?"

He took a deep breath, and then let Cora down to her feet to play. "Not yet. I just got your message. Sam had to take a detour to puke before coming to tell me that my wife's water broke. What a pussy."

"I did break my water on his legs." I said casually.

At that, he burst out laughing. Tears leaked out of his eyes, and I couldn't help but join in. This was entirely way too funny. Sam was so unflappable. There were times that he remained calm when no one else was able to. It took a lot of work to get him to smile at a joke.

"Do I have time to go take a picture really quick?" He quipped.

"He has to come back anyway. The girls are asleep at his house, and it's not possible for me to watch them anymore. If you hurry, you can get him coming back."

He took off to get the best blackmail photo of the century, and I dropped down on my haunches and blew a raspberry on the side of Cora's neck. She giggled and threw her head back laughing. It was hard to believe that she would be a big sister in a few hours.

Gabe came back in the room grinning from ear to ear; I knew he got the goods.

"We're totally hanging this up on the wall."

I gritted my teeth at the wave of pain that radiated from my tummy around my back.

"Sounds good. I think we need to go now. My contractions have started, and they hurt like a mofo. Where's Max?"

"Right here baby girl. I'll follow y'all up there as soon as I get Cora some stuff gathered up." Max said from the doorway.

I smiled and walked toward him, hugging him around the waist. "Thank you, Maximillian. I'll see you in a little while. Don't even think you're going to get out of being in the delivery room with us either. Don't dally."

Some people may think it's weird to have your brother in the delivery room with you; I didn't want him to look at my va-jay-jay or anything weird like that; I only wanted him to be there in case I needed him. He was the only family I had left.

"Wouldn't miss it for the world. Go." He said with a pat on the back.

By the time we arrived at the hospital, my contractions were one on top of the other. I'd called my doctor, and Cheyenne, on the way to inform them that my water broke. Lucky for me, Cheyenne's meeting was on the postpartum floor, and she would be able to help with the delivery when the time came.

Thirty minutes, four missed veins, and two blood draws later, I was hooked up to the monitor, and panting through the pain. I'd asked for an epidural as soon as I'd walked through the door. I wasn't the type of woman who got off on pain; when I was presented with the option to have that pain taken away, I jumped on it.

I was hunched over a pillow leaning into Cheyenne, while the anesthesiologist stuck a needle in my back the size of a Buick when I asked, "What does it look like?"

"Like a really long needle is being driven through your body." Cheyenne supplied.

We were weird like that. We found the most morbid things fascinating.

"What did you do with Gabe?"

"I made him wait outside; daddies-to-be don't respond well to this part. So they make us kick them out until the Epidural is in place." Cheyenne murmured.

"Alright, young lady. You're ready to rock and roll. There will be no moving until this baby is delivered. Page me if you have any problems." The anesthesiologist said right before he breezed out of the room.

I hope that he went to the screaming chick who was speaking in tongues down the hall. I don't know why she was torturing herself. This epidural was a-fucking-mazing.

Cheyenne helped me ease back into bed, and covered me up with the blanket when Gabe walked in. Followed by Max, Cora, Blaine, Justin, Payton, and Daina.

"I swear to God, if I hear one of you make a comment about my vagina, I'm going to bust a cap in your ass." I said grumpily.

"Oh, relax. There ain't nothing you got that I haven't seen. If you poop on the table, they'll just wipe it up real quick and no one will be the wiser. Except for those that are looking anyway." Payton supplied helpfully.

That was our Payton. Over the last few months, she'd grown closer to the group. She was wary of Max, but her eyes always drifted to his if he was in the same room as her. Max openly stared, but never made a move. They were playing a game, and it was funny to watch.

For the next few hours, we played Apples to Apples to bide the time. A nurse checked my progress regularly, but I was moving slow; which the nurses explained was normal with your first pregnancy.

It was four a.m., eighteen hours into labor when I finally felt the urge to push. Max came up above my head, because there were just some things he didn't need the knowledge of, and your sister's vagina was one of them.

Gabe was at my side, holding up a leg, while Daina was on the other doing the same. Payton, Cheyenne, and Blaine were all at the back of the room, watching avidly. I didn't mind in the slightest. My mind was wrapped around the fact that my epidural had worn off to where only my right side was numb instead of my entire lower half.

"This part is what they call the 'ring of fire.' It's where the baby's head is crowning." The doctor supplied.

He was right, too. It was the ring of fire. The left side was in agony. In the distance, I heard Payton singing "Ring of fire" by Jonny Cash, and I took enough time to grab the bedpan that was on the roller cart and chunk it at her.

Bitch.

It bounced off the wall and they all scrambled out of the way laughing. This was so not funny.

"There's no coming back from that." Cheyenne sniggered.

"In like a banana, out like a pineapple." Payton laughed.

"Gabe!" I wailed. "Make them shut up."

His look silenced them from the next comment they were about to make.

I was sweating like a hooker in a confessional. My hair was matted to my face, the gown was clinging to my chest, and I could feel droplets rolling down the sides of my temple.

Apparently, I wasn't going to be one of those cute women who don't misplace a hair during birth; nor would I have a wonderful afterglow. I was going to be lucky if I had any hair left after this.

"Okay, on your next contraction, I want you to push until Nurse Brady here gets to ten." The Doctor Robinson instructed.

Gabe and Daina's hand hoisted my legs higher to my chest, and I pushed with everything I had. Anything had to be better than the pain I was feeling right now. I couldn't even begin to imagine what it would feel like if I didn't have an epidural.

The doctor watched as the baby's head came down, but then went back up again. Each contraction was like that, and it was damn frustrating.

"You know," I panted. "I read somewhere women have orgasms during birth. I'm not feeling that right now."

Snickering filled the room, but no one said anything. Gabe gave me a kiss on the forehead before watching the monitors, and then the progression of the baby out of my ravaged vagina. Payton was right; it would probably never be the same again.

The doctor exchanged a look I couldn't interpret with the nurse, right before I started pushing again, but I didn't have time to think about it before the contraction claimed me.

I pushed with everything I had, but nothing happened. I did it constantly, until I fell back in an exhausted heap.

Suddenly the doctor yelled, "Shoulder!"

The room became a flurry of activity. Gabe was pushed out of the way, a button on the wall somewhere behind my head was hit, and the room filled with a shrieking alarm. Nurses and doctors rushed into the room at a sprint. The room was pandemonium.

I'd never seen anything like it.

I couldn't see Gabe, I couldn't see Daina, and all I had was the doctor between my thighs. Two nurses were at my legs, and another doctor was at my stomach pressing down. The breath left my lungs, and I couldn't breathe. The pressure was so intense that I felt no pain.

My heart was beating at a fast pace, and bile rose in my throat. The doctors were yelling at each other in some sort of code, and I just laid there helpless.

"What's going on?" I demanded breathlessly.

"It's okay, honey. What's happening now is what they call *'Shoulder Dystocia.'* It's when your baby's shoulders are stuck on your pubic bone. They'll get him out, don't worry." The nurse holding my right leg said.

The nurses at my legs brought my legs so far back that they were practically over my head. The doctor on my stomach pushed again, and the breath whooshed out of my lungs for a second time.

I watched in horror as my baby's face went blue. Dr. Robinson's whole fucking hand disappeared up inside me as he worked diligently to get the baby free.

Pain as I'd never felt before followed his movements, and the only thing keeping me conscious was sheer force of will.

"I'm going to have to break it." Dr. Robinson said, right before he used his hand to do something inside of me.

At the time, I wasn't aware what it was, but the sound made me sick to my stomach.

Once whatever he did was done, I was told to push again,

and I gave it one more. The baby finally slid out of me, but he was limp and unmoving. His coloring was blue and grey, his body was floppy, and they rushed him over to the incubator.

Nurses and doctors crowded around him, and they worked hard to get my baby to cry. I was sobbing so hard at that point that nothing registered. They were still doing something to me, but I no longer cared. I closed my eyes and prayed.

"Got him back!" A booming male voice yelled.

Strong arms curled around my upper body, and I automatically curled into Gabe, breathing his scent.

"He's okay, baby. He's okay. Shhh," Gabe consoled me.

I didn't know who he was trying to convince, him or me, but it wasn't working for either one of us. My eyes flipped open as I heard them rushing out of the room, and the voices disappeared down the hall. Glancing around the room, I saw my original nurse still at the doctor's side, working on me down below.

Cheyenne had Cora in her arms, trying to soothe and calm her down. Payton had a fist up to her mouth, tears were pouring down her face. Max was in the corner sitting on a chair. His head was between his knees with his arms wrapped over the back of his head. Blaine was cradling Justin to her chest, weeping quietly.

Daina walked up to us and wrapped us up in her arms, and I curled into her, sobs choking me. Gabe wrapped his arms around both of us, and we stayed that way for a long time.

"Gabe, go be with him. Please don't leave him alone."

He looked into my eyes, his cerulean blue ones boring into mine. Something profound passed between us in that second, and he nodded, gave me a soft sweet kiss, and left.

Max took up his position, gathering me close. I wrapped my arms around his waist, and continued to cry. He squeezed me tighter, and held me that way until a young male doctor came in a while later.

"Mrs. Maldonado. I'm the on call pediatrician. Your son is currently stable. He's breathing on his own, but we're going to monitor him for a few more hours just to be on the safe side. They did break his clavicle in order to get him out. You'll need to be very gentle with him, for that's going to hurt him until it heals. It will heal very quickly. Your husband's in with him now."

"Thank you." I whispered, and let my tears flow freely again.

Max shuddered around me, and I knew that he was crying with me. Terror was still in the back of my mind, but I had renewed hope that everything would be okay.

Ω
Gabe

I stared down at the sleeping boy in my arms. He was nestled in a blue blanket that Blaine sewed for him. He made a cute baby sound, and turned his head slightly to the side before falling back into his peaceful slumber.

I looked over at Ember, and marveled at how proud I was of her.

The memory of the birth was horrific. When the doctor had yelled that he had a shoulder, I knew immediately what was going on. I was pushed away from Ember, and watched from the other side of the room, while doctors and nurses surrounded her bedside. Thirteen people crowded around the small bedside, and I could see how terrified Ember was. I saw her eyes dart from side to side looking for me, but I knew she couldn't see me over the massive amount of people surrounding her.

I could feel the tears running down my cheeks, but I didn't swipe them away. Every second Ember experienced pain and terror, was another piece of my heart that broke off. I couldn't stand seeing her cry and not being able to get to her. My body ached to go to her, hold her, and comfort her.

I couldn't see what was going on below, couldn't see if the baby was making any progress, but when I heard him say he was going to have to break it, my stomach dropped. They only did that as a last resort. A last ditch effort to save the baby. I knew that they'd been working on him for three minutes now. At five minutes, lasting brain damage would occur, and the baby probably wouldn't survive.

The wall of people split as a young doctor took my son and transferred him to the station where they worked on the newborns. I watched as they crowded around him, and I prayed that he would be okay.

It was only when the baby was wheeled out of the room that I came unstuck and went to Ember. She was sobbing loudly; each one tore my heart in pieces. Gathering her in my arms, I cried with her. No one ever thought it would end up like this.

I'd absently read the emergency procedure on the wall above her head when she got into the bed earlier, but never thought that it would be needed.

Ember sent me to my son, begging me with her eyes.

Leaving her was one of the hardest things I'd ever done, but I couldn't resist the pleading in her eyes.

I saw them working on him through the glass of the NICU. They weren't scrambling like they were doing earlier, which was a good sign. From what I could see, they had him on CPAP. The mask was over his nose, and he was hooked up to multiple IVs and monitors.

The truly beautiful thing was the lusty cry coming out of him. My knees nearly buckled at the profound relief I felt. A nurse spotted me, and opened the door for me to come inside to see him. She handed me a yellow gown, and told me to wash my hands. Once done, she led me over to my baby boy.

The young doctor explained to me more in depth what happened. As it turns out, at thirty-five weeks, the baby weighed in at nine pounds two ounces. They wondered if his due date could've been off, but we'd never know for sure. His clavicle was broken during the birth to assist in delivering him. From what they could tell, Ember also had a narrow pelvis.

Throughout the next two hours, they weaned him off CPAP slowly, to make sure he did well on his own. I sent multiple texts to Ember, and she ooohed, and awed over every one of them. By hour three, I was finally able to hold him.

"You may take him back to the room to see your wife, if you'd like." A younger nurse said.

Like I was going to argue. Yeah, right.

Wheeling him down the hall, I peeked into the room to find Ember cradled against Max's chest. Her eyes were swollen, and still in her sleep, she was weeping. Every so often, her breath hitched, and each time my heart skipped a beat. She clutched her iPhone in her hand; it was curled close to her chest, and she looked utterly exhausted.

The room was filled with our family. Daina, with a sleeping Cora, sat on the couch next to Elliot and Blaine, who was holding Justin. Cheyenne curled into Sam's side; each had a twin in their lap. Jack had Phoebe curled against his chest. James sat on the floor playing quietly with Janie. Even Payton was there, leaning against the wall near the bathroom door. Each one of them broke out in smiles when they saw me wheeling in our son.

Lifting him out of the bassinet, I walked slowly to Ember, who was still sleeping. I placed the baby into Max's arms cautiously, and then helped maneuver Ember to where she was resting against me instead of Max. The jostling woke her, and she started crying anew when she laid eyes on our baby for the first time.

Max transferred him to Ember's arms carefully, and backed away to give us some privacy.

Everyone started to stand, but Ember stopped them with a staying hand. "Don't go. Please stay."

They all resumed their seats, and watched us rapturously.

"He's okay, baby. Stop crying, you're breaking my heart." I whispered into her hair.

"He looks just like you. Look at his little chubby cheeks!" She laughed.

I smiled. "He was nine pounds two ounces, and twenty two inches long. He's a big boy."

"What's his name?" Max finally asked impatiently.

"Gabriel Luca Maldonado, the third." Ember announced proudly.

My body froze, and pride burst through me. We'd never discussed naming him after me, and I never wanted to ask since my name wasn't a traditional American name. So hearing her say that, just now, was something I never hoped to have. We'd discussed that we wouldn't think about names until we saw him with our own eyes, but I had a feeling that she probably planned it like this all along.

Everyone stayed for a while longer, but left within the hour to give us time alone with Luca. Max took Cora home, who'd instantly loved her new baby brother. Unfortunately, she couldn't hold him yet since he was hurt, but she gave some great kisses.

After three days in the hospital, Luca and Ember were released, pending follow up appointments within the next week. Luca's collarbone healed fully within three weeks. The same couldn't be said for our hearts.

Ember suffered from nightmares about the delivery. I'd be dead asleep and her screaming would jar me awake. Her screams of pain would echo through me, reminding me of the delivery, of the terror I'd experienced seeing our son stuck, dying slowly. We spoke about the birth often. She told me that next time she was having an elective C-section, because there was no way she was going to experience that again, even though the odds were highly unlikely.

Each and every day, I thank God for sparing my family. I'd nearly lost Ember, my daughter, and then my son within a year's time. All of those times left marks on my soul. Something that I would never forget, even if I lived to be a hundred. I was one lucky son of a bitch.

EPILOGUE

Ember

"Thirty seconds." An electronic voice announced from my iPhone app.

Closing my eyes, I started thinking about all the crap I had left to do today. Since today's Cora's second birthday, we decided to hold a party for her at Air U. Air U is a large indoor area that had trampolines covering every available surface. However, this was not my idea. Gabe was big on trying to make up for his missing year in Cora's life.

He went over the top for everything, including the party. I had a little over three hours until we were to be there, and what was I doing? Nothing. I was working out instead of doing what I really needed to be doing.

I've slowed down a lot since Luca's birth. Savoring things that I wouldn't normally savor. Stopping to smell a flower on the side of the road instead of barreling past it at ninety. Taking the time out of my day to call Max and tell him I love him. Coming home at lunch to check on my babies, just because I missed them/; and yes, that included Gabe. Eating that second piece of chocolate cake, even though I know it will go straight to my love handles. I reveled in my perfect life.

It'd been nearly six months since I'd given birth to Luca. Our lives have settled down a bit since the birth. I'd started my job with the college back a little over two months ago. I didn't, however, do it full time. I'm more of an administrator now, instead of a full time athletic trainer.

I'd tried to go back to work, doing what I'd been doing before I had Luca. Unfortunately, it didn't agree with me. I was working long hours, and I never got to see my kids. I'd drop them off at daycare on my way to work at seven in the morning, and wouldn't be able to pick them up until late in the afternoon.

Once football season started, my hours got worse. The first away game for the football team I'd cried for nearly the entire bus ride. Four complete hours there. When I got home from the game at eleven that night, I was a complete mess. I knew from then on that I wouldn't be doing anything that took me so far away from my family anymore.

Kale and June's story wasn't a good one. Kale went to prison for his activities in the gang. His sentence was for five years, and he would have to serve two and a half before being considered for probation. Although, his sentence was significantly lessened when he gave up all that he knew, if they got his little brother into a good foster home.

June's still an assistant athletic trainer, but she lost her baby in the aftermath of Kale going to jail. She's a lot more quiet these days, and I let her be, because what can I really say other than it's going to be okay? I worried about her like crazy, but she was still loyal to Kale, and stuck by him even when he didn't want her to.

A droplet of sweat rolled into my eyes, distracting from my inner musings. Glancing down at the clock, I noticed I still had a minute left of this torture. Gritting my teeth, I moved faster.

"What, in the mother-fuck, are you doing?" Max asked, the door slipping from his grip and banging against the wall.

I glanced at him questioningly. "What do you mean, what am I doing?"

"That's what I mean, what are you doing?" Max said annoyingly.

Max hated it when I asked 'what do you mean.' He knew that I knew what he meant, yet I asked him anyway. I loved annoying my brother.

I was sitting in the chair in the living room. Max, Cheyenne, Sam, and Gabe walked inside. I had one of those shake weights I'd ordered off TV in my hands, and I was shaking it with all I had. I could feel my arms burning, and I was seriously about to pass out from the pain.

"She's working out her muscles. Gotta keep conditioned for later." Gabe said slyly.

"Does that thing work? All it looks like you're doing is jacking off the weight." Cheyenne said.

What could I say? I knew it looked bad, but the thing worked. It was going to keep my arms in shape so the tattoo that I planned to get in a few weeks looked good, instead of stretched out and flappy.

The alarm on my phone dinged, and I dropped my arms down to the arm of my chair.

"Sure as heck does. Here, you try."

Cheyenne took the weight from my hands, placed both of hers fist to fist, and started shaking for all she was worth. I corrected her position, and couldn't help but giggle at the sight.

"Oh, God. That looks awful! I should record this and put it on Facebook."

Luca started crying from the bedroom, and I got up to get him before he woke Cora. I'd gotten them down to a great schedule, and they both slept at the same times throughout the day.

Luca was gurgling and playing with his feet. Hoochie was on his tummy in the very corner, guarding Luca as he did every night since we brought Luca home from the hospital. It never failed, anywhere that Luca was, Hoochie was soon to follow.
I lifted him from the crib and gave him a smacking kiss on the cheek. "Hey there big boy. You didn't sleep very long."

Luca was now twenty pounds of chunky cuteness. He had Gabe's eyes, and the black curls that looked so much like his sister's beautiful hair. Today, he was wearing a shirt that said, "My dad can kick your dad's ass." Which was very true.

Max was a big believer in the onesies. Every time he found one he liked, he would buy it for Luca to wear. He had a whole closet full, and it probably wasn't going to stop anytime soon.

Changing him quickly, I made my way back into the living room. Max took Luca from me as I passed him. Laughing, I relinquished him to his uncle, and went to sit next to Gabe. He curled me close, and I buried my nose into his neck, kissing his collarbone where Luca's name permanently marked his skin.

The day after we were released from the hospital, Gabe disappeared for a little over six hours. All he told me was that he had an appointment, and he would be back as soon as he could.

I didn't question him, assuming it had something to do with work, and left him to it. I had help anyway, and planned to catch up on some much-needed sleep while I could. It was a little past six in the evening when he came back.

I was in the living room feeding the baby with all the girls crowded around on multiple pieces of furniture when his bike pulled up outside. When he walked in the door, I noticed the gauze over his neck instantaneously, and started flipping out before I saw the twinkle in his eyes. He walked right up to me and whipped his shirt over his head, revealing another large piece of gauze on the inside of his left bicep, and an additional one on the inside of his right bicep.

The girls and I watched in awe as he pulled off each piece of gauze. The one on his right arm revealed the words "My Ember" twined around the bulge of his bicep. On the other arm, a star adorned the majority of his underarm. The star was jagged and torn, and underneath you could make out the majority of Cora's name. It almost looked like she was buried deep, and the skin had been cut away to reveal it.

The last tattoo hit me the hardest, because on the left collarbone, the same one that Luca had broken, was Luca's name. It was simple lettering, and profoundly beautiful.

I wrapped my arms around Gabe carefully, and whispered into his ear. "I swear to God, we are never going to make it six weeks. I'd totally jump you right now if I could."

He let out a deep belly laugh, and I vowed that I would get a tattoo. That's when I started working on my arm flab; I wanted the exact same thing on my arms that he had on his, as well as the same tattoo on my left collarbone. I just hoped I wouldn't cry throughout the entire thing.

"Jesus. Do you think you got enough pictures?" Max asked, while bouncing Luca on his knee and glancing at the coffee table where I had some frames sitting.

"No. Never." I replied.

Gabe wrapped me tighter, and I glanced around the room.

Our whole living room wall was covered in 8X10 pictures. Six days after Luca was born, we had newborn pictures made. They were stunning. My favorite was of Luca swaddled in an American flag. In his hands, he clutched Gabe's dog tags. Cora was on her knees beside him kissing his head. It was a priceless photograph, because the rest of the shots were either blurry of Cora, who had turned into the Tazmanian Devil when it came to staying still, or Luca was crying.

When I wasn't getting professional pictures taken of the kids and ourselves, I was behind the camera, just as my mom used to be. Everywhere I went, now, I had my trusty Canon Rebel in my hands. I recently took a picture of the Gabe bent over a bike, wrench in his hand while the other supported his body on the seat of the bike. A red rag hung out of his back pocket, and another was slung over his muscular shoulders. Did I mention he was shirtless and sweaty at the time? That one I had blown up to a 10X14. I even considered having it blown up as an industrial print.

Another of my favorites was of Gabe changing his first blowout diaper. I'd come just in time to hear him gagging from the back part of the house where Cora and Luca shared a room. I, of course, pulled out my phone and took picture after picture. Gabe had his t-shirt up over his nose, and he was standing as far away from Luca as he could get.

Gabe offering sexual favors couldn't even keep that one off the wall. All admired it, and I would never take it down. He even promised he would never again bitch about the Twilight comforter I bought for our bed.

In the place of honor, on the mantle, sat a picture of Sam. His face looked like we'd kicked his puppy. Face pale, lips in a tight grimace, he glared at the camera. His knees down were wet. It was the one Gabe managed to get right after my water broke on him.

Cora's screeches filled my thoughts. "Mama, mama, mama."

Before I could get up, Gabe stood and went to her. My heart was full to bursting in my chest. She'd just started calling me 'Mama' on purpose this week. We were at Cheddar's, for Sidney's supervised visit, when it happened. Sidney was reaching for Cora, and instead of going into her arms like she did with everyone else, she buried her face into my neck and held on with a death grip.

Sidney, being the bitch she was, took her from me anyway. Cora was having none of it, and started screaming 'Mama' at the top of her lungs while reaching for me. Big crocodile tears rolled down her cheeks, and everyone in the restaurant watched curiously.

Sidney's face went from a shade of nicely hued tan to a mottled red in about three seconds flat. Gabe, sensing her hostility, took Cora back before Sidney could do anything stupid. That straw broke the camel's back. The next day, our lawyer called to tell us that Sidney terminated her rights.

Good riddance, we thought.

We were never able to prove that she set us up the day of the accident and kidnapping. Although we all suspected, nothing was done. Luke went through every gang member that was arrested, and didn't get a single word out of them about Sidney. Therefore, when she was released from jail last month, the judge made us do supervised visits. It was a horrid experience seeing Sidney with Cora. Something about the cold way she treated Cora left a bad taste in my mouth, even after the visit finished.

On a positive note, after a whole bunch of digging, the benefactor that paid Sidney to leave Gabe and lie about the baby was none other than Gabe's very own stepfather, Dorian. The day Gabe found out, he hopped a plane to Michigan to speak with his stepfather face to face.

Dorian never confirmed, or denied, but Gabe left that day with peace in his heart. He made a deal with his stepfather. Gabe wouldn't pursue the case if Dorian allowed Gabriel to move his mother to her rightful resting place next to his father. He agreed, and Gabe had it done before he left. We had plans to visit Michigan later on in the year.

Gabe and Cora just crossed the threshold of the living room when the monitor by our door pinged. Every house had this installed. When the new addition was completed, they put in a new security system. When someone pulled up at the front gate, the alarm would tell us that someone was there. The camera that was monitoring that part of the compound would shoot a signal to our panel and we could see who was there; we could choose to open it automatically, or refuse entrance.

On the monitor, we watched as James went to the gate to speak with the woman waiting at the entrance. His slow gate filled the screen, and then his voice asked politely, "Can I help you?"

The woman eyed him, and then nodded in confirmation and handed him a pack of papers. "James Allen. You've been served."

Ω

Watching six grown men bounce on trampolines had to be the highlight of my life.

Okay, well maybe the birth of my child came before that, but not by much. Their muscles contracted and bunched with each bounce on the trampoline. Swear to God, I was tempted to use Luca's bib to wipe my drool.

"This is one hell of a birthday for a two year old." Blaine concluded from beside me.

Her eyes were glued to the eye candy as well. Cheyenne stood at my other side, watching silently.

"Gabe got a little carried away. He wanted her to have the moon, and he settled for Air U after I explained that she would find no enjoyment out of the party he had planned." I explained.

"Sounds like Gabe. I'm surprised James is in such a good mood. I thought for sure he would be pissed off the rest of the day." Cheyenne observed.

I completely agreed. "You and me both, sister."

"Did he say what exactly it was?" I asked.

"No, he's being very quiet about it. I assume it has to be about Janie and Janie's mother." Cheyenne said.

I completely agreed. Janie's mother was a right bitch. I hope that she never has to experience the horridness that is that woman.

The rest of the party went off without a hitch. By the end of the day, though, I was ready to get the hell out of there. There's only so much screaming one could take, and in an enclosed gym with six million kids running around, I was lucky to escape with my sanity.

Max helped me load the gifts into the car, while Gabe stayed with Cora who'd finally given up the ghost, and fallen asleep on his chest. Luca was asleep in his car seat, and I silently wished they would go to sleep early tonight to give me a little alone time with Gabe.

We had to be more spontaneous since the kids got here. We had to do a lot more quickies, and a little less lovemaking, but that was okay in my book. I loved surprising Gabe at work, and having him take me into the back room, giving me the business, and then sending me on my way.

"Get that look off your face." Max growled from beside me.

I shut the door of the truck, and then looked at him innocently. "What look?"
He snorted in disgust, and then tossed an empty trash bag at my face.

"Hey!" I said indignantly.

He laughed and then took off to the party room. I did manage to jump onto his back and pepper his face with kisses. We entered the room with me on his back still, and Max walked up to Gabe who was still holding a sleeping Cora.

"Take this leach off my back, or I won't be responsible for what I do." Max demanded.

I laughed loudly. "Yeah, right. You wouldn't do a damn thing, and you know it."

He sighed long and loud. "I know. For some reason I like you."

I dropped off his back. "I love you, too. Now, let's gather the rest of this shit and get going. I'm whipped."

Ω

"When are you going to tell her?" Gabe asked.

Gabe and Max were outside on the back porch, sharing a beer. The sun was just setting, and they both watched it go down until it was nothing more than an orange red glow on the horizon.

"It's gonna have to be now. I report at oh-eight-hundred tomorrow morning."

What the heck was he talking about? I was about to ask when Gabe's voice broke the quiet night.

"I'll give you a few to talk to her."

He nodded and walked into the house.

He found me standing at the kitchen sink, window open, which was why I overheard their conversation.

Taking my hand, he led me into the living room, and held my hand. He looked me in the eyes and explained what was going on.

He was called back into active duty this morning. They were in need of his services. At this moment in time, he wasn't sure if it was for another tour, or if it was only an isolated service that was needed, and would be back as soon as it was taken care of.

Only time would tell.

I let out a low moan, and threw myself into his arms.

"No." I moaned.

He squeezed me tight, and let me cry onto his chest.

"Ax, Ax." Cora squealed from the hallway as she ran toward Max.

He scooped her up, and peppered her face with smacking kisses.

Gabe's arms replaced Max's, and I sunk into his chest. "Don't leave me, too." I whispered.

"I don't plan on it, booger, but you need to know that it's possible. It's possible for all of us. I'd never leave you willingly, though." He said.

"It's incredibly rare to be recalled back in to the military. Most serve their time, and then go on with their life. Only under special circumstances are soldiers told to come back." Gabe informed me.

I just hoped that those circumstances didn't take my big brother away from me. I needed him.

The rest of the night was spent doing family things. Everyone came over, but Max was subdued, which wasn't surprising. He was leaving me behind; I made him feel like shit for doing what he loved.

I would do it though, because that was the way of an American Soldier.

51788823R00200

Made in the USA
Lexington, KY
05 May 2016